KWACHA

KEN SWAN

 FriesenPress

Suite 300 - 990 Fort St
Victoria, BC, V8V 3K2
Canada

www.friesenpress.com

ISBN

978-1-5255-1707-5 (Hardcover)
978-1-5255-1708-2 (Paperback)
978-1-5255-1709-9 (eBook)

1. HISTORY, AFRICA, CENTRAL

Distributed to the trade by The Ingram Book Company

TABLE OF CONTENTS

Assistant Inspector Martin Robert Higgs-Briar. Born - Milton Keynes, U.K. 21 July 1937.

Tales of a young Englishman dutifully serving in the Northern Rhodesia Police Force, at the height of British Colonialism and the beginning of "The winds of change."

1

IT HAD TO BEGIN SOMEWHERE

England 1958, soggy, damp. For a young ambitious lad decent career opportunities were few and far between. Martin Robert Higgs-Briar, called Higgs by his friends, had graduated from high school in 1955. He then presented himself at college for three evenings, every week, for two years. He worked hard at a local garage in Milton Keynes, six days a week, repairing, servicing, riding, and enjoying Triumph Motorcycles. He loved his job but there were four men working there, the owner and his three sons. Martin's chance at getting anywhere career-wise, certainly in that motorcycle shop, was just about as close to none, as any odds-maker would bet. Having a few years of college under his belt meant Higgs could jump at any opportunity that arose.

Many people from England, at that post-war time, were leaving for warm and sunny distant commonwealth countries. Frankly, Britain's finest citizens were being encouraged

1

to leave by their own Government. These departures were a brain-drain with unforeseen consequences, for Britain anyway. Australia, New Zealand, the Caribbean, and Africa benefitted from these new keen arrivals who were first-class and hardworking. Jobs were abundant in those far-off places and it did not rain as much. Higgs figured his college education would help him find what he wanted, if only he knew what that was.

Meanwhile, Higgs did enjoy riding those Triumphs, especially the 650 CC Speed-Twin models and the Bonnevilles. The girls enjoyed riding with their arms hugging him like a bear, as their tight little thighs squished into the seat behind him, Higgs was over six foot, and weighed 185 pounds, with large blue eyes and sandy blond hair and the women liked him. Combine those assets with a big motorbike and there were "abundant babes willing and able to go on a date," as Higgs liked to say. Bikes and babes, only one thing was missing; okay, three things were missing: money, sunshine, and adventure.

One evening in the local pub, The Carrington Arms, he plonked himself down after a busy day, and ordered a Double Diamond beer. Higgs liked crossword puzzles and was thrilled to discover some patron had left today's edition of the London Times newspaper on the table. He glanced at the front page headlines: Archbishop Makarios of Cyprus still in exile in the Seychelles; Terrorists still attacking in Malaya and Surrey had beaten the visiting Australian's at the Oval cricket ground. Higgs ordered a second beer and flipped through the paper searching for the puzzle page. And there, on the very last page, was an opportunity to change his life, staring him in the face, a large advertisement that read:

> The Northern Rhodesia Police Force (NRP) needs men now. If you are at least 19 years of age and have at least two years in college, consider a career in Northern Rhodesia (NR), a British Protectorate. Successful applicants would have their passage paid to Lusaka, and undergo a fourmonth training course. Starting monthly pay is £32.18.4 pence. Subsidized living quarters and meals are provided. [Higgs earned £26 a month now and had to pay for living quarters and meals]. Every three years you qualify for six month's leave to your land of domicile, free return passage with full pay. If you return for another three-year contract you could be stationed elsewhere, or returned to your previous station and may be eligible for promotion.
>
> To determine if you qualify, contact: NRP - Crown Agents, St. Nicholas House, Sutton, SM1 1EL. This recruitment period ends on April 15, 1958. The next recruitment period will not begin until January 1959. If you qualify for this period, you depart U.K. on July 8th, 1958.

There were calls for almost the same offer for other colonial police forces in commonwealth countries, like the Bahamas, Bermuda, New Zealand, and Hong Kong. This had Higgs daydreaming; wondering where in the world he might be best suited. Higgs remembered all his relatives and the stories about their lives. Some had done absolutely nothing. Old uncle Gary was born in Liverpool. He was educated in Liverpool. He got a job in a print-shop, cleaning out lead type stacks. He married a girl in Liverpool; had two children, and 71 years later, died in Liverpool. Higgs wanted more out of life. He had to see the world and become "somebody." He relished talking to his other uncles. They had been pilots, Marines, or sailors. They had seen Europe, the Far East, New Zealand, the Cook Islands, and Canada, etcetera. Higgs wanted an adventurous life and this police ad seemed exactly what was needed. So, he made the decision.

Central Africa sounded great and the contract was for only three years. Hong Kong seemed appealing but that was for five years and, at the age of 21, five years seemed a lifetime if he discovered that he did not like Hong Kong. So he compromised and applied for the Northern Rhodesia Police Force.

The British government wanted more citizens from the U.K. to go and make their colonies fruitful. And they were willing to pay for it; the carrots they were dangling were hard to resist. After all, Britain had a large supply of red ink and they wanted all the atlases in the world to be covered in red, as it was now and as they intended for it to remain. For a young single man, the opportunity was too much to ignore. Higgs had deferred the National Service, where all young men over age 18 were to serve in the armed forces for at least 18 months. Because he was a fulltime college student, his recruitment was waived until after graduation. He could also waive entirely his National Service by signing up with a colonial police force. The choice was easy.

Higgs set about putting his plan into place. He made the call, filled in the forms, and put them in the post. Now, all he had to do was wait. From that moment, Higgs lost all interest in his job and his everyday habits. He visited the library for the very first time and began studying Africa and, in particular, Northern Rhodesia, Southern Rhodesia, and South Africa.

2

THE BEGINNING OF THE NEW LIFE

Three weeks later, Higgs received in the post instructions for reporting to the Northern Rhodesia Police Board. Three days later Higgs was in London, sitting opposite a tall elderly gentleman seated behind a large, oh so government-issue type wooden desk. The distinguished looking gentleman was a Director of the Crown Agents, a Mr. Farqhuar; he was checking Martin's forms before taking him through to a larger office, to be "grilled" by the Review Board. Once seated, Higgs found himself in front of the Director along with three men and a woman. The tough, third-degree interview began. A somewhat dishevelled gentleman in a blue blazer and grey flannel trousers said, "Now then, you say you are six-foot-one. Our minimum is five-foot-seven, so that's good. Hmmm."

Another man, in a chocolate brown three-piece-suit and a pencil-thin moustache spoke, "I see from your application that you are 185 pounds, which is just over 13 stone, is that right?"

"Yes, it is," answered Higgs.

Then the lady spoke, "You've answered here that you are not allergic to anything. Very good."

"Why do you want to be a copper, and in Africa too?" asked a small man, with a Harris Tweed sports coat, and a mustard yellow cravat. "Got some past history you are trying to get away from, eh? Hmmm. What?"

"No, Sir. None of that. I am simply looking for something meaningful in my life, that's all," responded Higgs.

"Yes, alright Jenkins. Let's move on to other questions, shall we?" admonished Farquhar.

"Can you ride a motorbike?" asked another board member, whose hair was very short, with too much Brylcreem. He also had a thin moustache. His large bushy eyebrows were literally twitching with excitement. He appeared to rather wish he was outside on an adventure, somewhere exotic.

"I ride and repair them and build them from scratch," beamed Higgs. "It is what I do for a living."

"Really?" enquired the man, sitting upright, his voice filled with enthusiasm. "What kind of bikes?"

"Well, BSA or Triumph are my favourites, but just about any," answered Higgs.

"Good Lord! That must be exciting! I love bikes myself. I remember once I owned an American-made Indian bike. It went like hell! Rode it in Arizona in 1946, but then........."

"Yes, all right. Major Billingsdale. Can we just inform Mr. Higgs-Briar where he stands?" admonished Farquhar.

"Okay, Sir," said the Major, sitting up and looking very pleased with himself. "If you can be ready to leave England on July 8th, 1958, I believe we can accept you for a three-year contract."

"Welcome aboard, Mr. Higgs-Briar. I need you to come through here with me," said the Director. "There's a little housekeeping to complete. I shall look forward to hearing about all your exploits in the future. Lusaka is a very exciting city and all I can say is I wish I was your age 'cos I'd be with you on that ship." And, two hours later, Higgs was out on the street; a new life ahead. He went to Austin-Reeds in Regent Street, to buy a new suit for £14. He felt a little numb when he got home that day. He could not have any way of knowing how his life was about to be turned upside down.

It had all happened so fast and now he had a short time to say his goodbyes, and hand in his notice at work. Of course, everyone told him how foolish he was being. How he would regret leaving such a great job, and so on.

His family consisted now of just his mother. She lived alone after his father had failed to return from WWII; he had been a Lancaster bomber pilot and the plane simply did not return from a late war flight over Germany. Higgs had to tell his mother he was leaving England for three years and she would have to be brave and stay close to her bridge friends because he had to go and she had to wish him well, and not be gloomy. She sobbed, as a mother would, but wished him well and chided him to write regularly.

There were no particular girlfriends to whom he had to say goodbye. He used the farewells to visit three women he had dated now and then. The farewells were racy but he did not feel too closely associated with any of them to promise them anything. He simply said goodbye. Young men have always found it exciting and easy to simply pack-up and leave, with little care for the past and a ton of optimism for the future. This was really little different from the ancient explorers who set off to seek new parts of the world. We can observe this and wonder but Higgs never gave the circumstances any thought. He wanted to leave and start a new life, and he was doing so; bring on the future.

3

THIS IS THE ONLY WAY TO TRAVEL

At 3:00 p.m. on Tuesday, July 8th, 1958, Higgs boarded the 20,120-ton ship, Carnarvon Castle, at Southampton dock, England. At precisely 4:00 p.m. she set sail, with 695 passengers on board, bound for Cape Town, South Africa. Martin had a single cabin on Deck 4 in the middle of the ship on the starboard side.

He had been handed an envelope at the ship's front desk and told to read the contents immediately. The young lady behind the desk, tall and gorgeous, in her Union-Castle Line navy blue uniform, who had handed him the envelope said, "Sir, my name is Yolanda and if you ever need anything ask for me."

"Oh, thank you," replied Higgs. "I will."

Yolanda said, "I see you have a double bed in your cabin, all to yourself. You won't have to worry about disturbing a roommate at any time of night," and she gave him a tiny wink.

There was only one urgent item in his envelope which was that he should dress in at least a tie and jacket, and make his way to the main dining room at 7:00 p.m. and show the maître d' the card noting he was one of eight to be seated at Table 12.

Higgs found his cabin, sorted out his wardrobe and bathroom accessories, then had a shower and picked out his clothing for the evening. Higgs was the first to be seated at Table 12, but within a few minutes seven other men had arrived, all about Martin's age of 20 to 30, and they all sat down and started introducing themselves to each other. Four were headed for Kitwe, in Northern Rhodesia, to work in copper mines. The other three had been hired to work for Impresit, an Italian engineering firm, and the main contractor for the new Kariba Hydro Electric Dam. This dam would be the largest in the world and was on the Zambezi River, which was the natural border between Northern and Southern Rhodesia.

Everyone introduced themselves. A big man with a rugby-players build and blond hair said, "Hello, I'm Mike Dunn. I'm off to Kariba, along with some friends here with me. My job is to be in charge of supplies, you know...how much cement do we need this week or how many gallons of diesel fuel each week, and so on. Nice to meet you." A lanky red-haired man, very tall, stuck out his hand, saying, "Lance Frazer is the name and I am going to Kariba too. I am a mechanic. I service the huge lorries that take cement to the vats pouring into the dam structure. Pleased to meet all of you." Higgs introduced himself, "Higgs is my name. I used to fix motorcycles and now I am headed for Lusaka in

Northern Rhodesia as a policeman. Just a natural progression, I suppose, motorbikes to police. Good to meet you all." "Lookout, lads! We have a copper here," retorted one of the Kariba boys, in a friendly tone.

The introductions continued as they ordered drinks from the wine steward. Mostly, they ordered beer and discovered a new brand, Castle, from South Africa. By the number of refills, it appeared that the lads loved Castle beer. They never ordered any other brand after that first taste. The table got noisier and the group seemed to have inherited very wide smiles on their faces. This 14-day cruise was going to be memorable and fun, thought Higgs. All of them expressed dismay that no women had been assigned to their table and they decided they would find some; perhaps not to sit at their table, but just to, well, you know.

Their steward arrived and introduced himself. "I am Stavros, your permanent main man for your table for the trip, sorry! If you no like we can exchange with Alexandros over here," pointing to the young pimpled water boy. Alexandros, who had a sheepish befuddled grin, carried on filling everyone's glasses. "I am from Loutraki in Greece. This young man is from Cyprus," said Stavros.

Stavros handed out the menu for the night, and it was impressive. Five appetizers and three salads. Two kinds of soup and five entrées. Three desserts and a cheese tray. Higgs choices were: Avocado Royale (half an avocado filled with fresh shrimp and drizzled with a tomato cognac cream sauce), then a mulligatawny soup, followed by tomato onion salad. His main entrée was lamb chops, served with roasted onions and asparagus on top of a mountain of mashed potatoes.

A light dessert of Cherries Jubilee followed, prepared at the table with huge flames reaching three feet above the copper frying pan. Then a platter of Stilton, Brie, and Havarti cheeses, with some crisp green grapes. Higgs thought to himself that this meal alone would cost nearly £3 back home. What a great start to my new life!

All of that was washed down with lots of black coffee. Everyone smoked, so plenty of exchanging various brands of cigarettes. Higgs stuck to his Pall Mall filters. Everyone had similar copious amounts of food. Fortunately for all of them, they were all under age 30. Perhaps by the end of the cruise, they may not be able to continue eating at that level but, then, why not? At 9:30 p.m. they all waddled down to the dance floor, to check out the ladies, more than checking out the dance styles. A five-piece band was playing music from "The King and I." A number of attractive ladies were skipping around the dance floor to "I Whistle a Happy Tune," some dancing with another lady.

Every man from Table 12 was mentally sizing up these women. Who were they? What were their ages? Would that one dance with me if I asked? Maybe that one. The band started playing "Jailhouse Rock" and suddenly a swarm of young ladies approached all the men and asked them to dance. All said yes and soon there were 20 pairs of bodies gyrating on the dance floor. The band never returned to the "King and I" again. About ten women had a bunch of tables pushed together for themselves, loaded with empty glasses. They were asking the men to dance. When a break was needed for the bathroom, booze refills, or just fatigue, the women would drag the man to the table, like a fly to a web, then leave him there as they rushed off to the bathroom or to get a drink or to strategize with their cabin-mates.

It was discovered that this bunch of charming women were all in their early 20s and were headed for Salisbury, in Southern Rhodesia, as nurses. They were pretty and intelligent and loved parties. The men could only hope they could keep on partying with them for the next 14 days. Soon there were six tables placed together and 20 men and women around them.

In between dances, the conversation got around to Africa and Northern Rhodesia. Of course, nobody among the group knew much about Africa. "Was it possible," someone asked, "say, to live in Lusaka and then go to Salisbury for a Friday night date?" Someone, who knew a little, suggested it was possible if one left Lusaka on a Thursday, drove through the night, and then stayed in Salisbury until Sunday. It was at least a seven-hour drive each way. Although at that age, with a good car and good luck, it was possible to leave Lusaka at noon on Friday, get to Salisbury at 7:00 p.m. and stay the night, and leave again sometime Saturday. It had been done but it was not really recommended. Africa was huge, and this was not the London-to-Brighton run.

So, might as well have fun on board the ship now, because the odds of seeing any more of these ladies after Cape Town were somewhere between slim and none. Devious plotting began so as to win over these women. Higgs being the smoothest man the world had ever known, and was getting smoother as the alcohol consumption increased, made a move.

"My name is Higgs, and yours?" Higgs enquired of the petite dark gorgeous woman. He had asked about her earlier on and discovered she had a German father and a Spanish mother, but she was born in Wales. She could easily have been a Miss World contestant. Using his smoothest pick-up line he asked, "What do you think of motorbikes?"

"Oh, Higgs," she sighed. "I would go anywhere on a motorbike if you were at the controls. And it's Gretchen, by the way." "Well, I used to be a motorbike mechanic," stated Higgs, proudly.

"I'm sure I could snuggle up and hold on tight as you wound your way around the roads," Gretchen giggled slightly and ran her hand up his arm.

"Okay, then let's make a date that somewhere in Africa I will pick you up on my bike, and then we can decide what we should do after that," said the ever bolder Higgs.

"Higgs, I really need to get out of these clothes and have a shower. That rock 'n' roll has got me all sweaty," Gretchen said. "Would you mind showing me to my cabin? I am still working on my bearings. I'm sure I will know my way around by our last day on board."

"Sure I can," responded Higgs, his hopes rising at a shot with Gretchen. "You want to go now?"

She grabbed his hand and said "Let's go!" They slid away from the rest of the group and headed for the central elevators and up to the Dolphin deck.

They were soon at Cabin 114 and she pecked Higgs on the cheek and suggested she would see him tomorrow. Then she slipped behind her door and locked it. Higgs was devastated. What a great start to his cruise! Still, he was a gentleman, and with no other plan in mind, he left. He had generally been a "ladies' man" and he had just been dumped.

He stopped off at the men's room and checked out his blond hair and boyish charm as he passed the mirror. As he meandered through the ship with his shattered ego, searching for the correct elevator to get back to his cabin, Higgs heard a piano playing and applause from around the corner. And there it was, "The Manhattan Piano Bar," smoky, noisy with great music and seemingly more women than men at the bar and dancing, perhaps a total of 30 patrons. Higgs figured a strong night-cap might be just the potion needed to get him up from his disastrous attempt at "being" with Gretchen.

The pianist stopped playing and announced, "Well, folks, I'm Bobby Gambol and I am your piano maestro for the evening. Any requests will be considered. No drinks can bribe me, unless they are Bombay Gin and Schweppes Tonic, with a slice of lime. I work for the Union-Castle Line but they let me play anything I want. So, if there is anyone out there with a request, just let me know."

A short little man with a toupe and a smart three-piece silver suit, somewhat inebriated, staggered from the bar, fresh new vodka tonic in hand and said, in a very haughty voice, "I say there, Mr. Piano Man [pronouncing piano as piaarno], play for me "That's What You Are.""

"You know, Sir, I would do so," replied the piano man, "but I don't think I know that one."

"I am excruciatingly surprised that you don't know such a famous tune," slurred the drunk.

"Okay," challenged the piano man. "Let's ask the crowd if they know the tune. I say, ladies and gentlemen, has anyone heard of the song 'That's What You Are'?'" Nobody knew the song.

The drunk said, "Hand me that microphone and I shall sing it to all and sundry." He grabbed the mike shoved at him across the white grand piano and, putting on his best Nat King Cole stance and voice, raised his glass, finished the contents in one gulp and sang *"Unforgettable, that's what you are."*

The crowd laughed. The bar seemed to explode with patrons ordering more rounds; even the drunk got a couple or more free drinks but he had no idea why. Higgs liked this place. He ordered himself a cold Castle beer and plonked himself down on a seat at the bar. Bobby was tinkling away with "That's Why the Lady is a Tramp." Higgs was tapping his feet and then a warm body slunk up beside him, and whispered, "Hello, Sir. I'm Yolanda, from the front desk. Remember me?" She really was stunning in a sparkling sequined and very short black and silver mini-skirt with a puffed long-sleeved cyan blue silk blouse. And he could smell her. She had a scent of bruised rose petals. Higgs loved her body smell. Her hair fell down to her shoulders, gleaming jet black.

Her long legs encased in black stockings and very high black patent leather high-heeled shoes to set them off. "It is my night off and this is usually where I hang out," she said.

Higgs gasped and stuttered a little while attempting to be cool, said, "You look absolutely stunning! Will you buy me a drink? I mean, can I buy me a drink? No, no, I will, ahem, I meant, buy one for you."

"Sir," she said sweetly. "I would love to have a drink with you, but put it on my tab, as I get a staff deal and you can save your money and use it to buy me, say, a new dress. You *are* planning to rip this outfit off me later tonight, are you not?"

Well, that got Higgs' attention. He had never known a woman so forward. He had always made the first moves, but this was very unfamiliar to him. He was not objecting but just now he felt very much in need of that drink, or six.

"Okay, something to think about over a Bacardi and Coke," he suggested, having composed himself back to his once and usual cool self. "Get me a double Jameson, on the rocks, "she requested.

The evening was wonderful. They liked each other. They had a lot of drinks. They danced much of the night on the ship's small dance floor. Yolanda whispered something to her fellow staff member, Bobby, playing the piano, and thereafter most of the music was romantic and mostly Latin rhythms.

She showed off her moves to Higgs, as she teased him a little by pushing her hips hard against him; she could feel he was becoming aroused. By 2:00 a.m. they closed down the bar and arm in arm went up to Higgs' cabin. He unlocked the door; she slid in then slammed it shut and then pulled him down onto the bed.

Her kisses were hot and plunging and Higgs slid his hand behind and up inside her blouse to unhook her bra, and she did not have one. She pulled his mouth down as she struggled to free herself from her blouse. Higgs slipped his hand to the silken skin above her black silk stockings.

Yolanda tugged at his leather belt, and unzipped him. Their tongues intertwined as she writhed under him. They slept until 8:00 a.m. Yolanda phoned the front desk to confirm that her shift was from noon to 8:00 p.m.

Higgs was now awake and each of them had a quick visit to the bathroom. Yolanda invited him into the shower with her. They stood and kissed and soaped each other and explored each other. Yolanda rinsed off both of them and took him back to the bed. Higgs was pushed flat on his back. Later that morning, she slipped out of the door. Higgs noticed his muscles were taught and very used. A few seconds later he went back to sleep. It was 1:00 p.m. when he awoke.

4

HAS IT ONLY BEEN TWO DAYS AT SEA?

Higgs showered and dressed in white linen pants and a pink shirt, with white sandals; very summery indeed. He did not know what selection of clothing would be available in Africa, so he had bought a lot of "summery" clothing, along Oxford Street, not so long ago. He made his way down to the dining room at around 1:30 p.m. and found he was alone at his table. Apparently, only three people ate lunch so it appeared most had a long hard evening the night before.

Stavros, the waiter, handed Higgs the lunch menu, which featured steak and mushroom pie but Higgs only wanted a plate of scrambled eggs and a Bloody Mary. He got the drink first and it was ice cold and quite spicy. He'd had a few Bloody Mary's in his life, but only English style, which was funny tomato juice from a teeny bottle (almost like red water), a splash of gin, and in a small glass and at room temperature. This Bloody Mary had vodka, tomato juice from real tomatoes, along with salt, pepper, Worcestershire sauce, and a dash of Tabasco sauce, all in a large glass and ice cold. It cured the remnants of last night's carousing and cried out for another one, which was gulped down and tasted as good as the first.

The scrambled eggs provided much-needed energy and, with two mugs of black coffee, he felt almost human. Higgs figured if this was the first night of his cruise, what adventures would he discover over the next 13 nights? He ventured out onto the promenade deck and strolled around it a few times to clear his head and take in the warm sea air.

As he passed one of the lounges on board, he heard the crowd muttering about the fun they were expecting at the, soon to start, general knowledge quiz. Higgs sauntered into the lounge, observed and listened to the crowd of about 75 people and joined a group of five returning citizens of Northern Rhodesia who needed a sixth person for their team. They introduced themselves and gathered a sheet of paper and a short pencil from the ship's entertainment director. The group asked Higgs to write down the answers, which duty he gladly accepted. He ordered an iced coffee to brighten up the brain. He offered but nobody else wanted a drink.

The quiz-master threw out questions. Their group was doing well, or so they thought. Then the quiz-master called out the correct answers, of which Higgs and company had only 11. The team across from them won with 16 correct answers. But Higgs' team were fourth overall, and there was a grand prize for total points for 10 quizzes over the length of the cruise. The team agreed to stick together and enter each quiz. Higgs got to know the family well and learned a lot about Northern Rhodesia, and the way of life there. There was Norman Blythe, a big red-faced farmer from Chisamba, a small town 30 miles north of Lusaka, his wife Carol, and their 18-year-old (going on 25) daughter Marjorie. Marjorie really was attractive, with large breasts and a small waist, sparkling green eyes and auburn hair, soft and flowing to just below the shoulder.

Higgs guessed she weighed about 130 pounds and was about five-foot eight-inches tall; a real farm girl!. The other couple lived in a suburb of Lusaka, named Woodlands, near government house; about three miles from what might be called the centre of downtown. They were Alfred and Dawn Mitchell; she worked for the government as a secretary and he was a foreman at a huge private trucking company, Hadley and Jarret, where he supervised mechanics maintaining the company's enormous fleet of 400 vehicles.

Higgs asked a lot of questions about life in general in Northern Rhodesia. He wanted to know how the public got on with police? Did they trust native policemen? Were all the roads paved? Did any white police date or marry local African women? Were there, in fact, any or many local women, or did most come from overseas? Did the white population have any fear of the natives in remote areas? What was a typical restaurant meal and its average cost? And how good were the restaurants? How much would a new car cost, say, a 1958 Ford Zephyr? Did they get the latest movies in their cinemas? All the questions a young single man and future policeman needed to know.

"Well," said Marjorie, "if you were taking me out for dinner to say, the Blue Boar Hotel, my favourite restaurant just outside Lusaka, I would probably order Peri-Peri chicken, which is very hot and originally a Portuguese dish. You might order steak and chips, we might share a bottle of wine. The total cost might be £5." At that point, her parents excused themselves to visit the bathroom and Marjorie and Higgs were alone. She leaned over and, in a hushed voice, said, "By the way, that Peri-Peri chicken may be hot but not as hot as I can get. I just love being picked up at the farm and driven into Lusaka. Often, I stay overnight. I tell my folks I am staying with Thelma, who is a good friend and covers for me often and well. Sometimes I spend a weekend at the Blue Boar Hotel. My folks would go crazy if they heard me being so suggestive, but any time you need a demo, leave a message at the front desk for me." And then she left with her parents who waved and headed to their cabins for a nap before the dinner party they had arranged.

Higgs was dumbfounded at the attitude of these women on board the ship. He hoped his stamina could take the challenges ahead. He ventured off into the ship's library and read a dog-eared book by a frontiersman, "Chirapula Stevenson" about life in the early days in Northern Rhodesia. That kept him engrossed for the rest of the afternoon. Then, after a warm shower, he dressed in a light blue suit with a white on white cotton shirt and made his way to Table 12 for dinner. All the newly-found friends were there and they discussed what they had been up to. None seemed to have the same type of evening he had, but maybe they were keeping everything close to their vests, as he was.

Higgs sat around with the lads and many told very funny off-coloured jokes. He ate a large steak and enjoyed one glass of Paarl shiraz wine to accompany the meal. At 9:00 p.m., he excused himself. With that, he went up to his cabin and had a shower then lay naked on top of the covers as he evaporated dry. At exactly 10:00 p.m., there was a gentle knock on his door and, half asleep, he opened it an inch or two and there stood Marjorie. Higgs tried to cover himself but Marjorie pushed her way in.

"Were you waiting for someone or will I do?" she asked. "I can see you are ready for action."

Higgs stammered a little and said, "Well, come on in, I guess!"

To which Marjorie responded, "Look. I am a grown-up farm girl and I haven't felt a man in ages. Just you and me, okay?" She pushed Higgs backwards onto the bed. Then in a magical move, she was out of her clothes and pulled him down on her. She yelped and moved under him; she really was a healthy girl with very firm eighteen-year-old breasts. Marjorie sighed and said, "If you are not planning to go out tonight, can we do this again?" Marjorie left the cabin at about 1:00 a.m. This was new to Higgs even though he had considered himself a ladies' man back home, these two women were a handful.

But he was just 21 years old and the cruise would only last a short while. Even so, Higgs realized that he would be dead by the end of the cruise if he tried to keep up with these two women. He showered again and dozed off in bed at 2:00 a.m. At exactly 11:00 a.m., he was awoken by the phone. "Don't forget the trivia quiz at 3:00 p.m." said Marjorie. "I will be there and it will be as if nothing happened. If it ever happens again you will have to initiate it, but just so you know, I will say yes every time you ask. Byeeee!"

Higgs could not decide who he would rather be with, Yolanda or Marjorie. They both had their charms. Yolanda was gorgeous and sexy with a night-club sophistication and a trim figure. Marjorie was young and firm, with a big farm-girl attitude, open and honest and so easy to love physically. He was on his way to start a new career and sex was simply a way to pass the time on what might otherwise have been a long boring trip. Oh, well, he figured, let the games begin!

He was as randy as they were and managed to have meetings so frequently that on one memorable day Yolanda left his cabin at 11:00 p.m. and Marjorie had him at 7:00 a.m. and again at 3:00 p.m. At 4:00p.m., Marjorie left for dinner preparations. Yolanda phoned and suggested they have room service in his cabin at 8:00 p.m. that night. How did steak and lobster sound? A special from her friend the chef. But first, she said, "I had a bad day at the front desk and I need you now. After dinner, you can have me for dessert!"

Higgs, who thought he knew all about women, was now getting laid twice a day. At 6:45 p.m., Yolanda knocked on his door. Higgs was naked and under the covers. Yolanda was in a navy velour one-piece jumpsuit and naked under it; she stepped out of it and fell into Higgs' arms. It was all over after a heated few minutes. They slept until room service arrived at 7:00 a.m.

Yolanda left the bed and hid in the bathroom until the waiter had left. Higgs stayed in bed and told the waiter to leave the tray on the dressing table. The two of them wolfed down the food and made love every hour or so until 3:00 a.m. Then Yolanda left and whispered, "Goodbye, my darling. Let us never forget this trip."

25

5

PLEASE GOD MAY THIS CRUISE NEVER END

Higgs spent the remainder of the cruise doing the perfunctory afternoon trivia quiz with the NR people, as he called them. They were a damn good team and they either won each day or were in the top three; they did not win the final trophy, however. Some group of library workers on a convention happened to win that. C'est la vie, figured Higgs.

There was a "crossing the line" ceremony on the 7th day at sea. All the hapless victims were presented with certificates for having been a volunteer as they crossed the equator. All slathered with chocolate, then plunged into the swimming pool; lots of fun and his first diploma he planned to keep, alongside his Triumph Motorcycle Company diploma for knowing all the ins and outs of the motorcycle "twostroke engine." Gretchen was there in a twopiece bathing suit and gave Higgs the eye, but he was not interested in her anymore.

He had enough to last him the rest of the cruise. Besides, he felt good ignoring her.

During the trip, Marjorie was just another team member with her parents during the quiz, without anyone realizing what went on just about every evening. This 18-year-old girl taught Higgs many things about sex. She came to see him on the last night before the end of the cruise. She was not sure if they would ever meet again but wanted to leave him "shagged out," and she did. It was also Higgs' 21st birthday, and he celebrated it quietly, in his cabin, with Marjorie, who remembered him saying when he was born during a trivia quiz one day. What a shame he did not have a big party. What a joy to be alone with Marjorie! How beautifully tiring! What a wonderful dilemma to be faced with!

He never saw Yolanda again on that ship; he missed her a lot. He was given an envelope at the desk on the day he checked out. Inside was a note from Yolanda, saying, "They have me in isolation. I picked up a bug. Nothing to do with us, but I cannot fraternize with passengers (tee hee, little do they know!) so I have not been able to contact you. I hope we meet again and again. No strings attached. Here is my phone number in Welwyn Garden City, where I live when these bastards allow me time off. I cannot believe my bad luck. I feel you every moment. Fate will get us together one day. Best wishes for a good life! Love, Yolanda."

Higgs was able to say farewell to the friends at Table 12. They all said they would meet up in Lusaka or in Kariba, when Higgs might come down for a fishing trip. They exchanged as much contact information as they had and most agreed to stay in touch.

6

WELCOME TO AFRICA

Later, in the morning, Higgs left the ship for the perfunctory immigration screening in Cape Town. He was handed an envelope at the South African Railways office that contained a letter from the Crown Agents, a train ticket, and a voucher for £20 (sundry for four days!) to spend on board the train on his journey to Northern Rhodesia.

Higgs had to be at the South African Railway station at 9:00 p.m. and it was not even noon yet. He asked to have his luggage stored and, on the suggestion of the local station-master, he took an afternoon tour of Cape Town. He enjoyed the wonderful scenery, the bright blue sky, and especially the visit to the top of Table Mountain. He walked barefoot along Clifton Beach and felt this was a place he could call home. He never noticed any armed-camp with soldiers and police. In fact, he wanted to ask a policeman a question about photographs, but could not find one. This was hardly the South Africa disparaged in the press back home. Higgs eventually asked a smiling young black man where he could find a toilet and the man showed him the entrance, some hundred yards along the street.

All too soon he was on the tour bus and heading back to get his luggage. He then took a taxi to the nearby train station. He was assigned to a first-class compartment, on his own, in which was a private shower, a toilet, and a washbasin that served as a fold down table for daytime activities, like reading or writing, or perhaps room-service breakfast or lunch.

Simeon was an old, what they called, "Cape coloured" man (there was a substantial population of this group of mostly Malay and white mixing in the early beginnings of the country). He knocked on the door and introduced himself as the compartment attendant for the entire trip. He informed Higgs, "Sir, the dining room stays open until 11:00 p.m. and it is now 8:45 p.m. I suggest you run along to the dining car which is three coaches back from here. I will put away all your clothing and toiletries. If anything is creased, I will iron it for you. Any particular bunk you want me to bring down and make up your bed?" Higgs had never had a servant but thought everything sounded fine.

Higgs replied, "Let me have a shower and get dressed then you can come back in 20 minutes while I pop off to the dining room. Okay? And that bunk there seems best for me," pointing to the forwardfacing lower bunk. Feeling fresh and clean and with a ravenous appetite, Higgs made his way back to the dining car, just as the train began to slowly move out of Cape Town Station. The dining car was magnificent and typical of the style introduced by Great Britain in the

1920s and refined by colonial architects. On one side were tables for four, with four padded dining chairs, and mirrored pillars between huge plate glass windows. On the other side was a row of tables for two diners; all tables had fresh linen tablecloths, with crystal glassware and sterling silver cutlery. The domed ceiling had brass metallic décor, with chandeliers every four feet. About half of the tables were filled and Higgs was placed alone at a table for two. More passengers began filing in over the next few minutes.

A tall handsome woman, with long legs, and dark hair folded beautifully on her head, came up to Higgs and enquired, "Would it be all right if I joined you? I find myself alone and you are by yourself at a table for two."

Higgs stood, clutching his serviette, and said, "Oh, please do. I welcome your company!"

The waiter pulled out the woman's chair and she sat gracefully.

She said to Higgs, "I'm Amanda De-LaHaye. I am travelling to Lusaka, where I live. My husband died a short while ago; seven months ago, actually. We had a small lot in Kabulonga, a suburb north of Lusaka, and we exported exotic flowers to Europe; we still do. I have just been a month in Cape Town, renewing some old business contracts and now returning home. Now what is your name?"

Higgs replied, "Well, I am Martin Higgs-Briar, born in England and on my way to Lusaka to join the police. I just got off the Carnarvon Castle this morning after 14 days of living the good life. I am pleased to meet you, Amanda, if I may call you by that name."

"Amanda is fine," she said. "I bet a young man like you had a lot of the good life on board the ship! I was alone on board a ship some five years ago and it was wonderful, but we shan't get into that. I need a drink. What about you, Martin?"

Higgs replied, "Oh, please call me Higgs. All my friends do. I just finished a Bacardi and Coke and I was about to order another. What can I get you, Amanda?"

"I need something exciting. How about a dirty vodka martini with two olives and a splash of olive jar juice?" she said to Higgs. "Now, waiter what's on the menu that I should not miss?" she asked the patient waiter still standing just behind her.

The menu was superb. They both had jellied consommé followed by grilled African sea fish, Kingklip, served with avocado and tomato. Entrées of petite filet mignon served with artichokes and roasted parsnips for Amanda and three Karoo lamb chops with grilled mushrooms for Higgs. Both skipped dessert but shared a half bottle of Paarl KWV port, deep purple-red. South Africa has some of the world's finest wines, and this port was as good as any other country's offering.

"Did you know," volunteered Amanda, "the Dutch settlers started wine growing in 1655, just three years after landing in the Cape. Then, in 1830-ish, the Huguenots from France brought with them some of the finest vines and so began the creation of some of the present day's world-class wines. After WWII demolished so much of the vines in France, South Africa had more French vines than they did. My late husband was a wine freak. That's how I know."

"I never knew that," responded Higgs. "Now there is my first knowledge of Africa that I can use."

After dinner they both strolled into the lounge car and sat in very comfy chairs and listened to a pianist tinkle away some Broadway tunes; "Lullaby of Birdland" was being played as they arrived. There was a dance floor and Higgs suggested they might dance, if she wished. Amanda smiled, but declined. "Dancing gets me in trouble." She grinned, "Here, let me get a couple of coffees and clear our heads, if that's okay, Higgs."

He nodded and they both sat feeling the warm breeze flowing through the open window. The train was climbing up from the coast and was doing little more than 20 miles per hour. Slowly, they felt the evening's meal and drinks affecting them and after an hour of chatting they both arose and went to their respective compartments. Both were surprised to discover they were in compartments number 37 and 38, in the same first-class coach.

"Goodnight, Higgs," said Amanda. "Let's see what tomorrow brings." She gave him a kiss on the cheek, shut her door, and locked it. Higgs went into compartment 38 and found all his kit put away and his bed was turned down and inviting. He was asleep at exactly midnight and awoke at 7:00 a.m.

He showered and dressed in tan pants with a green shirt over the top of his pants and strode off to the dining car. Amanda was already at "their" table and she waved at him with a welcoming smile.

"Good night's rest?" she asked.

"Oh, yes," he replied. "I must have needed that sleep as I hit the pillow about two minutes after we said goodnight and I woke at 7:00 a.m."

"Well," said Amanda, "I eventually got to sleep. I must say being alone doesn't help but I did get six hours of solid sleep, so am ready for anything. I say, do you play cards, Higgs?"

"Actually, I love poker," replied Higgs. "So if you ever hear of a game, let me know."

"In compartment 37 a great poker game begins at 10:00 a.m.," chuckled Amanda. "Will you be there?"

"Count me in," said Higgs. The two settled for freshly squeezed granadilla juice, smoked salmon on a bagel for her and two poached eggs on toast for him. Lots of coffee and at 9:30 a.m. they both left. She said as she entered her compartment, "It has started to rain so little to look at out the window. Let me have a few minutes and come and knock on my door at 10:00 a.m." Higgs went into compartment 38 and brushed his teeth and dabbed a little Jovan lotion on his neck and waited a while. At 10:00 a.m., he knocked on the door of compartment 37 and Amanda let him in and placed a "Do not Disturb" sign on the door. She had changed into a lighter dress.

"Now," she asked, "which side of the compartment do you want? Window on your left, or right?" He pulled down the opposite lower bunk and Amanda sat on her bed, and she dealt the cards onto the table folded down over the sink. So neither faced a window.

They played poker for about two hours. They were almost even except in the last hand, with a kitty worth £3. Amanda bluffed him to raise another £3 and then slammed down her three eights and two threes. He had two pairs, Queens and Aces, but her full house won; she grabbed the money and sat on it.

"It's safe there, I think," she chortled. "Look. I have a bottle of KWV Cabernet. Would you care for a sip and what do you want to do about lunch?"

Higgs replied, "I would love a sip of your wine. I'm not a big drinker during the day, but as it is your wine, I would love it. Also, you know, I am not very hungry; let's skip lunch, if that's okay with you. I would rather save my appetite for dinner. How about you?"

"Darling, I will do whatever you want. So get the wine from that cupboard and pour us a large glass each; the corkscrew is next to the bottle. Notice there is a bottle of Mellowood brandy in there as well. Perhaps for later?"

The two of them played cards for hours. Stopping now and then for some more wine and conversation that helped each get to really know each other. Amanda, by now, had most of Higgs' money and suggested a break.

"You are just a young man arriving for a policeman's job and here I am, quite wealthy, stealing money from you. What can I do to repay you?" asked Amanda. "I am surprised, I must admit, with you being young and me being the older woman. Well, not that old. I thought you might have tried something on me. I am both impressed and disappointed, if you must know. How old do you think I am? Be careful now, don't ruin your chances." She was, in fact, 40 years old.

Higgs replied, "I always was led to believe that the lady would show her intentions before I made a stupid move. And, I think you are 33. How old do you think I am?"

She smiled and answered, "33 is close enough. And you are about 28. Your build and the way you talk to people indicates a great deal of maturity. Am I right?"

"Close enough," he said.

Amanda got up and went into her bathroom. She seemed to be in there for quite a while and then emerged with her hair let down and a gorgeous perfume wafting off her. Higgs thought she resembled Ava Gardner, the actress. Her legs were long and her breasts beautiful and resembling those of a young teenager; her eyes stated loudly "Bedroom over here." She was tall and very sophisticated. She said, "You know we have had this damn table between us all day; you have more room over there. Can I come and sit by your side? I want to examine your hands." Without hesitating, she sat next to him and took both his hands in hers. She muttered some "heebie-jeebies" about lifelines and strength, then she took his right hand and placed it inside her robe, firmly on to her left breast.

"Unless you don't like me, treat me gently and I'll tell you when I'm ready." She kissed him hard on the lips and let him play with her tongue. He did not wait to be told. Amanda writhed under him but he held her firmly and then she jerked and writhed, seemingly forever, as if it was her first time. Then she raised herself up and lay back on the bunk and said, "I want you to make love to me for the rest of the day."

They heard the dining car attendant walking by, playing his little xylophone to announce afternoon tea was being served. They kissed a lot and Higgs ran his hands all over her body. She held his hand as they both dozed off together, squeezed tight on one bunk.

He woke at 4:00 p.m. and went into her bathroom and took a shower. He came out dripping wet and lay down on the other bunk and watched Amanda sleep. He watched a little scenery as the train slowly made its way up toward the Limpopo River but he then stretched out and fell asleep.

"Sweetheart," said Amanda "our train ride is another two days and there are perhaps some other women you could be with on board. I don't want to stop you having fun, but please let me know if you really want me. Don't just screw me because I am a convenient screw. Promise me that you really enjoy being with me. You don't have to fall in love with me or marry me. Just when you want me please really want *me*, okay?"

Higgs replied, "I am a healthy young man who has lived in a small town in England. Frankly, I don't think much about anything important, like relationships. To me, I like women in the first place. But you, Amanda, have made me feel very special and very satisfied. If there were other women on this train, I would still prefer to be with you. Alright?"

"Oh my, yes! That is alright. Since my husband died and counting the months he was ill before that, it has been almost 18 months since I have had sex. Well, I did have sex with a businessman in Cape Town, just a month ago. He came on to me, and I was desperate, so I let him have his way. It was a three-minute disaster. He kissed me and then without undressing me he simply pushed himself into me and it was all over in a minute. He was satisfied and I felt nothing. You, my dear Higgs, are kind and gentle and strong and young and experienced beyond your years and I am so satisfied now. You are going to have to come to visit me in Lusaka," she offered. "The police are in barracks and women cannot visit; well, I suppose they can but it is a small community and getting found out means your reputation is over; well mine, anyway. Now come here and kiss me all over."

It was now close to 7:00 p.m. and she said she had to kick him out so she could ready herself for dinner. He looked out the door, holding most of his clothing in his arms, and quickly departed compartment 37 for 38. He was absolutely "shagged out." What a great trip so far! And the exhaustion of the two on the ship had barely worn off. They met at 8:30 p.m. at "their" table in the dining car. They did not look at all like lovers. They chatted and casually enjoyed the offerings that night; both had porterhouse steak and mushrooms. This time, Higgs had a fresh fruit plate for dessert, with Amanda leaning over, revealing her breasts to him, and stealing portions of his fruit.

They went to the saloon coach and danced the night away to a good pianist accompanied by a terrific drummer on brushes; "Hernando's Hideaway" was perfect as they held each other tight. There was only one other couple still there at 2:00 a.m. when they drank some Uitkyk, one of the better brands of South African brandy, and walked off arm-in-arm back to their compartments.

They said goodnight, with a long kiss and went to bed. Twenty minutes later Higgs got up and with his South African Railway terrycloth dressing gown on he knocked gently on compartment 37's door. Amanda opened the door, dressed in a shorty nightgown which hid little. She said, "Somehow I knew you would call. I don't know what's gotten into me, except you, and I wanted you so badly before I went to sleep."

Much later, Higgs said, "Goodnight," as he kissed Amanda's soft lips and she was almost asleep when he slipped out the door. The two of them were like teenagers away from their parents and discovering sex for the first time. This activity carried on until they reached Bulawayo, in Southern Rhodesia. Lovemaking every day and dinner and dancing each night. At Bulawayo, the "official" train service changed to Rhodesia Railways. They kept the same compartments; only the engine changed to an enormous steam engine, a Garrett. The Rhodesia Railways did not have the electric service grid enjoyed by the more advanced South African Railways.

Nothing changed their routine. The two swore they would never forget each other and would try to meet often. Bearing in mind that Amanda was a very wealthy woman, she also suggested that she needed a strong manager for her on-going flower business and he would be hired if he should ever decide to quit the police. Higgs said he would think about it. Amanda also knew some of the "brass" in the police and she said if she could help in any way, simply to ask, but she would never tell any of her contacts that she knew Higgs. Just their little secret.

The first evening in Southern Rhodesia, after leaving Bulawayo, they danced until around midnight. Amanda came into Higgs' compartment and they opened the window as wide open as possible. Both of them had very little clothing on as they got hotter by the minute from the hot air blowing in. Both were leaning on the window sill, looking out at the pitch black landscape. They would be crossing the famous Victoria Falls Bridge soon and they wanted to see as much as possible. The bridge crossed the border between Southern and Northern Rhodesia; just a day or so to Lusaka. As they leaned into each other and began to kiss, and then explore each other, Amanda suggested they get completely naked as there would only be the odd elephant or giraffe that could see them anyway. Then as both became very aroused, Amanda said: "This is a spectacular view of the falls and I have seen it before but you should not miss it. I want you to make love to me. Here, sweet man, there is one way we can both see the falls." Higgs was pleased to oblige. A few minutes later the train slowed down to about two miles per hour and both felt a fine mist soaking them through the window. The falls could be heard more than seen. Both were soaked from love-making and the mist and they fell onto the bed in each other's arms.

"Higgs, my darling," cooed Amanda, "you have made me a very happy woman and I hope to see you once you can spare a moment in Lusaka. Of course, you may be posted to some far-off town in the country and that would be a shame. I promise I will not be the older woman chasing the young stud. I shall miss you the first night I am without you."

7

AND NOW IT IS TIME FOR THAT NEW CAREER.

And then it was all over. The train pulled into the Lusaka station at just after 1:00 p.m. and all those getting off, got off, perhaps 12 people in total. The platform was nonexistent and the day was hot and dusty. Amanda stopped briefly to remind Higgs that he could find her in the phone book, and to call anytime. She raised herself up on her toes to kiss Higgs on the cheek, then she was then taken away in a dark green Chevrolet, with a smart black man in a driver's suit, at the wheel.

The first thing that struck Higgs was the number of beggars outside the station. There were perhaps 20. Yet not one offering to help passengers with their luggage, where they would certainly get a tip.

Then a voice called out, "I say, old boy. Are you Martin?"

Higgs turned to see a red-faced man in police uniform, a grey shirt, khaki shorts, and socks up to the knee in khaki, with a navy top.

"Yes, that's me," replied Higgs, "but I am known as Higgs."

"Good. Alright, Higgs. I'm Assistant Inspector Peter Barclay. Call me Pete. I have been sent to pick you up and take you to our training headquarters, which is 11 miles away. We asked a few of our other chaps to make their own way on foot, but we have never heard from them since. Just kidding, of course. So, is this all you have? Two cases? Here. Let me put them in the boot and we can head out."

Higgs was ushered into a gray Vanguard saloon car and off they drove, through the main street of Lusaka, Cairo Road, then onto a narrow but tarred road at the end of town, around a large roundabout, and straight ahead for about nine miles to a place called Lilayi.

Higgs sat back and he said, "I have so much to get my head around. Do you mind if I just gather my thoughts for a while?"

Barclay responded, "Sure thing, old boy. Doze off if you want to."

Higgs tried to put his past three weeks into context. First of all, he thought, how the hell did I get into that sexual behaviour? It seemed to be non-stop; enjoyable, yes, but that has never been me. Maybe it was just the speed with my first ship cruise and then a damn good-looking pair of women, and they did throw themselves at me, he thought. Not that he felt guilty but he was in a state of shock. Then Amanda, on the train, that was really sensational, but it is all over now and my new life starts today. Hmmm...did I even tip Simeon on the train? Oh, yes. I did. I wonder if a few quid was the right amount? He shook himself as if to remove all those memories, and said to Peter, "My new life starts today. I had a trip on the ship and the train that was really quite enjoyable but now, a new era begins."

The two of them talked about what Higgs would be expected to do for the next four months and the end result possibilities.

Peter said, "You know, Higgs, this isn't like joining the police force in England. Here you are dealing with local African indigenous peoples, and you will be expected to learn their language, Cinjanja, it's called. Pronounced chin-yan-ja. There are dozens of different languages but the main one, Cinjanja, is what we teach you. You will encounter wild animals, perhaps not so many in the city, but in the bush; snakes are here in abundance. Then there is the European, by the way, all whites are referred to as "Europeans" but many, say half, are from South Africa, and have never seen Europe."

"Do the whites mix with the natives here?" asked Higgs. "You know, like in South Africa, it's against the law to do so."

"It is not at all like South Africa," said Peter. "It is not against the law to mix, as you say, with the local natives, who, by the way, are referred to as simply 'Africans.' But to be honest, nobody I know ever mixes with them. In fact, I would say it is identical to South Africa except they stupidly made laws from normal customs. I think they shot themselves in the foot by introducing the apartheid laws back in 1948. Our daily life here is, for the most part, the same lifestyle as you would find in South Africa. I find it quite paternalistic here. But don't try to compartmentalize the situation; it is extremely complex."

"So, this place we are going to, Lilayi [pronounced Lil-eye-ee], is it like say Sandhurst in the U.K.?" enquired Higgs.

Peter chuckled, "Ha, ha. I suppose a little. It is built to take raw recruits and in four months turn them into officers. When you graduate, you will have learned to put on three different types of uniform and learned to fire four different weapons, speak enough Cinjanja to get by, and march up and down a tarmac parade ground with matching steps to your 20 or so squad-mates. You will be able to rattle off the ten most commonly used sections of the law that most civilians break - like 222 Cap 6 is the act for assault on police, perhaps when some inebriated drunken cyclist takes a swing at you with a bicycle pump or some such event." At that point, Peter slowed down and turned left onto a gravel road, and suggested Higgs close his window as the dust would otherwise consume them both. Higgs wound up his window but not before taking in a gulp of dust.

About two miles up the road, they encountered a large squad of native recruits, about 99 in the squad, all marching toward them and with an enormous African sergeant yelling at them to watch out for the car and to stay left: "C'mon you total waste of skin, for God's sake, left, left, left, right, left. Can't you stay in a straight line while avoiding a car? Chipemba, I have my eye on you," he yelled at some poor hapless victim who was the right lead in the squad. "I'll have your balls for garters if you don't smarten up." Young Chipemba changed whatever he was doing and answered, "Ndi Sergeant" (meaning yes).

"Is that going to be me one day soon?" asked Higgs.

"I'm afraid so," replied Peter. "All the squad leaders seem to adore marching on this road. Ye shall not be spared. I don't mean marching a black platoon. I mean you marching in your squad, being yelled at by some mean drill instructor."

Soon they reached a number of buildings spread out at the end of a large fenced in parade ground.

"That big building facing the parade ground is called the Admin Building," said Peter. "It has all the offices in there; all the brass hang out in there. Even I have an office in there. Every now and then, like hermit crabs, one or more will stick their heads out and observe what the inmates, sorry, the recruits, are up to. The biggest threat in there is not the highest rank, it is Chief Inspector Oliver. Everyone calls him "Chiefy," but not to his face. He is harmless but he has made grown men cry. Just don't let him get to you. He is a fine man with a weird sense of humour but he does get carried away sometimes. Sounds racist but he usually picks on the African recruits."

"Tell me about the African police," asked Higgs.

"Look," replied Peter, "there's a lot you need to know. Let me show you to your quarters and then we can make our way to the bar which opens at 1600. By the way we use the 24 hour time here, so get used to it. You know, it is the same until noon then add an hour; so an hour after noon is 1300 Then you can ask as you buy me a drink. Okay?"

Peter parked the Vanguard outside a one-storey building and took Higgs' suitcases out of the boot and led him into the barracks. Inside was a centre corridor with six rooms on each side. Room 4 was Higgs' room, which he would share with a recruit from Pietermaritzburg, in Natal, South Africa, named Van Rooyen. He had not shown up yet but was expected that evening. Higgs dropped his cases down and said, "Where the hell is that bar? This hot dry weather is making me awfully thirsty."

The two walked to the nearby building that housed the mess and the bar and Anderson, a very black and very tall barman, took their orders:

"Two Lion beers please, Anderson. Now this is Bwana Higgs-Briar and you can start up a tab for him, and put both of these beers on it."

"Ndi, Bwana Barclay. Excuse me, Sir," he asked Higgs, in perfect English, "what is your squad number and room number?"

Higgs answered, "Room 4 and squad 27." And just like that, Higgs was now a member of the Lilayi bar and had a tab and was already in debt. Those beers cost one shilling each.

Higgs and Barclay took a corner table and Higgs asked, "You said Chiefy seemed to enjoy picking on the African recruits. Why?"

"It's not so much that he amuses himself. It's because it is a strategy. Let me explain. You see, the Africans are recruited back home in their villages. Some may have never seen a white man or some have never really seen any form of civilization. So, when they are offered a job as a policeman, they may think they know what it is all about but, until they have actually experienced concrete buildings, cars, uniforms, marching, writing, and reading, etc., we don't know how they will react. The world simply does not comprehend how isolated the natives live. For thousands of years, they really have lived a very primitive life.

The very first white people visiting Africa were Portuguese explorers, Vasco da Gama, and so on, in 1452. Inland, and not far from here, down to Victoria Falls, the first white man the tribes encountered was just in 1865, the missionary, David Livingstone. It has only been since the 20th century began that Britain really moved in to explore this land, north of the Limpopo River; north of South Africa, that is. Whether that was a great idea or not, who knows, but here we are and we try to make it all work. Frankly, I believe it is working quite well. Furthermore, when the Africans join the police they are generally banished from their tribe and, essentially they become members of the "police tribe." Most of them take to that like a duck to water, but a few cannot handle it.

So, what we do is divide their introduction to the force into three parts. The entire course is 18 weeks. They come here to Lilayi and enter the first six weeks of their course. During those first six weeks, if they change their minds, for any reason, they can quit and leave the force. In the second six weeks, if they have a reason to quit, such as proof of a dead parent or a doctor's letter claiming poor health, etcetera, after a review, they are usually allowed to quit. However, once the first 12 weeks are completed, they are contracted for three full years and cannot leave."

He continued, "Chiefy believes if you push them hard enough during the first six weeks, one can determine their character and "stick-to-it-iveness." The force is always looking for reliability and future leadership and Chiefy sends on the reports to headquarters, who then assess where best postings can be and which recruit might be selected to be promoted. The Africans are the constabulary, from constable to sergeant and sub-inspector. Europeans' starting rank is a cadet; assistant inspector after completing the course. In a way, you are no different than the African recruits, except you are already committed to a three-year contract from the get-go. But there is pressure and close scrutiny as to your future in the force. You are watched and reviewed and reported on quite frequently

Higgs asked if Peter wanted another beer but the offer was declined.

"I have work to do and I suggest you go back and tidy up your room and come back, next door to the mess hall, at 1800 for dinner. You will be told where to sit by the maitre d', a lovely man, a sub-inspector Chambula. Keep on his good side and you will be looked after; wink, wink," said Peter.

Higgs did as was suggested. He went back and found his roommate Van Rooyen had shown up. A big friendly chap, about six-foot three-inches tall, and heavy set, perhaps 235 pounds.

"Howzit, my man?" said Van Rooyen. "My name is Chris What's yours?"

"Higgs. Now you are from South Africa. Right?" replied Higgs.

"Yaa, man. Just flew in from Johannesburg, on a South African Airlines Viscount. Some young pommie. Oh, sorry! You are from England. Oops! I must stop using that word. Anyway, this pommie picks me up at the airport and drives me here about an hour ago. My family is all from Holland but I was born in South Africa. I think my career here, under the British system, is going to be better than it would be by me joining the SA Police."

"It is nearly 1800 hours. Should we saunter over to the mess for dinner?" asked Higgs.

"Yes, I am bloody starving and I have no idea where the mess is, so lead on, Higgs. I'm right behind you". The two walked over, were told which table to sit at, any seat was all right, and they sat down next to a dozen or so other men at the same table. These were all new recruits and they introduced themselves." Higgs liked all of them. There was Baldwin, Ferris, Dobbs, Hamlyn, Badenhorst, and Cantall. All so young and so keen. Higgs felt good about befriending these men.

There was a tinkling on a glass, and Peter Barclay was standing at a lectern at the main entrance, dressed now in a mess dinner jacket in white linen. "Good evening all and especially you first-timers to our mess. You will have noticed a menu on your table and see what choices you have for your food tonight. We like to keep it simple, so there are no choices; what you see is what you get. Sit back and enjoy your meal and wait for my message at the end of dinner. Thank you and enjoy."

Other men joined them at their table and it was determined they were all new boys for squad 27. Very smart waiters, wearing Northern Rhodesia Police colours of khaki and navy blue sashes, arrived with cream of carrot soup along with large chunks of fresh white bread. Then it was a large platter of roast pork, parsnips, and mashed potato. A bowl of lettuce and tomato salad was there to share. A dessert of banana pie and custard was last, along with coffee or tea. Peter Barclay then stood up and tinkled his glass again.

"For all new recruits, tomorrow morning you will be woken by a knock on your door, at 0600 you are to get dressed in civvy clothing and make your way here for breakfast; it will be quick. At 0700 you will leave here and get down to the Quarter Master 's Stores, that is out this door here, make a right turn and it is the fifth door on the left. All of you will be issued with all of your kit and, listen up, shown how to wear it. There is only one way to wear a uniform and that is the correct way; pay close attention.

Each of you will carry your kit back to your rooms and then put on your number one uniform and get to classroom number 3, at that row of buildings to the left of this one. Your first lesson will begin at 1100. Now is that all clear? Any questions? Yes, Hamlyn," pointing at a skinny young man with skin so milky white his fine veins were visible. He was seated at Higgs' table, so assumed to be a new recruit, especially with the question that followed.

"When you say put on our number one uniform, how do we know which is number one?" Hamlyn bleated out in a less than confident voice.

"You will be told as you are issued it. Alright now, everyone get a good night's sleep and we shall see you tomorrow. The bar is open now but be cautious about your consumption; tomorrow is a draining day. Don't say I didn't warn you."

With that there was a scraping of chairs and the noise level grew as they all mixed together introducing themselves and asking lots of questions. Most left the mess right away;

some ordered some small libations and got to know each other. Higgs and Chris had a cold beer and left about 2130. to stroll back to their quarters.

From a new boy in the morning to now a member of the Northern Rhodesia Police and a roommate who seemed a damn good friend. Life moves along quickly, thought Higgs, as he dozed off in his new bed.

8

WELL, THEY DON'T WAIT AROUND DO THEY?

Boom! Boom! The knock on their door was hardly a knock, more like a boot kicking the door. It was precisely 0600 and Higgs and Van Rooyen leaped out of bed, bumping into beds and suitcases and yelling. "Alright! For Christ's sake, we are up!" screamed Van Rooyen. "Bang that door one more time and I will be out there to bang you!" Oh, shit! He remembered that he was meant to be polite. "But forget what I said." The person outside their door yelled, "I want you out here in three minutes! Now move your arses, you lazy sods."

A quick visit to the bathroom and water splashed on unshaven faces, then a pullover and pants, and soon they were standing to attention outside their door. All the way down the hallway, other new recruits were stumbling and trying to remember if they were standing at attention, or even just standing.

"My name is Inspector Gary Portman and I am your nemesis. You do nothing without me approving it, and you will see me every single bloody day for the next four months. Now try to get into some form of line, in threes. There are 30 of you so that means ten lines of three. Got that, Van Rooyen? Now then, let's all march down to get some sustenance inside you so we don't have you fainting as we try to get through this miserable day. We will attempt now to do what is called a "march." You start with your left foot and swing your arms. Here we go! Quick march! Left, right, left, left, left, left, right. No, Hamlyn, swing your right arm when your left leg is pointing ahead. For Christ's sake, Hamlyn! I thought you were in the London Metropolitan Police before you came here. Didn't they train you to march there? Well, Hamlyn, did they?" Portman screamed into Hamlyn's left ear. They had now reached the entrance to the mess, so Portman yelled, "We shall continue this subject at a later time, Hamlyn. Now, all of you eat fast. It's already 0620, you slaggards. Assemble here at 0655, outside this door. Got that?"

Portman was very frightening, and his yelling did not help. Older men would have had to turn on their pacemakers; others perhaps an extra blood pressure pill. Nearly all these men had come from a military background, with a few ex-Palestine police and, like Hamlyn, three were ex-U.K. police officers, although Hamlyn had only been a Metropolitan Police cadet, with under one year's service.

All of them rushed in and grabbed whatever was the easiest or quickest to eat. Coffee or tea and a few pieces of toast was what most had. Hamlyn had bacon and eggs. They all managed to not be late and were all assembled before Portman showed up.

"Right, lads. We're off to Quartermaster's Stores, just a short walk down the road. You will all receive various items of clothing. We call them, Uniform 1, Uniform 2, and Uniform 3. If there is anyone who can't figure out which is which, there will be a class administered by Hamlyn, later today, and he will clarify everything. Right, Hamlyn?"

"Right, Sir," replied Hamlyn.

"Call me Inspector, not Sir. I am not an officer. Did you get that, Van Rooyen?"

"Yes, Sir," replied Van Rooyen, snapping his boots together like a Nazi officer.

That did not sit well with Portman, as his face reddened and he put it into Van Rooyen's face. "Listen to me you. Not only did you *not* listen to what I just said, but when you don't pay attention, you could put someone's life in danger during some dangerous police job in future. So, pay bloody attention and NEVER let me have to have this conversation with anyone here ever again. Got it?"

"Yes, Inspector," mumbled the group like 30 different religions saying a different prayer each, under their collective breaths. In any event, the 10 lines of three managed to march over to the Quartermaster's Stores with no yelling and no faltering. Maybe the good breakfast had kicked in by this time?

They all jammed into a cavernous warehouse, with long counters, like a stable with no horses. A group of African constables plus one red-faced white inspector, who was no doubt the man in charge, were behind the counters waiting to spring into action.

"Right!" yelled the very large white man. "I am Senior Inspector Older. I am the quartermaster here. I ask you all to listen carefully and stay out of my way, except for the one man at a time that I am speaking to. When I am finished, that man will move three paces to his right and one of my assistants will give him everything I suggested. Got it? Now then who is Baldwin? Get up here in front of me now. The rest of you, let's not stand around like gossiping fishwives. Just stand around with your mouths shut."

"Right then, you are Baldwin. Right. Six-foot and 42 chest. Waist 32. Inside leg 33. Hat 7 ¼. Shoes 11. Am I close?" All Older's instructions sounded like an auctioneer with a barrage of words at machine-gun pace.

"Well, waist 33 and inside leg 34. I am 6 foot 2 inches, but, other than that I'm quite impressed," responded Baldwin. "Oh, a clever lad. Hey?" sneered the quartermaster. "I am the person who keeps you well dressed so remember me, Baldwin. I will be keeping my eye on you in future. A slovenly uniform is an insult to all my hard work, so make sure you respect it and move over."

"Carlton, step up. Hmm! Five foot 10 inches, 44 chest, waist 34; better lose a little weight, laddie. 7 ½ hat and 31-inch inseam and 10 ½ shoes. Move along."

"Next, that's Dunbar. Are you a Scot, laddie? You have the appearance of a Scot. You are 6 foot 2 inches and a 44-inch chest and 34-inch waist. Size 12 shoes and 35 inseam with a 7 ½ hat size."

Dunbar nodded, saying, "You really should be a tailor on Saville Row."

"I was before I became a hard-working policeman, stuck with looking after you lot," replied Older.

"Donaldson, are you a Scot? Naaah! Yer only 5 foot 9 inches with a 40-inch chest, 28 inseam, size 7 ¼ hat, and 28-inch waist. Size 10 ½ shoes."

And so it continued for nearly half a day. Meanwhile, as they moved up the counter, the African constables were bringing uniforms in three styles and plonking them down in a heap in front of each man.

The constable said: "Now, Bwana, this is your summer uniform for everyday wear. A gray short-sleeved shirt and khaki shorts. Khaki stockings with navy top. Navy cap with silver badge. Blue lanyard for left shoulder, to hold your whistle. Here is the whistle. Black shoes for office wear and black boots for outside duty and training school. When you wear boots, you wrap puttees around the tops. This is your number 1 uniform. Also, you get a Safari khaki jacket and a full-dress pith helmet. Your instructor will demonstrate how to wear each item. The number 2 uniform is for winter and when you graduate from this course you will have a navy uniform tailored for you. Here is a white shirt and a black tie; also black socks. Keep these in storage until you have your winter uniform ready. That is your number 2 uniform."

"These running shoes are called Plimsolls and they go with these white T-shirts and navy shorts. This is your number 3 uniform and is used for PT [physical training] and all sporting activity."

All the men, carrying large bundles of clothing and caps perched on their heads, marched across the lawn to an empty classroom and each plonked all their "kit" on one desk each. Then they were given instructions on how to wear the uniform. Lots of repeated advice, such as, "Make sure your cap is straight and the peak is in line with your eyebrows. Ensure your cap-badge is lined up with the imaginary line between your eyes. Get the whistle and loop it on to that lanyard. Now place that around your left shoulder, through your shoulder strap, and tuck the whistle into the pocket on the left. Any questions? Right then. The top of your socks must be four fingers below the middle of your kneecap. Your shirt must be folded flat at your front and if there are any folds they are tucked into your belt behind you. Got that, Higgs?"

"Yes, I have it. When do we start chasing robbers?" responded Higgs sarcastically.

"You may never get to catch a crook, Higgs, if you insist on wearing your cap like that!" yelled out Portman. Higgs had his cap almost pointed backward as he tried on different parts of his uniform. The group got a good giggle out of that.

"Now here's the part you will like," announced Portman. "We are going to march over to your quarters, where you will drop off all your kit, and then we will have a late lunch; sausage and mash with baked beans, I hear. After lunch, you will go back to your quarters. Each room has a "batman" assigned to two men, and he will be laundering and pressing your uniform needed for tomorrow. This batman is well trained and is your personal servant for the duration of your course. Treat him well and your daily life will be smooth and hassle free. I will also be dropping by to each room to give you advice and to answer any questions you may have. Okay, pick up everything of yours and let's get out of here."

Higgs and Van Rooyen got to their room and found a 30-ish smiling light-skinned African man waiting for them. He was about 6 foot tall with a rugged build, with a row of teeth that resembled Hadrian's wall, when he smiled, which was most of the time. "Hello, gentlemen. My name is Petrol. I will take care of your clothing and cleaning of your room.

I am a Nyasa boy and I have done this job for eight years. If you need anything you just ask me and I will try to help you. I can see by the difference in size that I will not make a mistake knowing which laundry belongs to who. So you go now for lunch and I will see you back here at 1600."

It was a quick lunch. Everyone was very hungry and wolfed down the sausages and mash and lots of bread and gravy. Higgs and Van Rooyen were back in their room at 1550 and were surprised to see their shirts had been washed, dried, ironed, and hanging in each wardrobe. The drawers were filled with socks, underwear, and so on. In under two hours, Petrol had done it all. He had even taken their shoes and boots and polished them too.

Petrol said, "This footwear will pass inspection as they are mirror-like finish on the toecaps, and they will do for tomorrow. I am afraid that, officially, I cannot polish your boots and shoes. The big chiefs want you trainees to do that yourself. If you get asked today if you did these yourself, just show them your polish kit, in that tin under your beds, and say you used Kiwi polish and will do the rest tomorrow. Then I will not be in trouble and you will not be either."

Portman stuck his head in the open door about an hour later and told both men to take it easy. Have a nap and read the copy of Northern Rhodesia Police Force Standing Orders, which he handed to each man. "No tests on this material until next week, but you had better start swotting up now as you'll need an hour a day to finish reading it. Now tomorrow wear your khaki shorts, grey shirt, shoes, and socks. Wear your webbing belt and your cap. You can have breakfast between 0600 and 0730, then get yourselves to Classroom No. 3, by 0800. Jotters and all the writing material you will need will be in there. And, both of you, from now on do your own bloody shoes. Alright? Good evening. See you then."

9

THE COURSE COMMENCES

Everyone had a good long night's rest and all appeared in the number 1 uniform, in Classroom 3, before 0800. Most had the uniform on correctly. One had the whistle lanyard through his right shoulder strap and the whistle was dangling down his shirt. "There's no bloody whistle pocket in my shirt," he bleated.

Almost in unison, the squad yelled out, "'Cos it's in your left shirt pocket, moron!"

Quickly, and hopefully before Portman arrived, he scrambled to re-arrange the lanyard, and just did so as Portman and another Inspector walked in.

Portman announced, "This is Inspector John Brentwood. He will give you the first lesson and a layout of what your agenda is going to be over the next four months. I have other chores so will see you later in the day." With that he left the room.

Thirty men sat like little schoolboys, at attention, at their desks with their caps lying at attention too, on top of a blank jotter along with a few pencils and a couple of ball-point pens. Their eyes glued to the new teacher.

A man in overalls knocked on the door, walked in and whispered in Brentwood's ear, then left. "Right," said Brentwood. "This classroom is due for re-painting today. Bit of a mix-up, I'm afraid. Still, can't be helped. All of you, pick up your belongings and follow me to the classroom next door, Number 4. C'mon, lads, quick-march. Left, right, left." A minute later, everyone was seated in the other classroom, next door.

Brentwood started, "Now then, a useful skill a police officer uses a lot, is the power of observation. Our first lesson then is on this subject; how to look and how to see and then remember what you saw. When you've been around long enough it will become second nature to you. Right now, you are babes-in-the-woods, but you are going to learn. Take out your jotters and list everything you saw in the classroom we just left. In detail, no erasions please and exact numbers are required. Write your name, rank, and number on top line. Date and time on second line." One could almost witness the blood draining from everyone's faces. A quiet state of shock fell upon the room. Then there was a scramble to write. Afterwards, it was determined that a perfect score would have been 84 items. Higgs was second best with 26; the winner was Hamlyn, with 33. Van Rooyen had 5: desks, chairs, windows, green walls (they were pale blue), and small carpet.

Brentwood explained later: "Perfect score would have been,,four windows,each opening from left to right with eight panes of glass in each. The putty around each pane was badly in need of replacing. Then, 35 desks, all wood, 7 dark wood and the rest pale plywood. Also there were only 34 seats. A blackboard (that was actually green) with three sliding panels and nothing written on any panels. Three pieces of chalk were in the ledge in front of the blackboard, the two white pieces had been used and one piece of chalk was yellow.

The list went on and on: ceiling tiles, how many, what colour, what condition? Any pictures or maps on the walls? The detail was astounding and the squad was ever vigilant about observation from that day on.

Brentwood laid out their schedule which was a lot of hard work ahead. There was marching every single day, just after breakfast. Then Cinjanja language lessons each day, along with law lessons and geography lessons about Northern Rhodesia. There were tribal lessons on how each tribe operated, their dialects and customs. For example, if you were investigating a crime in a certain village, you would see the village chief first. You would go to his palace (usually a hut a little bigger that the rest of them) and some chiefs would welcome you by sitting on their haunches and clapping their hands, others would not clap and stand up. Some shook hands, many did not. Knowing this could help you solve a crime or be banished forever from a particular village. It paid to absorb this information, or at least read up on the chief on your way to the meeting.

Each day passed, with hard work, routine chores, too much food, and far too many laughs.

The squad melded very well and became a real unit. One for all and all for one, a la the three musketeers, just more of them.

They learned how to get into short pants that were starched and pressed so much they could stand on the floor on their own. The trick was to stand the shorts up, step gingerly into each leg, and have your roommate or batman pull them up to one's waist Then you could button the fly without creasing. One also learned how to sit down for breakfast, wearing sweatpants, and then rush back to your quarters to dress in uniform. Heaven help anyone with creases in their khaki shorts, especially if Chiefy had decided to come on to the parade ground and do a little inspecting himself. Chiefy was standing on the steps of the admin. building one day, next to a visiting Senior Superintendent. "You know, Chief Inspector," said the Superintendent, "I believe you and I have a lot in common." "Quite right, Sir," replied Chiefy, "except I press my shorts."

The third day, a Wednesday, the squad were advised that from now on they would jog down to the main highway and back, starting at 0630. They would all wear vests, running shorts, and Plimsolls. Then Dan Baldwin arrived wearing a silk paisley dressing gown, sunglasses, bedroom slippers, and a cigarette plugged into a long ivory cigarette holder. "I say, is this where we all start our little runsy wunsy?" he said in a very Terry Thomas-ish voice. The entire squad broke up laughing, including Portman, who said, "Okay, lads. Thanks to Mr. Baldwin, today's run has been postponed until later today, during your 1500 to 1600 break. Meanwhile, you can go back to your quarters and, within the hour, be prepared for inspection. I want your rooms spotless and your window screens polished, and just remember this is all courtesy of Mr. Baldwin." The men rushed back to their rooms. Soon all quarters were tidy. Beds were made taught like a drum. Everything was in its place.

The smart men cleaned their screens with "Duraglit," an impregnated cotton wipe. It cleaned anything brass but left no film. Those not in the know used "Brasso," which clogged up all those little holes on the screen. Some used toothbrushes to clean off the hardened paste. The screens were still partially clogged and the toothbrushes ruined completely.

Portman wandered around the recruit's quarters and could be heard congratulating some and berating others, "When your screen is free of all that bird shit clogging it up, you can go for breakfast" or "go for breakfast now and then come back and clean your screens." It was all done with humour as it really was not that serious, but the whole reason was discipline. Whatever one member of the squad did affected the entire squad. This really did work as they became a very solid team; mission accomplished.

10

HI, HO! HI, HO! IT'S OFF
TO WORK WE GO!

The weeks went by very quickly. Perhaps it did not feel that way each weekday morning as the squad ran seven miles down to the Kafue Road and back. Neither did the one hour of marching on that $#@#%* parade-ground every weekday. But, even though all men had presumed themselves fit when they first arrived, they had not been, but they were very fit now.

In spite of it all, the entire course was fun. From learning Cinjanja, understanding the law of the land, and shooting Sterling machine guns. Driving cars at high speed onto an oil slicked dis-used airfield and, turning 180 degrees using newly learned skills, was a hoot.

One particular day was purely fun – learning to shoot. All the men were taken to a firing range and an instructor handed each one a machine gun. A Regimental Sergeant Major, from the Northern Rhodesia Military, Duncan

Hampton, was the arms instructor that day. He was in camouflage uniform, beret on the side of his head, and looked tenfeet tall.

"Alright, chaps. Now this is a Sterling machine gun, made in Great Britain. It can fire 28 rounds in a second. See those telephone poles over there – five of them with targets nailed to the top? Right. I want the first five of you to step forward; stand on that white line and hold the gun pointing straight down. Hold it by the butt and have your index finger over the trigger guard," said the instructor. (Higgs wondered why all instructors spoke like auctioneers, rapid paced and loud.) "Now this is very easy. On my command, fire. I want you to raise the gun to hip level; with your left hand, grab that there little lever and cock it. COCK it, I said, Hamlyn! Not cock it up! Then place your finger on the trigger; make sure it's set to automatic. Then tilt the gun up and see how many shots you can get in your target. If the bullets go into the sky, we can't count them. Right? On my command, FIRE!"

Before he got to the word "FIRE," Dan Baldwin grabbed the trigger and 28 bullets went from a foot in front of him, bullets spitting up dirt, straight to the telephone pole, up the pole, past and through the target and into the sky. The instructor looked aghast. Very sarcastically, he walked over to Baldwin and started counting the bullet holes in the ground (5), then up the pole (6), and then in the target (2). "You have just wasted 15 bullets into the sky and the perpetrator is still alive shooting back at you. You are going to have to get a bloody hearing aid and wait for my order next time. Got that, Baldwin?" The group of men could hardly contain themselves, laughing hysterically, but Baldwin had given them a lesson and the rest at least got more bullets actually in the target.

Once, the entire squad was divided into two groups, along with a squad of 99 African recruits. The lesson was how to deal with rioters. Police designated as "rioters" wore a red band on each arm. "Police" were identified, as they wore a uniform. Bricks made from old sugar bags folded into about four-inch by six-inch bricks and tied with string, were thrown at the police by the rioters.

A rioter could "kidnap" a policeman and what that meant was the policeman would be escorted to a shady tree and, for him, the riot was over. Obviously, if the rioters were able to catch all the police, then the riot was over and the police had lost. But, the police could do the same thing and it was a matter of pride as to which side won.

Everyone was driven out into a clearing in the bush. There were many shady trees and a few empty and window-less pre-fabricated buildings. The police marched toward a rowdy crowd who were yelling, "kwacha," "Down with police!" and things like "Get out of our lives!" and "Kill all white people!" They would throw paper bricks at the police. They actually hurt if one hit you on bare skin, especially if one hit you on the face.

Police were told to use rifles but fired only dummy bullets and over their heads. This was, after all, just a training session. All the white police also carried tear-gas guns and three grenades, hanging on their belts. Tear gas was used in riots and headquarters wanted everyone to feel its affects so, should there be a real riot, they had at least that part of it out of the way, just like the army crawling under live bullets.

Yes, training could be dangerous but a real battle without experience was even more so.

But, as is always the case when competitive young men get into such a situation, it becomes real and personal. The first "arrests" were police running into the crowd and dragging out the ringleaders. They, as they would in real life, tried to not get dragged out, and they resisted. It got rough. Still, at one point, seven terrorists were sitting in the shade while only one policeman was under the shade of another tree, nearby. The police were "winning." Hamlyn was trailing behind his squad and very quickly a bunch of rioters had snuck up behind him and grabbed his arms and handcuffed them behind him. Van Rooyen was a designated rioter. He said to Hamlyn, in a very exaggerated German accent, "For you zee war is over." "Oh, no it isn't!" yelled Hamlyn and, he moved his hands and managed to pull a tear-gas grenade out of his belt clip. The idea was to pull the pin and drop the grenade on the ground amidst all the kidnapping rioters, while he ran full speed to avoid the gas. A clever plan indeed.

Hamlyn managed to pull the pin all right, but the grenade was stuck on his belt clip and he could not get it off. The cartridge started burning and the gas flowed out in a powerful cloud. Hamlyn started running; his hand feverishly struggling behind him, trying to now rip off his entire belt, but nothing worked. Now the phosphorous explosive started to burn through his belt, through his shirt, and searing his back. He was screaming very loudly as he ran through the bushes. The rioters who had tried to kidnap him were now running to help him. Hamlyn ran faster than them and it was like a cartoon one would see in the cinema – Bugs

Bunny running through the woods, with a jet of smoke running behind him.

The matter was deadly serious, however, and fortunately, in a way, the phosphorous explosive burned his belt off quickly and everything dropped to the ground, including his short pants. Eventually, Hamlyn was treated and rushed to hospital with first degree burns to his back and hands. He was kept in for three weeks. The riot exercise was cancelled and declared a draw. So, it was back to the training course.

The tear-gas episode was great for story telling but as Hamlyn was soon to be re-joining all of them, they decided not to embarrass him and all simply shut up about the subject.

Hamlyn arrived, seemingly none the worse for wear, except for a large bandage package on his back and some tape on a few fingers. He was back to marching and saluting and yelling, like the rest of them.

Then, sooner than they thought, it was all over. They had a rehearsal for a passing out parade. Van Rooyen said, "You know, man, I never saw one bloke pass out," displaying his brand of humour.

On one memorable day of marching practice, Chiefy happened to "stroll" by. "Morning, men," he greeted. "Mind if I try my hand at the controls?"

"Go ahead, Chief Inspector," said Portman.

Chiefy, using his deep authoritative voice, began: "Now men, you are not the first crew we have had here, and you won't be the last. This passing out parade is an ego trip for all the officers here working hard. The spectators are always concerned with how smart everyone looks, so make sure your uniforms are perfect. But also, your posture and timing as you march and salute are crucial. So let's see how you look. Squaaaad ATTENTION. Right turn. By the left, quiiiiiick march. Left, left, left, right, left. Squaaaad HALT. Now then, your marching wasn't bad but your halting was terrible. When I say HALT, I want to hear your last step in unison; one foot coming down not brppp, brppp, brppp, like a whole bunch of cows shitting in the fields. One foot as if all of you tied your right foot to each other and slammed it down once...Got that? Not brppp, brppp."

From the middle of the squad, a posh voice asked, "How did it go again, Sir?" It was Baldwin.

Chiefy had to hold his face together because he too found it as amusing as the rest of them. "It went brpppp, brppp, brppp and it is also going to cost you a drink in the mess tonight, Baldwin. Now did you get that?"

Everyone replied, "Yes, Chief Inspector."

With a smug look on his face, Chiefy yelled out, "Carry on, Portman!"

Then he marched off, up the steps to his office.

The days flew by and each one became an adventure. Three days of equestrian training. The bloody horses awoke early and had to be walked, brushed, and cleaned under the tail. Clean the floor. Clean bridles and saddles. Trot around the parade ground. Higgs wondered if he could sign something that excluded him from anything to do with horses, ever again. They learned to gallop and they learned how horses helped in crowd control. Then it was all over, with the horses, anyway.

In the last week, a driving instructor from London's

famous Metropolitan Police arrived and started teaching everyone how to drive a car. Everyone figured this was a bit redundant, that is until they were alone in the car, with the instructor sitting next to them. Higgs loved the whole two-day experience. Racing a Rover 90 at 80 miles per hour into a disused section of the airport; the whole tarmac apron had been slicked with oil. White-washed 44-gallon drums had been strategically placed. Higgs' job was to race the car into the oil and slam on brakes, all the while skidding through (not into) the white drums, and end up facing whichever direction the instructor said.

Then there was a drive through the residential streets of Lusaka. The instructor would yell out, "Look in the mirror 8 times a minute!" and "What gear are you in?" and, as he placed his hand over the speedometer, "What speed are you doing?" or, "Slow down and change gear, it's raining." It was an educational experience that never left you. Higgs thought it a shame, really, that all drivers do not take this course. The dolts on the roads today would be less doltish, if they did.

A few days later, in the late afternoon, a squad of 99 newly recruited native constables were being marched up and down the field. Chiefy was standing on the steps, dragging on a cigarette, watching the new constables marching. The drill instructor yelled out "Squaaad, left wheel!" (which meant the column of 30 x 3 made a left turn of 90 degrees). Unfortunately, the front two men either didn't hear or were day-dreaming. In any event, they found themselves marching together, in a straight line, while their other 97 cronies were rapidly marching away from them at a 90-degree angle to the left. Chiefy saw it all.

"That's right!" he bellowed. "You two wankers, keep marching, south of the bloody Limpopo River where you belong. Now get back in line!" The squad, was halted, facing the admin building. Chiefy had run inside and now emerged strapping on his Webley 38 revolver. He marched quickly to the first man at fault. Pushing his face into this man's face, he yelled, "Come with me now! The rest of you, eyes front!"

He marched the man behind the squad out through the gate and to the single railway track running behind the parade ground. Chiefy told the man to lie down between the tracks. (This was quite safe as there were only four trains a day and three had gone. The fourth was not due until 0100.) Chiefy then pulled out his revolver and fired three shots into the air. "All right, laddy, me boy, now you lie there and don't move a muscle." Chiefy then marched back and ordered the second victim to run to the workshop and retrieve a shovel, and then to run with it over his head to the railway. "Keep yelling 'I am a wanker' and then, bury your friend!" yelled Chiefy. This was all watched by two other squads of constables and Higgs' squad; nobody was marching. All were on the sidelines, under a row of shady mango trees, enjoying the event. One can imagine what the conversation was like at the railway track.

Recruit 1, "What are you doing with that shovel"?

Recruit 2, "I've been ordered to bury you."

Recruit 1, "But I am not dead."

Recruit 2, "I don't care. I have been ordered to bury you."

71

Who knows what was actually said? In any event, they were still there at sunset. Their uniforms were found in the bush the next morning. Police work was obviously not their cup of tea. They had left to go back to their villages, but Chiefy had got everyone's attention. No other squad would have anyone not giving 100% attention from there on in. Some may think Chiefy had overstepped his authority. But even the Africans thought the entire episode very amusing and a good learning tool.

A few days later, the passing out parade was on. The magnificent Northern Rhodesia Police band was playing and swaggering across the parade ground. The supply of starch became rapidly depleted. All uniforms were worn with pride. Full uniform and pith helmets adorned. Lots of yelling and saluting and marching. Applause from the onlookers. Some high-ranking government official was in attendance; in fact, very high; it was the Governor himself. Also in attendance were family members and the instructors during the course. Twenty weeks had flown by faster than they had anticipated.

Now it was the class photo and announcements as to where they were going to be posted. Many were going to Kapiri Mposhi, the mobile unit, or riot squad. Higgs, Baldwin, Van Rooyen, and Hamlyn were assigned to Lusaka Central.

Lusaka is the capital city of Northern Rhodesia. The Northern Rhodesia Police Headquarters are located there and Lusaka central is a downtown large all purpose police station. There are four smaller stations in the suburbs where one or two white officers may be stationed. These smaller stations usually have living quarters for unmarried personnel, upstairs.

11

LEARNING

Higgs left Lilayi on a Friday afternoon, along with his three friends and all were taken to Lusaka Central Police Station, in an NRP bus. They were assigned quarters in the building, which consisted of a small room each, similar to a small hotel room. It was about 325-square feet, with a bed, a wardrobe, a three-piece bathroom, and a coffee table with two arm-chairs.

A small card was on the dresser with some phone numbers on it; *Call extension 302 if you plan to miss dinner in the mess, 307 if you need medical treatment or advice, 311 for duty office. The bar is on the ground floor, open from 1600 to 0100 each day, 1100 to 0300 Saturdays. Call 308 for bar attendant.* The card had been typed and used by a previous occupant and had coffee cup rings on it; still, it served its purpose.

Higgs put away his uniform and civvy clothes. Then he had a shower and dressed in flannel pants and a blazer, and he went down the two floors to the bar. Higgs walked in at 1730 and there was a party going on; this felt like home, thought Higgs.

Someone with a broad Scots accent, still in uniform, but with his Sam Browne undone, looking as if he had lived in this bar all his life, was standing at attention behind a wind-up gramophone. In his hand he had a gin and ginger beer and was saluting so the contents drizzled, down into his right ear and down his tunic. Tears in his eyes as the record crackled loudly, playing "Land of Hope and Glory."

"Who or what is that?" asked Higgs of an officer in uniform whom he had not met. "I'm Higgs, new boy arrived today," he said, introducing himself.

"I'm Ian. Been here three years, and back to Blighty soon. That is Inspector Mike Cameron. The record playing and saluting ceremony has never been explained to any of us, as far as I know. He just gets blathered and out comes his gramophone. I don't believe he has any other records. Come over here and meet some of the lads, and can I get you a beer or something else?"

There were about 12 men in the mess, with three standing at the bar.

"This is our new boy, Higgs" announced Ian. "This is Pete Deale, traffic, Pete Sapphire, also traffic, Dickie Yates, mostly jazz pianist." They shook hands and welcomed Higgs, then turned to the barman, a large Nyasa man, with a beautiful black, almost purple face, and a grin that never ended.

"Philemon, this is Mr. Higgs and he is going to need a tab. Higgs, this is Philemon and he will take care of your account."

"You are Bwana Higgs. What is you surname?" asked Philemon. He scribbled down all the information he needed and announced that Higgs could now buy drinks, "You can buy drinks on the tab and pay every month. Your first payment is August 1."

"I'll have a cold beer. Is there a house special beer or a choice?" asked Higgs.

Ian said he had already ordered a Castle beer and it was on him. Higgs recalled that Castle beer was his choice on board the ship and he loved its crisp taste.

Higgs enjoyed the atmosphere. Then in came Chris Van Rooyen and everyone introduced themselves. Dan Baldwin was next to arrive, along with Michael Hamlyn. Pretty soon it was as if the four new boys with four new bar tabs had been there forever.

Mike Cameron continued his routine until nearly everyone left to go for dinner in the next door dining room, tears running down his face and gin and ginger beer flooding down the right side of his tunic.

One curious thing for Higgs was why each policeman in uniform had their Sam Browne's undone. Ian explained, "You can't drink in uniform. When one undoes their Sam Browne, one is not in uniform. Got it, Higgs?" Higgs tucked away that important piece of trivia into his mental notebook.

The next day, being a Saturday, Ian Bradley phoned Higgs in his room, at an early time, 0900. He volunteered to drive Higgs around Lusaka and show him around – the theatre, the cathedral, the restaurants, and so on. Higgs leaped at the opportunity and the two set off at around 1000. Ian had an old 1952 Morris Oxford that had at least 12 horsepower, but was comfortable and reliable.

Higgs could not believe that he was now a policeman and being driven around the city he was sworn to protect and serve; six months ago, he was a damn young mechanic in a small village in England.

12

SO THIS WAS LUSAKA

As the two drove around, Ian gave Higgs a lesson in what went on around the life there. In 1958 Lusaka was a city of about 15,000 Europeans and, with all the African compounds encircling the city, perhaps another 75,000 native indigenous. There were really no statistics for the natives, such as birth certificates, income tax returns, house numbers and numbers of occupants, for the natives. Precise data was simply not available, but a good guess was possible. Finding a particular native was a seriously difficult task for any policeman, and it was a big part of the job.

European family's would have a servant working for them. Most European houses had a separate building in their backyard, of about 400-square feet, with two rooms, a bathroom and a small kitchen, with running water and a sink. These small, stand-alone houses were called servant's quarters. Assuming one African family lived in each servant's quarters, this indicates there were about another 45,000 natives living within the city.

One statistic seemed to be right, and that was that a male servant would have his wife and two smallest children with him in the quarters. Usually, any child of age 12 or more would live back in their village, with a relative, and they attended school there. Servants were hired, not because the settlers were lazy or rich, but because servants were a necessity. In a typical European family, both spouses worked.

There were chores that needed being done and appliances were either scarce or very expensive relative to income. For example, a refrigerator would cost about six months typical salary, say £200 and more. Because there was no air-conditioning in homes, fresh bread, fruit, vegetables, and meat needed to be purchased almost daily.

Typically, both spouses left for their jobs at 0800. They would come home around 1700. The servant would have been given a shopping list to take to a grocery store where an account had been set up by the house owner. The servant generally rode a bike and picked up most items at one of a few, mostly Indian owned, general stores. There was quite a large percentage of Indians from India, who had filtered up from South Africa or arrived as immigrants directly.

Then there would be another trip to the butcher, frequently owned by an Afrikaans person and, with goods marked on the account, the servant would ride home. Then, potatoes, carrots, onions, etc. might be prepared. The meat might fit into a small table top refrigerator, often powered with paraffin.

When the family came home, all that was left was usually for the madam of the house to cook the meal. The servant would tidy up, clean the dishes, and then go home, 50 yards away, by about 1900. This was a good arrangement for all. Some families were wealthy enough to have a cook who did all that.

So, for an average family there would be a house-boy and a garden-boy. The houseboy generally supervised the garden-boy. There were African schools nearby and the servant's wife took any school-aged children to school daily, up to a possible twomile trudge each way.

The NR Government provided free education and medical assistance to everyone. Private medical help was for any who wanted some treatment and could afford to pay. All government employees and every member of the NRP got free or assisted accommodation, education, and medical, for themselves and their family under the same roof. The entire country was a fine balance of social welfare balanced with tremendous entrepreneurial opportunity; affordable to the government and private business.

Lusaka had one main street, Cairo Road. A dual carriageway a mile long with very large roundabouts at each end. Two lesser streets, Stanley Road and Livingstone Road, ran parallel to Cairo Road; the entire city was a neat rectangle. The city was where it was because the first settlers, less than 75 years ago, decided it was the right distance for a railway station to be placed. Except for this, Lusaka could have been a hundred miles north or south of where it was.

The African men loved their sports, especially football and, additionally, they enjoy their so-called beer garden, or beer hall, especially on weekends. Their beer is named "Kaffir beer" or "Tchwala." It is made out of a grain, similar to wheat. The beer looks like milk, and tasted awful but they love it and it's cheap.

We get a lot of work from those drinkers," explained Ian, "either common assault, or drunken cycling. They get motherless and, while most of them are lovers and not fighters, none of them are great at cycling home on roads filled with cars. So, we stop them, maybe detain them overnight, seldom charge them, but it seems to be a job that never ends. African women simply have little time for entertainment. They have domestic duties."

They were driving down Livingstone Road. Ian pointed at a building across the street and explained, "That is the Carlton Cinema and next to it is the Carlton Bar. Really only one of two cinemas in town, the other being the Twentieth Century, up the street. Both quite nice and clean and show all the latest films. The Carlton Bar seems to attract a lot of rowdies. You will attend a number of fights there."

They drove up to a drive-in café, called The Star, a few miles south on the Kafue Road. Higgs remembered passing it on the way to Lilayi. They pulled in for a hamburger and chips, and sat in the car chatting about this new country and Higgs' new job.

At that moment, a car, a 1956 Ford Zephyr, with a purple and black paint-job and swirling all over it some teenage louts, as Ian called them, screeched to a halt. As it did so, Higgs' tray, with his unfinished meal, was covered with a cloud of dust. Higgs yelled out of his open window, "Thanks a bloody lot for decorating my food. You should think before

acting so stupidly. Now what are you going to do about this?"
The teenagers were all in jeans and leather bomber jackets
and "Brylcreemed" hair, mostly in some duck-tail style.

The driver slowly got out of his car and walked over
to Higgs' window and carefully tipped over Higgs' tray, so
all the food and the unfinished milkshake were now on
the ground.

"Listen here, you jerk! Do not ever criticize me or my
driving, 'cos next time it will be you on the ground, not just
your food," said the teenager, rudely.

The young man was leaning on Higgs' door.

"Step back a little my man," requested Higgs. "I have to
get out of my car."

The teen stepped back about five inches and said, with
a silly grin on his face, "There you go. That should give you
enough space."

Higgs carefully twisted the door handle and then hit the
door fast and hard. The door swung into the young man's
knees and body and knocked him flat on the ground, with
his face resting in some hamburger and chocolate mixture.

"Oops! Sorry!" said Higgs, as the young man looked up
and realized Higgs, out of the car, was somewhat bigger than
Higgs appeared inside the car.

The teen weighed about 150 pounds and was about 5
feet. 8 inches tall . He got up, a little unsteadily, and threw
a £1 note on the ground and said, "Here is enough to buy
your bloody food." Then, he got back in his car, along with
the two others, and they raced off, shouting, "You'll be sorry
you picked on us!"

Ian and Higgs looked at each other, then burst out laughing.

"What do we do now?" asked Higgs.

"Oh, terrific! Your first outing and already you've made enemies of the local Mafia. Just remember what they look like, the car they're driving, and their licence plate number and save the info in the back of your head. You'll run into them again one day and that info could be useful. Meanwhile, let's get a new order from that pretty waitress," said Ian.

13

THE VERY FIRST DAY AS A POLICEMAN

It has always been assumed by the "know-it-alls" that run training courses that all graduates will be fully trained to handle any possible incident at work. This is especially true in the Military and Police Forces. All graduates who have been trained anywhere in the world, for any job, understand that there will always be something that comes up that was not covered in the training course. Imagine the new janitor at the New York Empire State Building on his first night of his new job; he went to janitor's training school for six weeks and not once did the course include what action to take should a large ape decide to climb up the building, let alone the way to clean up the damage from aeroplanes shooting at the ape. No mention either of the cleaning lady in the ape's hand!

Well, Higgs felt this way as he stood at attention, in front of the Lusaka Central Officer-in-Charge, the OIC. There was Van Rooyen, Hamlyn, and Baldwin; 12 other officers were present. All 16 would be the "A" Shift – 0800 to 1600, about as normal a shift as possible.

"Good morning, gentlemen," announced the OIC, Paddy Alton. "I want everyone here to welcome our four new men: Van Rooyen, Higgs-Briar, Hamlyn, and Baldwin." Each named man gave a nod and a small wave (although, by their very appearance, with their brand new uniforms etcetera, there was no need to wave to show themselves!).

"Now then, you new men will later-on go out on patrol in vehicles, and pair up with an experienced man, and get to learn about the job and each other. My roster shows Higgs-Briar, you will team up with Stuart Tunn. Van Rooyen, you with Duncan MacNeil; Hamlyn ride along with John Bullock, and Baldwin, you get to go along with Pete Deale. Now then, for you experienced men, you've done this before so you know the ropes. Teach these new men everything you know. Help them forget what they learned in training school and show them what reality is. Help them when they go on patrol on their own in a few weeks, and you new men, ask questions. Welcome to Lusaka Central and remember one important fact, 'NEVER embarrass me and your career is safe.' Okay, I will hand this over to Mike Cameron." Higgs hardly recognized Cameron, who was upright, cleanly uniformed, and his eyes very keenly focused.

"Okay, lads. Bugger off and get out of my sight," ordered Cameron, with a sly grin. "Stay out of trouble and, for the four new men, you and your partners for the day are having lunch at 1230 at Headquarters, in the officer's mess. A whole bunch of desk-bound Superintendents want to meet the new boys. Have fun and don't spill anything on your shirt. Now go."

With a shuffle of feet and papers, the eight on patrol filed out, down the stairs, to the outdoor parking lot where two Land Rovers and two black Rover sedans were waiting. Higgs and Tunn got into a black Rover 90 sedan

Higgs could not believe that such a luxury vehicle would be a "police car." In the U.K. this car would be what lawyers, judges, and doctors owned. Of course, it was perfect for hot, dusty Africa. A black exterior and lush red leather seats. Aaah! Well, they were supplied by the British Government, and they knew best!

Higgs settled in and Tunn got behind the wheel. "Here's the radio and that piece of tape with writing on it, stuck to the microphone, identifies us. See!" he said, pointing to the piece of tape, "we are Lusaka 3. They have an operator upstairs with a big table-sized map of Lusaka, with a glass top, and showing up to 50 miles of Lusaka's surroundings. They have little Dinky Toy police cars, both Land Rovers and Rover saloons. Each has a number on its teeny little roof and they move them around as we call in, periodically. I'll take you up there when we get back and you can check it all out.

"Headquarters is Lusaka Central and you are Lusaka 3. So it goes like this, 'Radio on, microphone in hand, lever on mike clicked down and say, 'Lusaka Central, Lusaka 3 on patrol toward the Great East Road. Over.'" From somewhere on another planet, an African's voice replied, "Roger Lusaka 3. Standing by."

And so, Radio Lesson 101 was done with.

Stuart was pale and slim with bright red hair and the two men conversed about everything and anything, as they drove up toward the Royal Show Grounds, some four miles away, and pulled over under some mango trees, and cut the engine. "This is a good place for a cigarette and a cool spot to be when the radio calls us into action. Also, take a pee break, as there no public toilets. If you need more than a pee, let me know and we can drive to another police station."

"How long have you been a copper?" asked Higgs. "Two years in Edinburgh and nearly two years here," replied Tunn. "I had to leave quickly – woman trouble. Well, her brother's trouble mainly. And you, what's your background?"

"Motorcycle mechanic in Milton-Keynes and boredom," responded Higgs. "Look, all the officers here seem so pleasant and friendly. Are they all like that or are there some bastards hiding in wait?"

Tunn replied, "No, they all seem genuinely nice. Mess them around, embarrass them, as Paddy warned today, and they will come down on you like a ton of bricks. Keep your nose clean and show up for work and you'll be fine."

"Lusaka to Lusaka 3. What is your position?" blared the radio.

Stuart grabbed the mike and replied, "About five miles up the Great East Road."

"Roger. Attend immediately to a death of an A/M (police jargon for an African male) on corner of Cecil Rhodes Drive and the Great East Road. Ambulance heading there now. Possible murder and assailant, with weapon – possibly an axe – is on site."

"Higgs, hold on," said Stuart. "Hit that red button above the glove box."

Higgs hit the button and nearly jumped out of his seat as the siren began wailing.

"No heroics when we arrive. Common sense and be observant. Let me know anything you see that might prove important," demanded Stuart.

On arrival, lying in the entranceway to a three-story apartment block, was a young African male in jeans and a blue checkered shirt, with blood everywhere, flowing out of his head, and very obviously dead. He appeared to be in his mid-twenties? Lying next to the body was a short axe, with flesh and blood all over the blade.

Higgs strolled over to the bushes at the side of the entrance and called out, "Stuart, there's someone hiding in here!"

And then the bushes came alive and a very petite African woman came running out at Higgs with a large kitchen knife. Higgs side-stepped her and she ran at Stuart, who had just retrieved his notebook and was about to write notes. At that point the ambulance arrived and the two attendants, both African police constables, along with the driver exited the vehicle and ran toward the berserk woman. The three surrounded her, as Higgs reached under her arms and kneed her from behind.

Then she dropped the knife and she was on her back. She gave a parting kick right into Higgs' privates, before she was handcuffed by the constable. Her feet were also shackled. She got thrown into the back seat of the Land Rover. Higgs threw her in with a little extra enthusiasm.

A Land Rover pulled up with a plain-clothed Inspector Rob James driving and two black detective constables. Higgs explained the set-up, discussed the important lunch date, and James said he would take over. They all agreed to complete the paperwork later on, after lunch, at the station.

"Okay, let's go and take her to lock-up as we don't want to be late for lunch now, do we?" yelled Stuart. The assailant was removed from the Rover saloon and transferred to the Land Rover and each vehicle left to go where they needed to be, leaving behind a detective and a camera at the death scene. Higgs figured the detective had a means of getting back to the station.

"Bloody hell! What a first day on the job!" exclaimed Higgs. "I hope my balls survive that kick! Right now they're numb."

"Do you think a doctor should check you out?" asked Stuart.

"No, just get me somewhere I can have a drink," pleaded Higgs.

Almost exactly at noon Stuart dropped off Higgs in the parking lot of the Northern Rhodesia Police Headquarters officer's mess. "I'm off, so get a ride back with one of the others," yelled Stuart, as he raced off. As Higgs entered the building, he was met by the other men in the vestibule. Higgs' uniform was muddy and a few blood stains on the front; the rest appeared to be dressed for parade. The head steward called them in and, there, around a very large table, that could hold 16 diners at a stretch, stood five senior officers. Introductions were made and all sat at the places where their name cards had been placed.

Assistant Commissioner Hatfield stood and raised his glass, "All rise please, to the Queen." All and sundry mumbled, "To the Queen."

Then a ruddy-faced man, looking much like a Royal Doulton character jug, stood up and said, "My name is Punch Ramble and I am Chief Superintendant of the Lusaka Division. I have been proposing toasts to our new men now for over 20 years. Please raise your glasses to "the new graduates." None of the new men knew, as they were the ones being toasted, whether they should stand or sit or drink, so they stood and drank.

The wine was very good and the African wine steward was very attentive and poured constantly; nobody had a chance to run out of wine. It was from Constantia and it was truly delicious, one of South Africa's best shirazes. Higgs remembered that Napoleon said his desolation on Elba was made more pleasant with Constantia wine.

Deputy Commissioner CID Dennis Bitwell asked, "Nobody has mentioned this, but did you have a fight today?" nodding toward Higgs, "Your uniform is smudged with blood and dirt. What happened?"

Higgs answered, "Today was the very first day I wore this uniform and we ran into, what appeared to be, a domestic that went terribly wrong. Looks like wifey axed her husband to death. CID has the case now and I am sure they will have sorted it all out when we check with them later on."

A Superintendent Rider sat back and pushed his bowl of jellied consommé away from him. "I can't stand this bloody soup," he moaned. "Waiter, bring my curry would you? Lamb vindaloo, not that bloody cauliflower stuff." He seemed to have had a lot to drink but nobody was about to tell him so. "Look here, chaps, I think it's bloody marvellous that you can come for lunch with us old pricks after a run-in with a murderer. I bet your appetite was increased, hey, what?" Rider said.

After more curry and then canned peaches and Bird's custard, for dessert, lunch was over. There were questions about where people were from and their impressions of Africa, and so on. Then it was over. Everyone stood as Assistant Commissioner Hatfield announced they were going back to their duties and so should the new boys, "The streets of Lusaka are not safe without you lads. So get back out there and wave the flag, so to speak." Higgs scrounged a ride with the men returning to Lusaka Central.

All of them were far too bloated from the heavy lunch, and frankly, all had a bit too much to drink. Still, it was just 1500 and in an hour they would be off-duty. Higgs contacted CID when he got back to the station and signed the papers that had been drawn up. He simply completed the blanks, confirming his first arrival at the scene and the subsequent scuffle. Apparently, it was learned, from a confession and witnesses, that the arrested woman was the victim's wife. She was jealous of the laundry girl working in the same house, where her husband was the houseboy. With that completed, Higgs retired to his room and opted to not attend the bar that night.

Higgs got undressed and showered. His head hit the pillow at 1800 and he slept soundly

Once during the night, he was awoken up by the sound of male voices, emanating from the bar two floors below, singing something about "never let your bollocks dangle in the dust." Higgs smiled and went back to sleep until 0600. Then he got up, dressed, went down to the mess and had a very hearty breakfast. Stuart was already there and they sat together at a table for eight.

Ian Farmer sat next to them: "Hello, Stuart. Is this the lazy prick you were partnered with yesterday?" he asked. "I've just been told he has to go out with me today and you are with a Michael Hamlyn. Hello, Higgs. I'm Ian. Don't worry about Stuart's comments. He thinks everyone is a prick! I will take you to a nicer part of town today. Now, eat up; parade is in ten minutes."

Higgs looked at Stuart, who nodded his head and raised an eye-brow, and they parted company. Farmer was a terrific jokester, all day long he told silly but very funny stories. Higgs liked him a lot. Farmer also tried to teach Higgs some Cinjanja. "It will come in very handy if you know just a couple of questions," he said. "Mudzi yanu alikuti?" means, "Where is your house?" and "Oopi wena hamba," means "Where are you going?" (in fact that was not pure Cinjanja but what was known as "Kitchen Kaffir, or "Chilapalapa"" a patois that most understood). Both men chuckled and came up with other useful tidbits of language.

A while later, Higgs noticed a black Ford Consul in front of them, licence plate that read "TIT." Ian said, "Let's pull him over to check him out." Higgs hit the siren and the Consul pulled over. "You handle it," said Farmer. "Your first episode."

Higgs approached the car owner and asked for his papers. "What is your licence number?" he asked. The driver, a handsome young white male, answered, "T 11." "Get out of your car, Sir, and read your rear licence plate." The driver did so and then stood in shock when he saw 'TIT.' Someone had taken a paintbrush and drawn over the second 1 to form a T. The driver figured he knew who had done it and everyone laughed.

"Get it cleaned up today. Here's your papers. Tell whoever did this that he is a twerp. G'day, Sir," said Higgs.

"Well handled," said Farmer, and off the pair patrolled.

Higgs was summoned to see the Assistant O.I.C. later that afternoon. He was standing in the office when this red-faced man with a big moustache, very skinny and very tall, and seemed quite old, maybe aged 40ish, Inspector Franklin started questioning him. "Did they teach you how to handcuff a person at training school?" he asked. "Well, of course, Inspector," replied Higgs.

"I presume you were taught the section of law surrounding assault on police?" asked Franklin.

"Yes, I was...that would be 222 Cap. 6 Para.1," replied Higgs.

"And did they teach you the best way to clean a police vehicle that had puke all over the back seat, from a drunk?" Franklin enquired.

"Aaah! No, Inspector. Not part of the course," said Higgs.

"Bloody shame that," blurted Franklin. "I've always said they should teach real events. You see, Higgs, we have a car downstairs right now that has that problem So use your noggin and get down there and figure out the best way to clean it. And have it all sparkly and shiny and with no pongs, and by 1600, ready for the next shift. Move along, laddy."

Higgs trotted down the stairs to the parking lot. There was a Rover parked close to the hosepipe He assumed it was the pukey vehicle and opened the back door. It was. The smell rocked him back on his heels. He opened all doors and then grabbed the hosepipe. Beautiful red leather seats with cheap clear vinyl plastic covers at least made it easier to clean. Higgs turned on the hose at full blast and sprayed through the passenger side back door, across the seat and forced all the "puke" out the other door.

Franklin appeared, yelling, "Initiative? Using your noggin? I think not! That's not how you do it, you wanker! You go the cells and find out which prisoner puked in the car. Then you get a constable to guard him while he comes out and he cleans the car.

That bloody training school never teaches anything that is reality. I will show them all when I take over, as soon as Chiefy leaves. Alright, you are dismissed, Higgs, and stay out of my sight."

Higgs walked back to the mess, next door, and stripped himself completely and stood in a lukewarm shower for half an hour, and then lay naked on top of the bed and fell fast asleep. About 1800 there was a knock on his door. Higgs got up and opened it and there was his batman from Lilayi, Petrol.

"I have been transferred here to look after three men and you are one of them," beamed Petrol. "I will now take all your laundry and clean up your room. You may now concentrate on being a best policeman, now that Petrol is here."

Higgs welcomed him and shook Petrol's hand. "Now I don't have to train a new man," said Higgs with a sigh of relief. Petrol reminded Higgs to get dressed and go down for dinner. Shepherd's pie was on the menu. Higgs was hungry and had stories to tell. He ate ravenously and enjoyed the company of his fellow policemen. Life was good, in spite of that damned dirty car. Petrol was there and he felt good about that.

At dinner, one officer said he had run into a group of men carrying political messages, mostly about jobs and housing. The men were rude and looked ready to riot. This was his first run-in with anything political in over five years with the force. He had found it very disturbing and hoped it was an isolated incident.

14

DAY TWO

Ian Farmer was a jolly man. He was about 5-feet 10-inches tall and maybe 170 pounds. He always had a joke and a smile. He was driving the black Rover sedan, Lusaka 4, as they patrolled the early morning streets. They turned out of Lusaka Central Police Station and up the hump bridge that went over the railway tracks, and down onto Cairo Road. There were two lanes of traffic on a dual-carriageway and in the middle was a row of jacaranda trees, planted 20 feet apart, for the entire one-mile length. British colonialists had designed the whole city, so it had to be neat and tidy. Ian lit a cigarette that he had scrounged from Higgs, and the two sat back and enjoyed just driving around.

Ian said, "I'm from Somerset, in England, and I have been in the force for five years. I absolutely love it! The weather is perfect and the job is terrific. Now look at those jacaranda trees lining Cairo Road. They are in full bloom now and will be full and that gorgeous pale mauve colour until year end. Imagine, in England, in mid-November, the bloody drizzle and no sun until April, maybe. We are blessed to be here."

Higgs asked, "Do you ever wonder if we are here lording it over the indigenous peoples like we Brits did in India? I mean, we simply arrived one day and suddenly we are the bosses and our laws are to be obeyed, and that seems a bit like fighting the Germans because that's what they wanted to do to us." "Good question," responded Ian, "but think of it this way. When we arrived around the turn of the century, we did not arrive with a party of men armed to do battle with some army protecting the land.

There were a few men from South Africa and Mashonaland, now called Southern Rhodesia. There was no clear border although the Limpopo River was clearly a good place to start. We rode up to the nearest village and met with the chief, who, by the way, was an invader himself. He was a Zulu, named Lobengula, who was Chaka's cousin (Chaka was a ruthless Zulu leader in Natal, South Africa). Lobengula had run away from Chaka, over a rulership dispute. He then invaded Mashonaland, bumped off most of the Shona tribe, and now was, de-facto, in charge of what is now called Southern Rhodesia.

But now that he thought of himself as a 'God,' he had mellowed out a bit and was quite a friendly host. He invited the white guys to stay. He had no guns and the visitors had a few. The man in charge of our lot showed off what his rifle could do by aiming at a bull Kudu, one of the biggest deer we have here. One shot and it fell dead. The group of Lobengula's men were shocked at the "thunder-stick (the rifle) and bargaining took place. Mostly, you give us six of those thunder-sticks and you can have all gold metal stuff in the ground.

The chief summoned his men to skin and butcher the animal, and they had a great feast. Nobody got angry at anyone and so the white man had arrived, with the chief's blessing. Just a short while later, a bunch of men rode over the Zambezi River into what we now call Northern Rhodesia. It wasn't like the U.S.A. where wars happened daily between the colonizers and the native Indians. In fact, it was quite a peaceful takeover, although there was not much of any value to takeover." "Yes," said Higgs. "But why did we come here in the first place? Why was colonization necessary? Why didn't the natives throw us out eventually?"

Ian responded with a quick short reply, "Don't go trying to re-write history. We are the last of the explorers. Every country has been either invaded or colonized; and England as much as any. It's like them talking about visiting the moon one day. Mankind is simply an inquisitive bunch who want to know what's over the horizon. Frankly, I don't know why England wants this place. It's nice and it's a great place for about 80,000 Brits to live, settle, raise families and then what? They send us over here to police the laws they invented and in a missionary-like zeal.

Perhaps they want to make the whole world just like them. Lots of Brits living everywhere, eating fish and chips and drinking tea. And I suppose our job is to steer all these natives in that direction? Then some mining began and copper was found in the north and a huge change came about in lifestyle and wealth."

"Didn't work in India though, did it?" sighed Higgs.

"Well, it actually worked well in India," said Ian. "But Indians seem to be a more progressive race, more educated and clearly prefer to run things themselves; almost a love/hate relationship with us Brits. The indigenous here are completely different and not as established or as educated as the Indians. I don't think anyone can say that the British being in India was worse than them never having been there. And I believe this colonization here will be more beneficial to these people than us never having been here. Only time will tell, I suppose. Anyway, enough of this crap.

Look, there is an A/M (African male) riding his bicycle in a strange way. Methinks he has had a snootful of booze today. Pull over and sort out the problem," said Ian.

Higgs saw the man' eyes were as glazed as a doughnut. "And where have you come from?" asked Higgs. "Yes, Bwana, I have come from church to pray for almighty God," slurred the swaying man desperately trying to hold himself and his bike upright. "Did the church give you something to drink?" questioned Higgs. "Bwana, Mr. Polishimaan, they gave me a chance to celebrate and told me to rejoice. So, me and my friends celebrated with some beer." He slurred.

Ian yelled from the car, "We have to go! There is an accident! Let him walk home."

"Well, the Lord has helped you again but he is watching you, my man. Now push your bike and walk home off the main road. Do you understand that? Jesus himself is watching you and he will report you if you try to ride your bike? Understand?" And with that the drunken cyclist staggered off, pushing his bike. He tripped and fell into the roadside bushes as he turned to glance back and wave at the police car.

"Seems like a pretty bad accident on the Broken Hill Road, about six miles north of here," Ian announced, as they raced off with the siren blaring. "Apparently an E/F [European female] is dead or dying so call in and check if an ambulance has already been summoned. If not, get one on its way."

At over 90 miles per hour, they reached the scene in five minutes. A long low hill was in front of them, and at the peak of the hill a small crowd had already gathered. Around the world the public is attracted to accident scenes, due to morbid curiosity. But in Africa it seems the entire populace turns out; perhaps as they have little else to do to pass the time? Here, in the middle of the lane, on a two-lane major road, at the very crest of the hill, a huge Bedford lorry was jacked up. The driver had a flat tire and had stopped right there.

A woman, driving at tremendous speed, in a new Vauxhall Cresta, and on a glistening wet and slippery road, was obviously not paying attention and rammed right into the back of this lorry. No occupants of the lorry were hurt. They were sitting off the side of the road having cigarettes and lunch, deciding what to do next. Higgs looked into the wrecked vehicle; it was empty. "Where is the driver?" Higgs asked the lorry driver and his crew.

They had no idea, so Higgs crawled into the shallow ditch where her car had wedged itself and found the lady's handbag, which he searched for her identification. As he was crouching down in the ditch, Higgs looked up into the face of the deceased driver who was flat on the bench style driver's seat and half-way out of the passenger door. She had been covered with a blanket which was why Higgs thought there was nobody in the car.

Needless to say, Higgs jumped a mile and his heart rate jumped. He also found a half bottle of Mellowood brandy in the foot-well of the car. This was the very cheapest South African brandy one could buy; this in itself told a story.

The lady's car was doing 87 miles per hour when it hit the lorry. No skid marks were apparent and her speedometer was jammed at 87. Higgs and Ian spent over two hours in the drizzling rain clearing crowds, directing traffic, measuring distances, arranging a tow truck, issuing a ticket to the lorry driver, arranging for the deceased to be transported to the morgue and, then, they managed to get back to Lusaka Central, by 1700, and completed their paperwork.

At 1830 they slipped off-duty and into the bar. Both of them had a quick scotch and soda, then went to their rooms upstairs, to shower and get ready for dinner. Higgs started a healthy discussion at dinner as to why that African driver would stop in the middle of the road, and not put up a warning flag, or a person with a flag, 100 feet behind the lorry to warn people.

Everyone had their theories but the cops who had been hired from South Africa all said the same thing, "It's because they are Africans. Nobody will ever figure them out, so why bother trying. They simply do not think ahead and their logic is way different than ours, so there. They will not change in a thousand years."

"Isn't that a bit harsh?" asked Higgs. "Sounds to me like racism."

A grizzly 12-year veteran, Duncan McIntyre, born in Port Elizabeth, South Africa, responded, "Hey! How long have you been in Africa, Higgs? Wait until you work with the Africans, get to know them, if that is actually possible, and then, maybe after five years, come and talk to us about our thinking. You do know that British politicians came here a few years ago, stayed for a day and a half, then left having discovered 'everything' about Africa. Then they make decisions that will affect all our lives, based on that minimal knowledge.

One British chain-smoking female politician, back-bencher, Barbara someone, stayed a day or two, then told us all off because of the way we handled Africa – US! What a bloody nerve! You can't do anything in Africa unless Britain says so. Nevertheless, she went back to London and was made Minister of Africa, or some such title, because she was now the expert. Sorry, Higgs, my man. You just struck a nerve there, but do remember this discussion, as you will change. One day Britain will be repaid by all these natives wanting to live in England, and they will, mark my words."

"Let's agree to disagree on this subject, but thanks for the information," replied Higgs. After dinner Higgs went for a walk along Church Road, a mile long each way. He walked in the African dark. It gets very, very dark and you can hardly see your hands in front of you. Fortunately, there were dim orange street lights every 500 yards and the walk cleared his head.

Higgs had now been three days as a policeman and had seen a murder and a gruesome accident, as well as that dastardly drunken cyclist. He wondered what else would unfold as the days flew by. In fact, Christmas was just around the corner, and he wondered what he might experience during that period. Also, it was nearly five months since had been with any woman, and he realized that he had just started thinking about that and he started making plans to rectify that situation.

He got back to his room and found a note stuck under his door. It was from the batman, Petrol. It was a scrawled handwritten note, on a piece of ruled notepaper, and it said:

> *Bwana Higgs. I am pleading through God's intervention that you allow me to order you some more uniforms. I am very busy cleaning your two uniforms because they are filling with mud and blood. Some of the other Bwana's here can wear the same uniform for three days before washing and ironing, thus I am working three times harder doing your laundry than for the other men. Maybe we can talk about this matter tomorrow?*
>
> *Yours respectfully,*
> *Petrol Mutenga*

Higgs' first thought was how neat the writing was and the spelling was perfect. He would ask Petrol where he got his schooling, and okay an order for a third uniform, just a pair of khaki shorts and a grey shirt, for the summer, which was starting now. Higgs also was happy with his life. The next day Petrol knocked on the door and had a big mug of hot steaming tea for Higgs.

He woke Higgs up and asked if he had read his note as that day was a good day for him to order the new extra uniform. Higgs drank enough tea to get his brain in gear and then excused himself as he visited the toilet. Ten minutes later he emerged to find Petrol standing in front of his dresser mirror, holding Higgs' dress jacket up to his chest. "I want to see if I look as good as you, Sir. Maybe one day I will become a policeman."

Higgs asked, "Where did you learn to read and write English so well, Petrol?"

"By the English teachers at school in Zomba, Nyasaland. For five years they made me write exactly between the lines and they made us learn spelling and grammar. Some of my friends refused to go to school and now they can't find work or they work for one quarter of what I am earning. I do not understand why they were so stupid. School was free and also we got fed twice a day. They are just a waste of skin."

Higgs agreed that Petrol should order an extra uniform and he signed a requisition form. He also suggested that he would help if Petrol needed any advice on English or other problems in the future.

Higgs asked Petrol, "By the way, Petrol, what do you and your friends say about the Europeans being here in your country and making all the rules? Do you just tolerate them or do they all want the white man to get out?"

"Well, it is not for me to say, Sir. But when you see what the Europeans have done here, we should be thanking them. Before, there were no rules and everybody had to fight for food and our people were still living the way they have lived for thousands of years. Now we have education and medicine and a way forward. And I am not from this country, you know. I am from Nyasaland, but the Europeans don't mind. If I work and stay out of trouble, I have a good life," said Petrol.

"But you can't vote!" exclaimed Higgs.

"Yes, Bwana, but nearly 90% of the African people live in the bush. Many have never even seen a white man. They want to hunt and fish and get babies from their wives. Do you think they are worried about a vote? Even if you explained what a vote is, do you think they will care? The only ones who care are a few nuisances who have been overseas and they want power. They cannot be a chief, so they want white man's government, but with them in charge. These few live in the cities and are causing trouble. So, we like you being here." Answered Petrol.

Higgs nodded and had a lot of food for thought with that education from Petrol. Higgs also noticed tthe relationship between white South Africans, was quite paternalistic and seemingly respectful, on both sides. So, for all the talk about racism and apartheid, they actually learned to live together. Certainly, he was finding Africa to be quite a dilemma. Yet the South Africans had lived with the race issue since 1652 and, while some tasteless laws had been passed, somehow they got along with each other. It was not an easy issue to resolve. Perhaps, he thought, I should tone down my opinions until such time as I have real experience and not just preconceived ideas.

15

FITTING IN NICELY

Higgs had a versatile week. Here it was, a Friday, and his last day before the weekend break. His week had gone so fast because he had done so much, and each event had been so different that he hardly had time to breathe. All along he had planned to write a diary so that he could reminisce when he one day returned to England as a retiree. But time to write a diary? Hah!

He was now driving a Land Rover, with Senior Inspector Bill Campton in the passenger seat. Campton had come into the office at 0700 and said, "I want to get to know our new officers this week. Now then lad, what's your name again?"

"Higgs, Inspector Campton," answered Higgs.

"Right, let's patrol. We'll use Lusaka 2 today; you drive. Let's just drive around the suburbs."

So here they were, two men who really did not know each other, stuck together in a hot vehicle. Higgs noticed that the weather was getting hotter, perhaps 90 degrees

Fahrenheit. It was very sticky and no rain to cool it down. Campton was around 28 years of age, which seemed very old to a young fresh 21-year-old lad just arrived from overseas. Campton himself had arrived from Manchester, just five years before. He was on his second tour. A 'tour' was the term used for each three-year contract. He noticed that this new man, Higgs, was very relaxed and was proving himself a very good driver. As Campton was in charge of the local Traffic Unit, he was always on the lookout for new candidates to be persuaded to apply to join the Traffic Unit. Higgs may just do fine, he thought. He would wait a few days to make suggestions.

Just at that moment a yellow Ford Zodiac convertible, top down, and driven by a long-haired blonde woman, raced across the intersection in front of the pair. Campton flicked on the siren and ordered Higgs to follow her and pull her over.

They pulled her over just about a mile away. Campton, in his slow "up-north" accent said, "Alright, Higgs. Follow me to the car. Keep yer bloody mouth shut! Listen and learn."

The two approached the car. Campton said to the driver, "Now then, Madam, you were going a little fast back there." At this point it must be remembered that no radar or stop-watch or timed distance had been used, but it was obvious to anyone watching, that she had been speeding.

"Can I have your licence and papers?" asked Campton, with his hand stretched out.

The driver was a very attractive society lady, with flowing blonde hair and a slim figure, great teeth, and a lovely smile.

She was dressed in a tennis skirt and top and was about 35 years old.

"Do you know Colin Cunningdale, the lawyer?" she asked.

"No, but I have heard of him," replied Campton.

"Oh, my husband and I play bridge with him and his wife every week."

Campton stood there reading her documents.

"Do you know Commissioner Forbes?" she asked cheerily.

"Yes, of course," replied Campton.

"We were on a cruise together last year. The four of us have become very friendly," she cooed. "And what about Superintendent Ramble, do you know him?"

"Yes, I do," replied Campton.

"My husband and I see him and his wife at church, every Sunday," she stated, flashing her eyelids at Campton. Campton tore off the ticket he had written up and handed it to the driver.

"Do you know Senior Inspector Campton?" he asked.

"No, I'm sorry, I don't," she replied.

"Well, that's me. Now that's who you should have known. G'day and slow it down!"

They both walked back to the vehicle and the lady drove off to her next adventure, with her blood level crawling up her cheeks. "She knew she was speeding," said Campton. "I just gave her a £3 fine for driving 5 miles per hour over the limit. If she actually takes it to court, she'll win, but I doubt she wants the publicity. So, another dastardly criminal gets put right."

Higgs thought the entire scene was wonderful and he attempted to incorporate it throughout his career, but never found the right circumstance. Oh, well! They slowly drove around a part of the city that Higgs had never seen. He was very impressed at how clean the houses were and how neat the lawns and foliage, with manicured hedges and bright green grass. The area was known as Woodlands. In fact, the whole City of Lusaka had an air of cleanliness to it. For such a small place with a small population, the city government kept everything neat and tidy. There was one small area that was somewhat less clean and that was the "second class market" at the bottom of the huge King George Avenue. Here were shops especially designed for the native trade.

Stores were generally all owned by Indian shopkeepers, mostly named Patel, which is the name for shopkeeper in India. Here would be many shops selling "seconds," clothing that was let go by a factory somewhere because the item did not pass the grade. Appliances, bicycles, and anything else one needed could be purchased there. It was a little scruffy and there was a lot of petty crime.

Campton asked Higgs to drive slowly around the six-block market. They did so and Higgs was introduced to the very opposite of the trading areas on Cairo Road, Lusaka's main street. This was an area that nobody seemed to care about. There was no tarmac so the streets were all either dusty or muddy and filled with potholes and had not been graded in years. You took your life in your hands if you drove at more than 20 miles per hour.

There might have been shops owned by other races, but as far as anyone knew, they were entirely owned by Indians. They were small shops that sold just about everything. Most store windows still had the sun-stained posters saying "Going out of Business Sale," which were placed there on the day the store first opened for business. That could be 20 years ago, but nobody cared. Each store carried the name of the owner above the front door, Patel or Naik.

As they were slowly patrolling the area a call came across the radio. "Lusaka to all cars. Is anyone near the second class market?" Campton picked up the radio microphone and answered, "Lusaka 4 Lusaka. We are right in the middle of the second class market. What do you need? Over."

"Lusaka 4, can you attend 312 Norman Street? Shopkeeper reported a stolen wife. Tread carefully! Over and out." After a block or so, they found the address; a typical Indian store with a big 1952 Cadillac parked outside. The store was perhaps 600-square feet in size, and sold, from what was on the banners over every square inch of window space and the glass door, products such as "Nestle," "Zambuck," "Dunlop Tyres," "Pepsi-Cola," "Sunlight Soap," "Mars Bars," "Vaseline," and so on.

A posh, short perhaps 5-foot 4-inch Indian gentleman, in a dark brown three-piece suit with a shocking pink tie, and highly polished shoes, ran out of the shop waving his arms, and yelling, "These bloody Europeans! They come to my house and walk my garden through. They tie my dog loose. They eat my chili bites, and they play around with my wife but I am going to give them a blow they will fail to see, with a letter from my solicitor," he said, sounding very much like an English extra acting the part of an Indian, with his distinct accent.

Campton asked what had transpired. Mr. Naik explained. "I was away doing business, but my next door business neighbour told me that two young Europeans had driven up to my store in a red American convertible car and came into the shop asking for a CocaCola. My wife said we only had Pepsi-Cola. So they asked for a bottle of Pepsi and poured some rum into the bottle and then each drank some. Then they offered a drink to my wife, who is only 26 years old and very beautiful, but naïve to the ways of the western world. She is not allowed to drink alcohol.

She should not have drunk any, but she did. In fact, even though she was protesting, she drank some more. Then they all got into the red car and I have never seen her from 11 o'clock this morning. Who knows how many natives would come into my store and steal things when my drunken wife leaves it abandoned?"

Campton said, "Can't help. It is a civil matter, mate. Call your solicitor." It was later discovered that a red and white 1956 Ford Starliner had been found in a ditch that afternoon, with nobody present. The vehicle owner was tracked down the next day; he knew nothing, of course. Nobody saw the wife again, at least not in Africa.

"Right," said Campton, "there's a bloody fantastic take-away down this street. Best chili bites ever. Let's go get some. I am starving. It's nearly 1300.

Higgs commented, "Me too, but what exactly are chili bites?"

"I think they are officially called 'bhajias' and they are like tiny doughnuts, spiced with chillies, cumin, onion, and garlic. That's what Naik was upset about. Those blokes had eaten his chili bites."

You could smell the spices a mile away. Campton bought a dozen chili bites, and they parked under a shady mango tree, and wolfed down their lunch. Campton explained to Higgs that most of the Indian store owners would rather have a fancy car parked outside their stores, in full view of other storekeepers. They then usually slept on a mattress on the floor of the shop.

"Also, while we are in training mode," said Campton, "the surname Patel means shopkeeper, in Hindi, which is why you will see that name many times, over their doors." They got back to Lusaka Central around 4 o'clock. Their mates began faking illness and gagging. "Been at the old curry munchers in the market, have you? That smell will take days to vanish," they teased.

16

NOTHING REMAINS THE SAME

Higgs had been in Northern Rhodesia since July. It was now December. He had been a street cop for just over a week and, added to the over four-month training course, he had not had much time to think about himself. He knew he needed his own transportation so he could get away from "everything police" and find a social life somewhere. Not that hanging around with cops was not enjoyable, he just needed an outlet. He made getting a decent used car a top priority. He had never met his bank manager. His pay had been automatically deposited at the local Barclays Bank, and he had hardly spent a penny; over £300 must be in there, he thought.

He needed to determine what interest he might have to pay and how much advance he could get, should he find a car. Also, no women! Grrrrr! He would have to do something about that! Christmas was approaching fast and the station had a list on the notice-board asking for volunteers to work over the holidays:

> *Married officers with children should spend time with their families. Married with no children were next in priority; all single officers would surely understand. Sign your name. Days off later in January will compensate for your thoughtfulness.*

Higgs ordered a third beer, as other officers barged into the busy Friday bar. Van Rooyen sat down next to Higgs, looking exhausted, and downed an ice-cold Castle beer in about 12 seconds.

"Hey, Higgs! I've missed you, man! Christ! We're in the same police force and the same mess. We sleep three doors apart and yet I have not seen or heard anything about you since Tuesday. What the hell have you been up to! And, yes. I need a re-fill...Castle please," said Van Rooyen.

Then Baldwin trudged in saying, "Hey, you two! How about coming with me to the Northern Rhodesia Regiment (NRR) Military Rugby Annual 'do'? Lots of food, lots of women! We get to meet men who aren't cops and we can talk rugby, while we drink their beer. Just £1 cover charge and you get to eat. Leave here at 1900 hours; my car, out the front. At least a Blazer and tie are required." They all nodded.

Baldwin drove his 1956 Austin Somerset with Van Rooyen in front and Higgs sprawled across the back seat. It was only four miles; right on Church Road left on King George Avenue to Government House. A right turn into NRR Regiment Headquarters to what was called KG6, the mess for the military. There were about 20 soldiers and perhaps six policemen huddled around the bar. The trio were welcomed at the front door, ushered in, and introduced to a Sergeant Duncan Hundale, who tried to get everyone introduced.

The noise level was high as a Colonel Dirks grabbed a microphone and asked everyone to take their drinks to their assigned tables. The trio were at a table for ten, where they discovered two couples and one single female, with a single male. They introduced themselves and sat back as a few speeches were made. Then the order was given to go to the buffet table and help yourselves. If you needed help with your plate of food, one of the native soldiers, on duty, wearing magnificent white starched mess uniforms, with a red sash and a red fez, would give you a hand.

From the frantic activity at each table, one would have thought that world-wide food rationing was going to be imposed the following day. Everyone stuffed their faces with the meat, vegetables, and breads. Roast pork with crackling skin, and roast beef with Yorkshire pudding. Also rack of lamb and an enormous 30-pound glazed Gammon ham. Potatoes were mashed, roasted, scalloped, or as chips. Veggies were Avocado and tomatoes along with artichokes, red onions, stuffed mushrooms, and corn on the cob.

Breads were crunchy baguettes, Italian Ciabatta, and huge dinner rolls. Whatever was there at the start, little was left at the end. Well, perhaps an artichoke, or two? Desserts were sticky toffee pudding, trifle, flambéed bananas, or chocolate cake. Every liqueur, beer, or spirits known to mankind were available, along with coffee and tea.

A military quintet had been playing softly during the meal. It was now nearly 2130 hours, the eating frenzy had ended, and a young tall black corporal, stood up and started playing on his clarinet Benny Goodman's "Moonglow." The four-piece group behind him joined in and the beautiful music persuaded virtually all attendees to get up and sway across the enormous parquet dance floor. If you closed your eyes, that band was as good as any in the world. In their day jobs, they were all members of the military band, marching around with bluster and John Sousa music.

Higgs, and his cronies, without female company, sidled up to the bar and did what all young men do at times like these; they lean, look, leer, and bullshit. But it was not long before the bandleader called for a lady's request dance. "Stompin' at the Savoy" began playing. All the "old" husbands gratefully collapsed at their tables as their younger, friskier, and eager girlfriends and spouses whooshed to the bar to grab the nearest and best single man. Most men were unwilling but all were dragged to the floor and the wild dancing began.

The moves were spectacular and the sweat was very apparent. The alcohol consumption was taking hold and, if there had been any inhibitions, they had now all disappeared. Some of the ladies had abandoned their shawls and boleros and were now dancing like young teens at the high school annual. There was gyrating, swinging legs, and intertwining moves with their partners. Surely the beginning of some marital spats and future adulterous events! There were about 200 people at the dance with about 175 on the dance floor, performing various moves with marvellous flexibility, all that alcohol consumption allowed. Higgs finally got an opportunity to break free from the lady who had forced him to dance. She was about age 50, probably the oldest woman there, and definitely wanting more than a dance from Higgs. After half a dozen gin and tonics, she excused herself and Higgs galloped away to a table in the corner. Two other men were at the table. The conversation turned to going home now and meeting tomorrow for lunch and cold beer at the Majestic Restaurant to recover from the night's ordeal.

Higgs interrupted Baldwin snogging some pretty young thing on the dance floor. He told him he had a ride home and said to say cheerio to Van Rooyen. Higgs and his two new friends drove off around 0100 and he was dropped off, at the central mess, 20 minutes later. They all agreed to meet at the Majestic Restaurant, Saturday at 1700, and Higgs staggered into his room and was asleep almost before his head hit the pillow.

Saturday was Higgs' first weekend off, as he was not due to work until Sunday, B shift, at 1600. A Land Rover was about to leave on patrol so Higgs scrounged a lift to the Majestic. His new friends were already there and Higgs ordered a round of Castle beer and joined the two. Both men were mechanics in the NRR.

Bryan Lygard was a young Rhodesian, from Bulawayo, a Corporal. He owned a Matchless motorcycle; Higgs was impressed. The other man was 30 years old and soon to be a Sergeant. He had come from England 10 years ago, and had done the same job since: "Bill Withers is my name. I can strip a Land Rover and put it back together in two hours. I can do it in my sleep. I need some fun, or change my life...hmmm! Wonder what it would be like to become a transvestite?" Higgs thought to himself that would be horrendous with those hairy legs. He set aside the thought as he finished his Castle beer.

Around 1800 they decided to order something to eat. Each had a whole peri-peri chicken with chips and salad, and Castle beer to wash it down. By 1900 they decided to leave and check out Bryan's Matchless. It was at the back of the NRR garage, a lovely machine. While admiring the bike, Higgs noticed a wooden crate in the corner which looked suspiciously like a motorcycle packing case.

"What's in there?" asked Higgs.

"Oh, that belonged to a Regimental Sergeant Major Wobbly Willy, who had to return to England. He said to sell it to anyone who was interested, but they would need to be a motorcycle mechanic," said Lygard.

"Hey, I'm a motorcycle mechanic and I need transport," responded Higgs. "What is it?"

"It's a 1956 Norton 500 ES2, and it needs work. He said send him £200 and keep the balance. It's been there for a year. I will tell him I only got £125. Let's rip it open and if you are keen, I can let you keep it here until you fix it up," said Lygard.

The three men tore the shipping case apart and there stood a black Norton, in perfect condition. "Let me at it," said Higgs, as he began tinkering. In an hour he had the bike running and, after finding some light bulbs and fuses in the regiment's tool shop, Higgs jumped on the bike and rode around the huge parade ground.

"I'll take it!" Higgs screamed. "Let me sign the papers and I will give you the money when the bank opens on Monday. Okay?" "Well, only because you are a cop, and you are going to drink with us again. Yes, we can arrange everything on Monday and you can take the bike now if you like," said Lygard. "I have the papers and you can sign them now."

And so Higgs now had his bike, and a damn good one at that, and he had just a little more independence. He also discovered that there was a shed in the Lusaka Central Police Station parking area and he received permission to park his Norton in there. Now he could come and go as he pleased. Just to be able to tinker with his bike, every moment he was off duty, had Higgs excited and he was a very happy man. He knew a few tricks with fine-tuning and he had that bike performing better than the original factory specs had ever predicted, or promised.

Sunday was the first "B" shift for Higgs; 1600 to midnight. He reported to the Lusaka Central office along with 12 other officers.

Forty-eight African Police "The Constabulary" reported to their SubInspector Chimfwembe, in their room. They heard their Inspector Hargrove explain that the day had been quiet, and the evening promised to be the same. Then, at 1620 a mighty crash was heard right outside the front door.

The Public Works Department had dug a trench across the main road, Church Road, some 75 feet from the front entrance to the police station. They had made a large ditch to hold a new 60-inch concrete pipe for the new water storm drainage system. The ditch was cut from one side of the road to about 25-feet across; leaving about 12 feet on the edge for a single lane of traffic to get by.

The ditch was well lit for night time with two telephone poles going across in front of the ditch, set up atop four 44 gallon drums painted white, with six flashing red lights, lit up 24 hours, so that any idiot could slow down, and detour to the single lane, when able to do so. Some idiot did not even see the barrier, as he was asleep across the front bench seat of his Ford Prefect, and the car was now nose down into the 8foot deep ditch and he was still asleep in the car.

All the officers had gone outside to rescue the driver whom they recognized as Bobby Marshall, a well-known drunken driver in the city, and he was keeping up his reputation, even on a Sunday. He had chosen a poor spot to demonstrate his skills and was immediately taken to hospital for a check-up, just in case he had been injured. The police officer who drove the ambulance waited at the hospital and then brought Mr. Marshall back to the station, an hour later. He had been breathalysed at the scene earlier where the reading was .235, nearly three times the legal limit of .08. Mr. Marshall spent the night in the station cells. He would be charged with driving while under the influence and had a one-year driving suspension and a £75 fine, after a brief court appearance, a week later.

At 1800 a call came in to Lusaka 3 to announce that someone had thrown a rock into a local bar window. The Lusaka Bar was a small popular bar and patrons enjoyed the casual atmosphere. They also enjoyed, like Tombstone, Arizona bars, regular fisticuffs. The bar was renowned for the fights and virtually four times a week someone was arrested there for assault. Higgs was in Lusaka 3 and responded to the call.

He parked right outside the bar and walked in to a mob of drunks, all yelling, "Mind your own business, copper!" and

"You're not taking him with you!" and also "You better get out of here before we take you on!" Mostly the populace of Northern Rhodesia, all races, were polite and respected the Northern Rhodesia Police. This was the booze talking here.

Higgs noticed a man flat on his back, with his feet wrapped around the chromium legs of the cymbals of the drum set on the small stage. The stage was there for a band to play whenever there was no fighting going on. The man was unconscious and had a few blood issues with the scars on his nose and eyes. A big man, about 6-feet 4-inches tall with a white forehead and a deeply tanned face, with arms shaped like baseball bats, knocked back his beer and stood up from his bar stool and yelled, "Okay, Mister! I was the bloke who hit him, because he is a pommie! So what are you going to do about it?"

Higgs now wished that he had some backup, but it was too late now. He had to decide what to do.

"Well, I'm a pommie too," announced Higgs. "What do you do – just hit every pommie you see?"

"Yes, man! I don't like you pommie bastards, and I would hit you too if you weren't a cop," replied the man.

Higgs answered, "Well, that is bloody decent of you! You just sit down over here, at this table, and I will use the phone to get me some officers to get statements from all these witnesses."

"You know what?" the drunk slurred. "I am Boet De Groote and I don't care! So take this!" He stood up and swung a big haymaker at Higgs. Higgs simply grabbed his fist that was still making the swing and helped him on his way. The huge drunk could not keep his balance and fell on the

120

floor, next to the, still unconscious, victim, and then could not get up. Higgs put his foot on big Boet's neck and said, "Anyone else want to play pommies and drunks?"

There was a hush in the bar, and the barman shouted to Higgs that he had phoned for backup. "I am very familiar with 79315, the police phone number. They said to hang on for two minutes."

About a minute later the door flew open and in walked Chris Van Rooyen, who was about the same size as Boet De Groote. With his strong South African accent, and perhaps putting it on even stronger for the drunks, he stated, "Okay, you! Ou's what the blerry hell is going on here?"

A drunken old man then stood up. He had grey hair, was dressed in grey flannels and a blue blazer. He had a regimental tie and a badge sewn on to his blazer pocket. All his clothing was wrinkled and stained. He stated, in a perfectly upper class English accent, "I say, old boy. That man on the floor likes to hit pommies. I'm one of those you know, pommies, that is. I would have done something about it but I hadn't finished my gin and tonic, otherwise I would have slugged him myself. "A chuckle ensued from all the patrons,

Van Rooyen said to Higgs, "Alright, my friend. Let's get him to his feet and get the constable in my Land Rover to cuff him to the roll-bars and then we can get some statements from these fine people."

As he got De Groote to his feet, Chris Van Rooyen looked him in the eye, and said, "Listen, man. You can't go around hitting pommies. That war was over in 1901 and this is British Territory. But Higgs is also my pommie friend and you are very lucky he was in a good mood, because he would have put you in hospital, Verstaan jy, (Do you understand?) you bloody shameful specimen?"

With that Boet De Groote was handcuffed by an African constable, which Boet did not find amusing. Higgs and Van Rooyen went around and got details from a handful of people. The first victim vomited all over his jersey then got up and refused to press charges. De Groote was charged with obstructing police and assault on police. He was subsequently fined £50 and placed on one year's probation with visits to any pubs in the country not allowed during the year.

It was now 1900 and Higgs and Van Rooyen agreed to get together at the Star Drive-in restaurant for a hamburger and a coffee, after they had dropped off Mr. De Groote and the constable.

The two police vehicles were parked in the drive-in lot, among at least eight other vehicles. Both cops were sitting in the same car. Their tray had just been delivered, with meals and drinks, at the passenger side window of the Rover sedan, Higgs' car.

A teenager approached the car and said, "There is a gang of six inside the restaurant and they are plotting to knock your tray off your car and, if you get out of your cars, they will beat you up. I am leaving on my motorbike right now. I'm on parole. Please don't tell them it was me who told you." Then he started his BSA motorbike and rode off.

Van Rooyen said, "Are you thinking what I am thinking, Higgs?"

"Let's go inside and see what can be done," suggested Higgs.

The two got out of the car and walked quickly into the restaurant. Six so-called thugs were seated around a table, filled with chips, Coke, hamburgers, ketchup, and so on. The young men were around age 17 to 25. Their faces all drained of colour as these two big uniformed officers suddenly appeared. Van Rooyen stumbled and knocked a lot of "stuff" off the table. Most of it spread over the young men. Now most of these "tough guys" had some sort of food or drink over their faces and clothes.

"Oh, sorry! I have big feet! Here, let me clean this up," said Van Rooyen, as he grabbed a handful of serviettes and started wiping milkshake and ketchup all over the ringleader's sweater and jeans.

They had guessed this man was the ring-leader and asked his name so they could send him a cheque to pay for damages.

"Will £5 cover the food and dry-cleaning?" Van Rooyen asked. "And your name and address is?"

"Bbbasil Waters," stuttered the man, "at 271 Livingstone Road."

"Okay. Cheque's in the mail," said Higgs. "Anything else?"

Everyone shook their heads and the two cops left to finish their snacks. A few minutes later all the "thugs" filtered out of the restaurant, looking at their feet, getting into their cars and driving off.

"Shit! I thought we had another Valentine's Day massacre there for a moment!" said Van Rooyen.

They both burst out laughing all the way back to the station for some paperwork to be finished. Van Rooyen said to Higgs, "You know, we should work together more often. I miss your company!"

Higgs agreed, saying: "every bloody time I come here I end up in some argy-bargy; we should go somewhere else." At the station, they asked the Inspector if they could go out on patrol together for the rest of the shift. It was now 2045 and they were told they could, as long as they did not get into any trouble.

"Well, it should be a quiet evening, Inspector. We will be fine," said Higgs. And so it was.

The next day Higgs was on patrol with Constable Phiri. A TR4 green sports car, with a young single driver at the wheel, dashed through a stop sign, without even slowing down. Higgs put on the siren, pulled the driver over and told Phiri to give him a ticket. The white driver was furious at being ticketed by a black policeman and was waving his finger and shouting, "For God's sake! I can see up the road a half mile and there was no traffic. I can see down the road half a mile and there was no traffic. Why aren't you out catching bank robbers or something?"

Higgs exited the Land Rover and said, "Now listen here." Phiri interrupted Higgs,

"Let me explain, Bwana Higgs." Then looking down into the driver's face said, "Do you see this sign? It does not say if there is no traffic you can go. It does not say if there is traffic you stay here forever. It just says S T O P, and you didn't. Here is your ticket." Higgs nodded as the TR4 drove off and said to Phiri, "You could not have explained it any simpler. THAT is precisely what the Road Traffic Act stipulates. Good for you, Phiri. I am going to use that explanation from now on." Every day one can learn something new and different, thought Higgs.

17

ENGLAND WAS BECOMING
A DIM MEMORY

Higgs realized that he was fitting into his career extremely well, and enjoying the whole experience. He had been on the streets for nearly four weeks and Christmas was just a day away. Maybe he should not do it, but Petrol, his batman, was a Christian and Higgs was going to get him a gift.

Higgs had been notified that he would be on a shift change on Thursday, December 25. He had signed the volunteer sheet, as he was a single man.

At 0800 Petrol came in to wake him up and had a small parcel, wrapped in Christmas wrapping, and proudly gave it to Higgs, "Merry Christmas, Bwana Higgs. This is from me to you."

Higgs opened the small package and in it was a leather strap (actually a plaited necklace of five strands of elephant tail hair, with a lion's tooth, set in a metal ring).

"This is a good luck symbol for you so that nobody will hurt you when you wear it around your neck," explained Petrol, very proudly.

Higgs felt very touched and thanked Petrol profusely. "Now," he said, "I have something for you. I saw you one evening looking in the mirror, wearing my suede jacket, which fitted you perfectly. I want you to get it out of my wardrobe and put it on."

Petrol carefully removed the jacket from the hanger and put it on. It fitted as if it had been handtailored for him.

Higgs said, "Petrol, I want you to have that jacket as yours, and in the pocket is a note from me saying I had given it to you. That way there will be no trouble if questioned by anyone. Merry Christmas, Petrol." Petrol was over the moon. One would have thought he had won some lottery. With two hands he grasped Higgs' hands and squeezed them.

"Thank you, thank you, Mister Higgs. This is such a beautiful and warm jacket. I will be the proudest man of all the batmen working here," responded Petrol with a tear in his eye.

Higgs was on patrol, this Christmas Day, with Chris Van Rooyen. They were in Lusaka 3, the newest Land Rover 90 sedan; Higgs at the wheel. There had been reports of a gang of A/M [African male] youths throwing rocks at cars driving by on the Great East Road, some 12 miles from the city and past the show grounds. Chris was infuriated, and yelled as he punched the dashboard, "Can you believe these bloody guys? On Christmas bloody day! Why don't they stay home and sit around the fireplace, waiting for Santa bloody Claus? Shit! Some poor bastards have to go to work, while these sods are up to mischief. I hope they are still there. I need to speak to them."

About eight minutes later they saw a car racing toward them and the driver waved at the car to stop them. Higgs pulled over and noticed three young children in the back seat and the driver had blood running down his face. "Back there," he yelled, "a bunch of kaffir bastards broke my window and glass just missed my eye! I hope you get them! They are hiding behind an old building near a clump of willow trees. Arrest the sods and bring them around to my place. I'll show them who the tough guys are! My name is Bezuidenhout and I am going to the station on Church Road to report this. Okay?"

Higgs yelled back, "We are on our way now, so we must go. Make sure you report this incident and don't try any vigilante-type revenge. Thanks, Sir, we will be in touch." They drove off without using the siren.

As the road curved left ahead of them, they both saw a gang of youths standing together on the side of the road. A car was driving by and all of the gang threw rocks at it, as the car swerved and drove on. The group had picked up some more rocks and were waiting for this shiny black car to use as a target. They had not noticed yet that it was a police car. When it dawned on them that it was the cops, they dropped their stones and stood around, as if they were a bunch of tourists.

Higgs drove right up to them and Van Rooyen jumped out before the car skidded to a halt on the gravel. He put his face into the face of the obvious leader.

"Okay. Who is the leader here? Who is in charge? Is it you, you cheeky looking sod? What are you all doing here? Do you know someone has been throwing rocks at cars? Maybe they think they are tough guys! You, are you a tough guy? Have any of you thrown rocks at cars today?" demanded Van Rooyen.

All of them looked aghast. "What? Us throwing rocks? Never! We are not rock people." They shuffled around and stared at their feet. Higgs called in and said, "Lusaka 3 to Lusaka. Can you read me? Over."

"This is Lusaka. What do you need Lusaka 3? Over."

"Send the paddy wagon up to mile 11 on the Great East Road, for seven suspects to be transported to Central. Over." With that announcement being heard by the gang, some tried to make a run for it. Van Rooyen had anticipated this and had even correctly guessed which direction they would try to escape.

He managed to grab two men in each fist and, with his size compared to theirs, it looked as if he had two wet blankets in each hand; even their feet were barely touching the ground. Higgs carefully approached the remaining three men and said, "Better you come with us rather than run away and have the police dogs get you. We can have them here in less than ten minutes. What do you think?" Van Rooyen threw his captives down into the gulley by Lusaka 3 and said, "Don't you blerry move, you nuisances, or I will kick your arses so hard you will not walk again for the rest of your lives! Do you understand me?" They nodded. They understood.

Higgs asked, "Why are you throwing stones?"

The gang knew English and one said, "Last week a car ran over my chicken and killed it, so my family will not have meat."

"We call that 'road food' in South Africa, so you could have taken the chicken and eaten it that day. You cannot take the law into your own hands and throw rocks at other completely innocent people. I don't buy your story anyway. I can smell drink on you and I think you were all drunk and thought this was amusing," chided Van Rooyen.

Within minutes the Bedford paddy wagon arrived and all seven gang members were loaded up and handcuffed to the rail in the back. Higgs told the driver to take them back to Central, where he and Van Rooyen would be soon, and they would complete the paperwork surrounding the charges laid.

The truck drove off and a short while later Higgs' vehicle overtook it. By the time all the routine had been completed and the seven gang members in an appropriate cell room, it was nearly 1300. Van Rooyen and Higgs were told to report to the mess for their Christmas dinner.

Inside the mess dining room, 20 officers had just begun their late lunch; the food was spectacular, as Dickensian as one could get in hot Central Africa. There was roast chicken, almost half a chicken for each man, along with tons of stuffing. Of course, there was a pile of mashed potatoes and gravy, and sausages, brussels sprouts, peas, and other christmassy stuff. The tables and walls were covered with decorations and a record player supplied jolly christmas music. The dining room staff were called in and they were applauded and each of the five men, all trained chefs and servers, were each given a new £5 note as a gift. This was about equal to their monthly salary, so £5 would allow them to buy gifts for their families, while also giving them enough for a few pints of beer for themselves. It was a happy occasion.

Higgs had shovelled about a half-cup full of hot mashed potatoes into his face. Van Rooyen had a chicken leg in his hands and was ripping into it with relish. Inspector Hawley, on duty, took a phone call from the standard black phone extension in the mess. "Yes," he said. "Right away." Then turning to the table he said, "Sorry, lads. Higgs and Van Rooyen, take Lusaka 3 and go to Chilanga Club. Murder E/M [European male] on E/M. The suspect and victim are still there, waiting. Violence is not expected. I'll get the morgue truck there with two constables. Keep your radio on full blast and I will update you before you get there. Understand? Now move!" Higgs grabbed a piece of chicken breast and his cap, and the two leaped into the long-wheel-base Land Rover and headed out with the siren blaring and all lights lit up. Chris Van Rooyen was driving.

Chilanga was a large cement factory, some eight miles south, on the Kafue Road. About 6,000 people worked at this plant, 300 or so were white. Most of the white males were single, from overseas, or from South Africa, and lived in bachelor's quarters, each in about a 300-square foot room.

There was not much to do so the corporation had built a club and that is where one could find the mostly single men, playing snooker, darts, cards, or just propping up the bar. Christmas Day was apparently no different. Opening at 1000 hours, there were some 70 men occupying the club.

Booze was flowing freely and by about 1230, the usual suspects had reached the "My Dad can beat yours" stage.

Nobody remembers who started it but when the two police-men arrived they began asking. C.I.D. arrived at the same time – two detectives, Detective Chief Inspector Terry Sythe and Detective Inspector Sweet. Sythe took control, and told the rest of them to not let anyone out of the building and to determine if anyone who had been there during the incident might have already left.

A pale, middle-aged man, was sitting at a table by himself and had a Smith & Wesson .38 revolver on the table, within arms length. Higgs approached that gun quickly. He moved it away with a pencil in the barrel. Inspector Sweet thanked him and placed the empty pistol in a paper evidence bag.

The man at the table spoke up. "I'm the one what did it," he explained in a Manchester accent. That is my gun and all it has in it is six empty casings."

Meanwhile Sythe was examining the dead body of a heavy-set white male, lying on his back under a nearby table. His face was clean but his chest was riddled with bloody holes. Sweet asked the suspect, "Can you tell me what happened? And don't go too fast. I've forgotten how to understand Manchester blokes. I've been here for seven years. So, let's start with your name."

The pale man was trembling a bit and said, "Look, my name is Dougie Weldon and I killed him. Alright? He was a bloody drunken Dutchman who kept on teasing me. He called me a 'soutie,' he called me a 'rooinek,' and he called me a 'kaffir-boetie,' (all three insults came from the Boer war era and were typically Afrikaner against Englishmen). He said he was going to shove a carrot up my arse when the sun went down. He was relentless. Then he came up to the snooker table and shoved his hip into it, which caused me to miss my shot. I had £5 riding on that shot, and he caused me to lose. I warned him to stop but he was hell bound to make me look foolish. I told him to stop drinking and leave me alone, but he kept on. So, I left. Then he started yelling out the door:

Go on. Run away, you bloody pommie!' I ignored him but when I got home I poured myself a strong Scotch and it took over my brain. I went to my top drawer and unlocked it and took out my Smith & Wesson, loaded it up, and shoved it into my belt. Then I walked back to the club and found that arsehole sitting right here in this seat, with a beer in his hand, telling all his mates how he had thrown out that cowardly Englishman. 'That's it!' I yelled at him, 'Enough, now then, stand up and face me.' I pulled out my gun and shot him in the chest until there were no more bullets. Then I asked someone to phone the cops and here you are. I don't want to burden the taxpayers with the cost of a trial. Just take me away and hang me and get it over with!"

DCI Sythe had the man handcuffed and ordered Higgs and Van Rooyen to take Mr. Weldon to Lusaka Central and have him processed and locked up. He and Detective Inspector John Sweet stayed behind to question witnesses and clear up details. They also supervised the taking away of the deceased, a Mr. Louis Meyer, in the morgue van.

Driving back to Lusaka, Weldon was in the back seat, conversing to both officers, about his dream of becoming a police dog handler, and how he had come from England in 1953 and taken the well-paying job at the Chilanga cement factory instead.

Both Higgs and Van Rooyen agreed afterwards that Weldon was a decent bloke who they felt sorry for, but a murderer nonetheless. As Higgs locked him into his cell, the lock-up guard said, "Well, Mr. Weldon. You will get a Christmas dinner tonight. Mr. Higgs, I'm afraid *your* shot at any Christmas fare has gone. But I gather they are putting on a mulligatawny soup and cheese sandwich meal, because the chefs believed everyone would be too full after their late lunch Christmas meal. Sorry about that, Mr. Higgs. But the dining room opens at 1800, so enjoy!"

Higgs grabbed Van Rooyen and suggested the two go out to the Majestic Restaurant, the popular local Greek establishment. So they did. They shared a bottle of wine and ate arni psito (roast lamb) and finished with two crème caramels each. Higgs excused himself and used the phone in the back office and phoned a number he had been given about six months before. His call was to Amanda. She answered. Higgs spoke quietly into the phone, "Are you able to speak? It's Higgs.

"Good God! I never thought I would hear from you again," replied Amanda. "Look, I have two guests here from lunch time and they are about to leave. I have an early morning meeting tomorrow. Yes, on Boxing Day, I know. I was planning to stay overnight in the Ridgeway Hotel, where the meeting is to be held. I couldn't face a long drive in before breakfast tomorrow, so resting up tonight makes good sense. Can you meet me at the Ridgeway at about eleven tonight? Just ask for my room number. Yes, you can. Oh terrific! See you soon!"

Higgs hung up and told Van Rooyen he had a date and he was taking him back to the mess. Higgs got out of his uniform, had a shower, and dressed in a dark tracksuit, and at about 2245 he jumped on to his Norton and drove the mile journey to the Ridgeway. He asked for Amanda's room number at the front desk and then leaped up two flights of stairs to her floor. He knocked gently on room 218 and Amanda answered the door.

She was dressed in a terrycloth robe, with her hair under a towel and she smelled of lavender. She was as lovely as he remembered her from the train. Higgs did not know what moves to make, but it did not matter. Amanda rushed to him and kissed him very hard. "Oh, my sweetheart! You are here! It's been five months. Come, tell me all about your career so far."

They both sat on the edge of the bed and Higgs said, "I need you so badly! Maybe we can talk later, perhaps?" At which Amanda opened her robe and Higgs ran his hands everywhere and kissed her very hard and all over her body. They made love twice and then shared a shower and sat on the loveseat in the room and talked.

Amanda rang room service and ordered a bottle of port wine, which they sipped until almost three in the morning. Amanda wanted to stay awake all night and make love every few moments. Higgs had to report for duty at 0745 and she had a breakfast meeting at 0800. She was taking in a corporation as a partner for her flower business and could not miss it. Reluctantly, they agreed that they would have to end this reunion.

"Just one more time and leave me feeling ravaged and sore," pleaded Amanda. "Then we can arrange another meeting with more time for each other."

Higgs dutifully obeyed, and he ravaged her, as promised, and left her sleeping as he slipped out of the room at 0400. He parked his Norton in its shed behind Central and was asleep in his own bed by 0430, with the alarm set to 0720. Three hours sleep would be enough. He joined his fellow officers on parade at 0745; all of them with that morning-after appearance. Higgs felt the tiredness he felt right now was worth it. Not a bad Christmas at all!

18

WINDING UP 1958

December 26, Boxing Day, was very quiet. You could have fired a cannon up Cairo Road and not hit any vehicle. Higgs was patrolling on his own in Lusaka 3, the black Rover Sedan. He was always bemused at the cheap clear vinyl seat covers, protecting the luscious red leather seats, but it was not his duty to question things.

Higgs had been a street cop now for five weeks, yet he felt he had been there much longer. He knew Lusaka and its suburbs quite well and he studied maps and everything about the country, whenever he was alone in his room. He practiced his Cinjanja language skills, testing them out on African policemen and Petrol. He was becoming very proficient, especially with the accent.

He had also used his Norton to explore the city and found areas of very smooth and straight highway, such as about six miles north on the Broken Hill Road, where he could open up the bike and reach great speeds, and one late afternoon reached 120 miles per hour. Other than a few stinging bugs in his face and gloopy mosquito remains on his goggles, he was so invigorated it became a habit, almost weekly. This day he even had the Rover at 105 miles per hour and realized how thrilling that was.

Near the Rhodesia Railways goods yard, some five miles north of the city, was a wrecking yard on a 50-acre site. It was owned by a Mr. Ferranacci, the sign at the huge fenced gate read. Higgs noted the gate was locked with no guard in the guardhouse. Four cars were parked outside the main office, one of which was a distinctive white Jaguar 3.6. Men were inside the office with a few outside, leaning on the cars. Higgs made a mental note of this as it seemed unusual, on a holiday, that so many men were present. Still, working on a holiday was not a crime so no action was needed.

There was a rugby game on at the NRP Headquarters grounds. Higgs parked under the shady avocado trees. The NRP team were playing the Broken Hill Mine team and were tied nil, nil. Higgs noticed a bunch of offduty Central officers so he joined them for the company. Most were CID. Detective Chief Inspector Sythe was there and he asked Higgs to join him on a deckchair as he had a spare. "Tell me about yourself, Higgs," said Sythe. "I appreciated your efficiency at the murder scene yesterday and realized I know nothing about you. I asked around and very few people know you and now I hear you just joined us six weeks ago, at Central. Is that right?"

Higgs got grilled for 40 minutes, then had to excuse himself to recommence patrol duties. Sythe said, "I like you, Higgs. I might want to use you one day. Cheerio for now." Higgs left, called in to Central, and went on his way patrolling Lusaka.

Higgs got into the habit, when on night shifts, of riding his Norton up to the local swimming pool, and swimming as many lengths as he could; 72 lengths equalled one mile. It took him almost three months to be able to swim that much. He was becoming fitter than ever and he was very tanned and, also, more muscular. He now weighed almost 190 pounds. He had to get Petrol to let out his shirts as they were a little too tight, especially at the shoulders and upper arms.

At the pool Higgs noticed the cars parked outside the main entrance. One car, in particular, was a 1956 Mercedes Benz 300 SL, silver with doors that opened like a gull's wing. This was a very expensive car and he kept a lookout for the owner/driver. On one particular day, he arrived on his Norton and parked it under a tree, just as the driver was emerging from the Mercedes. He was an enormous man, perhaps 6-foot 5-inches tall and weighing at least 300 pounds.

"Eh, you, man. Is that your Norton?" the man asked Higgs, in a strong South African accent. "I have a 1956 BSA 650 Road-Rocket and I need a good mechanic. Who works on yours?"

Higgs answered, "I love bikes too and I just got this one. I work on my own bike. I am a qualified bike mechanic, trained in England on Triumphs and BSAs. My name is Higgs, by the way," and he stuck his hand out.

"My name is Swanny," said the man, introducing himself. "Well, Swanepoel, actually, Koos Swanepoel....Swanny is fine. I own a road construction firm here. Anytime you curse detours and heavy equipment on our highways, it's my firm causing the delays. Look here. Can I buy you a drink and can we can talk about bikes inside the pool hut?"

"Glad to, but you must give me a ride one day on this magnificent bike!" pleaded Higgs.

"Alright, we will make a plan. Now let's talk," replied Swanny.

The two changed, had showers, and then sat at a table under the shady thatched roof of the small hut. There were lots of children, shivering in their wet bodies and sagging little swimsuits as they screamed and ran in circles inside the hut. Swanny gave them a brutal stare and, amazingly, all the children left. "At last, bloody silence!" said Swanny. "I have been told that our local dealer has a 1958 BSA Super Rocket, 650 twin, and I am on the fence about fixing my '56 bike or trading for the '58. What would you do, Higgs, assuming money is not an issue?"

Higgs replied, "Well, if I was you I would fix the old bike and sell it, then buy the '58. It is possible to get more horsepower from your bike with maybe a new plug, tightening up everything, adjusting or replacing the exhaust, but for a big guy like you, the SuperRocket is best." Swanny said, "Look. How about you looking at my bike? And then give me an estimate as to the cost to bring it up to first rate, and maybe we can make a deal to share any profit, after expenses? One day we will get you up to my place. I live on a farm just off the Leopard's Hill Road. I don't actually farm. It is just 20 acres, but it was my Dad's place and its home to me. Chickens and a couple of cows is all there is. But I have a big garage with all my vehicles in it. You could checkout the bike and work on it in your spare time. By the way, what is it that you do for a living?"

"I'm a cop," replied Higgs.

"Oh, well. In that case I can leave you unattended in my garage. Let's swap phone numbers and arrange a get-together. Maybe you can come for dinner one night and try my kudu steak and mushrooms. Okay, Higgs?"

"Okay, man that sounds good," replied Higgs.

They exchanged phone numbers and then sat at the pool for a few hours. Higgs did his laps while Swanny promised he would swim next time.

This was the beginning of a very good friendship. They parted with a promise to get in touch soon. Higgs began to feel that he was fitting in very well in Lusaka. He had made friends outside of the force and he felt more familiar with the populace each day.

Higgs had a note under his door, back at the mess. He was advised that starting on December 27, he would report to the "Charge Office" at 0800 and he would be on permanent day shift, attending to matters in the office, for the next 30 days. He would have Saturdays and every other Sunday off. This pleased Higgs as he would get an opportunity to meet more of the "behind the scenes" while giving him a rest from the somewhat chaotic shifts he had worked in his first few weeks. Mind you, he had enjoyed the excitement, but now he could settle down and maybe start some "non-police" activities; and Amanda was a big part in that, too. He had not been to a cinema, or a sports event (well, a little rugby one day), or been to a restaurant, or on a date (Christmas Day with Van Rooyen did not count!). And, even though he had ridden his bike, he now had more time to play and look over Swanny's BSA, as well as use his Norton more often.

Working in the office every day was a very different atmosphere. Certainly, during quiet moments, there were funny incidents, some practical jokes and, still, because very senior officers dropped by periodically, one had to be disciplined and not be caught out playing the prat in the office. Higgs like it. He learned many new skills and, in fact, was placed in charge of an entire department, with African Constable Mafuli as his assistant.

Without any ceremony, Higgs was now Officer-in-Charge of the "Stolen Bicycle Section." Every time a bicycle was stolen, which would be about ten a day, the report showed: date stolen, colour, manufacturer, serial number, owner's name and address. Mafuli entered this in a special book, made out of 8x10 paper sheets, cut in half. He would have a pile of 5x8 paper, which he would punch two holes into and draw lines with a pencil and ruler across each page, half an inch between each line, with room for ten entries. Five lines were drawn vertically with headings over each section. Then Mafuli would enter the data and undo the hinge and slip each filled form into the very thick register. The daily grind was archaic and the "system" medieval.

Of course, if a bike was ever recovered, Mafuli would cross it off, enter the date of recovery and contact the owner (well, at least the person who had reported it stolen, if he was still living). With possibly two bikes a week recovered and about 75 a week stolen, the register became filled very quickly. There were, in fact, over 60 registers, dating back to 1953. Police work at its finest. Higgs began scheming to make improvements, with no urgency. Certainly, Mafuli had a fulltime job.

Every morning, all officers reporting for "A" Shift (0800-1600) assembled in the main charge office, checking the mail, gossiping, or just waiting around for something to happen. Lusaka was not Chicago or Johannesburg, so the days started slowly. One other officer on regular office duties, like Higgs, was a fellow trainee, Assistant Inspector Hamlyn, who had been a cadet in the London Metropolitan Police (for about six months), and made sure everyone knew it. Anytime Hamlyn was given an order, he would somehow squeeze in a retort about being in the "Met." Inspector Harley was the usual Officer-in-Charge, at least of the charge office. He mainly directed which officer would get which duties. For example, he would say, "Hamlyn, get down to the garage and check each vehicle's mileage and service due date."

Hamlyn would reply, "Yes, Inspector. But we didn't do it that way in the 'Met.'"

Harley would get red-faced and say, "Never mind about that, laddy. Just do it!"

On another day, Harley ordered Hamlyn to go to the Armoury and scrape off all the colourcoded paint, on the tear-gas grenades, as the paint jammed up the barrels when it got hot. Hamlyn said, "Alright, Inspector, but we never kept our grenades in the Armoury, in the 'Met.'"

All of the men in that office knew that Inspector Harley was going to explode one day, and have Hamlyn's balls for garters. That day happened soon. One morning, at about 0830, the phone rang and Harley answered it. "Yes, yes. I have it. Soon, very well. Twenty-five minutes perhaps."

Harley looked at Higgs, then looked at Hamlyn, and said, "Right. Listen carefully, Hamlyn. Get down to the Armoury. Take Constable Mafuli here and Constable Tembo from the car pool. Issue each constable with a 12-gauge shotgun, with four cartridges each. Take a Sterling with four clips and a pistol. Take a Land Rover, one that hasn't been cleaned yet, and the three of you head out 12 miles down the Kafue Road. Local farmer, Jackie Fourie, was in his Chevrolet truck when a male hippopotamus, apparently previously wounded by gunshot some time ago, ran out of the bush and hit Fourie's truck. Now the truck is demolished and off the road. Fourie is not hurt. Your job is to track that hippo and destroy it. It is going to injure many others because of that wound. And, Hamlyn, before you say it, ... do NOT tell me that's not how you did it in the 'Met!'"

Blood drained from Hamlyn's face, which was already a pale milky-white, and he slunk out of the door, saying nothing. Everyone in that office, exploded with laughter and Hamlyn never mentioned the "Met" again. He did, however, track down that hippo and killed it; leaving the carcass where it lay. It would soon disappear with all the scavengers around; first a Leopard or Lions, then Cape hunting dogs, then hyenas, and then the vultures. It would quickly be a mound of white bones left in the sun.

Higgs reflected on his new lot in life. The camaraderie was terrific and Higgs just loved going to work every day. He was called upon to go to court and testify on the few cases he had been involved with. His very first day's excitement resulted in a guilty verdict for the African female who had stabbed her husband and tried to harm Higgs. She got 15 years in prison.

The men who had been stoning cars each got 12 months in prison. Higgs took it all in his stride. His life in England was a fading memory. Every day as a policeman brought new challenges and different adventures. Office routine was extremely active, with the public coming in frequently to complain about something or another. Mainly, it was the Africans who came in during the day, and their issues were sometimes sad, often amusing, but all were treated respectfully and officially.

The country of Northern Rhodesia was filled with very nice people. The Africans were pleasant and there did not seem to be any racial issues. The white population were very much united and productive. They went about their lives without any social issues disturbing them. Mostly, the whites were of British descent, but there was a fair share of Italian, Polish, and South Africans, both of Boer descent as well as English. Everyone just got along.

The South Africans treated their African servants and labourers with respect and helped educate the adults as well as their children. Higgs was pleasantly surprised at this, because, coming from England, all he knew was about apartheid and how poorly the government treated the black population there. In fact, while there were racial laws on the books, the manner in which the races lived together, in that era, was not dissimilar to that in the U.S.A., who had apartheid but not on the books; a distinct difference. Still, even though the blacks could not vote in South Africa, neither could they anywhere else in Africa; well, in Ghana, perhaps?

That is the way it was and, frankly, other than a handful of, generally overseas-educated sophisticated blacks, nobody cared about the vote. At least, the police had no reason for concern, at this point, about any agitators causing trouble.

Higgs thought the entire country was idyllic with respect to the population digging in and getting on with each other. Most of the Africans accepted the laws of the white man. Prior to the white man's laws that were steadfast and true, their previous laws were laid down by the village chief. You stole a goat and the chief was in a bad mood, you got either a public rebuke, or a week of working for the chief, or sent on some shopping chore. If the chief was in a good mood, you got sentenced to cleaning the chief's quarters for a day or two. Chiefs were what kept villages in line. Killing anyone was not a good idea. Public lashing or execution, were all part of the chief's bag of tricks. The white man's laws were comparatively mild. Steal a goat or a bicycle and you got maybe seven days in jail, with free meals, no nagging wife, and maybe a guitar from the prisoners-aid society.

Hard labour was for more serious crimes such as burglary, robbery, and assault. Mostly, hard labour meant whitewashing the round stones surrounding the prison circular driveway. In fact, many prisoners committed some other crime on the day they were released from prison, just to get back to the prison "good life"!

The general demeanour of all the public Higgs had dealt with so far was kind, and they were happy with their lives. The police were all very friendly and united and the general public, both indigenous and ex-pats, seemed to be satisfied with their relationship with the NRP. Still, he had noticed in the Central African Post and the Northern News, two daily newspapers, that more and more political news filled the pages. There seemed to be a movement afoot with some African leaders reaching out to China and Russia more than their traditional leaders, the village chiefs. Nothing noticeable on the streets but just that feeling that "something" was in the works. A new religious movement headed up by an African woman, named Alice Lenshina, was causing some disturbances. Ironically, she had a "bee in her bonnet" about voting and democracy. She did not like the idea at all. But her anger was directed at fellow Africans who fancied joining or starting political parties. This was just the beginning of some very unpleasant events.

For now, however, Higgs was pleased that a New Year's Eve party had been arranged, but as he had volunteered to work from 1600 to 2400, his night was pretty much taken up with police work. He might be lucky and find a party going on well after midnight and, if so, he would head there.

Higgs had been given Monday, December 29 and Tuesday, December 30 off. Also, he had Wednesday off because he only had to report for duty at 1600. He contacted his new friend, Swanny, and arranged to go to his home, so the two of them could fix up bikes and go for rides. As usual, he gave a contact phone number to Lusaka Central, in case he was needed. His leave might have to be rescinded if the world was coming to an end. He gave Swanny's phone number 77223. He packed a small kit-bag and filled it with clothes and strapped to his Norton and took off for the eight-mile ride to Swanny's place. It was about noon on December 29, when he arrived. Swanny was outside his backyard playing with his two massive Rhodesian Ridgeback dogs.

"Hello, Higgs, my man!" he yelled. "Park your bike in the barn here, out of the sun. My other bike is in there. Used to be cattle and chickens, but they are too much work, so now its bikes and tools, and a small fridge. By the way, meet Simba and Nyoka (lion and snake), my two dogs. Fancy a cold Castle beer?"

Higgs grabbed the beer and slugged it back, ice-cold, hurting the back of his throat and enjoying every minute and every drop. He played a while with the two dogs and then said, "I need a ride today. So let's finish off the work we started a while ago. Did you get those new plugs?"

"Yup. Here they are and I also got new lines for fuel. What can I do or should I just sit and watch?" said Swanny.

"Just sit there and talk to me. I like working alone but don't like being alone," suggested Higgs. Then he got to work on the BSA motorcycle.

Swanny sat in the shade with his beer and said, "Okay. My wife, Cindy, has put on a splendid dinner tonight and she wants you to be here. No running off to be with someone more fancy than us. Also, I expect you will have a skinfull of booze, so no riding off drunk or I will report you to the police. We are Boers, you know, so we always have lots of bedrooms and we have a nice comfortable guestroom for you and a very attentive muntu who will look after you. His name is...wait for it...Butler!"

Higgs thought that was so funny he fell on the ground laughing. "Alright," he said. "I shall work all day and stay all night. But don't send in Butler to wake me up. Okay?

By the way, Swanny, did you hear about the best name for a manservant, from New Delhi? Listen to this. His name was Mahatma Coat! Get it? Great name for a butler, hey? Ha! Har! Dee! Har!"

The two men laughed, fiddled with their bikes, and talked for hours. The two got on each others' bike at about 1700 and drove slowly on the dirt road, that led to the narrow tarmacked road and then they opened them up. The sun was low on the horizon and there was no traffic and they had almost ten miles of tarred road to ride on. Both exceeded 100 miles per hour and then pulled over under some trees to chat about the performance and so on. Spitting a few bugs out of their clenched teeth and wiping their faces, the two were grinning and puffing a little. The ride had been exhilarating and their heads were clear. They turned and raced back. Swanny said, "I am having a shower and then a nap. I will see you down in the lounge at 1830. Okay, Higgs?"

Higgs did the same and, feeling very fresh and hungry, he arrived in the lounge, fighting off the two friendly Ridgebacks as Cindy, Swanny's wife, came in, shooed the dogs outside, and offered Higgs a drink. Then there was a knock on the door and two couples arrived who were Swanny's dinner guests. Introductions were made all round; Butch and Gwen Fabrolet and Tim and Carol Huntington, all small lot farmers living in the surrounding areas. They arrived in one car so Higgs assumed they lived close to each other, and he was right. They were neighbours and lived about ten miles away.

Higgs enjoyed every moment. Great food, with Boerewors (a farmers sausage) as an appetizer, followed by crispy roasted Guinea fowls, and tiny roasted potatoes alongside a fresh tomato and avocado salad. Dessert was a fresh fruit salad, with banana, pineapple, orange, and passion fruit. The wine was South African, a Nederberg Pinotage, and seven people consumed five bottles. The place became funnier and noisier as the evening continued.

Swanny, Tim, and Higgs got into a discussion about Ferranacci's junk yard. Higgs perked up as he had seen that place weeks ago and was already suspicious of the goings on there. Tim was saying that he had worked there during the drought, a year ago, as he needed money to get through his inability to make money farming at that time. Swanny said he had just this past month been contracted by Ferranacci to grade, level, and pave the entire area because of the mud. He wondered how the firm had so much money from a simple wrecking business. His fees were going to be high. Tim said, "There is something going on there. I was in charge of the car crusher. Basically a load of cars, maybe 12 at a time, were driven, or lifted over to me. I picked them up, one at a time, and dropped each one into the jaws of the crusher. But every now and then, maybe three times a day, a car from inside the warehouse, on its own, would be brought to me on a forklift truck, and it would be tipped into the crusher. I don't know why that car was special, or why it came from the warehouse, or why I couldn't crush it, but the whole process seemed weird."

Higgs asked if he left them since the drought was over and Tim said he had. Swanny said he was starting his contract on January 15, and had already assembled a crew of 35 labourers. Higgs made a mental note of this discussion. He was slowly but surely beginning to always think as a policeman. One never knew when any information, no matter how it was gleaned, might prove useful one day. At midnight the other guests left; the driver was the one who was the most sober. Higgs stayed out of the discussion but Tim volunteered, "Carol's okay. We never knew she drank until we found her sober one day. Ha! Ha! Ha!" Tim staggered around at his own attempts at humour.

In any event, they all drove off, with Carol at the wheel, and Higgs and Swanny had a great 'Oude Meister' cognac (one of South Africa's finest), before retiring. Swanny said, "You know, Higgs. I'm glad I met you. Not only can I put a notch on my belt and tell people I have a pommie friend, but also a cop pommie. They will be aghast, but I will be proud. Now goodnight, my friend. Breakfast is about 0900. See you then."

The next day, after a refreshing swim in Swanny's pool, Higgs ate an enormous breakfast; a mixed grill of bacon, pork chops, and Boerewors, with fried bread, eggs, and tomatoes, and a lot of coffee, very strong with all milk and way too much sugar, but great tasting and refreshing.

"Swanny, I need a drive in your Mercedes 300 SL," pleaded Higgs.

Swanny responded with, "How's about you ride my BSA down to the dealers and I will be in the Merc? Then we can see what deal we can get for the '58 BSA Super Rocket, with the trade for my '56. Okay? Then we can leave the bike there and both drive back in the Merc. You can drive."

They set off to the dealer at 1100. The deal was Swanny's '56 plus £100. Swanny rode the Super Rocket home; Higgs followed in the Merc. Both had grins a mile wide. Higgs refused to take any offers Swanny made. He flat out said he enjoyed the time and Swanny's hospitality and wanted nothing. Higgs had a quick ride on the bike, which was fantastic but still not quite as fast as his own Norton. He promised to keep in touch but finally left Swanny at 1900, after a lovely dinner, and rode his Norton back to the mess. He dropped in to join the lads having a beer. Van Rooyen was there and so was our Scot, Mike Cameron, tears in his eyes, stains down his shirt, standing at attention and saluting, as he played his little 78 record, "Land of hope and glory."

19

THE NEW YEAR BRINGS
NEW OPPORTUNITIES

Higgs finished his humdrum New Year's Eve shift at midnight and heard a few yells from the mess bar, so he slipped down and celebrated the New Year at the bar, for about 20 minutes. Then he phoned Amanda. She wanted to celebrate with him and said by the time he arrived at her place, her last guests would be gone. There would be just the two of them for the whole evening; by 0100 he was knocking at her door.

The two spent the evening making love and talking and drinking Moen Champagne. They finally drifted off until 0900. Higgs had to report for duty at midnight but then had no shifts until 0800 on Monday, January 5. He promised to return the next morning and stay until Sunday night.

Higgs was about to tell Amanda that he was in love with her, but he decided not to rush into a serious relationship, even though she was a gorgeous woman and he did love her. There was no doubt she loved him. There was this age difference, though?

They met up frequently, perhaps twice a month, while Higgs attended to his career and now had a membership in the NRP rugby team. He also started making enquiries about becoming a full-time member of the motorcycle traffic division. Senior Inspector Campton wanted Higgs in traffic but could not commit to a full-time motorcycle rider position.

Around the same period, Detective Chief Inspector Sythe summoned Higgs to his office. He had heard, on the infamous "grapevine," that Higgs wanted a transfer. He had a suggestion for Higgs. "Listen, my boy," he said. "Once you have had about a year of regular police groundwork under your belt, and are finding yourself, and fitting in with the lads as well as grounding yourself in your off-duty social life, I think you might like the CID. But, if you do think you are interested, just remember that the job is all-consuming. You get involved in a mystery and you cannot bring yourself to leave your work and go home. It is a terrible life for a family man with a young wife and kids. On the other hand, the work is so fascinating that if you do become embroiled in some mysterious case, then, as a single man, it is the greatest job you will ever have."

Higgs answered, "When does the year start?"

"Well, how about you come and see me around June? It's January now and you started in July, so that seems a good time to see if you are still interested. Okay?" Higgs agreed, but asked if there was anything going on at the Ferranacci junk yard. Sythe nearly slid off his chair.

"Why would you ask about that specific case?" Sythe wanted to know. "Do you know something?"

"Not really, but if you ever needed someone to work on anything that arises there, I would like to be involved."

"Hmm...very strange! I'll keep that in mind. Now, off you go and don't disappear completely. Understood?" Sythe went back to the files on his desk as if Higgs was no longer there.

Higgs was becoming well known in the communities where he patrolled, as well as a name well known within the ranks. It was July; Higgs was wearing his warmer, and more formal, navy uniform. Winter days were comfortable but when that sun set it could become cold. He had become involved in so many relatively minor cases lately that his court date appearance diary was filling up rapidly; housebreaking, stolen bicycles, assault, arson, and domestic violence. Usually these types of cases were with the constabulary, somehow Higgs ran into them. Cases seemed to jump out at Higgs, no matter how he tried to avoid them.

The previous day he had attended a housebreaking. He was there before the CID, and he was making a quick survey of the house. The owners were away for another week, on vacation, so someone knew this and broke in, and stole, who knows what, but a lot of things. Also, right outside the window that was smashed and was the entry point was a very large turd, on the ground, very smelly and very fresh. African Detective Constable Nkoma arrived shortly after. He introduced himself.

"Good day, Mr. Higgs. I am Detective Constable Nkoma. This is our first time working together. I am the very one that is called most often for housebreaking. Now, have you found anything unusual around the premises?"

"Well, as a matter of fact I have," replied Higgs. "C'mon look at this." He led Nkoma around to the giant turd.

"Ahh!" said Nkoma. "It seems that the phantom shitter has struck again. That name was given by Detective Chief Inspector Sythe on a previous case. We now have five. What happens is the culprit gets a nervous stomach while they survey a property. This then becomes a bowel movement and the result is a turd. This one seems to be similar in colour and size to all the others. Now, if we only knew who the shitter was, we could solve five open cases. Unfortunately, they shit and steal, then they run."

Higgs was amused at the attitude and the lingo of Nkoma, but could not argue with the facts.

On his way back to the station, Higgs asked his constable in the car, "Is Nkoma a good detective?" Constable Phiri answered, "Yes, Sir. He is very bloody good but Detective Chief Inspector Sythe says he cannot seem to get his shit together. These five housebreakings are the only ones he cannot solve. Can I trust you do not repeat what I said? I just heard it at the last break-in and Sythe was telling another detective and I overheard." "Your secret's safe with me, Phiri," replied Higgs.

Back at the station, just as Higgs entered the charge office, a drunken ex-convict was yelling at the officers on duty, "The judge sentenced me to seven years in jail for assaulting my neighbour. Today, I was told that I can leave. That is only four years that I have been in jail, not seven. I trained in jail to become a religious preacher and I still have a year to go for completion of that course, which is only available in jail. Also, I was getting food three times a day and also getting ten cigarettes each day. Now I am nobody, not a preacher or anything. What kind of justice is this? The sun is going down and I have had nothing to eat since breakfast. And how do I get cigarettes?"

"Do you want to go back to jail?" asked Constable Cephas.

"I demand my whole seven years. I want to see the magistrate who makes promises but he does not keep them."

"What is your name?" asked Cephas.

"J.G Jack Smart is my name and I am bathing [he pronounced it baffing] 11 times a day," was the response. Perhaps he thought frequent bathing cleansed the soul?

Constable Cephas, using his initiative, suggested to the man that he be dropped off on Cairo Road and then he can decide how to get back into jail. He asked Higgs if he would not mind driving the man to Cairo Road, and leaving him there. Higgs responded, "Just lock him up downstairs. Give him a cigarette to smoke while he's in there. He's in time for prisoner's dinner in an hour or so. Then when he sobers up, release him, in the morning, after breakfast."

And so the saga ended. Just another decision Higgs had made; he was beginning to feel like he was really a cop. He felt all warm and fuzzy inside. He was glad he had chosen this career.

20

EVERY DAY BRINGS SOMETHING NEW

"Where was the time flying to?" This was the question Van Rooyen kept asking in the mess each night he was in there. Okay, each night was when he was in there. Higgs thought he could put the beer away, but he was an amateur compared to Chris Van Rooyen

"Holy God, my man! It is Monday, March 24, 1959 and I am still alive and still a cop and not in jail! I suppose life can be beautiful," said Van Rooyen.

Higgs brought two beers over to the table and he said, "Hey, Chris! It is better than you think. I just read on the notice board that you and I are to report to the Officer-in-Charge at 0900 tomorrow. I've done nothing wrong, how about you?"

"Well, I got some blerry woman upset with me on New Year's Eve. She didn't mind me removing her bra but did not like it hanging from the chandelier at the rugby club. But, other than that I am squeaky clean."

"Hmmm!" Higgs sighed. "Something seems fishy here. Oh well, one more beer and I am off. It is almost 2200 already."

Both men were almost out the door, when Dan Baldwin jumped up and started singing. "Oh, Mr. Fisherman, Fisherman of the sea, have you a lobster you can sell to me?"

Then everyone in the bar, about 12 men, sang the chorus, singing, "Oh, tiddly, oh, shit or bust, never let your bollocks dangle in the dust."

Higgs and Van Rooyen joined in then Baldwin bought beers for his entire choir. It was way past midnight when the bar closed down and Higgs hit the hay just before 0100. The next day, at 0900, OIC Paddy Alton, asked both men to come into his office. "Look, lads. Yer not in trouble. I know most of yer mates are out there wondering why you are in here. Well, I'll tell ya. I believe every officer should be exposed to each and every type of situation that us policemen encounter and sometimes not everything crops up. We can either use fakery and train you at the training school, or grab a real event when it happens, and send somebody to see it from beginning to end. I know both of you have the same length of service, since July correct? And I hear good things about both of you. Well perhaps, Higgs, you are not quite as experienced in ladies underwear as our friend here, but still you are both good men. So I chose both of you to go together on this rare event. You can learn a lot and then report back to me and tell me all about it on Friday."

"Sir, the tension is mounting. What is it?" blurted out Van Rooyen.

"Well, I'm glad you asked. It is an exhumation. An American geologist has been living with his family, in Lusaka, for about four years now. He has a wife and three-year-old daughter. They had a pretty young Shona girl, about 18 years old, as the little girl's nanny; been with them two years. Now apparently, the nanny was given ten days leave to go back to her village to visit her relatives. While there, they discovered, she had been put under a spell by the local witchdoctor. He willed her to death. It is not frequent, but it happens enough for us white men to know it is a fact; if the witchdoctor says you are going to die, you do. They simply stop being alive; no food or drink and they fade away.

In any event, she was buried right there in her village, which also happens to be a mission. And we believe there might be grounds for an investigation. We have all the known facts and the Catholic Church is pretty upset at us wanting to dig her up. I said to the priest, 'Jesus Christ, I'm a bloody Catholic too, ya know, but I have a job to do. We're both stuck in jobs we have to do. Take this bloody warrant and keep it handy in case the Bishop asks for it.' So, at 1000, go and pick up Detective Constables Phineas and Ndlovu, downstairs. They are waiting for you at the garage. The CID Land Rover is also waiting for you and they know how to get there; you follow them. Have a nice day and you will also be attending the post-mortem tomorrow. Good day, chaps."

By 1000 the two Land Rovers set off for Kasisi Mission, some 30 miles east of Lusaka. The trip took them up the Great East Road for 26 miles, then there was a sharp left onto a dusty trail for another four miles. The CID vehicles were up front spewing dust in a corkscrew so it blanketed Higgs' vehicle.

In the CID vehicle were DCI Sythe and DSI Maxwell, up front. DC Phillimon was bouncing around in the back seat. Higgs was driving while Chris Van Rooyen was bouncing around in the front. Phineas and Ndlovu were also hanging on for dear life as they jumped and bounced around on this trail of dirt.

They arrived at the gravesite at 1130 and the grave, with its heap of loose earth piled up high. Phineas and Ndlovu started digging, while DCI Sythe tried to pacify the priest who still believed he could stop the exhumation, which he could not. In the awful hot sun, the only shade was inside the vehicle, which was like a hot oven. The digging was easy until one reached just below ground level. As you shovelled up, half came trickling back down. The constables needed a break so Higgs and Van Rooyen decided to get in and help.

Four feet down, the work was awful. You would throw up a shovel full of earth and another shovel full slid down back into the grave; it was hot down there. The bluebottle flies buzzed around knowing something nasty would soon be revealed. By 1400 Higgs and Van Rooyen gave up and the two constables got back in to finish the job. Then Phillimon grabbed a shovel and started to push away the newly dug earth so that avalanches were prevented and the work proceeded at a faster pace. Now, in addition to the hundreds of flies, there was a distinct smell of death.

DCI Sythe warned everyone, "If you have never smelled death before, it is a smell you will never forget for the rest of your lives. You'll never get used to it. I haven't and I have been smelling death now for over 20 years. Nothing to do but keep going. By the way, you are all going to the post-mortem tomorrow and it will be worse. May I suggest you pour a little methylated spirits onto your hanky and if you begin to feel nauseous, take a whiff of it and you'll be okay."

Just then Phineas yelled up," We are at the body, Bwana! Now we need some rope to lift it out."

A length of rope was retrieved from the Land Rover and the body was lifted out of the grave. It had been buried fully clothed and without a coffin. A plain blue blanket was wrapped around the body. At that moment, a vehicle approached the site and the American who had reported her missing was driving. He had been told to arrive at 1430 to identify the corpse.

The body was partially unwrapped to expose a woman's face and chest. She had been buried for four or five days, and the earth had flattened out all her features. She was a black woman but her skin looked like flat green marble. One could barely make out that this was a woman, her breasts were also flattened. Higgs reached down and pulled back the flimsy blanket off her face. His fingernails scraped grooves of flesh off the girl's forehead. Gruesome was not enough of a word to describe the scene.

The American man, looking very sick and not really wanting to do this, looked at her closely, and said, "I cannot identify her face but she is wearing a dress that my wife had given her to go on her vacation, so it must be her. Her name was Mary Chiloma, by the way, and that murdering bastard, the so-called witchdoctor, is responsible. I hope you get him and shoot the bugger! She was a lovely and decent person. Can I go now?" he asked DCI Sythe, who agreed, but said he would be in touch again.

The American drove off. The body was re-wrapped and placed on the floor of the long-wheel-base Land Rover of the CID vehicle. Higgs asked the constable to drive with him so he would not have to endure the body bouncing around, or the smell. He gladly accepted the offer. The two vehicles drove off to the African mortuary. On arrival, two hours later, Higgs went inside to see what the inside of a morgue looked like. There were about 50 refrigerator doors, five high and five wide, so 25 spaces on one wall and the same on the opposite wall. It was after 1600 so no attendant was available.

The constables had the body on a trolley and asked, "Bwana Higgs, can you please find us an empty spot?" Higgs dutifully opened the first door and there was a large pair of feet with a tag on the big toe. He slammed that door shut. He wondered why they did not have a label on the outside showing it was occupied or empty. Still, he opened seven or eight more; all full. One had a baby, all wrapped up in a towel, which had been placed on top of an adult, perhaps its mother or father. The baby fell out and Higgs had to pick it up and place it back. This was a smelly dreary and poorly lit place, and very scary.

Finally, Higgs found an empty space and the two constables eased the body from their trolley into the sliding rails which were then pushed back into the fridge. Higgs wrote down the number on the door and all three rushed out to rejoin Van Rooyen, who was dozing in the Land Rover.

"Where do you men want dropping off?" Higgs asked the three constables. All three replied that their bicycles were at Lusaka Central, so there is where they all wished to go.

"Do you all need a beer?" Higgs asked.

"Bwana Higgs, right now I wish to have a bath in beer, but the bar is quite far from my quarters," replied Phillimon. Within 30 minutes, they pulled up outside Central. "You three wait here for a minute," ordered Higgs. He rushed into the bar at the mess, and ordered three bottles of ice-cold Castle beer, in open bottles. He took them out to the waiting trio.

"Here," he said. "Knock those back and have a good evening. Leave the bottles in the hedge when you leave. And never tell anyone that I gave these to you; especially you from CID."

They all grinned, took the beer and knocked it back within 30 seconds. And with very noisy belches, threw the empties into the hedge and grabbed their bicycles and went on their merry way. Higgs then went up to his room and threw his uniform on the floor and had a cool refreshing shower. He then slipped into some civvy clothes and made his way down to the bar, where he glugged down three beers.

Two men were going out to the Majestic Restaurant for a steak, and Higgs joined them, as he, like them, were not interested in the lasagne in the mess. Higgs got to bed at 2230 and slept like a log; up and ready for the post-mortem at 1000. Oh joy, thought Higgs.

Then Petrol knocked on the door and saw Higgs' uniform from yesterday's grave-digging activities. "Oh, Bwana Higgs. Again, your uniform is covered in dust and crap! Why do you play rugby in your uniform? I will need to take this to the drycleaner so it will not be ready until the day after tomorrow. Today you will have to wear long khaki trousers and a khaki shirt with a jersey. Maybe you should have worn that yesterday, Bwana."

Higgs felt chastised and simply replied, "You are a good man, Petrol. Just keep looking after me."

It was a brutal morning. Higgs cut himself shaving and then struggled to get dressed in an unfamiliar outfit, all the while thinking about what kind of day this was going to be, with the post-mortem and that smell of death. God, thought Higgs, I haven't had any cereal or a cup of tea yet.

He trudged down to the dining room, grabbed a cup of tea, and decided on a piece of dry toast. He joined bleary-eyed Van Rooyen at a table and very slowly both of them woke up.

It had taken a number of grunts and sighs but the tea got to them and their eyes opened. It was now 0930 and they grabbed a Land Rover outside and drove off to the mortuary laboratory where the autopsy would be held.

When they arrived, they parked and found the right room. The two stood at the slab of stainless steel, on which there was placed a naked Mary Chiloma, the very girl they had unearthed the day before. Also present was DCI Sythe. A door swung open and a middle-aged man, in an undone flowing white long coat, followed by a girl in nurses-type uniform, with a clipboard.

"Good morning, gentlemen. For those who don't know me I am Dr. Phillips, the local pathologist. Hello there, Mr. Sythe! Haven't seen you in a coo...in a long while." He was cheerful and loud. He strapped on what looked like a buffalo horn on black straps. Underneath that contraption was a tape recorder, flat on his stomach, hooked up to what was a microphone that was on his chest.

He checked out the body, running his hands over it from head to toe. "Right. We have here a black female, of approximately 25 years of age. Susan, my large scalpel please." The nurse handed him a huge, what looked like a carving knife, scalpel. Dr. Phillips plunged it into Mary's neck and cut her open all the way down to her pelvis, like cutting into a 100 pound slab of butter. Then, he gripped the two sides of the rib cage and folded them out with a loud crunch, as the bones snapped open. He put his gloved hands inside and checked her stomach, and started humming, mindlessly and tunelessly. Higgs tried to figure out the tune; he thought, perhaps, 'White Christmas', or was it 'Rule Britannia'?

It was at exactly that point in time that Higgs remembered that he had forgotten the advice about a methylated spirit soaked handkerchief. He and Van Rooyen rushed for the outside door exit. They found a whitewashed 44-gallon drum and both threw up into it until they were empty. After a rinse and a gargle, under the hose-pipe sprinkler, and a thorough drink of the cold water, they slowly moved back inside. They had only been outside a minute or so, and Dr. Phillips was now at his happiest.

"La dee dah," whistling another tuneless tune (Higgs finally recognized it as "ta rah rah boomteeyay") and talking into the buffalo horn he ripped out a piece of internal organ. "Appendix normal and she's not pregnant. Da da dee dum." Then he shoved his hand under the ribs and said, "Jar please. There you are. Liver seems normal. Have that checked please, nurse," as he plopped the liver into a lidded jar.

DCI Sythe said, "I need a cigarette," and left through the exit door. Then the whole show was over. Dr. Phillips said he would have his report for Sythe in two days. Then he left. All police officers gratefully left, as well. The report later said she had died of natural causes! All was for naught. This event really told the real story about good old police work. A report is made by someone and it has to be recorded and investigated. Nobody knows what the end result will be. No stone is left unturned and every lead must be followed. Higgs realized that each case was a puzzle and he simply loved doing puzzles.

21

THIS POLICE WORK IS ALL CONSUMING

The next day, Friday, Van Rooyen and Higgs went to Lusaka Central and called the Officer in Charge Paddy Alton. He invited them up to his office for them to relate their Kasisi Mission experience. As they were relaying their story, one could see that Alton would really prefer to be a street cop, instead of being Officer in Charge. But he had his job to do and so did they.

It was 1100 before the two reported to the charge office to check what their work would entail that say, and what their shifts were next week. Van Rooyen had been summoned to the Broken Hill detachment for a week, probably vacation schedules up there? Higgs was still on "A" shift 0800 to 1600 for the next few weeks, which he liked.

The stolen bicycle section now had a new system, thought out by Higgs. All stolen bicycles, when reported stolen, would be written up on a whiteboard with a black marker. Frequently, a bike is reported lost and a day later it is reported found. Beer consumption by the owner, and/ or the thief, was usually the reason. If the report had gone into the little file, it was too much work to then have it "erased officially." Now, when the bike was not recovered within ten days, it was erased from the whiteboard, and entered into the file. One would have thought Higgs had broken the Nazi ULTRA code by the praise he got for this outstanding ingenuity.

Higgs was also becoming a white African. He knew the smells of trees; the beautiful lilac jacaranda. He relished the avocado pears, so abundantly available. Here was something he had never heard of in England, let alone eaten it. Then there was the enormous kidney mango; so big and juicy, it was deemed best eaten naked in one's bathtub; which he tried and enjoyed. Then he discovered the granadilla, or passion fruit, that grew everywhere on hedges. When they were deep purple and wrinkled, as if they had dried out, they were ripe and easy to pluck one off its bush, rip the end off with your teeth, and suck out the tangy contents. Having a giant paw-paw for breakfast, with a squeeze of lime over it, was a feast that Higgs really enjoyed.

Northern Rhodesia was addictive. The climate was perfect and the people were terrific and so was the abundance of fruit and vegetables, in season. Add to that the wild and domestic meat and fish available, this place was truly a land of milk and honey. Higgs had fallen in love with this country, as well as his job. It was now at the end of June, 1959 – a year since arriving; almost nine months as a policeman. Higgs was doing well at the native language. He picked it up quickly. He was always curious and made a habit of learning three new words a day. He would overhear a constable saying something and, without being intrusive, he would ask what a particular phrase or word was.

He would get the pronunciation right and practice saying it, with the dialect. He read as much as he had time for about the different tribes. He also tried to speak only Cinjanja to any African complainant, who came in to the police station. If he got stuck, then he had a handful of constables handy to help him out. He seemed to be able to get through more than half the conversations before he needed help. His first few days, months ago, he would last 30 seconds before calling for help; now it was two or more minutes.

Another thing Higgs noticed, at those times he was naked in front of his mirror, he was getting tanned. He had, at the very top of his forehead, a white patch where his police cap rested. The balance of his forehead and all of his face was very bronzed. His body was lily white but his arms were deep brown up to just above the elbows; his right forearm almost deep bronze (resting his arm on the window ledge while driving). His legs were tanned from about four inches above the knee to four inches below the knee. He was becoming Rhodesian.

The months had flown by and Higgs found his days extremely busy. He had seen Amanda every few nights, maybe twice a week, where they just treasured each other's company and made love often. Higgs was not sure where that relationship was headed. He loved her but did not want marriage. She felt the same way; she needed space but would marry Higgs if she thought that would keep him. They both liked their "arrangement" as it was.

Higgs spent many hours visiting Swanny and the two of them riding their bikes out on the main roads. They biked 100 miles south on the Kafue Road one day, and up a 100 miles to Broken Hill, north of Lusaka, when both of them hit 125 miles per hour on one straight-away where one could see for seven miles and the road was dead straight, with little traffic. Swanny had no fear at all. He would open up to maximum whenever he could. He played by the rules, however, as he respected his friend Higgs was a cop. He never sped where Higgs would be in a compromised position, as in racing up Cairo Road in rush hour.

These two friends really liked each other. Higgs attended a number of weekend visits to Swanny's braais. He explained to Higgs that once he had visited Dallas, Texas, where they had barbeques, whereas in Africa, he said, "Us white blokes call it a braai-vleis. Vleis is meat in Afrikaans, the language of the original Dutch settlers in South Africa, the Boers. Basically it's just grilled, or barbequed meat. We've got it down to just one word now, braai, pronounced 'bry.'"

Higgs had to say no a few times because he was simply too busy and Swanny would have had him over twice a week. Still, he was there often enough. Days were getting busier as Higgs had to attend court for cases he was involved with, and he had a few: traffic violations, the phantom shitter (they finally got him....caught in the act, so to speak!) – where he was called as a witness. A few assaults here and there.

One day at court there were seven police officers in attendance, and they all sat together at the back of the courtroom, until called. On this day Van Rooyen had to return from Broken Hill as he was the officer in charge of a very serious vehicle accident, some two months before. This was now a fight for damages between two insurance companies. One car had hit the other head-on, and had crossed the white line. Obviously, the car that crossed the line was at fault. That driver's lawyer asked Van Rooyen, "How do you know *exactly* where the actual impact took place?"

Van Rooyen removed his notebook from his tunic and asked permission to refer to his notes. It was given. Van Rooyen had to flick back through the pages of his note book. Then he found the notes about that day and the accident.

"Yaah! Here it is, Sir. I noticed exactly where the impact was by the position of the derbis on the highway."

"The what?" asked the lawyer.

"The derbis," responded Van Rooyen.

At which point six policemen at the back of the court were hanging on to each other trying to suppress their schoolboy giggles. Someone near Van Rooyen whispered, "Say debris."

"Yaa. The debris was about three feet on the wrong side of the white line but the car was now bounced back into the donga (a ditch) on the side of the road. My spelling doesn't change the facts," said Van Rooyen. He was on the winning side that day but he never lived it down. Even as he drove off later to go back to Broken Hill, his mates were yelling, "Watch out for the derbis!"

Then Higgs had to have his turn. He had arrested a shoplifter, The man, a young African male, had stolen a socket set in a red metal box and tucked it into his shirt. He ran out of the store and right into Higgs who was on a rare foot patrol that day. When Higgs asked him where he got the red metal box of assorted tools, the man said, "I have never seen them before, Bwana." Higgs stood up when his name was called. The magistrate asked the clerk to bring up Timothy Tembo, the accused. When he arrived a few minutes later, he recognized Higgs and yelled out, "Good day, Bwana! Thank you very much for giving me a chance. I have been three weeks in prison and it is very nice." The magistrate said, "Well, then, Mr. Tembo, you can have six months more. Next."

Court could provide some humour. But when Higgs got back to Central he was summoned by DCI Sythe, who informed him that he was needed on the following Monday, June 23, for the Doug Weldon murder trial. Higgs had almost forgotten about that. Weldon had been in prison since that dreadful day and now he was to pay the penalty. As he would plead guilty, the trial would be a one-day event, if that. The trial was in front of a high court judge. Weldon had been appointed a great lawyer, but Weldon fired him. Higgs was called and he simply relayed the events of that day, and was gone in ten minutes. Weldon pleaded guilty and as there were no mitigating circumstances, Weldon was sentenced to death by hanging. And, indeed, nearly three years later, in the Livingstone prison, Mr. Weldon was hanged. One could not help but feel sorry for Weldon. It was said that he was the last white man to be hanged in Northern Rhodesia.

One late afternoon Higgs was asked by Inspector Bradley to accompany him to a domestic case. Nobody else was available and Higgs was pleased to get away from the clerical duties that bored him lately. It was 1700 by the time the two men arrived at the address in the Matero compound. It was busy as hundreds of workers from the city were arriving home from work, and riding bicycles everywhere.

Higgs called in as they arrived, "Lusaka 2 Lusaka. Arrived at number 1247 Matero on the domestic complaint." There was no reply from Central, but there was no time to check the radio as there were loud shouts and screams coming from the laneway, behind the house. Higgs ran to see what was going on and found Inspector Bradley in a heated discussion with an African female who wanted us police to go away. Bradley was trying to tell her she was the one who reported the complaint, that her husband had a knife and was threatening to kill her.

In perfect English she screamed, "Go away, you police! I never called you! My husband is a peaceful man and would never try to kill anyone!"

"Well, alright, Mrs., but I have to check out your house. Is he in there?" asked Bradley. At which point, a man with glaring eyes and no clothes came running out of the house, screaming, "Leave my wife alone! She does not want to sleep with you!" and plunged a large chef's knife into Inspector Bradley's stomach.

Bradley dropped to the ground holding the knife handle and spurting blood out of his mouth. Higgs ran behind the Land Rover and opened the rear door. As the very large African male came around the back, Higgs hit him with a fire extinguisher across the man's head and knocked him out cold, and may have fractured his skull. Now the wife began attacking Higgs but two off-duty African constables, who were drinking in the Matero Bar, had heard the noise, phoned Central and now arrived on the scene. They were able to subdue the wife. Bradley was dead. Moments later, the morgue transport had arrived along with a detective sergeant, followed by Detective Senior Inspector Woolton, in his private car.

Higgs was now throwing up in the bushes nearby. His partner for less than an hour was dead and the adrenalin from fighting for his own life had got him to this stage. Bradley was just 31 years old. At least he had no family, which was a blessing of sorts. Still, his death was awful, painful, and so unnecessary. Detective Sergeant Bwalya was told to drive Higgs back to Central, while a small crew stayed behind to clean up the site, and interview witnesses. The honeymoon was over. For the very first time, Higgs began to realize that what he had thought of as a "lark," that being a cop in Africa was like belonging to a fun boys' club, at this moment Higgs had simply never thought about getting killed on the job. Much like a smoker who cannot see that the habit is killing them, Higgs had to really come to terms with the dreadful event that had just happened.

Higgs was ordered by the office in charge to take the rest of the week off. "Be available if we need you on this case, but take yourself off until next Monday. Report to duty for 'A' shift next Monday. Leave a number where we can reach you.

Don't drink too much, alright," ordered Superintendant Jack Mead. Higgs thought it all unnecessary but he went along with it. He contacted Amanda and asked if she could have him for five days. Of course, she agreed. Higgs packed lightly and jumped on his Norton and to her house, just past the convent school in Kabulonga, on Leopard's Hill Road.

She was waiting for him at her front door. She hugged him and kissed him gently on the mouth, and ushered him in. "Sit down here on the couch," she suggested, "and let me pour you a drink." Higgs asked for a very large scotch and soda. Amanda brought him a silver ice-bucket filled with cracked ice, a bottle of Johnny Walker Black, and a heavy crystal glass. "Here we are, my sweetheart. You look after yourself. Now tell me all about this event that has you quivering so."

Higgs filled the glass with whiskey and drank half of it in a long gulp. He then told her about his day and the way Inspector Bradley died. He teared up at first, took another drink, and then sobbed like a baby. The two cuddled and Amanda hugged him and gently held his head as she rubbed his back. Amanda said she had let the servants go for two days, so they were on their own. Today was Friday and she would do whatever Higgs wanted to do. He wanted to have Amanda right now, on the couch. He carefully removed all her garments and she lay back on the couch. Her hands reached down to him but she could not arouse him.

Amanda suggested that his shock today was affecting him and she was not concerned. The two of them went to bed at an early 1900 and both slept until the sun hit their bedroom window at 0600. Higgs got up and had a shower, leaving Amanda naked and drowsy in the large bed.

He returned to bed and she woke up and saw him. "What do I see there?" she murmured, as she reached out and felt him. "Did you have some woman in the shower with you? She got you all aroused? Just wait a few moments and I will make you feel so much better." Amanda rushed into the bathroom, had a very quick shower, splashed a sprinkle of eau de cologne on her neck, and returned to bed. True to her word she made Higgs feel so much better. By 1100 they had both made each other feel better three times. Amanda made them eggs benedict and then she dressed in jeans and a Tshirt. Higgs dressed the same and then they slipped on leather jackets and rode the Norton into Lusaka to the 20th Century Cinema, and watched the matinee. The film was "Vertigo" with James Stewart and Kim Novak. They sat upstairs, loaded themselves up with popcorn and Coca-Cola, held hands like teenagers, kissed, and did a little groping.

When the movie ended, the two jumped on to the Norton; Amanda, looking 17 years old, tucking her thighs in and hugging the breath out of Higgs. They sped off, down the Kafue Road and headed for the "Blue Boar Inn," about seven miles south of Lusaka.

They were a little early for dinner so they booked a table for 1800 and enjoyed a few glasses of Paarl sauvignon blanc, on the terrace. They enjoyed a three-course meal, with avocado and shrimp, followed by locally caught bream in a burre blanc and a light crème caramel for dessert.

The ride home took 25 minutes, with Higgs taking it up to over 100 miles per hour, on the main road. They both ran into the house, dropping clothes off as they ran for the shower. They laughed and played and kissed and touched each other until they were so aroused they jumped onto the nearby bed, both soaking wet, and made love for hours.

On Sunday morning, at the breakfast table, Higgs poured his third cup of coffee and raised his cup to Amanda and said, "My sweet, sweet, Amanda. Both of us have to admit, that we are highly compatible. I am in love with you and I believe we could spend the rest of our lives together. I don't know if you see other men. I do not see other women and when I need to see you I call you. But I wonder if we should consider making some permanent and formal relationship?"

Amanda got up and sat on Higgs' lap. "Are you asking me to marry you?" she said.

"Yes, I suppose I am," said Higgs.

"Well then, as long as you can wait a few weeks, so I can arrange my affairs, I would love to be married to you. You are a sweet and kind man. Our sex is so good and you are exciting in bed but also in your everyday life. In fact, you are exactly my kind of man. If you were wondering, that was a 'yes.'" The two spent that Sunday planning their future, talking all day then making love all night. Higgs left at 0600 on Monday morning and rode back to his quarters, to get ready for duty at 0745. He promised to phone Amanda later that night.

Nearly all day Monday, Higgs was interviewed by senior officers and CID, regarding Bradley's murder. The entire station was simply a gloomy place to be. Police around the world do not like one of their own to be murdered, and in this smaller community the mood was extremely angry.

Higgs was also asked to change shifts to "B," 1600 – midnight, starting Tuesday afternoon. This had nothing to do with Bradley's death but because of vacation schedules by two officers normally on that shift. Higgs phoned Amanda and told her the latest news. They agreed that it would likely be past the weekend before he could get to see her.

Monday evening, he went in to the mess bar and joined up with a few cronies in there. Once again the mood was sombre but the beer went down well; the shares of Castle Brewery went up that night. On Wednesday, July 8, Inspector Bradley's body was flown back to England, at his family's request. A moving service was held at the Anglican church, with over 300 officers attending. Then the body was taken to the airport.

On Tuesday night Higgs was on patrol at about 2000 when he was alerted to a fight going on in the Lusaka Bar, one of the smallest and shoddiest bars in town. When he arrived, he discovered that the owner had closed the bar early and gone up to his room after throwing out the last three customers. "Anyone know this guy's name?" asked Higgs. One drunk said, "Du Toit." One of the small crowd assembled on the street said he had heard a loud gunshot. Higgs decided to call in to Central and asked for back-up.

Higgs knocked on the door yelling, "Mr. Du Toit, are you alright?" but got no response, then he kicked in the main door. He cautiously went inside, then up the stairs to where he guessed he would find the owner's living quarters.

All doors were closed. He opened the first door which was the bathroom and empty. The second door was the bedroom and he opened that door. Sitting on the edge of his bed was Mr. Du Toit, a shotgun on the floor resting on its butt. The barrel was pointing upwards, and Mr. Du Toit had his right shoe and sock off. His head was on the floor and blood was spattered over every place visible. Higgs went down to his vehicle and reported the apparent suicide.

By this time another officer arrived and within just a few minutes CID and three more vehicles showed up. They never did discover why he had committed suicide, and it was obvious he had. But Higgs thought of Du Toit's last seconds on earth, pulling off his shoe and sock so he could pull the trigger with his big toe. Death played a big part in Higgs' mood that week. He drank more than usual, both in volume and frequency, not dissimilar to many police officers around the world when the job affects them and then their family is affected too. Higgs had just himself to get over his mood.

22

SOMETHING ON THE HORIZON.

Swanny phoned Higgs at the station around 2000 on Thursday night.

"Howzit, Higgs, my man?" Swanny yelled down the line. "Listen. I heard about you and that Bradley guy last week and I am so sorry that happened. And you found Du Toit! Jesus, man! You must stop this meeting with death thing. Soon you will have to come visit and we can make you feel better. Look here I have something to tell you about that job I am nearly halfway through, at Ferranacci's wrecking yard. There is something going on there and I think you cops would be very interested. Do you think I should continue on the phone or can we meet somewhere tomorrow?"

"That sounds very mysterious," replied Higgs. "How about tomorrow for lunch?"

"Okay, sounds good! How about we meet on our bikes at the Star Drive-In?" said Swanny.

Higgs said, very enthusiastically, "Okay, but make it early as I am on duty at 1600. I'll have to leave there by 1500. So how about 1130? See you there. I have news as well. Totsiens, hey!" Higgs was now picking up some Afrikaans, the language of the original Dutch settlers in South Africa. "Totsiens" simply meant "Cheerio."

For some reason, the barflies were really in the mood and it was just a Thursday night. When Higgs dropped in for a nightcap at the police mess, just past midnight, there were about 15 men, mostly pie-eyed, and singing as loud as possible, "One red one, one white one and one with a little shite on and the hairs from his dicky dido fell down to his knees." Then, as Higgs slugged back a cold Castle beer, he joined in, but they had changed songs. "Rule Britannia, marmalade and jam, three Chinese crackers up your arsehole. Bang, bang, bang." The lyrics were rude and crass but bloody stupid and funny. After all, it was men only and they had to let off steam, and most were under age 30. Also, it was a police mess. No neighbours were nearby and who was going to complain anyway? I guess this is what cops do to ease stress; they did here.

Higgs joined in and started feeling less sorry for himself and, in fact, became a happy, giggling drunk that night. It was around 0100 when a detective, Dave Weeling, was about to leave the bar. He had been on call for the CID and had been called to a burglary case. He was riding a Triumph 650 Speed-Twin motorbike, with no police markings on it, so nobody could guess that he was a detective, even though the licence plates read NRG (Northern Rhodesia Government), the same as all other police bikes. Dan Baldwin grabbed hold of Higgs and said, "Stall our detective for a few minutes."

Baldwin, and a few cronies, all ran up to the parked motorbike, took the petrol cap off the tank, and took turns urinating into the tank. One at a time and giggling like schoolgirls, they almost filled that tank. How much beer a human bladder can hold must be a lab question somewhere. In Northern Rhodesia, at the police mess, at past one o'clock in the morning, with young strong men, all in their mid-twenties, drinking beer for hours, the answer is bloody gallons.

Then Weeling emerged from the bar, and solemnly said, "Sorry, lads. I must go." By now a crowd of a dozen, or so, were gathered to see him off, trying to suppress their giggling. They watched as Weeling cocked his leg over the seat, pulled on his gloves, and then strapped his helmet to his head and adjusted his goggles. Then he turned the ignition key and kick-started the bike, which caught first time. The crowd encircled him so he could not just drive off. The crowd were saying things like, "C'mon, Dave. Stay and have another beer." Higgs asked, "How fast have you been on this bike?" Another said, "Wait here and I'll run in and get you another beer." And the crowd continued on with their comments.

All the while, the petrol in his lines was running fine but he had been idling now for about ten minutes and soon the petrol began diluting with the urine. The engine started to sputter and Weeling began twisting the throttle and he would get a roar then a sputter. Eventually, the motor died. All the lads were holding on to each other, giggling; some fell into the manicured hedges.

"Oh, no need to panic," said Weeling. "I can fix this. Probably some gunk in the fuel line." He pushed the fuel button a few times and then kicked the starter; no go. Now the men were waiting for the next move and had to stop giggling to catch their breath. At which point, Weeling got off the bike, leaned down, and pulled the fuel line open and sucked a lot of fluid out.

The men all roared with laughter, falling about like idiots on banana skins, into the hedges, and unable to speak and getting sick into the hedge as their giggling stopped their breathing. Weeling never did figure out what was so funny. He scrounged a ride in a patrol car that was just leaving, driven by African SubInspector Bwalya. He announced that he would have the Public Works Department pick up his bike the next day, and was whisked home to forget his evening.

Wednesday morning, Higgs had a large orange juice and a coffee for breakfast, then rode his Norton to the Star Drive-in restaurant, arriving at 1130. Swanny arrived three minutes later. They sat on the veranda at the shady table at the back. The waiter took their order; both ordered steak and eggs and a cold Castle beer. "So what's this big secret?" asked Higgs.

Swanny looked around to check nobody was listening and said, "That wrecking yard is spending more money than it gets for its wrecked cars. My job alone is costing them £20,000. They get £30 for each wrecked car; they sell one hundred cars a week to customers, so that's £3,000 a week they earn. Then from that minus expenses such as maintenance, salaries, transport, acquisition costs – do the math my friend. Unless they have another source of income, how do they survive?"

Higgs responded, "Yikes! Those figures are not sustainable. But what do you think they are up to?"

Swanny hushed up as the waiter delivered their food. Both men took a long drink of ice cold beer and then dug into their brunch. Swanny doused his steak with chilli sauce and Higgs splashed HP Sauce over his eggs. They ate a few mouthfuls then talked again.

"OK, Higgs, it's like this," says Swanny. "I noticed yesterday that the driver of the huge lorry taking the wrecked cars away was a driver that used to work for me. I got talking to him, remembering stories from yesteryear, and I asked him about this job. He said something strange. He said every time the crushed vehicles were loaded on, ten rows of five cars high, there was always one last car brought out of a warehouse that was loaded on last. All the others were brought to the lorry on a forklift truck, five at a time. Then, a crane lifted them off and the pile placed in the lorry. This was repeated ten times, except only four cars on the last pile. The last vehicle always came separately on another forklift, and was then placed on the top of the pile of four, to complete the load.

I asked him where they were taken. He said always to the Rhodesia Railway goods yard, and put on a freight train to Beira, in Mozambique. The final destination was always Albania. He also said the last car always had chalk markings on it that none of the others had.

Higgs gulped. "Well, it sure looks like something out of the ordinary is going on there. Do me a favour, Swanny. Do not mention this to anyone, and I mean anyone, and, do not attempt any detective work on your own. I am going to discuss this matter with our CID blokes. If I need you for anything I shall call. Okay?"

"Yes, Sir. Trust me to keep schtum. Keep in touch mate. Cheers, said Swanny, as they finished off their brunch at about 1300 and rode off together on their bikes.

Higgs went around the south roundabout, down Cairo Road to his mess. Swanny turned up King George Avenue, towards Woodlands and to his residence in Kabulonga.

Higgs showered and dressed in uniform and walked along the hall to the administrative side of the building. He left a message for his shift boss that day that he had reported in but was now with DCI Sythe in CID. He had phoned Sythe and asked for a short discussion. "Sir, I think something big is happening at that wrecking yard owned by Ferranacci." He went on to detail what Swanny had told him.

Sythe was very interested and said, "You know we have suspected something going on there for months. You actually mentioned some time ago, so this is very timely. I think we need our African detectives working undercover at the yard and also another working at the rail yard. Between the two of them, we should be able to figure out what's going on. It may take a while, Higgs, before we zero in on what they are doing and what we can then do about it. So don't get antsy and decide you and Swanny are going to solve this alone. Relax, keep quiet. We will call if we have anything. And, Higgs, thanks man. I've made note of this."

It was just after 1600 and Higgs reported to his shift, and then started the evening rush, with phone calls and complainants dragging themselves in from afar to report some crime. Nothing was big and few patrols were reporting much more than the odd drunken cyclist or reports of break-ins.

Higgs had time to phone Amanda and they chatted like teenagers talking nonsense and giggling often. He had seen her a few times, but was looking forward to the shift changeover at the weekend, when he could spend a night with her.

Then, at about 2100, Lusaka 1, with Chris Van Rooyen driving, reporting from the Matero compound that housed 28,000 Africans and their families, called in to say they were experiencing a rash of arsons. Five residential buildings had been torched and accelerants had been used each time. They needed the fire department, as well as a few officers to deal with an unruly public. It was possible there were deaths, but none he could confirm.

Higgs had not been out all evening so he volunteered to go. He took Sergeant Ngoni with him in Lusaka 2. As they raced out of the station yard, the ambulance overtook them and up ahead they could see two fire engines, with lights flashing and sirens blaring.

They made it to the scene in under 20 minutes. Chaos surrounded the burning houses. These houses were not the typical two-bedroom, half-bathroom huts that were prevalent in Matero compound. These five burning homes were larger, with two or three bedrooms and a full bathroom. African VIPs lived in these houses.

Higgs recognized the large figure of Chris Van Rooyen framed against the flames, and pulled up close to him. He yelled out of his driver's window, "Hey, you bloody South

African! Hoe gaan dit?" (How's it going?) Higgs was picking up more Afrikaans words each day, and Van Rooyen turned and yelled back, "Lekker, you bloody pommie!" (Great, you bloody Englishman!) "Look at this crap happening here!. This is the type of shit you get in Jo'Burg, not here."

By now the fire brigade was turning on hoses and trying to get into the burning buildings, to see if any victims were trapped. An African mob surrounded the police vehicles yelling, "There are people inside! We saw the gangs that started these fires. They poured petrol onto these five houses because they are paid to kill anyone who is opposed to UNIP." (The newly formed United National Independence Party.)

Because the houses all had tiled roofs, the fire was contained inside the dwellings and anyone inside would be unable to escape. There were about 1,000 Matero residents surrounding the fires and most were asking the officials if there was anything they could do to help.

Higgs told them to find, identify, and seize anybody they were positive had started the fires. "With no violence!" he yelled at them. Ten or so youths ran off, seemingly knowing where to run. By then two senior officers had arrived, Punch Hamble, the regional police Superintendent, and Colin Gillis, the fire chief. They began some sort of organized chaos and set up a van with a table under a tent to get this incident resolved. They knew what Higgs and company did not know, and that was that the family of the leader of the newly emerging opposing political party was in one of these houses.

It took about 90 minutes for the last embers to be extinguished. Now came the news from one tired and sweaty fireman. "Bwana, there are five bodies in the first house and three in the last house. All the others are empty." Higgs passed that news on to Superintendent Hamble.

Van Rooyen took two constables with him into the first house and Higgs did the same in the fifth house. They had called for body bags earlier on, in anticipation, and now they were put to use.

Van Rooyen watched as the two constables picked up the charred body of Horace Namakula, a senior member of the ANC (African National Congress). The smell of burned flesh is sweet and unforgettable. Also, placed in bags were Mrs. Namakula and the couple's three-year-old daughter, five-year-old son, and eight-year-old daughter, all stiff and black and with horrific facial features, all living breathing humans a few hours before.

Higgs and his crew removed a man a woman and a teenage boy. "Remove" means actually picking up a stiff charred body and placing it in a rubberized bag and tying the top so bits do not fall out. It is very hard and very unpleasant work. Nobody could identify any of the bodies, at this point.

Political parties were new to the African people and, having spent thousands of years of living under tribal rules, with loyalty only to the village chief, they were introduced to "democracy" and "voting" by leaders who had only just figured all this out themselves.

These newly formed parties were phenomena that started slowly as the British tried to make a Federation of Nyasaland, Southern Rhodesia, and Northern Rhodesia in 1953. Nobody thought the "Federation" would work, especially the indigenous native politically-active Africans in each country. Even though the Federation's Prime Minister, Sir Roy Welensky, thought the idea of a federation was terrific, it may be that he was the only one who thought so, outside of Britain, that is. The political activists had learned about "sedition" and acquiring votes in the majority, from their teachers overseas, China and Russia being the main two countries who would gain the most from kicking out the western colonial powers from the lucrative land they wanted.

This was an era where the Iron Curtain and the Cold War seemed to only get attention in Europe and the U.S.A. But here in Africa, there were enough spies and pretend tourists whose task was to disrupt, by any means, so the Brits would abandon Africa and let them have it. By now, and after granting independence to Nigeria and Ghana, Britain simply could not and did not want to manage any more issues in Africa. Frankly, they really were useless at handling anything in Africa. The "winds of change" were coming and the U.K. wanted to get out. Of course, Higgs could see why Russian would want to leave their beloved country to live in Africa. Why not?

Meanwhile, the police forces, with little or no workable guidance from Britain, or not much anyway, had to carry on regardless and keep the peace. All the while both Russia and China denied being present anywhere in Africa and Higgs had not witnessed any such issues since becoming a policeman. But they were there. This was the first time Higgs had encountered political subterfuge. Frankly, it upset him. The happy life he had enjoyed in Lusaka so far was becoming unpleasant. To Higgs, this was a sad situation and the facts depressed him.

It was 0130 when all the police got back from the fire in Matero, completed some forms, and finally got to sleep.

Two days later, on a lovely sunny day, well, they were all sunny days but this one was spectacular, a very sad incident arose. Higgs was summoned to go with two senior CID officers to a small plot of land, filled with blue gum trees, about 10 miles south of Lusaka. This African male had committed suicide by hanging himself from a high branch of a gum tree. From the ground, one could only just see the body very high up, almost hidden from sight by the branches.

Higgs was wearing his winter, navy blue, made-to-measure uniform. He felt very posh and was told by the "brass" to always try to keep it "neat 'n tidy." The two CID senior inspectors told Higgs to climb the tree and get the body back down. Higgs detected a somewhat smug attitude from both. Certainly, climbing a sticky blue gum tree would not help his uniform. But an order must be obeyed, and who else was there to do it?

Police standing orders stipulate that if a body is found hanging, one should hold the body, cut the rope, and gently lower the body to the ground. Then check for a pulse, and if there is one, perform cardiopulmonary resuscitation. Higgs grabbed the axe out of the Land Rover's firebox and climbed the tree. He took forever getting to the top. He looked below and both detectives were smoking and chuckling. The body was reached and it was obvious the man was dead. He had used residential electrical cord to tie around his neck. He died slowly from strangulation. There was no way Higgs could "gently lower the body." He raised the axe and, checking first to determine the branch was not the one he was sitting on, with a swift blow to the cord, the body dropped rapidly to the ground. It dropped within a yard of where the two senior inspectors were standing. It hit the ground and immediately gushed, like a fire hydrant, about a bucket full of Kaffir beer. It sprayed all over the two men who could not jump out of the way quickly enough.

Higgs had climbed down from the tree and said nothing. He brushed off some gum particles and walked over to a bicycle he had seen from his tree-top vantage point. It was propped up on a nearby tree. Attached to the rear spring-loaded carrier was a small page torn from a notebook, with a handwritten note scribbled in pencil.

The note read:

> 'To my wife and children, I have gambled all my
> paycheque away. I cannot feed you. I am sorry
> but I cannot live anymore. Please forgive me for
> what I did. Goodbye my love and my babies.'

Such a sad note; all the men were teared up. They radioed in and waited for the "death squad" to arrive and they then cleaned up the scene and took the body to the morgue.

Higgs grabbed the bike and tucked it into the Land Rover. The drive back to the station was very quiet and seemed to take forever. The smell was awful. Then there was a lot of paperwork and relaying events to the CID bosses. Higgs thought just how diversified police work was. For two days, Higgs had to wear his khaki uniform as the drycleaners and then the tailors fixed up his tree-ravaged winter blue one. But it was returned as good as new, so it was not an issue. He did glance admiringly in the mirror as he walked by in his winter uniform. My God, you are a handsome devil, he thought to himself.

The next few weeks went by with very little excitement: a drunken cyclist here and there, a few driving misdemeanours, and a couple of house-breakins. But one dreadful Tuesday morning, Higgs was summoned to an accident about 10 miles from Lusaka, on a side road in a mostly-farming community. Higgs arrived to find a new Wolsely sedan lodged into the front of a 10-ton truck, filled with milk cans.

Inside the car was a European middle aged couple, both killed as a result of the accident, a Mr. and Mrs. Boudley. He had the steering wheel column through his chest; she was half-way through the windscreen. Both were civil servants and were on their way to work, as they were every weekday. Apparently, on this particular day, they were a few minutes early and speeding towards them was the truck that picked up milk cans left at the end of a farmer's driveway, to take into the cooperative creameries in Lusaka.

The truck was a few minutes late and, with the morning sun in their eyes, and a slight rise in the road, inevitably they collided. This was a bad scene for Higgs and he called for tow trucks and two ambulances. The truck driver survived but was injured badly. His two assistants had been riding, illegally, on the back of the truck, and they were catapulted over 50 yards to their deaths, on a clump of rocks ahead of the truck.

Higgs took possession of all the belongings on the bodies, such as watches, rings, et cetera, as well as wallets, a handbag, and papers. Later on that week, on a Sunday afternoon, Higgs began the "B" shift. He had just started work behind the desk when an attractive blonde woman entered. She wanted to meet the officer who had possession of her parents' personal belongings. "My parents were killed in a car accident on Tuesday. I was attending Edinburgh University and heard about this on Wednesday. It has taken me this time to get to London and fly Central African Airways to Lusaka."

"Coincidentally," said Higgs, "I am the officer you are looking for. I am so sorry for your loss and if you have any questions, I will try to answer them."

They spent an hour going over her questions and getting her to complete the documents that enabled her to take away all the possessions. Higgs reflected on how sad it must have been for this only child to have to now go to her parents' home and sort out their estate.

Still, this job was so diverse that on the very same day, Higgs was summoned to the Lusaka Railway Station. A young 25-ish African male was found dead in a first class compartment on board the train. This was not a place where any native would be found.

There was no law banning them; there was no "apartheid" in Northern Rhodesia. It was simply too expensive to travel first class, especially for natives. No, this one, apparently, had been willed to death by a witch-doctor. It was not a frequent event, but, if you got into some disagreement with a witch-doctor, they would, and did, will you to death. And such was the devoted belief in the "system," it happened. The victim would not eat or drink or sleep and, sometimes up to a week later, they simply died. Higgs had only been at work for three hours and already his day could not have been more diverse. The morgue van was summoned and the paperwork completed and then it was on to something else.

Higgs got called by his mate, Van Rooyen. "Hey, man! I'm working out of Woodlands police station (a satellite station some 4 miles away in the posh suburbs) this week. Why don't we patrol together next week, when I'm back at Central?" The plan was set.

The next Monday, both Higgs and Van Rooyen were on general duties, at Central, on "C" shift 0001 to 0800. On that day, some new African constables had been training to be radio operators, pushing Dinky Toy cars around on a large table. This was somewhat based on the more sophisticated London Metropolitan Police control method. Most of the constables were very good. They listened to their trainers and read the manuals. But one particular man, a Constable Bwalya, had been dismal and annoying.

He was lazy and could not get the car ID number right; he was often not at his desk when called (this is no big deal for routine calls but an officer in trouble, and alone miles away, would be in a perilous position if there was no response).

In any event, the African sub-inspector wanted to give Bwalya a lesson, so he set up a prank. He asked Van Rooyen to be his accomplice and instructed Van Rooyen exactly what to say when he radioed in, later that evening.

At about 0300, Higgs and Van Rooyen were in Lusaka 4, patrolling the back streets of Lusaka. Van Rooyen called in, "Lusaka 4 Lusaka. Come in."

Bwalya answered an agonizingly 15 seconds later, "Lusaka to Lusaka 4."

"Lusaka 4. I understand a suitcase full of pornographic magazines was misplaced in the station today. I now am told it is actually under your control table. Can you see it? Over."

"Yes, it is here," replied Bwalya.

"Lusaka 4 Lusaka. Please get under the table and open the suitcase to verify contents. Leave the microphone switch on so I can ask you questions while you are under the table. Have you read me? Over."

"Yes I read your instructions," yawned Bwalya.

The two officers had no idea what would now happen. They heard the noise of a chair scraping back and then a muffled, "I am opening the suitcase now....aaaaargh, myway, Jesus, man! What is this?" in loud and very panicky screams. Chimfwembe had put a 12-foot python in the suitcase (someone's lost pet handed in earlier in the day). And then they heard guffaws from about six African police in the background, who were witnessing Constable Bwalya trying to get out from under the table while also trying to close the suitcase. Bwalya requested a transfer back to patrol duties after that incident. A satisfactory conclusion, indeed.

Then, later in the week, on a day off, Higgs awoke with the sun blazing through his window. He got dressed and went downstairs for breakfast. Three officers were eating and Higgs joined them. The conversation quickly trended on politics, the Matero fires, and would the bullshit ruin their rugby do on the weekend? Higgs explained that he had a weekend appointment, so no rugby for him.

Higgs went back to his room to read a book about the Nyanga Mountains, in Southern Rhodesia, as he was thinking of going there with Amanda, for a week or so, when his two-week vacation came about in July. This part of Africa was a most beautiful spot and used frequently for honeymoons. Higgs' mates had told him about this and he was very excited about going there one day.

His phone rang and DCI Sythe was on the line. "Come down and see me ASAP, would you, Higgs? I am in my office. No uniform required, come as you are." Higgs was in Sythe's office within five minutes. Sythe got up, closed the door, and sat next to Higgs.

"You know that story about the wrecking yard and Ferranacci? Well, I have had two undercover constables working at the rail yards for the last three weeks and they have a story of their own. Apparently, Ferranacci's men also work at the rail yards. They are bullies and powerful. They get what they want and pay bribes. It seems they are smuggling something in the wrecked cars. My men couldn't find out how the smuggling was done, so it seems that part is done at Ferranacci's yard before they transport the crushed cars to the rail yard.

I have asked the officer-in-charge if I could have you working undercover for me for the foreseeable future, starting right now. He has agreed, so unless you plan on quitting the police force, you are now a detective, working in plain clothes. It's not a big deal but tell your friends you have a clerical job and are working on a project for me. Your uniformed friends don't need to know either; you are now a clerk. If they figure it out, that's okay, but try to keep it quiet, as we don't know if anyone has big ears and a skinny wallet, now do we? Right now, I have a meeting set up for noon. Come back then and join us at that meeting.

I'm ordering sandwiches and tea and that's our lunch, and yours too," said Sythe.

Higgs realized that from now on he would be working strange and plentiful hours, in CID, and he had to warn Amanda that plans would be hard to make, for at least a while. He phoned her immediately. He told her a story that skipped the details but was enough to keep her happy!

She was happy for him getting work he had always wanted, yet sad for their relationship. She said, "My darling, I love you so much and I'm so lost without you here in my arms. Please call as often as you can. And do not forget who I am. Okay, doll?" Higgs was sure he could get to see Amanda often.

23

A CHANCE TO SOLVE A CRIME

Today was Wednesday, July 22, 1959. Higgs had spent a wonderful weekend with Amanda. They celebrated his birthday the previous night and this day she had to fly to London to seal a contract to deliver flowers over a three-year period. With Higgs immersed in his new job, she felt a two-week absence would be healthy for both of them. She left Lusaka airport on a BOAC Lockheed Constellation, at 0800. (British Oversea Airways Corporation long before it became British Airways).

Higgs showed up at Detective Chief Inspector Sythe's office at 0900, wearing cavalry twill pants, a white shirt with a maroon tie, and a Harris Tweed sports jacket. He was thrilled to be able to wear civvy clothes.

Sythe took him in to the meeting room where eight officers were seated around a large table. Three women and five men were the total CID unit for Central Division. Higgs was introduced to them all, many he had met over the course of the past month work, none in any official capacity. Someone else, Petrol, Higgs' dutiful batman, was also pleased that Higgs was wearing civilian clothes, as they were easier and not as laborious as cleaning a uniform. Now it was just underwear, a pair of socks, and a shirt each day.

Sythe said to Higgs, "I have put you together with Fred Sampson. He is that good-looking devil over there, with the receding hairline." He then said, "Inspector Sampson, meet Assistant Inspector Martin Higgs-Briar, known to all as "'Higgs.'" The two shook hands and they could tell their relationship, work, and social life was going to be just fine. He continued, "Fred will be your mentor and will be doing a lot of hand-holding during your first few weeks here. You will find that we, as a group, are a bit more informal than you were in the uniformed branch. We still have rules, and we are still police officers, but we turn more blind eyes than the other lot. OK. So, what do we have today?"

Shirley Watts spoke first. "There is something going on at the school for the blind, in Woodlands. One nine-year-old boy was found playing with a gun last week. He said he found it when he broke into the headmaster's cupboard, looking for biscuits. Then just last Friday a teacher at the same school was climbing up into her bus that takes her home, and a pistol fell out of her handbag. After checking over the weekend, I determined that a new wing of the UNIP party had a contact in the school and they were blackmailing or threatening that person, to allow them to keep a cache of arms in the school. It would be easy to get a warrant and search the place. We could take a lot of weapons away, but I thought there may be an opportunity to infiltrate that school and keep tabs on the politics. So, I am seeking advice and ideas." "Okay," said Sythe. "Let's keep that on the table and let's hear from Charlie."

Charlie Hogarth, a Senior Inspector announced, "There are thugs out on the main streets who are entering stores and distracting staff while they steal expensive electronics, record players, etcetera. The fence they take this equipment to for cash is in the second class market. We have a warrant and we are visiting the fence tomorrow. We know he is a local Indian businessman and I am sure he is scared stiff of these gang members, all of whom are native teenagers. We believe he will cooperate with us and give us names of these thugs. Details next Monday."

Sythe thanked him and then pointed at a scruffy man. "Alright, Chalky, what about the railways?"

Detective Inspector Chalky White, who worked under-cover, mostly as a drunk in almost every bar in town, reported, "The railways have encountered more and more obstacles on their lines, especially on the Broken Hill to Livingstone lines.

You know that there are hundreds of silver coins, the three-penny bit and the six-pence, thin and pure silver, that are placed on the tracks so the trains flatten them out from a half-inch coin to a three-inch coin. Then the natives make filigree jewellery for sale to train passengers. It is all illegal but, frankly, as you know, we haven't got the time or the inclination, to stop it. And the crime is hardly any threat to the populace. If we stopped it altogether we might save the British Government nearly a £1,000 a year, after we have spent £10,000 on the investigation. So there has been little or no coin activity. However, there are reports of other items being placed on the tracks, such as horseshoes, shovels, an anvil, all to try derailing trains; in other words, terrorist activity. This is new and frightening. With utmost urgency, I believe we need a team and a plan to stop this activity."

Something was happening to this beautiful friendly country. Higgs was listening to these reports and he realized that these issues were not some trivial happenings that could easily be fixed. India had been surrendered in 1947 and Africa seemed to be on that same trajectory. The British were losing their influence and a world atlas would have less red ink on it now, as each commonwealth country began leaving the club. The CID meeting went on for another hour or so. Higgs was alert and paying attention to each detective's cases. Sythe then introduced him.

"This man, Higgs, has been asked to become a detective, on a temporary basis, because he has contacts that will help us delve into a mystery case that has been a bit smelly over the past year. We've had our eye on it for a while and nothing has happened. Frankly, I feel a bit like Christopher Columbus with this case. When he set sail, he did not know where he was going. When he got there, he did not know where he was and, when he got back, he did not know where he had been. Welcome to the CID, Higgs. You will feel like that for quite a while. Higgs has found out some small issues that, should we say, have put the corners on our jigsaw puzzle. Now we can start searching for the right pieces. Okay, meeting adjourned."

Higgs was to follow Sythe into his office. He wondered why Sythe had not given out much detail regarding the

Ferranacci case, and Sythe responded that he liked to keep everything close to his chest until the perfect moment to spill the beans.

Sythe continued, "Right now, Higgs, I want you to come up with a plan whereby we can get you closer to the enemy. We have had reports from our two constables, working at the railway depot. We need you working in Ferranacci's workplace, or getting in and out of there, with a legitimate reason. Let me know tomorrow if you have any great brainwaves. Thanks, Higgs, you can go now. Drop by Senior Inspector Barbara Hazelton's office now; she has an assignment for you. Cheers."

Higgs dropped by Barbara's office and she invited him in. "It's like this, Higgs. You are the new boy today and you want to go out and be a detective, but we have paperwork and training to do. So, sit down and spend a couple of hours with me, and for God's sake, take that frown off your face! Enjoy yourself. Look, Higgs, I don't want to beat around the bush. The NRP likes to shuffle new men around to different departments to see where they seem to be the most useful.

I would like to think that if you were transferred to the political wing of special branch, and you loved it, and were good at the job, the NRP might transfer you there permanently. That would make sense, but it rarely happens. They move you to the Library and you become a great librarian, and after a year NRP moves you permanently to the Transport Department. Don't ask why, 'cos nobody knows, perhaps just bloody mindedness?"

Higgs was now a detective. He was now known as Detective Assistant Inspector (DAI). After reporting for duty at

0900 on Tuesday, August 4, 1959, Higgs realized he was fitting in very well and now had a lot to learn. DSI Barbara Hazelton was assigned to show Higgs his role, and to hold his hand as required. She was about 5-foot 5-inches tall with very black hair and wore too much make-up. She had huge buck teeth and was married with three children over age 20. Nobody had met her husband, and it was rumoured he had left her years ago because she was too bossy and hardly ever home; sort of a mixed blessing really. However, all the personal stuff aside, she was a damn good detective, with nine years' service.

Barbara took him to an office that was like a Hollywood back-stage. It could be, and was, rearranged every week to emulate a crime scene. That day it was set up for training purposes, but it did represent a real crime scene of some months past. She told Higgs what the crime was and got him to go through the room and write down his observations.

"Just outside his workplace lay a dead body, an E/M, named Larry Hopkins, 35 years of age. Here are photographs of him taken on the morning of the crime." She handed him 15 8x10 black and white glossy photos. "He was a grader driver, working for the Lusaka Municipality, Roads Department. It had been raining for three weeks without pause. He parked his VW Beetle in the parking lot about 100 yards away. He then walked to the office of the local municipality here, our crime scene, and retrieved the keys for the grader. He was found, as you see in the photo, face down in the mud. He had been run over by the grader after he had started it. The keys are still in the grader. It is possible he got it started and somehow slipped and the grader moved and ran him over him. He usually was the first person to arrive at work, about 0600, as his job was to grade the dirt roads, or, in this case, remove the mud so that traffic could get by. The first worker after him was the manager, who drove up at 0815, to find the body, as shown in the photos. He called us and the first police to arrive did so at 0830. We fingerprinted the keyrack in the office and all over the grader. We got the deceased's prints and a couple of others which we have not identified, yet."

Higgs asked, "Have you now solved this incident or is it still open?"

Barbara responded, "We think we know what happened but let me hear what your comments are after you spend a while looking over everything."

Higgs studied the photos; the same scenes but at different angles. He asked, "What is there between the parking lot and here?"

"Nothing but trees and lawn. On that particular day it was mud," replied Barbara.

Higgs said, "He was killed somewhere else and deposited here."

"How do you know that?" asked Barbara.

"Well, he is wearing very heavy work-boots with at least one-inch-deep rubber cleats on the soles. There is absolutely no mud on the bottom of his boots, and there would have been had he walked through all that mud. Also, your photo of the inside of the office, where the vehicle keys were kept, shows no sign of muddy boots from the door to the key-box. So now it's murder. Who killed him and why?"

Barbara made a mental note of this man's powers of observation and intelligence.

"Okay," said Barbara, "why don't you get back to your quarters and put on that thinking cap about how we can get that Ferranacci case solved. See you in here at 0900 tomorrow. Good afternoon, Higgs, and may I say welcome to our little corner of the world, at CID."

Higgs went back to his room where he lay on the bed and slept until 1800. Upon rising, he had a quick shower and ran down to the dining room. He was ravenous and that night's dinner was curried chicken with samosas. Higgs ordered a large glass of milk and polished off all the food within minutes.

At the table were some traffic officers. They were telling a story about what had occurred that morning. Apparently, traffic lights had been installed for the first time at the corner of Cairo Road and Church Road. To make sure the locals became familiar with the workings of these lights, a constable was assigned to stand on what looked like half a wooden wine barrel, painted white, of course, and with the word "TRAFFIC" painted on it. He then helped direct the traffic. When the light went red, he stopped all the traffic affected; when it turned green, he let them go, and so on. Rocket science was not required.

It seems that one African male cyclist, pedalling flat out, paid no attention to the red light, or the constable's outstretched hand ordering him to stop; he whizzed through the intersection. Constable Reuben did not like his orders being ignored. He leapt off his box and yelled at the cyclist to stop, which he did. Reuben then yelled into the cyclist's ear, "I should have let you kill yourself. You are a cirombo!" (Pronounced – cheerombo - translation from Cinjanja is: wild beast, weed, animal or useless thing.) Then he promptly leaned down, removed both valves from the cyclist's tires, admonishing the cyclist to push his bike home; and went back to his "traffic control box."

Higgs thought cirombo was such a perfect word and appreciated the good laugh; he needed a humour boost. Police officers usually laugh at silly or sick jokes, as the pressure valve from their jobs needs releasing every so often.

Higgs was very interested in the case of the dead grader operator. He loved the mystery and was frustrated at really not knowing how or where to start solving the murder. But, he knew he would.

24

THIS GAME IS SERIOUS

August 3, 1959 Higgs called Swanny and asked if it was possible to get a job with his company, as he needed undercover credentials. Swanny agreed but needed to discuss the deal with him.

"Come to my place for dinner tonight. It's a bank holiday today so nobody is working, except COPS. My wife is visiting relatives and I'm on my own until she gets home around ten p.m. I'll get our cook to make us a Boerewors and Mealies (Farmers sausage and corn on the cob) dinner. 1800?"

"I'll bring my bike," said Higgs.

Then he reported to DCI Sythe and asked for a confidential meeting. They entered Sythe's office and shut the door.

"Okay, Sir. I have an idea," said Higgs. "I am going to work for Swanny while his company is finishing off their contract. Not quite sure what the exact duties will be, but I meet with Swanny tonight and, by tomorrow, I will have the precise plan. Whatcha think?"

"I believe that is a great idea. I want you to spend a while with my two undercover constables today. They have been let go for a shift change and have three days off. The whole railway is virtually closed down until Friday. Find out what they found out. Okay, Higgs? Oh! And go and see Barbara, now," Sythe said.

Higgs was told that he would now be in charge of the re-opened case of the deceased grader driver, the Larry Hopkins case. All he had was a file and the man's photo. Fortunately, there was a very good picture of the man's face, taken from his employment file. Higgs was now a detective trainee and had no idea where to start. Fate would intervene.

At Swanny's place that night, his wife, Cindy, arrived home around 2100 and the three friends sat around the comfy lounge and chatted. Cindy was complaining about her brother, Daryl. "He has become a real gambler!" she exclaimed. "Higgs, do me a favour. He is coming for drinks any minute now. Would you say something about how bad gambling is, not letting on that you know about him. Okay?" Higgs was a bit reluctant to get involved. He was 22 years old and thought a little harmless gambling was all right, frankly. But he said he would go along with her request. Daryl arrived in his pink and cream 1958 Vauxhall Cresta, in a cloud of dust. He was about 26 years old. After introductions and a few beers, Higgs started asking questions. "So, Daryl. What do you do for a living? I mean it must be working for you to drive a fancy car like that Cresta."

"I farm pigs and sell them to the Cold-Storage Commission. They butcher them and sell bacon and sausages to the public. That brings in a nice income. I am also lucky gambling so that helps too," Daryl replied.

"But where do you gamble?" asked Higgs. "It is illegal here and in South Africa, right?"

"Yes, of course. I fly to Beira, in next door Portuguese Mozambique, or sometimes to Lourenco Marques and sometimes I win big and seldom lose. You have never been there, I assume?"

"Nope," replied Higgs. "I am curious. Is it modern or just a dump?"

"Very modern." said Daryl. "Here, in my briefcase, is a tourist brochure. It shows all the hotels of both cities, and on the front cover is a picture of the new airport at Lorenco Marques. Here. Look it over," he said, as he passed the brochure to Higgs.

Higgs studied the 10-page brochure filled with pictures of all the 4 and 5 star hotels. "I'm impressed," said Higgs. "Say, who are all these guys on the front cover?"

Daryl replied, "They were a bunch of regular gamblers who fly down once a week. The casino gave them a free flight and that is them in the departure lounge waiting to fly home. Some others are locals flying out to Jo'Burg or Lusaka. I am there with two locals flying out to Lusaka, those two with silly grins on their faces."

Higgs studied the picture carefully as he believed he recognized one man in the crowd of eight people. He was right and, it was his deceased grader operator. "Daryl, do you know this man?" asked Higgs, pointing to the man with the big grin in the new airport picture.

Daryl replied, "That is Larry Hopkins who is a big time gambler. He was always down there whenever I went. Haven't seen him for a while. Maybe they banned him. Not as lucky as me though. I think he has an enormous credit line and the casino is not amused at his debt. That's what I hear, anyway."

Cindy, noticing her task she had assigned to Higgs was going nowhere exclaimed, "I hope you see what trouble gamblers can get into!" Little did she know, and what did that mean, anyway?

Higgs asked if he could take the brochure. He would return it soon. "No, keep the bloody thing," said Daryl. "I don't want it." Higgs knew it could wait a few days, but it appeared he had solved the who and the what. Now he had to solve the why. He celebrated all night with brandy and Coke. The meal was terrific and with way too much meat. He later he got up, saluted, and slurred, "Alright, you sods. I am off to bed." He ran to the bathroom and, following many jungle sounds, jumped into bed, still fully clothed. It was after midnight and the rest went to bed right afterwards.

25

NEW RULES

The CID found a desk for Higgs which was in a large office, with two other detectives sharing. Each had a typewriter and a phone, but everything else in there was shared. He was anxious to contact Barbara Hazelton and tell her about how he solved her cold case; well, almost solved, we should say perhaps. As Churchill once said during WW II, "This is not the end, or the beginning of the end, but perhaps the end of the beginning." At least Higgs now knew who the victim was and he had a hunch as to the reason for his death - gambling?

Barbara was impressed but also teased Higgs a little about good luck, while partying. "Now," she asked, "what do you plan to do now?" Higgs suggested he would interview family members, coworkers, pub-crawling friends, and other fly-to-Mozambique fellow gamblers, to see if they knew any persons who had been visiting Larry around the time of his death. Perhaps he had introduced a new friend to someone? He also would recruit the help of Detective Inspector Chalky White, the undercover detective, who might guide him through the minefields of pubcrawling and inconspicuously interviewing patrons. Barbara thought that was a good start.

That afternoon DCI Sythe held his round-table meeting. It was announced that Rhodesia Railways (RR) had adapted a new system of security. All trains would now be escorted by a four-seater railcar. There had been a quietly held series of meeting between RR, the police, and Special Branch to try to stop the threats to the railway.

It had been determined that six special trolleys would be built by a factory near the copper mines in Ndola. They were diesel powered and held four persons. The driver would be a RR engineer, and he would be joined by one European policeman and two African policemen, all very heavily armed.

There was not a lot of rail traffic, but what there was could not be assumed safe by itself. There were four trains a day through Lusaka, in each direction. One passenger train, with usually eight or nine coaches, headed north and arriving in Lusaka around 1400 each day. Another passenger train, headed south, would leave Lusaka at 1700, plus two freight trains travelling in each direction.

The freight trains were deemed more valuable targets, initially. Passenger trains may be more of a valuable coup at a later date. Freight trains were to be placed on staggered departure times. A team of police officers was assigned to be the guards to ride in these railcars. The railcars, called "trolleys," were built in Ndola, about 200 miles up north in the copper belt.

Five were ready for action within six weeks. All the officers were sent to a quick, one-week training course, where they were taught about terrorism and what to look out for. More importantly, they were taught what to do should they encounter any problems.

The first trolley to depart from Lusaka station was at 0100 on August 10, 1959. Dan Baldwin was the first to go. He arrived with two constables.

Dan carried a Very pistol, a Sterling sub-machine gun with a pouch, and six 28-round cartridges, as well as a Webley 38 revolver in a holster on his hip. Each constable carried a 12-gauge shot gun and a truncheon. The two constables occupied the back seat and Dan sat next to the driver in the front seat. At 0100, the passenger train to Bulawayo, Southern Rhodesia, was ready to leave and our little railcar headed off, about two minutes ahead. Their trip would take about eight hours to Livingstone. There they would get a rest for eight hours until the next northbound train arrived.

Two days later, they all returned. Their trip had been uneventful and afterwards a few beers were consumed with Baldwin, with him explaining every detail about his adventure. He did say that it was quite cold inside the railcar so they had the windows closed. He suggested that either the driver or both constables had eaten rotten eggs before the trip; the smell was simply unbearable. Some days later we heard from the driver that he believed Dan was the guilty 'farty.'

These car security trips became as routine as apprehending a drunken cyclist. They happened every night and they became a non-event. Nothing ever happened. If there were any terrorists, they were on vacation somewhere else? And then came the night where fireworks began.

It was John Bullock's turn to be on patrol at 0100. He was in the mess bar most of the evening and decided to go up to his room, at around 2100, to have a quick nap before reporting for duty on the trolley.

Those still in the bar at midnight noticed Bullock had not shown. A search party went up to his room, and he was still fast asleep; almost in a coma. The five or six men decided to get him up, dress him up, and take him down to the Land Rover waiting to take him and the two constables to the railway station.

Bullock was so out of this world that when someone threw a bucket of ice water on his face, he opened his eyes, but they were under two pools of water; he never even blinked. After struggling and arguing, he was dressed. His weapons were on his belt and someone carried his Sterling machine gun down.

Four men went in their own vehicle to the station, in case the need for assistance of some sort might arise. One went in the Land Rover with Bullock, who was now singing, "I'm 'Enery the eighth I am. 'Enery the eighth, I am, I am. I've been married to the woman nexsht door and I don't know the words...Ha! Ha!." The station was less than a mile away.

There were no passengers waiting and it was doubtful whether any would be getting off, when the train arrived at 0045. It was pitch black with a very weak overhead light from a poorly lit lamppost. Bullock, still beyond any legal limit for driving a car, pulled himself together.

Someone told the constables that Mr. Bullock was feeling sick and, if he fell asleep, not to wake him unless terrorist activity commences, and watch out for his Sterling machine gun.

The driver was there, and opened the door for Bullock and got into his side behind the controls. The two constables got in the back seat. John Bullock said, "Look here. Honest to God, honeshtly, I am okay chaps. No need to worry! I'm not driving. Au revoir." He slurred every word but he looked fine (police officers seem to hide inebriation very well; if he kept his mouth shut, so would the rest of them). And he really was not breaking any law, so he was allowed to go. Surely, if he was not acting sensibly someone would have called the cops?

Then Bullock stepped into the car and slipped. His Very pistol trigger got caught on the door handle and went off. A hot stream of red fire went into the car. The occupants left the trolley, should we say, rather quickly. The trolley and every bullet and shotgun shell remaining behind exploded like a New Year's Eve fireworks display. Bullock sobered up quickly, and all agreed they had never seen anyone move as fast as those two! Frankly, no one could recall ever seeing Bullock move so quickly either.

The train driver, who had witnessed it all, said he would leave without an escort, as he believed it was safer. And he did. And, for that night at least, it was! The car was not repairable and a substitute was called for, from Ndola. The new car arrived ten days later with a note from the manufacturer stating, "Fire-proof paint has been used both outside and inside, as a precautionary matter."

Higgs was one of those involved in this matter and faced numerous interviews from senior officers. Mostly they tried to show they were angry but most were simply bemused. No action was brought against anyone. After all, the entire group of witnesses was united in their opinion that a poorly made Very pistol caused the problem. Alcohol was never mentioned.

26

UNDERCOVER

Higgs had not seen Amanda for a week. Since returning from England, she was busy implementing new ideas for her flower business empire. Meanwhile, Higgs had been working fiendishly on his mystery death case and had started work for Swanny so he could get into the car wrecking yard, legitimately. Swanny hired him as a driver and Higgs was now taking wrecked vehicles to the rail yard. He was able to stop for gasoline on the way, and do a quick check of the crushed cars, for his records. Something was up and he was going to discover what it was.

Higgs recollected a story his uncle had told him, at the end of World War II; apparently, the occupied forces were in Hamburg and they were using a member of the Dutch army as an interpreter. This man would leave for Holland each Friday afternoon to see his family. He always pushed a wheelbarrow over the border and each time was thoroughly scrutinized by Dutch Customs Officers. Every wheelbarrow was searched carefully but nothing was ever found that would suggest he was smuggling. On each Sunday night he would leave Holland for Hamburg by train. He did this routine for ten months. Finally, when his services were no longer required and he was de-mobbed, he settled down in Holland and started a wheelbarrow business; he had over 40 wheelbarrows as a beginning inventory. All along he had been smuggling wheelbarrows. Higgs went back to that story to help his thinking. He knew that somewhere in the wrecked car business something devious was going on and he felt he could find the illusion and solve the crime. Little did he know what would transpire over the next few weeks.

Higgs had driven five loads of crushed cars to the railway goods yards, since working for Swanny. He was seeing Amanda on Friday night and called her to remind her that he would be staying the weekend. Even though he was busy, he now had no shift work and sometimes managed to arrange his time more efficiently than when he was in uniform. This was one of those times.

Amanda had decided that she too wanted to be a motorcycle rider and had applied for a licence and now suggested that Higgs teach her how to ride. Swanny arranged for his dealer friend to lend Amanda a 1956 BSA 350, in red and cream with cargo bags and hand shields, for three months. If she liked it, she could buy it for £145. For the first time, Amanda met Swanny. Higgs got her on the back of his Norton and drove over to Swanny's home for a braaivleis. They arrived about 1400. Higgs felt comfortable with Swanny and his wife Cindy. They all hugged and shook hands and Swanny brought out wine. They sat in the shade of a gum tree. The quartet was having a small party as if they had known each other for decades; such was the lifestyle of typical Rhodesians.

They wolfed down the juicy Boerewors and cut into the rump steaks as if they were vultures on a fresh kill. They ate grilled mushrooms almost the size of their plate. A huge salad of lettuce, tomato, and avocado, with freshly squeezed lemon juice and thinly sliced red onion was also on the table. They drank Paarl shiraz and Roodeberg, a thick and fruity wine but, to Higgs, the best dish of all was the green mealie bread. Cindy sliced the uncooked corn from the cob and stirred the milky mush into a bread recipe. The result was a heavy bread, smelling and tasting of luscious fresh corn, and a delight that was as good a gourmet treat as any imaginable. He must have eaten five slices slathered with half a pound of butter. And as the sun settled below the trees, the brandy was produced and they sipped it for hours. Cindy left to get a bowl of fresh fruit salad with English custard. After a meal with a lot of meat, a fruit salad helps the digestion. Their fruit salad contained pineapple, granadilla, mango, paw paw, orange slices, and banana. A truly African tropical fruit salad, with each fruit picked, on Swanny's land, just hours before consuming. Where else could one enjoy such a feast? Everyone simply sat back with that sated look and sighed a lot as the evening cooled.

In the trees at the end of Swanny's garden, the pigeons cooed goodnight as the bright African sun sank quickly and all that was left was a cool breeze and pitch black evening time. Twilight did not exist in Africa.

Stories unfolded and the wine helped with the humour and exaggeration. Swanny had a zillion stories about his job and his labourers. He had introduced a trophy to the labourer who had attended the most mother's funerals in a year; one man had nine funerals and was proud to accept the trophy, which was a pee-pot adorned with ceramic baby soothers (nine in his case). The labour force did not really see the humour. Swanny kept records in case he had to fire one of the trophy winners in the future. Then Higgs had a handful of police-related incidents to relate. One about the African male bringing in a 200-pound brown paper bag, filled with marijuana (they called it dagga), and so high himself he was wondering where he was as he started his sales pitch to the dozen or so bemused police officers.

By about 2200, they were all so mellow and tired. The two house-servants came out to tidy up and everyone was asleep in their cozy beds by 2210. What a lovely life! Higgs had to stop kicking himself as to the smart decision he had made in England just over a year ago.

The next day they had a small breakfast of a two-egg omelette and a gallon of black coffee and, at noon, Higgs and Amanda were off for home. Amanda all excited about picking up her bike on Monday.

.

27

SO MUCH TO DO, SO LITTLE TIME

The weather was changing. Soon it would be October, called "suicide month" by the white population, because the cooling rains did not arrive until about November and it became so hot many drank themselves to death or found some other way to bump themselves off. This is not to say there were dozens but, over the decades, enough had done themselves in that the reputation was established. Higgs found he was almost drenched in perspiration constantly.

This was Thursday, 24th of September, 1959, and Higgs was in his office. Air conditioning was a luxury not found in Northern Rhodesia at that time. At least the offices were in the shade; the windows were open, there were fans, and usually a breeze. But patrolling in a car was very uncomfortable. Lusaka was at 4196 feet above sea level, so it was not as bad as many other countries in Africa. Still, it was bloody hot. The ancient and enormous black telephone rang with a ring that could have been heard in Calcutta. Higgs was daydreaming, as detectives do, and was startled by the ring. He reached over and said, "Higgs here."

"Is this a bloody pommie who fixes motorbikes?" the man on the other end of the line asked.

"Yes, that's me. But I am a policeman now. Who's this?" replied Higgs.

"It's Mike Dunn. Now then, if you remember me I will buy you a case of Castle beer," said the crackling voice on a poor long-distance line.

Higgs responded, "Right, you bastard! You are working in Kariba and we met on the ship, over a year ago."

"Oh, shit," replied Dunn. "There goes my beer budget. How the hell are you, Higgs, old boy? Listen. Me and Lance Frazer, remember him, the lanky redhead? Well, we are both coming up to Lusaka for some R&R, and wanted to come and visit. We don't want a room as we have a free weekend at a place called the Blue Boar Inn. Do you know it? Tell me it isn't some dosshouse out in the bush somewhere!" Higgs was enthusiastic, and said, "Look, that would be great! When is this going to be?"

"Pretty well a set date. There is a bunch of us meeting there for a convention on concrete. Well, actually we all belong to a poker club and concrete will never be mentioned. I checked to see if it was all legal, as I knew I would be talking to a copper. And it is, as you probably know. It is a private club and in a private suite, and paid for by each member. Say, are you a player? Wanna join us?" asked Mike.

"Not really," replied Higgs. "But I assume you take breaks during the day and we could meet for lunch or something.

Hey, listen. I'm really glad you called me! I am working hard and need a break."

"Okay," responded Mike. "It's just that we are not quite sure of the timing. The whole thing was set up by some Portuguese bloke and he has two friends flying in from Beira. They seem to be the ones who know what's going on. Look, we're driving up from Kariba and will be at the Blue Boar around 1600. The others fly in from Beira and get here at 1000 on Saturday. So how about meeting up with us for dinner on Thursday, at the Blue Boar, around 1900? We can talk everything over at that time. Okay?"

Higgs responded quickly, "You're on. I will ask for you at the front desk of the Blue Boar. See you in your room, say 1830? See you then, looking forward to a catch-up."

Now Higgs was excited. This incident was too good to be true. Surely these were the two men who had killed Larry. He had fingerprints and he would soon have them together in a room full of poker players, and now he had to figure out a way to marry their prints with those on file. He needed to dwell on the methodology so he did not lose the chance of a lifetime. Hmm... what would Hercule Poirot do on a case like this? Higgs had about six weeks to put his plan into place. The next day Higgs realized that DCI Sythe would probably be the person to speak to, rather than wondering what Poirot might do. He called to arrange a meeting and relayed the incredible lucky circumstances he was in.

Sythe could not believe it and began shuffling some papers around, piled high on his desk. "Papers make me think more clearly, not that these have anything to do with this case. Just the act of shuffling papers. Now, where was

I?" he said. "It seems to me that we have certain knowns and many unknowns. For example, you saw the picture of these two bastards on an airline magazine. You are convinced, and by the way, so am I, that these are the two killers. But we don't know for sure, right? Which airline was it, by the way?"

Higgs replied, "I am sure we will find out these two are the perps. The airline was LAM, something something Mozambique, I think."

"Yes, it is a perfect coincidence, and I believe we are on the right track, but it is not a fact," said Sythe. "Our main goal here is to get these two identified. And, that identification has to be that we marry the prints we took at the crime scene and 100% prove that they belong to these two men. Then we have to make sure that we get to keep these two men. So we need to know exactly when they arrive; flight number and time. And, straight into Lusaka or say via the copper belt? How long are they going to say as guests of Northern Rhodesia? When do they actually arrive at the Blue Boar Inn and when do they pack their bags and leave? Is it at night and are they having dinner somewhere before they leave, or not? When they leave, whose car will they be in? I haven't heard of any airport service limos from there to the airport; it's not bloody New York, you know. Who will be driving them and what's his, or possibly her, background?"

Higgs had been writing down all of this in some strange Higgs-type shorthand. He looked up and said, "It seems that there are definites we can determine beforehand, while other details may only be determined as the game begins. For example, we can use our border control agents to give us the time of the flight that departs from Beira that arrives in

Lusaka at 1000. I'm sure there would only be one morning flight a day. It would only be about a two-hour flight. We could get a list of names of all passengers on that flight and what passports they are holding. We need to know if it is indeed LAM; could be SAA or even Air India. Fine minutia but each piece of the puzzle has to fit. Then, we could check those names against any rooms booked at the Blue Boar. There could be one name but with, say, three rooms booked under his or her name. If so we can heavycheck that person of interest. Once the game begins, literally, the poker game, my friends can give me some details, but I really don't them well enough. I believe they are as pure as the driven snow, but they could be untrustworthy, even if a tongue slips 'cos they're pissed."

"Yes, good points there, Higgs," said Sythe. "I think we need someone inside, and not you, I'm afraid. I know that may be disheartening to hear but you are not ready. We need a devious bastard like Chalky White. He could drink them all under the table while keeping his senses about him. The poor sods would not stand a chance at beating Chalky at any card game. And, should fisticuffs come about, then Chalky – he used to be an unarmed combat instructor for the Royal Marine Commandos. He cleared a room once with 11 people who wanted to kill him. I think all had to be taken away by some vehicles with red crosses on them; Glasgow, just after the war. No, Higgs. I'm afraid we have people like Chalky so we can use them.

Let me tell you just sigh with relief that he's on our side and sit back and watch. Never fear; this will be your case and your ego will be massaged. Okay, old chap? Let's meet on this Monday the 28th at, say 1700, right here. Okay with you? I will make sure Chalky is available and hasn't planned to be off swanning around with mates at Buckingham Palace. He has some, you know. He is always flying off to London; never pays. He must have some incriminating photos of the airline manager? One way or another, Chalky seems to have some hold on these chaps. We also need to get him invited to the game so he appears to be simply a keen but legit card player. Something to work on."

Higgs spent the balance of the day doing a bit of shopping. He bought flowers and a kilo of freshly caught shrimp. He had been checking at the airport, on and off, for a few weeks without revealing he was a detective investigating a crime that had flight implications. Anyway, he got to know the LAM business development manager. Higgs asked if any fresh shrimp were ever flown in to Lusaka. He was given the names of three restaurants where fresh shrimp were delivered daily: The Rendezvous, The Blue Boar Inn, and The Woodpecker Inn. If Higgs wanted some he could get him a kilo or two of freshly caught, and never frozen, shrimp, on Friday's flight. Higgs' cost would be the same as the restaurants paid, which was eight shillings a kilo. Higgs jumped at the offer and picked up his kilo on Friday, after lunch time, around 1400. A quick stop at the liquor store, where he purchased two bottles of Mumm champagne, and off he rode on his beloved Norton, to arrive at Amanda's around 1600. With her gift for him – herself: and his gifts for her, a busy romantic evening.

28

SOLVING HIS FIRST CASE.

Monday afternoon was hectic. Amanda would not let Higgs out of bed. She begged and then she no longer needed to beg. She had him where she wanted him and at 1500 Higgs actually had to pretend to be cross. "No, for Christ's sake! You know I have an important meeting at 1700!" he yelled. "And every time you show me your naked body and then kiss mmrrrrggghhhhhhh! me. See, now I need you again."

"C'mon," cooed Amanda. "Just a quickie to clear your head, my big, ooh! bigger, beautiful man! Here, let me hold you tight. Under me. Hold on, dear man. There now what was all that fuss about?"

Higgs reluctantly ran for the shower and was dressed in jeans and a T-shirt and leather jacket, within minutes. He was on his bike at 1620 and sitting in Detective Chief Inspector Sythe's office at precisely 1700.

Chalky White dropped in and slumped into one of the office chairs. "Sythe about?" he asked.

"He's supposed to be here now," replied Higgs, "and look, here he is. Right on time." As Sythe walked in, shut the door, flung his jacket on the desk and turned on a huge electric fan. The three men looked at each other and finally Sythe said, "Well, okay. Let's have a beer." He opened a cupboard and behind that was a small fridge and he extracted three bottles of Lion beer. He slammed each one on to a shredded corner of his desk, and passed the capless bottle to each man. "Cheers! I've been looking forward to this for the past hour. On a tour with Punch Hamble, in his Humber Super Snipe, to determine what potential terrorism risks could be reduced at eight train crossings around the city. Hot and boring. Still, had to be done. Now then, where are we at?"

Chalky piped up, "Why am I here?"

"You tell him, Higgs. I need a recap anyway. This is bloody interesting, Chalky. I think you're gonna like this," said Sythe as he grinned.

Higgs related what he knew. "This all started with a grader operator found dead and first assumed to have been run over by his own grader. Since then it has been determined that he was, in fact, murdered. The hit was from a gambling casino in Beira. He owed them some £6,000, hadn't even made payments so, you play with the big boys and that's what happens. Two hired killers, lived in Beira, related some way to the casino. They flew in here, bumped him off somewhere, then propped his body where we found it, naughty chaps trying to deceive us police. I got involved with CID for another case but was tested on this one and now I am involved here. Coincidentally, a good friend's wife has a brother who likes gambling. He told me a lot about his lifestyle and then, out of the blue, showed me an airline magazine, LAM, with a picture of a crowd of men at the new Beira terminal. One just happened to be Larry Hopkins, our deceased. In there are two faces which I believe are those of the two killers. At the crime scene, there were three distinct sets of finger prints: over the key rack, over steering controls of the grader, and a few on the front window. One set was Hopkins' and we cannot identify the other two.

The employees who work there have all checked out. So my first job was to identify two males whose fingerprints matched those we have on file. Where to start? Then, two friends, whom I hardly know, met them on the ship coming over a year ago, phoned me up a week ago. They are coming here as tourists in five weeks – November 6. They wanted to see me and all that, but they are checked into the Blue Boar Inn, because some mate of theirs has set up a poker game over a two-day period. They like to gamble so they jumped at the idea. Now then, listen to this....ungodamnbelieve- able ....two men from Beira are into gambling and their mate is flying them in to join the game. There are so many coincidences in this story and I am guessing at least one more; these two guys are the killers.

Higgs continued, "So we need to find out what passports they travel with. I'm guessing Portuguese, but I could be wrong. Then we will have their names and we can get border security to check every time those two have travelled here, on those passports. If one of the dates is around the timing of the Larry Hopkins' death, then voila!"

"So, why am I here?" asked Chalky, very drolly. "That was a grand tale, Higgs, but I only have a few years left and long stories eat away at my life expectancy."

Sythe sat up and said, "We want you in the room with the gang and to gamble, chat, drink, smoke, anything, but mainly get information and pass it on to us. We shall be somewhere close by, in another room, I suppose, planning what to do next. You can help."

Higgs said, "What we have to do, without raising any flags, is to be able to get everyone's fingerprints in that room, positively ID the ones we get from the two we suspect. Now I have to actually see them first so I can at least say they are indeed the two on the airline magazine cover. If not, we aren't quite back to square one but now it is fingerprints alone to make a case. Am I right, Chief Inspector?"

Sythe replied, "Hmmm.... That leads me somewhere. We are owed many favours from Pat McCullough, the Blue Boar owner. We could have shut him down years ago with his licence squabbles and his stretching the open pub hours. So I am going to get you a job, Higgs, as the manager on shift when they check in. You can ensure their rooms are first rate and then take them to the main salon where they will be gambling. You can check them out and let us know they are or are not the men on the magazine cover. Then you will also be able to get close to them, asking about delivering drinks and food supplies during the gambling hours. A reason to enter the room without raising any suspicion. And, on more than one occasion too.

Chalky, we shall work out a few choice words you can use. We will have the room bugged and we need to know a good time to enter the room so the waiter can clear up and bring refreshments. Let's say the lads are all drinking beer. There will come a time when you notice the two, let's call them Beira boys, have finished their drinks, maybe a bottle or a glass needs refilling or replacing. You could talk out loud, say, finish your own drink and say something like, 'Can we phone to get another drink or are they coming routinely?' We can then get one of our African detectives dressed as a waiter to, at a suitable timely delay, knock on the door and say 'steak sandwiches' and he can simply enter, and place the plate of sarnies on the table. He can take away only the Beira boys' drinking vessels and identify whose was whose. He comes out of the room and walks down to the kitchen area, where the vessels are handed to our fingerprint expert waiting in the shadows. Okay so far?"

Sythe continued, "Our waiter can return immediately and bring replacement drinks. He can befriend the patrons by saying something like, 'I brought you back the very same drinks you had before but maybe you want to change. Whatever you wish, Bwana, I will do for you.' They would probably just wish he would leave the room so they can concentrate on their cards. In any event, we can do this and get the prints off four or five sets of glasses to make sure we get clear prints. One way or another we will be able to compare our new prints with those we have on file, and in our kit at the Blue Boar that day. If all goes well, we will have a match and then will not have to care about etiquette and how to treat them; we cuff them and take them away.

Also, Chalky, we assume you'll still have horseshoes up your arse and that they will be a bit upset with you winning all the time, so they won't be thinking of waiters and finger-prints, etcetera. Any other input?"

Chalky surmised, "I guess if we find the fingerprints we have on file bear no relationship to the ones we take off their glasses and bottles, then this was all for naught. We simply walk away?"

Sythe retorted, "Well, nothing is for naught. This is just one step in our investigation and what if it didn't work out the way we thought it would? Higgs will have to start again and we shall move on. Surely, Chalky, you of all people should know, you stop a vehicle for a broken tail light and the next thing you find a dead body in the back seat. Police work is simply trying one thing after another, baby steps. Besides, this may be the real deal, and we nab the sods in one fell swoop. Okay, let's make a plan for next week. It's 1900 now. Let's get out of here."

Higgs wanted to know who would arrange for a couple of African detectives to work undercover. "I am guessing that would be you, Sir?" Higgs asked. "Yes, yes, leave it to me, said Sythe, "now come up with some ideas as to how to get Chalky into the game. Both of you let me know what you decide, next week. But don't do anything yet; just come up with a plan. Okay?"

Chalky left for one of his sleazy bars to continue his undercover work. Higgs left for the police mess to have a drink with his mates, whom he had not seen for a while. The buzz at the mess was about an African who had been molesting women, mostly white women, as they went about their daily business, right on Cairo Road.

Five women had reported that this young man had reached inside their bras or put his hand up their skirts and was attacking them, roughly. Anyone who had tried to stop him had been attacked. There must have been some mental issue here, but the man was strong and had avoided capture.

At about mid-day, outside Moffat's department store, stood a lady with her arms filled with gifts. She was waiting for her husband to pick her up and take her home. This sex offender came out from behind a pillar and attacked the lady, just as her husband arrived. Unfortunately for the attacker, her husband was off-duty Inspector Triggs. The attacker was still unconscious some ten minutes later when the wagon arrived to cart him off to jail. Apparently, a chop to the neck with the right hand and a knee to the groin were all that was required. The rule is very simple, world-wide too – do not mess with policemen's families.

Days went by and Higgs was driving for Swanny each day. Nothing was apparent; nothing uncovered and actually quite boring. What should he look for and where to begin? And then, one day, Higgs got to meet Mr. Ferranacci. He was waiting for his truck to be filled with crushed vehicles when Ferranacci drove into the yard in his 1957 Alfa-Romeo. "Who are you?" he asked. "Are you the driver for Swanny?"

He appeared quite short behind the wheel of his car, had long dark grey hair, and was wearing huge aviator sunglasses. Higgs noticed an enormous diamond in a gold ring, on his left pinky finger.

"Yes, just waiting for a full load for the rail station," replied Higgs. "Say, what year is that Alfa? I love motorbikes and Italian sports cars."

Well, that put a smile on Ferranacci's face. "Oh, you like my car, huh? One day, when I'm in a good mood, I might give you a ride. Ciao." And he drove off to his assigned parking spot in front of the administration building. Higgs had managed to at least break some ice; he phoned Swanny that evening and told him about the encounter. Swanny warned him that while he should use the meeting to his advantage, to be totally aware that Ferranacci was a snake and very venomous. There was no doubt in Higgs' mind that it was so.

Sythe was informed that same evening and he showed a lot of concern. "Look here, Higgs. That man is going to want to know about you. He has a very suspicious mind and, from past reports, he will not be taken down without a fight. He'll want to know your background and where you live now, and why did you come to this country, and so on. I hope you have a story. But, in the meantime, I don't think we want a tail on you and one of his contacts reporting you entering the police station each night. Maybe it's time for you to move out and go live at Swanny's place. Do you think he has room?"

"Room?" gulped Higgs. "Christ, he could house everyone currently staying in the mess. But whether or not it's a good idea, I'm not sure. I believe you are right about moving out, but where to?" Well, it was a "no-brainer," he moved in with Amanda the next day. He asked Petrol to stay on, working for the other men, until he returned, and to let him know if he ever wanted anything.

29

IT IS ALL IN THE DETAILS

They had a week to finalize all the details before the poker game began. African Detective Constables Reuben and Nyarenda were recruited to be "kitchen staff," and were taught by the maître de of the Northern Rhodesia Police officers' dining room the subtleties of being a good waiter. They would be picked up at 0500 on Saturday, November 7. They would have a few dress rehearsals showing where to deliver food and drinks and where to drop off specific glasses and china for fingerprinting.

The "Kariba boys," Mike Dunn and Lance Frazer, were informed that they should not expect to meet up with Higgs until after the game, Sunday the 8th.

Perhaps they should only show up Friday night, November 6? Also, that Mike had a friend, Chalky White, who needed to be invited to the game. A phone call was made and it was agreed. They would NOT mention to anyone that

Higgs was a COP; better still, do NOT mention Higgs at all. The rest thought an extra man to play along was a great idea as long as he had money; CID had floated Chalky with $4,000 US dollars. So, there would be seven players; the two Kariba boys, the two Mozambique boys, Chalky, and two unknowns, except they were helpers for the two from Beira.

Higgs had a fingerprint expert along with his portable kit so he could take prints and compare immediately with those on file. Higgs and Sythe would be in a nearby room, while the fingerprint team was next door. The waiters would be in the real kitchen, where Blue Boar kitchen staff would prepare and plate room-service items. A short menu had been prepared for food.

After examining a choice of rooms, Sythe and Higgs decided on 207; on the same floor as the kitchen and which had room enough for an eight-foot table with eight very comfortable chairs; perfect for a poker game. There was a fridge and a bathroom in the room with a window facing the forest at the edge of the hotel grounds. The fingerprint team were in 216; Sythe and Higgs in 215 (same floor but around the corridor). The kitchen had no room number but if it had it would have been 214.

The game would begin at 1300 and the arrests were assumed to be around 1400, if everything went according to plan. Also, room 207 was bugged the night before, by Special Branch, professionally done, with state of the art equipment. For example, one strand of wire in a screened window was a microphone.

Unless Beira people had Scotland Yard sophistication, nobody could detect the numerous devices hidden in devious parts of the room. Equipment in 215 would record every word. By 0900 on Saturday, everyone was in place and comfortably ready.

All officers on site were watching the main entrance driveway, from room 215's window, when a large American Oldsmobile pulled up at 1045. Airport surveillance police had radioed to say the plane had landed and that these four men had entered an Oldsmobile. The Blue Boar contingent saw the two men they wanted get out of the back seat. Importantly, the two African detective constables, posing as waiters, got to see the "bad guys" so they could get their glasses and have them in for checking.

Then a quick scramble to get everyone into their assigned, and out of the way, places. Both African detective constables got the giggles as they checked out each other's waiter uniforms. But they soon settled down and now it was simply a waiting game. The new arrivals checked into their rooms. All of them had showers and changed clothing and made their way to room 207. They introduced themselves and found out just who was who. One of the Beira boys, Paulo Fereira, did a quick walk around the room, trying to look casual as if he was not looking for anything really, checking under the obvious places for listening devices such as lamps and window latches. Of course, nothing was found because nothing was there, not to amateurs, anyway.

"I am quite hungry and would love a cold beer," announced Chalky White.

"Me too but I want a brandy and soda," said Paulo. "Look, there are grilled prawns on this menu. I'm going to have a plateful of those. Anyone else want prawns?'

"Why don't we get a tray of sandwiches and potato chips and a large bowl of prawns then we can all grab what we want?" suggested Johnny Lucca, the other Beira boy. "And a decent red wine, some cold beer, and your brandy and soda."

There was a bell on the wall and Johnny pressed it. Within minutes African Detective Constable Nyarenda arrived with a notepad and wearing a fez, and took their orders. He was back in a few minutes and put the orders on the table. "Texas holdem?" Johnny suggested. "We can play with US dollars or English pounds and we can use $3 to the pound, when we tally up at the end. I have chips in this box and we can buy them now. Any objections or suggestions?"

"Chalky, you haven't said a word," said Lance. "Anything wrong?" Chalky said, "Well, there is actually. I have finished two beers and I need another one. Then I need a piss and then, for God's sake, I hope we can start playing. It is nearly 1300 and I've been ready since Tuesday."

Mike said, "Let the games begin. Five-card draw. Minimum bet a blue chip worth $3 or red worth £1, maximum bet each round is $60 or £20. Everyone familiar with the rules? Remember, all players put their ante in the pot and each gets one card down and one face up. Then you bet. You get a third card up and you bet again. Your fourth card is up and you bet again. You get a fifth card up and you bet again. All the surviving players who haven't folded show your hands and the winning hand wins. Simple enough! OK?" asked Mike. Paulo's friend Greg said, "I have a printed sheet in my briefcase showing the rank of winning hands, just in case any arguments come along. But you guys are pros so all this is meaningless. Let's get on with it!" His accent was strongly South African.

The other man was very short, perhaps five-foot four-inches tall, and he was the other of the foursome from Beira. His name was Guido Jones (he had a Welsh father).

The cards were dealt. Paulo won the first round with three jacks. The kitty was worth $155; Paulo was smiling. Not so much smiling after eight rounds, as Paulo had not won again. There was no clear winner. It seemed everyone had won at least once, with Chalky White not winning at all. Guido said he needed fresh drinks and some more prawns. The bell was rung and African Detective Constable Nyarenda arrived. The glasses and sandwich plates were removed; he dusted crumbs off the table and took the new order for drinks and food. It was way past 1400 and the room was filling with smoke. Gambling fever had taken hold of the group.

Nyarenda handed the new order to African Detective Constable Reuben and took the Beira boys glasses to the fingerprint room. Detective Inspector Sheila Hodgkins carefully examined and then processed each glass.

Reuben, meanwhile, took in the new order to the gamblers, who were in the middle of a side bet. "C'mon, Chalky. Say do they call you Chalky because your name is White?" asked Guido. "Well, duh!" responded Chalky. "Don't try to avoid your bet now. You said you would bet me on the side for $100 that you would have a better hand than me; I agreed. So, are you on? Where's your $100?"

Guido placed a $100 bill in front of him, while Chalky did the same. At the end of the round, Mike won the kitty but Chalky had three threes, while Guido had two aces. "Hey, we have a new waiter," noted Greg. "No, Sir. I am not a new waiter, I am a different waiter," replied African Detective Constable Reuben. "Cheeky bugger!" retorted Greg. "But you have good refreshments so here, take this $10 bill and spend it on some cheap women."

"Aah, Bwana, all my cheap women let me have them for free. But I will use the money to buy some drinks for my friends," replied Reuben, with a huge grin.

Sheila Hodgkins knocked on Sythe's door. "Bingo! We have a match for each of them."

Meanwhile Chalky White had just lost another hand. "You guys seem to have experience," he said. Then he asked of the Beira boys, who had won a lot in the last three hands, "Do you play here a lot, or is this your first time to Lusaka?" Paulo responded, "Actually, this is our second time to Lusaka. But this is the first to this hotel. Last time was in August and we were just tourists but also looking for a business associate." "Oh really," Chalky grunted, "did you find him or her and was your meeting successful?" Johnny said, "Well, let's just say it worked out the way we had hoped."

At that point, the door was flung open and there stood Higgs, Detective Chief Inspector Sythe, Detective Inspector Hodgkins, and three other policemen. Also coming into the room were Reuben and Nyarenda. It was 1520. Sythe took charge. "We are from the CID. We need you all to stand up and back up against that wall by the window. Who are you, Sir, and what do you do?" he asked Chalky White. "I'm a lounge lizard, Sir," replied Chalky with a silly grin on his face. "Well, get out and wait for me with this lady officer Hodgkins!" shouted Sythe.

"Now who are Dunn and Frazer?" The two identified themselves. "Right," said Sythe. "You two are wanted urgently, step outside and Assistant Inspector McIntosh will escort you to our vehicle. Which two of you are Paulo and Johnny? Well, you two are to go with Inspector Higgs, who will take you to your rooms and discuss your issues. Now you two, Guido and Greg, if I was you, and this is only a suggestion, mind you, I would get the hell out of here, pack your bags and get on the first flight out of Northern Rhodesia. I don't care where you go to, just don't let me see you in this country, ever again. Now get out and do NOT bother waiting for Johnny and Paulo; they plan to stay here for quite a while."

Higgs spent a while explaining to his friends from Kariba what had just transpired. He gave them as much detail as he could and apologized that they were unable to get together, unless they could stay over for a few days. They could not. They explained to Higgs that when concrete is being poured 24 hours a day and 7 days a week, shift work was crucial and work habits especially essential, but they invited Higgs and Amanda down to Kariba and to stay at the fabulous new hotel. They also had contacts for luxurious houseboats and fishing tours. Higgs took the offer under consideration.

Later, Paulo and Johnny were charged with murder then handcuffed and taken away in the back seat of a Land Rover. Over the next few weeks, the court case became a beehive of barristers, paperwork, and typing. In the end, however, the actual trial was child's play; there was so much hard evidence as well as circumstantial, as well as two ex-casino employees, brought up from Beira, who testified against Paulo and Johnny. Of course, the two accused both denied ever being in Lusaka before, but their own voices were recorded telling Chalky White that they had.

They both denied ever being at the site of the municipal grader garage, but could not explain why their fingerprints were there, in abundance, and taken before anyone knew who they were. And, of course, they both denied being sent by the Beira casino to kill a gambler who had not paid his $6,000 US debt which he had accumulated over four years. The two culprits also denied knowing LAM airlines or had even been in the new terminal in Beira; the publicity magazine cover plus copies of original tickets put that defense attempt to rest. So, three weeks later, and after only one full day's deliberation, the jury found them guilty of first degree murder. They were sentenced to death by hanging. No appeal was forthcoming; most thought the two despicable and nobody seemed to care about their fate.

Higgs had his first case solved and he could genuinely take credit for its resolution. A very contented Amanda noticed a renewed vigor in Higgs that night and most of the day after. Higgs had to drive his Norton for two hours just to get back down to earth. He also discovered the vast amount of paperwork back at the office, when he arrived for duty at 0800 Monday morning.

"Good work on that case, Higgs," said Sythe, and the handful of detectives in the office stood and applauded.

"Oh, really, thanks, but I just followed NRP procedure," said Higgs.

"Yes, yes, we know. Now what have you done on your other case?" said Sythe, sarcastically.

30

AN IMPORTANT CASE LEFT TO SOLVE

Higgs had informed Swanny that he would not be working on Wednesday through Saturday. So this would be his first day back driving the big truck filled with crushed cars. Swanny assured him that he had told Ferranacci of the temporary driver change. Higgs finished off the dozens of pages to be done on the gambling murder case, then at about 1100 he got on his Norton and rode up to Swanny's yard where the big vehicles were kept. He found his red truck had just been washed and ready to go, and he drove to Ferranacci's yard. He was parked and in place by the crane, at 1230.

He made two trips; both uneventful. Again, he could not figure out what was going on. Each time he either stopped to offload or to fill up with diesel, he walked around the loaded truck to see if anything stood out. Nothing was that obvious. It was now Thursday, December 3, 1959. There were no crushed car deliveries today, so Higgs decided to drive by Ferranacci's yard in an impounded, and thus incognito,

Austin Westminster. Nobody would see or recognize either him or the car.

Higgs noticed a grey Vanguard, a typical government-issue car, but no identity as to whose government issued it, parked off the shoulder right opposite the yard. A large elderly man was inside the car, sitting in the passenger seat with a pair of binoculars focused on the administration building inside Ferranacci's establishment. The occupant did not seem to notice Higgs drive by.

That night was Dan Baldwin's birthday and the celebration was to be held at the Star Drive-In restaurant. About 20 cops were going to be there in about five cars. Higgs missed his mates and phoned Amanda to tell her he may not be home tonight, or if so, very late. She understood.

Higgs arrived on his Norton before anyone else. He kicked his stand and was walking into the outdoor veranda area, to commandeer all the tables, when a young man with a duck-tail hairstyle approached him and kicked Higgs in the groin. "You are the guy who knocked my mates' food on the ground. You bastard! Now we will see who is so tough."

Higgs was trying to get up when a fancy purple and black 1956 Zephyr Six pulled up and screeched to a halt in a cloud of dust. Higgs gulped and looked at his watch, the rest should be here by now if he could hold off any confrontation for a few minutes. The driver got out and said to Higgs' attacker, "Do you know who this chap is?" To which the attacker replied, "No, I don't care and why don't you just get the hell out of here. Our gang owns this restaurant and they will be here in a jiffy."

The Zephyr driver had metal tips on his jazzy boots and he lunged with a kick to the man standing over Higgs. The boot caught him under his arm-pit and lifted him a foot in the air. He landed whimpering.

The driver said, "Hey, copper! Remember me! I thought you treated us OK last time when we had an altercation here. That is my payback and if you are ever in trouble, here is my card, call me and we will all come to the rescue. Now get the hell out of here before his gang arrives."

Higgs saw the card said "Basil Waters" Panel-Beaters and Spray Painters, Stanley Road, Lusaka. He slipped it into his pocket, examined the unconscious man on the ground and said to the Zephyr driver, "Thanks. And when you leave here do not speed or show-off on the road back, as my gang are coming here as we speak. OK, I will remember this. Now go." The Zephyr screamed out of the parking lot and Basil saluted as he disappeared, just as two cars and seven cops arrived.

Higgs explained that this young man tripped and was going into the restaurant to wait for his gang to arrive. Actually, he skulked out, got into his two-tone rust and dust 1950 Ford Anglia and spluttered out of the parking lot. He nearly hit two cars filled with cops, just entering the lot. Eighteen cops got caught up with all the tall tales they had encountered in the last few months. They drank beer, ate hamburgers and chips, and laughed for hours. Higgs left following the last car, at 0100. He drove to the mess and slept in his own room, which had still not been assigned to someone else.

Higgs called for Petrol, who came very quickly. "Are you back with me permanently?" gushed Petrol.

"No, I'm afraid not, but I want to make sure you never leave without talking to me first. Do we understand each other? I am involved in a special clerical project and so I don't need a uniform for a while, and I cannot stay here for a while. Okay? When my special job is over, I will probably be sent back here and back into uniform," explained Higgs. He actually did miss the camaraderie of the uniformed friends and regular police work was a bit more fun, especially less paperwork compared to CID.

Petrol nodded and said, "I miss you, Sir, but if I must wait then, I shall do so." He also noted that Christmas was nearly upon them and he worried that Bwana Higgs might just forget Petrol (in other words don't forget my Christmas present)! Higgs assured him that Santa would visit. He then phoned Amanda and explained his change in routine. She understood, "So, see you tonight then," she said. Higgs replied, "Yes, late-ish, say 2200, and I will have eaten. 'Bye, doll. I love you."

He ate at the mess that night and rode his Norton home at about midnight. Amanda was in bed and Higgs slept in the guest room, so as not to disturb her. The phone rang at 0230 and Higgs was needed at an incident past the Ferannacci yards and he needed to pick up a Land Rover from CID that was being driven to Amanda's house and would be there in five minutes. Higgs had to do a quick change. It was a cool night and he wore a sleeveless sweater under a tweed coat, over cavalry twill pants and, the obligatory veldschoene (desert boots). He was soon driving the Land Rover with African Detective Constable Ngoni next to him.

Ngoni knew where the scene was and in the darkness of an African night, they saw the headlights of other police vehicles, off to the side of a shallow hill, about four miles north of the city.

On arrival, Higgs discovered he was the only CID member, so de facto in charge of this entire incident. First, he had to find out what exactly was going on. Apparently, A/I Dan Weeling was on traffic patrol late the night before and had simply pulled over a vehicle with a smashed tail light. As he approached the driver's side of the car, the driver, a 35-ish European male, reached over for a shotgun and pointed it at Weeling.

The driver sped off. Weeling radioed in the licence plate number, then gave chase, with his siren blaring and lights flashing and requesting assistance. The driver pulled off to a dirt road and then drove over a barbed-wire fence and up a deserted hill. Weeling pulled up behind the car and saw the man running away toward the crest of the hill. The man turned around and fired his shotgun at Weeling, who, wisely, ran back to his patrol car and radioed in all the information. Then he pulled out a loud-hailer and called upon the man to surrender, which prompted two shots from the shotgun.

Higgs was looking inside the man's car and found a receipt, dated that day, from the Stanley-Day Arms Co., in Lusaka, for eight boxes of cartridges for a 12-gauge shotgun. As there was no ammunition in the car, it could only be assumed the man had them all with him; it could be a long dangerous night, thought Higgs.

All night there were calls for surrender to which there was a response of shots. Now a sniper had arrived with an

FN rifle and was positioned to take the man out, if he could see him and only if the situation warranted it.

There was no response, well, except for the shooting from the man, as to just exactly what his problem was. Nobody knew him, and apparently he resided in Lusaka, as details were obtained from his car's licence plate. Officers were dispatched to the home address listed on the car's ownership details, but the house was empty and in darkness.

One police officer was stopped as he backed out of the man's driveway. The next door neighbour told him that this man had just lost his family, a wife of 14 years and two daughters, in a major car accident in Spain just the previous day and said if he were the police, he would put out an APB (all points bulletin) because he figured the man was so distraught he would try something stupid, cumulating in suicide. "In fact," the neighbour said, "that's what he was probably trying to do now, Suicide by Cops." That information got passed on to Higgs by radio.

At close to 0430, there about 20 police officers in attendance and no sign of this problem being resolved. No communication in either direction with the armed man. 30 shots had been fired at the police and remarkably nobody injured. But this had to stop. Then, roaring up the hill in his personal car, Superintendent Punch Hamble arrived in a cloud of dust. He leaped from his car and said, "I have been listening to this bloody shambles for the past two hours and I am here to stop it. Which way is the sod?" he asked.

Then, wagging his cane high, he walked up the hill toward where all assumed the gunman was located and, in his very broad Lancashire voice, yelled, "C'mon, laddie. What are you damn well thinking of? We have a lot of bloody decent police officers here and they all want to get home to their families. I know you have suffered a loss in your family but this will not help you. Now don't make me come all the way up there on my gammy leg. Just put yer gun down and come and let me get you a cup of tea and we can chat about what to do next. Do it now, before you are in trouble."

Amazingly, a voice was heard from about 50 feet away. "Okay. Don't shoot. I have put my gun down and I am walking towards the only one person I can see, with a waving cane above his head."

And down the hill came a young man aged about 35 and ran into Superintendent Hamble, hugging him and sobbing, "I'm sorry. I didn't know what to do and I was going to get one of you to kill me. Please help me."

Higgs took the man into custody and left the scene. Punch Hamble, with a wink in his eye said, "Now then, not by the book but I can still handle a crisis." Soon the hillside was empty; someone picked up six boxes of shotgun shells and the shotgun, and took them to be locked away.

The courts were very lenient with the man, under the circumstances. He was allowed bail under his own recognition, mainly so he could sort out the funeral and had been determined to not be a threat to society or himself. Four months later, he was found guilty of attempting an assault on police and of trying to evade a traffic violation. He was sentenced to four years' imprisonment, suspended for ten years. He went back to his occupation as a chemical engineer; sold his house, and left Lusaka to live in Kitwe, a northern town in the copper belt.

By the time Higgs had finished all the paperwork and processed the prisoner, he got back to Amanda's at around 0900. He greeted her, had breakfast, and fell asleep for most of the day. At 1500 DCI Sythe phoned him and asked him to come in at 0600 the next morning. "Things are beginning to develop on Ferannacci," is all he said.

Higgs took Amanda to the Rendezvous Restaurant that evening, where they enjoyed a slap-up dinner of crispy roast duck in black cherry sauce. They rode together on his Norton and were back home by 2200. That night, Amanda was demanding and rough.

31

RIGHT, LET'S GET THIS OVER WITH

Feeling somewhat shagged out, Higgs managed to wake up, shower, get dressed, eat a bacon sandwich, and get to his office on his Norton, at 0600. Sythe was sitting at his desk eating a soggy egg sandwich and drinking his fourth cup of coffee. "Grab a coffee and grab a seat," ordered Sythe. "Listen here, we have had a report from MI5 that one of their operatives has been working in Lusaka and thinks he has cracked a diamond smuggling scheme."

"I bet that was the guy I saw with the binoculars!" suggested Higgs. "So what is his theory?"

"That's just it!" exclaimed Sythe. "He doesn't really know! Here's what he believes so far. Africans are taking in "found" wild diamonds, or rough diamonds. You know there are parts of the country where a keen eye can find a diamond simply lying on the top of the ground. The finder knows that the government has encouraged them to bring the diamonds into them and they will be paid the going rate, for that particular diamond, in that particular condition. Historically, the government has been squeaky clean in their assessments and pays a fair and going rate. The bad guys, those who want to bypass the normal way to get a diamond, have convinced most of the Africans that the government are a bunch of crooks who pay less than half what they pay. Russia and China play this game as they try to disrupt the standards for gold and diamonds.

Sythe continued, "So, this MI5 bloke believes that Ferannacci is a buyer. Don't know where his seed money comes from or where or how he gets the diamonds out, but he is positive that Ferannacci is a crook and is an illegal diamond buyer. It is on our turf and MI5 do not want to be seen, so we have to solve it, and I believe we can. The only item that ever leaves Ferannacci's yard is wrecked cars. No parcel post being sent out and no visible people driving out of the yard with pockets stuffed full of packets of diamonds. So diamonds are somehow hidden in the wrecked cars. Agree?"

Higgs answered, "I do. And you know there is always one car that is loaded on my truck last. And it seems that car comes directly from the warehouse and not from the crushing area. Well, it is crushed then taken away then comes back as the last car to be loaded. Something happens to that car in those moments it goes from A to B."

Sythe pours two coffees and sits with his feet up on his desk. "I'm guessing they have a bag of diamonds and they are hiding it in the car, but where? Oh, yes. I forgot to tell you, Higgs, one of our African detectives has been closely observing Ferannacci's men at the rail goods yard. He found out that a telegram is sent for each trainload of wrecked cars that goes to the docks in Beira. Then that train's contents are loaded onto a freighter. That freighter then departs for Durres, Albania. Every trainload only gets to be on a freighter to Albania. So we have to ask ourselves, what the hell does Albania want with so many wrecked cars?"

"Can the African detective constable get us just one copy of one of those telegrams? Any pressure he can bring to bear on the railway telegram operator? Perhaps he can be casually watching where the copies are kept and he could steal one from the middle of the pile, get it back here for photocopying, and we could study it. He surreptitiously takes it back and slips it back into the pile. Hmm ... do you agree?" asked Higgs.

"Right, it is 0730 and our two boys are going to be at work at 0800. They phone us before they leave home to get special instructions. They will be phoning any minute now and I will tell one of them to get us a copy and today, if possible," replied Sythe.

"Oh, by the way, Mr. Sythe, why in hell did you want me here so early today?" asked Higgs.

"Oh, that. Well, we're are having a CID Christmas party and wondered if you would like to bring your special friend, Amanda, and introduce her to us, that's all," said Sythe, with a bemused smirk.

Sythe gave clear instructions to his detective during his phone briefing. He wanted to see if there were perhaps two telegrams to someone. Perhaps one went to the port-master who got the wrecked cars on the right ship, going to the right place. But surely someone on the other end must be told which ship and the estimated time of arrival. Hopefully, this second telegram had other news as well.

Meanwhile, back in the uniformed world, a report comes in that three white males have been arrested for a prank. It seems that the United National Independence Party has a new headquarters. Outside that three-story office building is a flagpole and a huge flag was swaying in the breeze. Now, most institutions lower their flags at sunset, along with some ceremony (you have a flag you need a ceremony!) but apparently not the UNIP. So, with a little help from Johnny Walker and Schweppes, three men climbed the pole and removed the flag.

Because they were observed by a UNIP vice president and the police were called immediately, the three were caught red-handed. They were all Lusaka Central Division police officers. A court date was set and the best lawyer in town volunteered his services and defended the three without a fee. The case lasted 20 minutes and each man was found guilty of a misdemeanour and fined £2 each. The UNIP was not amused and vowed to seek "revenge." The flag flew again and the entire world sighed with relief.

It was now Friday, December 11, 1959 and Christmas decorations started to appear in the department stores and some in police offices. Invitations to parties began arriving. Certainly, a calendar was required as there were so many opportunities to get one's dates wrong. Christmas day was two weeks away, on a Friday.

This Christmas was very different from 1958. This year Higgs felt more like a civil servant than a police officer. He had no dinner with his uniformed pals and he spent a lot of time at home with Amanda.

Higgs was also able to socialize a lot with Swanny and friends, as well as parties at the regiment with his motorcycle friends there. Higgs liked the new life but did miss the uniformed camaraderie. It was a dilemma he would consider often over the next few months.

After a number of "braai's" and quite a few parties, Higgs also attended his formal CID Christmas party. He introduced Amanda to all his detective associates. The music and the food were great but the two got themselves home by 2300 and collapsed into the bed, unable to do anything but sleep until 0900. Refreshed, the next morning the two went for a ride on their bikes. Amanda was getting lessons from a retired British South Africa Police instructor, who had been a cop for 33 years, in Bulawayo, Southern Rhodesia. She was gutsy and competent and could almost keep up with Higgs. She had finally settled for a brand-new Matchless 350 and chose a purple colour and leather saddle bags. She looked great, especially in her jeans and leather bomber jacket. She loved her purple helmet and enormous tinted goggles. The entire male population in Lusaka loved her outfit as well.

On Friday, January 8, 1960 Higgs and Detective Chief Inspector Sythe were pouring over some papers brought in by African Detective Constable Nemiah. He managed to slip into the telegraph office and dug down in the pile of copies. He found three copies of everything sent over a two-day period the previous week.

The evidence was photocopied and the copies returned to Nemiah, who promptly returned them to the drawer in the telegraph office. He had a doctor's appointment, he told his boss at the railways. He had been away less than two hours. Nobody blinked an eye.

The first copy was from "F&Assoc's" to East Asiatic line M/V Java. "Train load 343. Arriving Beira 2300." The second copy was from "F&Assoc's" to Majur Corp. "Red Fiat SX564877." The third copy was from "F& Assoc's" to JB Ltd. Durres, Albania, confirmed to Majur. Right there, in writing, was the evidence they needed, obviously telling the freighter the train to load up. Then telling the receiver to look for a specific car, the type, colour, and serial number and then confirming, presumably, to the bankroll.

They devised a plan. On the next truck ride, with the "late" car identified, there would be a minor accident. Police would immediately surround the vehicle with canvas, so the CID could work within the tent-like structure, unseen by any prying eyes outside the canvas perimeter.

Sure enough, two days later, Higgs was able to phone Sythe and confirm he would be leaving with a blue Austin A40 as the subject vehicle. Sythe advised Higgs to prepare for his "accident" just before the road leading into the railway goods yard. Higgs would feign injury and an ambulance would whisk him away from the scene (just in case they still needed him for future disguised work).

It happened quickly. An old, unidentified Land Rover swerved into Higgs' truck and he veered off the tarmac into the bush. Police were on scene surprisingly quickly and had the scene canvassed off within minutes. Some government vehicles with the ability to rip metal off metal, like Van Rooyen ripping meat off a chicken leg, began removing one particular car, the blue Austin. The car was in shreds within minutes.

Three or four minutes later, a canvas bag fell out of the empty gasoline tank of the Austin. Sythe grabbed it and unsealed it. It was filled with very ordinary looking but certified diamonds that needed a little cutting and polishing and worth, in the region of, £2 million. The case was solved. Now, to put it all together to get a conviction.

Higgs was able to phone Swanny from Amanda's house. He warned him about the impending raid and that he should stay away, if possible, and get his employees away. Swanny was promised all the juicy details, but not yet. It was confirmed that Ferannacci was at work this day, and his two henchmen, a vice president and the managing director, were meeting in the main office. They were all up to their eyebrows in this scheme. Little did they know how their day would end as they smugly sat around smoking huge cigars.

At exactly 1600, three patrol cars and two unmarked cars drove through the gate and halted outside the main office. Sythe brushed his way past the young lady at the reception desk and entered the office where Ferannacci and company were meeting. All were arrested and taken away.

Over the next few days, the CID thoroughly went through every piece of paper in Ferannacci's buildings, even finding a cache of nearly 50 canvas bags containing diamonds. The trial was six weeks later. The sentences they received were very high, from 15 years to 45 years for Ferannacci himself. Diamond smuggling was a serious offense and MI5 would not tolerate it. The MI5 were informed; apparently Sir Percy Sillitoe, a former Northern Rhodesia Police officer himself, headed up MI5 and he had actually been investigating Ferannacci personally since the late 1940s. MI5 also had contacts in Albania but the outcome of their involvement was never known as it was all handled "diplomatically," communism being a secretive society and a hindrance to law and order. This case was one more that not only involved Higgs but truly was his to own. He was awarded honours for his work, in person, from the commissioner.

Sythe called Higgs in on March 25, 1960. "Higgs, my boy, today is not a good day for me. I have been told that uniform needs more manpower. There is a looming problem on the border with the Belgian Congo and the brass in HQ need someone to do a little "recce" up near Jadotville and Solwezi. Superintendent Punch Hamble specifically asked for you. He said you were a great detective but with all the recent publicity, poker games, murder, and MI5, you could hardly go undercover and your work might simply be reduced to heavy duty research, in other words, a clerk. I agreed with him and I want you to get ahead as a policeman and not be in a boring back office. So, I agreed to let you go back to uniform, just temporarily, mind you. I said I would take you back as soon as your new venture was completed and it was what you wanted."

Tears were running down Sythe's face; Higgs noticed more tears came from Sythe's left eye and wondered why. Then he realized he too was tearing up. "If that's the way it is, then so be it," said Higgs. "I have never worked with anyone that I have so respected. Mr. Sythe, you are a class act and I shall miss our relationship a lot. The moment I can, I will apply to come back to work with you."

"Oh, bloody hell!" said Sythe. "Don't get me all emotional; shake hands on the deal and if you find info along the way, let me know. Okay? For the greater good, you know." The two hugged, a very un-British thing to do, and an un-police thing too.

"So long, Higgs. Take the week off and report to Hamble on Monday, April 1st. Take Amanda away for a few days. Use my cottage on the Kafue. Here are my keys and here's how you get to it. I need it for April 4th. You can go there today if you want. Shit, I am going to miss you! Now, goodbye." They chatted about provisions and the weird neighbours down by the cottage and some various notes, and also a private telephone line which Higgs could use. Higgs left the office quickly. He was soon on his Norton and back at his room in the mess. He had a chat with Petrol, then went down to the bar and enjoyed a rare evening with most of his mates. Sythe slammed his door and retreated to his crossword puzzle in the Central African Post, the local daily newspaper.

Higgs explained to Amanda about the Kafue cottage and his new job. It was not a secretive job but he had no bloody idea what the job was; he would find out on April 1st, at Punch Hamble's office. The two packed up freezer bags of ice and frozen meats, some rough clothes, and a case of various libations. They drove the 35 miles to the cottage in 45 minutes and arrived at 1430.

The cottage had three bedrooms and a huge veranda. It had a one toilet en-suite and a large four-piece bathroom that had very modern tiled vanities and shower, with a bidet and a toilet. All the water came from a clear spring nearby, with a Honda electric motor generator to provide all water to the house, as well as ample electricity for lighting.

The stay was idyllic. If they were tense beforehand and needed a rest, the two had five days of relaxed bliss going out on the small boat, swimming in the river, fishing and eating the fish, love-making, reading, and listening to plays from the BBC on the tinny radio. But, it was over quickly and now Higgs had to report to Hamble on the 1st of April, the next day. He was waiting for an April Fool's prank, but it did not happen.

32

A GLIMPSE INTO WHAT MAY COME

He wore his uniform for the first time in almost a year. It was still hanging up covered in a bag as Petrol had left it. Hmm... he needed to talk about where he was to live and about Petrol, especially if he was back in uniform; the servants at Amanda's house could not keep his uniform up to snuff.

He parked his Land Rover outside headquarters and was shown to Hamble's office by the guard. Hamble stood up and said, "Oh my God! No need for you to be in uniform, lad, next time just plain clothes, and I mean just plain. I have no idea what your job is going to look like, and so we don't want you messing up a perfectly good uniform while we plot and plan."

"Sir, whatever you need me for, I am ready. Can we start with just exactly what the goal is?" asked Higgs.

Hamble called for his assistant, a beaming corporal in uniform, and asked for some tea. "You too, Higgs?" he asked. "And how do you like it? Tell Njovu here and he'll get you what you want." The tea arrived shortly thereafter (Milk and two sugars for Higgs). The two men walked over to a very large table which had three or four large scale maps on it.

Hamble began, "Look here, lad. This is all very hush, hush and I expect you to make up whatever cover story to keep all of it away from everyone. And I mean everyone. Even if another police officer wants to know what you are doing, refer them to me. Use your cover story, otherwise. "Now then, we are getting accurate info about a number of political parties being formed and they have sedition in mind. They want our government out. They want all Europeans out; they want to run this country themselves. They say they want democracy but are not much interested in majority rule. Some have a slogan 'one man one vote,' but we are of the opinion they mean 'all vote for one man and that man better be me.' We need to be prepared and we need to have a plan that will work. In fact, we need more than one plan, as we don't know exactly what or which party will emerge the strongest. As you know, there are rumblings in the Belgian Congo, and they sit on our northern border; bound to be crossover issues there."

Hamble continued, "Then we have the railways under extreme threat from either a lonewolf terrorists or henchmen for some political party. We need a shit-disturbing risktaker to lead our anti-terror squad, as I like to call it. And, your name came up four times. I met you when you had blood, shit, and mud all over your new uniform, when you had lunch with all of us on your first day as a copper. I must say it was a novel way for you to introduce yourself. Hey, what! Then I saw you up on the hill a while back when that man with a shotgun was threatening you all. That was your first CID case where you were the lead detective. You handled it well, of course, once I showed you how to do it. But I hear you got a murder case solved and now an MI5 diamond smuggling case too. So, I asked for you and the Commissioner said yes, and here you are.

Frankly, if I was 20 years younger, this is a job I would have liked to head up. I was informed by the brass upstairs that I was too old and too level-headed to come up with plans."

"Oh, thank you, Sir. Does that mean the brass believe me to be some kind of whacko?" asked Higgs. "Like, only I with my devious mind could outwit the terrorists?"

"Yes," replied Hamble. The two grinned at each other and got down to planning.

"Firstly, we need to sell the farming community on our plan, without giving too much away. We have heard about the Mau Mau, in Kenya, and how their tactics are to get to the farmers and their families and scare the beloving Jesus out of them. Using surprise and then unthinkable brutality, they attack the homes, kill off the servants and the dogs, and then rape and then kill the wife, and kill the children, while the husband is away or, if he's home make him watch, then torture and kill him last. That is not going to happen here, under my watch. We have a map here that shows every home within a 100-mile radius from Lusaka. There are others beyond that circle but we will get to them later. We will have available two helicopters and, if we hear of any home being attacked, we can get to them within 20 minutes. Each farm will have a code and each will have a phone radio installed. And each will have their code painted on both sides of their corrugated iron roofs. Look, this one here, the closest one; he stabbed a huge finger at the map. That farm belongs to Jannie Uys, he's A1. If attacked, he will call in immediately and say A1. The helicopter crew will scramble, and have three heavily-armed officers on board and they will know where to fly to and where to land. There, just four miles away, is Brent Fogherty's chicken farm; he is A2, and so on."

Ramble continued, "Within a week, I need you ready to visit all the farmers in section A, 34 of them. Make sure you provide them with their code and they understand that they need to paint that code on each side of their roofs. Here is an artist's rendition of what size and colour it must be, and on the back are the procedures to follow in the event that some attack is occurring. Remember, most farmers will be complacent about this, as they have lived a very peaceful life so far. On one hand, we don't want to panic them but we must caution them about the possibilities. The Kenyan community had no idea what hit them, and were sorely unprepared. We will not be caught with our pants down. You will use horses and take with you one African sergeant and two African constables. The two constables will carry FN Rifles and be responsible for carrying two tents and supplies. The sergeant will be your helper and translator, if required. You will carry a pistol and a Sterling machine gun; your sergeant will have a 12-gauge shotgun. Well, Higgs, so far what do you think?"

"The farmers will likely offer to put us up, if it is close to sundown while visiting them, and they will probably offer us food. Should I accept it and should I volunteer to pay for it?" asked Higgs.

"You have no rules in this regard, so act responsibly and do what needs to be done. You will be provided with government vouchers, which the farmers can claim at a later date. On the other hand, if they insist on being generous, then accept their offer and thank them on behalf of the NRP. It really is these little things that can make this a nightmare or a simple exercise. That is why I believe you are the man for the job." Hamble further explained, "You seem to have the know-how on how to fit into a situation never ventured into before."

"Do you have any timetable in mind, Sir?" inquired Higgs. "Any time you want to begin and end, at least section A?"

"Section A, for you is only yours to complete. You may select others for the remaining smaller sections, B through E. But first I need you to visit the stables and see Senior Inspector Bryan Arthur, who is expecting you, and get yourself four horses. Check out the constables he has available and select the two you prefer. You will be using Sergeant Amos. He knows horses. He is from a village where most of the farms are located, which is very useful, and he can read and write English better than me. But, more than that, he has a sense of humour and is a decent bloke. He will be good company for you. That's it, Higgs. Oh, and by the way, while you have all the time on your hands as you cloppity clop along the farm roads, think about a plan should these bastards decide they want to take us on, head to head."

Higgs said, "I hear these sods – what are they calling themselves? 'freedom fighters' – are receiving arms from

Russia and China. My latest escapade was involved with railway use for smuggling, and coming out of Albania via Beira. If they could send diamonds out, then surely someone could bring weapons in. My first plan will be to stop that as soon as possible and, secondly, track down where they are being stored and either capture or destroy them. Southern Rhodesian Intelligence will gladly help, and the South Africans will not mind sharing data with us if they have us fighting a battle that they will face one day."

"I like your thinking, Higgs," beamed Hamble. "Now, would you join me for lunch and let's get to know each other a bit better, alright? I believe they have a mixed grill for the menu today."

Over lunch, with other senior officers frowning and wondering who this young whippersnapper was alone with Punch Hamble, Higgs brought up two subjects. "Sir, what do you suggest I do about living arrangements? My room at the mess has been given to another officer and I had a great relationship with my batman. Now I am living with my girlfriend, at her home, which is fine but my batman works for someone else now. Any help or suggestions, Sir?"

Hamble said, "That is going to happen frequently during your career. It is simply the nature of the beast. Roll with the punches and get over it."

"Okay Sir. I can do that. Now, should we be involving the Northern Rhodesia Regiment at all? If sporadic fighting takes place, we do not have the manpower to spread ourselves across the country. The military does. I am thinking that maybe one soldier that I know, a corporal, would be the right sort of bloke to come with me on the farm code trip. Good idea or not, Sir?"

Hamble replied, "Damn good idea but not yet. We are concerned about the natives in the army. Unlike our blokes, there is a small faction that could be spies as they sympathize with one or more of the political parties. Naturally, I too have strong contacts and slowly they will be told." The mixed grill was a lamb chop, a pork chop, an English sausage, and grilled kidneys, with mashed potatoes and a mountain of green peas. Sticky toffee pudding and custard followed. Higgs could hardly walk as he headed back to the Land Rover. He drove a mile to the stables and spoke to the only white officer in sight. "Senior Inspector Arthur?" he asked.

"Yes, that's me. You the Punch Hamble bloke?" responded the 40-ish balding, tall man with nicotine-stained fingers.

"Yup, A/I Higgs-Briar. They call me Higgs," explained Higgs. "I need four horses for about two weeks. I gather you have it all arranged. Can I also meet the constables, so I can select which two seem compatible?"

A sergeant came in saying he had been asked to accompany Higgs. He was a tall, lanky man with bright eyes and skin the colour of light coffee. He had a grin spread across his face and Higgs liked him right away. Five constables appeared and Higgs questioned each one. He immediately found the two that had, in his opinion, the right qualities to fit in with his team. A quick concurrence from the Sergeant, and they were selected.

Higgs addressed the three men and told them they would be leaving on a journey that might last two to three weeks. They should inform their families and be ready to leave very early on Monday, April 4th. They would have the horses and all the equipment trailered out of town to the nearest farm, A1. The trailer would leave them and they would saddle up and proceed to their first assignment. He explained the sleeping arrangements; a small tent for him and the three others in the large tent. All would use sleeping bags and food would be basic sadza and mostly tinned foods. Fresh eggs and chickens, etcetera could be purchased en-route. Tea or coffee and tinned milk would be abundant. Higgs had to explain to Amanda his uncertain absence.

Amanda announced that this would be a perfect time for her to fly to Spain, as she had a new contact there with the promise of a huge purchase of her flowers and a long-term contract. She would fly out at mid-day Monday, after a passionate weekend. Amanda and Higgs were alone all Friday night, and every moment until he left at 0500 on Monday morning. She smiled as he bent over the bed and they kissed, deeply and passionately. "C'mon, baby, time for one more just for you. Lie back and let me get you so shagged out you will only just be ready for sex when I return on the 14th," she whispered. "No fair," he pleaded. "I can hardly walk as it is. I must set off on my journey."

33

SHIFTING GEARS

The Land Rover he had ordered for 0600 was waiting for him in the driveway. Sergeant Amos was at the wheel. They assembled at the headquarter stables and loaded the horses into a large trailer. And so, they all set off at 0700 on Monday. The men were joyful and chattered with themselves. At 0830 they were saying goodbye to the trailer driver as he drove off. They were on horseback and arriving at Mr. Uys' farm at 0930. All officers were wearing uniform, wearing jodhpurs, riding boots, and pith helmets.

Laundry had not been discussed but it was assumed that the farmers' servants would offer to do the laundry every few days. It should be remembered that the attitude of these farmers and their families was firstly, very friendly toward police, and secondly, pleased to talk to any visitor to their homes. It was a lonely life for most and, frankly, their only entertainment was visiting neighbours or having neighbours at their homes. Three or four times a year, they might visit the city. This might be only a two-hour journey but it was a terrific morale booster and an opportunity to buy scarce items needed to run their home.

The dogs began barking as they entered the front gate. Five Rhodesian Ridgebacks ran out to greet them. They were huge and friendly but would eat one's leg off if their owner instructed them to attack. Mr. Uys came out and yelled at the dogs, "C'mon, you guys, get back! Hello, police. What am I accused of?" he laughed. Higgs explained their purpose and Uys asked him to come in and join him for a coffee.

"Tell your men they can ask for Mathew down at my staff compound and he will give them refreshments. They can also tie up the horses down there, and let them drink from our trough."

Sergeant Amos understood everything said and, tipping his helmet said, "Thank you, Mr. Uys. We will take advantage of your offer. Come on you two, we are off to the staff compound. We will take your horse too, Bwana Higgs, and let us know when you are ready to move."

Higgs enjoyed a real Boer cup of coffee in a very large enamel mug – very strong coffee filled with sweetened condensed milk. In fact, he had two. He and Uys discussed the instruction card and Uys confirmed his code A1 would be painted on his roof by that night.

Of course, Uys had a radio phone, locked up, as well as a party-line telephone. Uys then showed Higgs a shortcut across his land, to get to the next farm, owned by Brent Fogherty, A2, in 30 minutes, compared to nearly an hour by road.

Within half an hour, the team was crossing over fields to Brent's farm. Mr. Fogherty welcomed them and understood what he had to do. Twenty minutes later, the team was making its way to A3, a farm owned by a very British ex-major, from India, Michael Hazelmuir. He farmed flowers.

"Come in, old chap," he beamed as he shook hands with Higgs. "Tell your men to go and visit my compound down there where the smoke is. Tell them to ask for Rajah, my foreman. He just went down there for his lunch. Whatever they need they can get from good old Rajah."

Over a cup of tea and some ginger snaps, he explained that he drove into Lusaka three times a week to deliver his flowers to Amanda de la Haye. "Do you happen to know her at all, Higgs?"

Higgs said he did, but did not elaborate, not for any particular reason; he just liked to keep some stuff close to his vest. He did think it was a small world, however.

Soon the team was at A4, a small pig farm that smelled bloody awful. Constable Phineas said, "Bwana, I think this farmer should take some of that awful perfume some of my girlfriends put on, and put it on the pigs." All got a good laugh out of that. Mr. Engelbert ran the farm and invited all of them to come into his house and have a late lunch. "You must be starving! It is nearly 1330. I have just roasted a whole pig and was about to send some of it down to my compound. I have 15 labourers who look after my farm and they have gotten to like pork. We can eat outside under that willow tree at that picnic table. If you wish, you can refresh the horses at the barn, in the shade, and give them hay and a drink. We can rip this pig apart here and have some tomatoes and corn bread with it."

Constable Ngoni took the four horses to the nearby barn, then joined the men at the table. They devoured the food and drank many glasses of iced lemonade. The purpose of their visit was explained and at 1400 they recommenced their journey, over to A5. Once again they were given permission to take a shortcut across Engelbert's small farm of 15 acres.

A5 was a huge cattle ranch, over 1,000 acres. It was owned by two brothers with two distinctly different houses, driveways, and garages. The brothers were Dutchmen, grandsons of Boers who had left South Africa in 1900 to escape the tragedy of the war. As if they were on a timer, both brothers emerged from their respective houses as soon as they heard their dogs barking.

"Jannie van de Merwe," greeted one and stuck out his hand. "Gert van de Merwe," said the other. Both men came up to each policeman, who had now dismounted, and shook each man's hand. "Hey, we were nowhere near the bank when it was robbed, so that charge won't stick. To what pleasure are we expecting from you police blokes today?" asked Jannie. Higgs asked for 20 minutes of their time. Gert said, "Tell your men to go and refresh the horses and if they need anything just ask either Luke or Lifebuoy, our two head boys down at the servants quarters. Let's sit here on our veranda and we can talk," suggested Gert. "Can I bring you a beer or a soft drink?" Higgs went through the details of the mission as he sipped a large glass of iced tea. They were on their way to A6 within an hour. As they were leaving,

Jannie brought out a very large brown paper bag. "We are renowned for our biltong (dried beef similar to jerky). The best way to advertise it is by word of mouth. Here is enough for all of you to share, maybe for your dinner tonight." The bag was gratefully accepted and tucked away in a saddlebag, until dinner time.

Higgs read the farmer's name out as he checked his map. "By God," he said to the men, "I actually know this farmer. I met him and his family on the ship when I was coming here from England." Indeed the farm belonged to Norman Blythe and his wife Carol. Of course, there was also Marjorie.

Blythe was a corn farmer with nearly 800 acres. The team arrived at 1700. Blythe was not in the house but Carol came to the door. "Yes, officer, what can I do for you?" she asked. "It's Higgs!" came a scream from behind Carol and there stood Marjorie, in sweat pants and a man's white shirt, looking slightly slimmer and very pretty. "And just exactly how can I help you?" Marjorie asked, with enough innuendo but not enough to give away her secret to her mother.

Frankly, Higgs was speechless. "I am here on official police business and may I ask how long you guess your father may be before he returns?"

Carol explained, "To be honest, I can't believe he will be more than a few minutes....in fact, look, there he is now in that cloud of dust driving his truck home. But please, do come in and get out of the sun. Your men can rest the horses down there about 100 yards away, and they can use the stream to give them water and to refresh themselves. Aah! Here's Norman now." To her husband, she said, "Hi dear, what a surprise visit! You remember Higgs from the ship and now he's here on official business."

Norman smiled and shook hands with Higgs and ushered him into their living room. "Oh my, what a surprise! It has been a long time and we had so much fun, didn't we, Marjorie," glancing aside at his daughter. "Did Carol tell your men where to rest up?" he asked.

Higgs nodded as he took off his headgear and plonked himself down at the huge dining room table, where Norman had pulled out a chair. Once Higgs had explained his purpose for being on this mission, Norman understood and asked if Higgs had plans to visit anyone else that day. "It's getting near to sunset and almost impossible for you to head out now."

Higgs said, "We have tents and supplies and will camp out tonight."

Norman would have none of it. "Look here. We have a vacant guest rondavel for you. It is right next door and it is a comfortable 200 square feet with a great bed. I know, I have slept in it myself when Carol said I was snoring too loudly. I will make sure I don't snore too loud tonight otherwise I could be cuddling up to you in that big bed...right, Carol? Also, I have just finished building a large 400 square foot rondavel down in the servants area, as I plan to hire six more men this season. If your men have sleeping bags and blankets, they can share that new big place and I will tell my head boy to also feed them and the horses. In fact, let me do that right now. "

He pressed a buzzer on the wall and a few minutes later a smiling middle-aged man wearing jeans and an old Harris tweed sports jacket, with no shirt, came to the house. "You buzzed for me, Bwana?" he said, addressing Norman. "What do you need, Sir?"

Norman said, "This is Chevrolet, my number one man. Chevrolet this is Mr. Higgs, a man I met on the ship nearly two years ago." Higgs and Chevrolet shook hands. Norman continued, "You saw those three policemen and their horses. I want you...." Chevrolet interrupted, "I have given my son the job already to look after the four horses and make space for them in the barn. I have told my wife to make extra food to feed the three policemen and put all their katunga [their belongings] into the new house. I just need to know what time in the morning you and your men will be leaving, Mr. Higgs, so I can arrange food and horses for you."

Higgs could not get over the lovely relationship between an African servant and his boss, and the respect for each other's position and the common-sense working elegance.

Norman said, "Chevrolet, thank you for thinking ahead. Higgs, what time tomorrow?"

Higgs said, "About 0700."

"Oh, that late?" grinned Norman. "I shall have been up two hours by then...." All laughed, as did Chevrolet on his way out.

"This is also your lucky day," explained Norman. "Our neighbour just brought over this morning about 15 pounds of beef bones. Carol has had them in a slow-cooker for eight hours and the meat is literally falling off the bone. So, of course, it's corn on the cob, beef bones, along with roasted carrots, potatoes, and onions. Is there some dessert, Carol?

Aah! Yes, I see it now, that enormous strawberry pie in the cooler."

The first to bed was Marjorie. "Goodnight, Mr. Higgs. It's eight o'clock," she smiled suggestively. "I have to go into town early as I have a new job. I'm living in town, at Longacres, and working at Lusaka Airport in the weather office. If you like clouds and weathery stuff, give me a call."

The rest sat back drinking Van Der Hum (a Dutch liquer, made by the Boers, attempting to duplicate Grand Marnier. They actually surpassed it!). They reminisced about some of what went on on the ship. But Higgs also got a feel for what the farming community was feeling about these new disturbing activities, all politically motivated by a handful of "shit-disturbers," as Carol called them. Over the course of the evening, while they reminisced about their ship travel, Norman and Higgs also poured over maps and Higgs was given a lot of information about shortcuts and personalities of whom he was calling on the next day. Very useful.

By 2000 all were in bed. Higgs barely got out of his clothes and he was asleep in a warm bed, in a warm room. He prayed Marjorie would not pull any stunts that night; she did not.

At 0600 Higgs was awoken by a servant who had a huge bacon sandwich and a large mug of very strong and sweet coffee. He was also given two large towels and was shown how to use the en-suite shower. At 0630 he was dressed and ready to go. Carol brought some cold beef sandwiches, enough for all four policemen, and gave him a huge thermos flask full of hot coffee.

"I would like the flask back one day," she explained. "You could always drop it off at Marjorie's at Longacres and she can bring it back one day. No rush. Goodbye, Higgs," she blushed and kissed him gently on the mouth. His men were waiting impatiently with all the horses. They saddled up Higgs' horse and packed away all the stuff Higgs seemed to have accumulated since arriving, and soon they were on their way.

About ten minutes later, they came across Norman's truck and waved at him. Norman walked out of the cornfield and shook all their hands. "Come back for a visit any time. Now, you men didn't find any girls down in my quarters that you wish to visit again, did you?" he joked. The men all grinned and sheepishly replied, in unison, "No, Sir. We were all on duty, so no time for womanizing. But thank you for the wonderful food and the new house we slept in."

A7 belonged to a chicken farmer, Nick Potgieter. He had a small acreage and was very busy. Not that he was anti-police, just busy. He came out of a shed, wiping his hands on an oily cloth. "How can I help you cops today?" he asked. "Sorry, I am busy fixing my small two-stroke tractor and my mechanic is away for two weeks in Jo'Burg. Let's get on with whatever it is...not another brain-wave plan from the British Government, is it?"

Higgs dismounted and asked if he could see the type of tractor he had been working on.

"Ja, OK. It's a damn home-made thing from a motorbike engine. The wheels and body are from a jalopy that was lying around and we bought the engine at an auction for £20. You think you know engines, you go ahead and tell me what's wrong," said the exasperated Nick.

Higgs went into the shed and fiddled with the engine. Then he found the electric start button and pressed it just once. It roared into life. Nick was so surprised that his glasses fell off his face. "How the bloody hell did you do that?" he yelled.

Higgs said, "When you have a tricky engine made in England, then you need an English motorcycle mechanic to fix it. Your fuel line was reversed; open position actually was the closed position. If I were you, I would take it off and put it back the right way. No charge, Mr. Potgieter. Just make sure you paint your roof." It was as if the mouse had removed the thorn from the lion's paw.

Nick stood there with his hand out and said, "Saved by a bloody Englishman! God has wondrous ways. Thank you so much! I feel so foolish not to have figured that out myself. Can I get you anything?" "Sorry, we must be on our way," said Higgs. "Totsiens meneer!" Higgs yelled to an astounded Mr. Potgieter (Van Rooyen's Afrikaans lessons were useful, mused Higgs).

A8 through A20, were all very close together and they were handled very quickly. In fact, by 1730 they called it a day. The last farm they visited, A20, was owned by a woman in her 80s, who had over 300 sheep. She supplied some milk and live sheep to an Italian butcher in Lusaka. She had only a large yard and a rondavel for her living quarters.

She offered a corner of an unused field for the police to use as their overnight camp. She was a vegetarian and had no meat to offer the men but she gave them a steaming hot loaf of bread and refilled Higgs' thermos with hot tea.

The men had their tents set up, while Higgs explained what Mrs. Wilson had to do. She had a radio telephone as well as a regular party-line phone. She also had a foreman who would paint the code on the roof by the next day. She did not want to be told what to do or how to live, but this idea she liked.

Higgs and the three men sat around a nice fire and ate the sandwiches given to them. They finished nearly all of the biltong and most of the fresh loaf. Constable Ngoni sat back, leaning against a tree, feeling very sated, and said, "Bwana Higgs, here we are in Africa watching the sun dropping behind the earth. We are filled with food and hot tea. We are wearing clothes given to us by our employer, and we are being paid money for us to enjoy all this. No wives and no drunken neighbours. Do you have this in England and can you ever leave us?"

Sergeant Amos piped up, "Mr. Higgs can never leave us. We will not let him go! But we will not even have to try too hard because he will never leave. He likes us and he likes Africa and he wants to stay forever. Isn't that right, Bwana Higgs?"

Higgs said, "I like everything about this place. But most of all I like all the policemen and how nice they are. I wish I could stay forever but one day I may be forced to leave. Sometimes we don't always get what we want. Now let's go to sleep. It is nearly nine o'clock and we should try to get going by 0630. Bathroom and toilets are downstream from the spring where the horses are tied up. Ngoni, when you are down there farting, do not come back here and blame the horse." All of them roared with laughter. They all took turns to go down to the spring for ablutions. They all blamed the horses at some time or another.

They visited 12 farms that next day. Actually five farmers were having a card game in a large tobacco barn, owned by Blondie O'Malley, so each one was told the reason for the visit. It was close to 1800 and the men were offered a corner of a field for their camp that night. O'Malley had a fridge in the barn and he offered each policeman a cold Castle beer. They gratefully guzzled it down and set up camp in the field. This time Ngoni set up a fire and emptied three cans of tomatoes and two cans of cannelloni beans into a large pot. He had a packet of rice and he threw that in, along with some spices – salt, hot chilli-flakes and curry powder – and the balance of the biltong, which he had sliced very thinly. Within an hour they were eating. "What do you call this, Ngoni?" asked Higgs, wiping red sauce off his face.

"I call it 'gunge' because every time I make it there is something different, and gunge covers every dish. Do you like it, Bwana Higgs?"

"I absolutely love it," answered Higgs.

At that point, there was a noise in the nearby bush and Sergeant Amos suddenly picked up his shotgun and blasted a shot into a nearby thorn tree. "Jesus Christ, man! What the hell are you doing?" yelled Higgs.

Amos turned on his torch and reached into what was left of the tree. He brought out the remains of a very long, perhaps six feet in length, green mamba; one of the deadliest poisonous snakes to be found in Africa. Had that snake bitten anyone, they likely would have died within 24 hours.

"A gift for you, Sir," Amos said, handing the shredded snake draped over the barrel of his shotgun across to Higgs. "And I hope you will do the paperwork for me when we get home as to where one shotgun shell was used." All laughed nervously then thanked Amos and were all asleep by 2100.

On Friday, April 8, 1960, the team had just 14 farms left to visit. A21 was a farmer who had been on this land of 1300 acres since 1934. This was the Wilkins farm, run by the old man in his 80s, along with his three sons. They raised cattle, and grew wheat, corn, and potatoes. They also supplied eggs and chickens to the main city, Lusaka. Each son had their own house and really their own farm; one grew crops, one raised cattle, and the chickens were raised by the youngest, who was about 28 years of age. "Paint A21 on the largest house roof, not each one," said Higgs.

They also knew that most of the other farmers were meeting for their monthly "what can we talk about?" session. Normally one of the Wilkins would be in attendance, but today they figured they had too many urgent chores. Higgs was directed across their field to A26, where they got to deliver at least six messages. They found 10 of them. A22 through A31 were all inside an enormous house. Higgs pulled up and asked permission to give his presentation. They all listened carefully, asked a few questions, and took their specific code card. They understood the situation and did not seem overly concerned. Most had inherited their farms from their grandparents, and knew their area well. They knew Africa well and they felt they knew the local Africans well. They were also a tight group and would help each other out should a situation arise. Frankly, they represented a tough "circle the wagons" type of group, and were well armed.

By 1300 they were on their way, with only three more farms to see. One of the horses, a chestnut mare, became a bit skittish; something was bothering her. Once again, eagleeyed Sergeant Amos noticed something in the bush, walking about 15 feet away and keeping pace with them. It was a huge rhino, blind as a bat but he too was unsure of the strange smell coming from the four strange animals, or was it their riders? Amos suggested they should maintain their pace and eventually the rhino would become confused and leave. Twenty minutes later, the rhino stopped, tried to remember what he was supposed to be doing, and wandered off from the road the Higgs' team was using.

Soon, they could see A32 a few hundred yards away. In fact, it was not a farm at all, it was the home of the district commissioner. The British had set up offices to help anyone needing a form or a stamp, or a driver's licences renewed, etcetera.

This was an inexpensive way to have their laws complied with and so that the populace could feel comfortable with their "owners," there would be none of that "no taxation without representation" malarkey in a British colony ever again. An old African man in some type of soldiers' uniform, told the men to refresh the horse down under the Acacia trees surrounding a small pond. He then escorted Higgs into the house.

It was so that British Higgs expected Sherlock Holmes to enter at any minute. There was dark furniture and silverware all over the enormous living room. Mrs. Hackworth, the lady of the house, greeted Higgs. "Sorry, my husband is away until next week; we don't often get tall young men visiting. Can I get tea for you?"

Higgs explained his mission and urged her to get someone to paint the code on her roof. She agreed that she would and first thing tomorrow. While Higgs was enjoying his third cup of tea and, perhaps his fourth cucumber sandwich, with the crusts cut off, of course, he noticed something quite peculiar. Each door in the house had a large mouse hole shaped hole cut at the bottom of each door, maybe eight or nine inches around. Mrs. Hackworth noticed Higgs frowning and said, "You are probably wondering why we have a hole through each door?"

"Well, as a matter of fact, I am," answered Higgs.

"Oh, it is only for Griswold," she said.

"Griswold?" asked Higgs.

"Yes, Griswold. You see....Oh! Here he is now." An enormous python slid through the hole in the closed living room door, that opened up to the dining room. "You see, it gets very drafty around here so we need to keep all our inner doors shut. Then we acquired Griswold because we were having a problem with rats and mice and insects.... Ha! Ha! Not any more though, do we, Griswold?" she bent over and scratched the snake's head. "We were having to get up every few minutes and let the snake enter. He doesn't settle down you know, not like a cat would, say. Hmm ... we had a cat once, never did know where it went. So our solution was to cut those holes. Now everyone is happy, especially Wilfred, the Commissioner, that is, my husband. Now, he can sit there, where you are, in his comfortable leather chair and tune in to the BBC, for his favourite radio shows. Do you ever listen to 'Much Binding in the Marsh' or now it's that dreadful 'Goon Show.' Wilfred splutters so much he gets pipe tobacco all over his waistcoat; Griswold likes it. He eats up anything like that on the floor. Just ignore him, Mr. Higgs. I see he's climbing up your left boot. I am about to have a gin and tonic, would you care to join me? We won't be disturbed, I can assure you."

It was already 1300 and Higgs figured he was in a bit of a spot now, without the addition of alcohol. "No," he said, "I must go, plenty to do, carry on and all that." He stood up, thanked Mrs. Hackworth and called for his men from the front porch.

They finished the last farm, A34, at 1500. They were at Dairyland, an enormous milk farm, and Higgs asked to use the phone. He got hold of Superintendent Hamble and asked if he, Hamble, could arrange the trailer to drive out to A34, and take them all home. Hamble was shocked at how speedily Higgs had managed to finish the first section. He told Higgs to unsaddle the horse, find a cool spot to have a nap, and the trailer would be there within two hours.

Ivan Thrush, the dairy owner, showed Higgs a cool shady spot to wait for their transport. He invited Higgs to join him in the main house, and also told the other three to wander over to the stairs leading up to the office in the dairy and ask his daughter, who ran the show, for whatever they wished for, milk or ice cream, and, if they promised not to tell anyone, it was free, a freezer pack each for their families. Each pack contained a litre of cream, two pounds of butter, and a quart of ice cream. The three African policemen could not believe their fortune. Sergeant Amos asked if the freezer packs could stay in the freezer until their transport arrived, so it would still be frozen when they got home. Constable Ngoni could not believe he could also have ice cream and milk now, as well as the gift pack. He must have swallowed three pints of cold milk, as well as a very large cardboard cup of chocolate ice cream.

Higgs also had a large thirst and drowned two pints of cold milk and a small bowl of passion fruit ice cream. Barbara Thrush was a very handsome woman, about 30-ish, with chestnut hair and very long legs. She fussed around the kitchen and talked her head off, as they discussed politics, Higgs' life story, and his current mission. "What a shame you have to leave us so soon," she sighed. "We seldom have visitors but this weekend we are throwing a party for Ivan's 40th. Why can't you stay?"

At about 1730, the trailer pulled up and the men all cackled and laughed as they put away the horses, packed all their katunga, and retrieved their freezer packs from the office.

They were back at the stables by 1900 and they all departed from there to their own homes. Higgs phoned Swanny from the stables and explained that Amanda was away and could he drop by. Typically, on a Friday night, Swanny was having a braai and invited Higgs over. "There's only five of us. Come and join us now. Come as you are, shower here, and stay the night if you want," suggested Swanny. With friends like that, figured Higgs, how does one say no? He asked the constable driving the Land Rover to drive to Swanny's.

While he could not go into detail about the real purpose of his trip, Higgs was able to tell a version of the mission and what transpired during the week. All enjoyed the Griswold story. "You bloody Brits are so filled with wanting to stay British, wherever they are. Imagine living in a house like that. I feel sorry for any bloody muntu that burglarizes that house and he's all alone in the dark, when Griswold finds him.... Ha, ha, ha! Byeeee burglar! I bet the bloody floor was spotless too, and not any vermin in sight. Hey, maybe the cat vanished that way?"

Higgs felt so African this night. He still had on his jodhpurs, but he had borrowed a shirt that Swanny could not get into anymore. And he was barefoot, having kicked off his black shiny riding boots. He was sitting at the picnic table eating corn on the cob and rump steak, and drinking cold Castle beer. How could life be better?

He presented his freezer pack to Swanny's wife Cindy and asked her to accept it as a gift from him. She took it and kissed him quite hard, on the mouth, twice.

It was unusually late as they all staggered into bed. The three guests had driven home around 10-ish and now it was near midnight. Saturday was bright and cool and Higgs was up and looking at Swanny's bike. He tweaked a few knobs and, then, when he saw Swanny wandering over, he started it up and opened the throttle. Swanny said he thought it sounded smoother. Higgs said, "That's why it pays to have a decent English mechanic around to tweak it, now and then."

Swanny put his arm around Higgs and walked him to the back porch, off the kitchen, where Cindy was making Boerewors, bacon, and scrambled eggs for a late brunch.

"You know we both like you a lot," said Swanny. "We cannot imagine you not being around and being such a good friend. You make sure you stay the way you are, okay?"

When Higgs got home that afternoon, he had Amanda's houseboy grab all his kit and wash and press it. He then had a tall rum and Coke and went to bed at 2000, letting the servants know they could go home and only Timothy, the head boy, was required the next day, Sunday, at 0900.

34

CHANGES

The phone rang loudly. Higgs was in a deep sleep. He woke up and stared at the little alarm clock with a lace cover, which Amanda forgot to take with her on her trip; she'll have missed that, thought Higgs, as he realized it was three o'clock in the morning. "Is that Lusaka?" asked a woman on the line.

"Yes, it is. What do you want?" asked Higgs, as he tried to figure out who and where he was, at that hour.

"Are you Mr. de la Haye?" she asked Higgs. He got asked that quite a bit because of his living arrangements and so on. He did not bother to explain. "Yes, I am he."

"Are you with someone now?" she asked. "Are you seated somewhere?"

"Yes. Look, what is this? It is almost dawn here, so get to the point." Higgs was irritable now.

"Sir, this is the London Metropolitan Police Headquarters. I am Senior Superintendant Muriel Burrows. I am afraid to inform you, Sir, that there has been a dreadful traffic accident today on the road from the Hilton Hotel to London's Heathrow Airport. A Mrs. Amanda de la Haye was a passenger in a taxi cab heading for the airport when the accident occurred. I regret to inform you, Sir, that Mrs. de la Haye succumbed to her injuries and passed away at 1600 hours Greenwich Mean Time, today. I am very sorry, Sir. We found a note in the lady's handbag with instructions on whom to call. Do you have a pen at hand? Our number here is 00 768 554 3677. Please contact us within 48 hours for more details and what your wishes are regarding her personal possessions. Refer to File Number 04/12/60-MPT 78H.

Higgs was kneeling on the bed. He started to vomit. He screamed and then he cried like a baby. Sobbing non-stop. Deep breaths, then more sobbing. "Oh, no! My baby!" he cried. "My sweetheart, darling little baby. No! Please say it isn't so! Mistakes are made all the time. I bet they mixed up it all. But maybe it is right? Oh, my baby, my lovely, lovely doll. Please do not do this to me. God, please help me."

He hung up the already silent phone and he phoned Swanny, who was not amused at being awoken at after four in the morning. "Who the hell is this?" asked Swanny. "Swanny, it's Higgs. I am sorry, man. I need you. Please come here now and take me back to your place. I must get out of this house, NOW! Too many memories. Amanda is dead. England. Car accident. Please come quickly!"

"Hang tight, my man, I will be there in twenty," responded Swanny. And in twenty minutes he pulled into the drive-way, with Cindy, both still in their pyjamas. They rushed into the house and found Higgs lying on the floor like a baby, sobbing over an empty suitcase, he had been attempting to pack. They both pulled him upright and the trio stood hugging each other for a good ten minutes, saying very little. Then Cindy broke away, went around the house and packed a week's supply of Higgs' underwear, socks, shirts, etcetera. She then left a note for Timothy to phone her as soon as he arrived for work on Sunday morning. She and Swanny ushered Higgs outside into the warm car which had been left running.

They got Higgs into bed in the guest room, and gave him a sedative and a brandy with warm milk. "Hush, sweetheart," Cindy said as they got Higgs covered up. She kissed him on the forehead and told him they would talk about it all tomorrow. Swanny left the guest room sobbing uncontrollably. It was 0630 when all three finally got to sleep. Cindy had left a note for her houseboy, Simeon, to not disturb them at all. No way was he to take tea or coffee into the guest room. He was not to prepare any food, just tidy up silently and wait outside on the garden furniture until at least noon, and no noise please.

Higgs staggered into the living room, after a shower, at almost noon. Cindy had been up a few hours already and had been busy on the phone.

She had spoken to Timothy, who had been Amanda's houseboy for nine years and he too was distraught. Cindy ordered him to get together Mr. Higgs' clothing and separate it into police and civilian and she would have someone collect it today. He was also told to stay in the servants' quarters and be in the house during the day, to answer the door or receive any post. He would be called every day to let him know what was going on.

Cindy held out a mug of coffee to Higgs, which he gratefully accepted. "Did you get any sleep, babe?" she asked.

Higgs said, "Surprisingly, yes. I had a good eight hours and everything would be fine if my sweetheart was here. Now, I must use the phone. He grabbed it and dialled a number. The man on the other end said, "Hamble here."

"Sir, it's Higgs...I just wanted...."

"Higgs! Oh, my God! Higgs, there you are. I am so sorry to hear about Amanda; it's all over the Sunday papers. How are you and where are you and what do you need?"

Higgs explained his whereabouts and gave Hamble the phone numbers where he could be reached. "Sir, here is what I need. Number one, please don't take my new job away from me. I can handle it and I need it to keep my mind off this issue. Secondly, I am staying with such good friends and I am sure they are going to ask me to stay with them forever, and I could, but I need to be with my police chums. Is there any way you could get my old room back in the mess, or at least any room in the mess? I need the company of all those reprobates who live there. Please, Sir?"

"Son, your job is secure and when all arrangements are done with, I need you in my office for a few days. The mess and the room...hmmm! Let me see. I shall be back to you at this number, by 1600, today. Keep your chin up and always call me, at any time, day or night, if you need anything. Cheerio, Higgs. All the best. Keep me in the loop, okay?"

Higgs hung up and immediately the phone rang. Cindy answered and the caller asked if a Mr. Higgs-Briar was there. "It is for you Higgs, or should I tell him to just leave you alone?"

Higgs took the phone. The man said "Barry Huntington here, Higgs, Amanda's lawyer. We met once at her house. I have some documents here that were sent priority courier from the lawyers in London. Can I come to your house, or at least where you are now, and can we go over them?"

Huntington arrived at 1400 and the two men sat outside under the shady trees and discussed Amanda's will, business dealings, and, frankly, the rest of Higgs' life. Firstly, she had made a deal with the largest florists in England, that unless Higgs objected, they could buy her entire empire for £24,000, which meant there would be no business debts for Higgs to pay. The house was not included in the sale and Higgs could live in it forever, if he wished. If he wanted to sell the house, it was worth about £2,000.

All other items such as her jewellery, her car, and her new motorcycle, furniture, etcetera belonged to Higgs.

Amanda wanted to be buried in the new cemetery on Kabulonga Rad, in Lusaka, not too far from where she lived. Her body would be flown from England on Tuesday. Barry had a funeral time and date for Saturday, April 16th at 1500, if Higgs agreed. He did. In looking through all the papers in Huntington's possession, Higgs saw, for the very first time, Amanda's date of birth. It was December 25, 1918. My God, he thought, she was twenty years older than me! Bloody amazing! She looked, acted, and felt like a woman in her mid-twenties. He did not know how he felt about knowing that fact. She hid her birthdays well because it was on Christmas day. Higgs did not think it was an important issue, so he had never asked.

Higgs got up, thanked the lawyer, took his business card, and asked if he could be with the hearse at the airport on Tuesday. That being confirmed, Higgs went back into the house and threw up until he had nothing left. He sobbed himself to sleep.

The phone rang and Cindy woke Higgs up. "It is a Mr. Hamble," she said. Higgs made a motion for a mug of coffee, which Cindy understood. Higgs said, "Hello, Sir, any news?"

Hamble said, "Look, here's what I have done. I needed a young lad to go up to the mobile unit, in Bwana Mkubwa [roughly translated that means 'Big Chief; the name given to the Mobile unit or riot squad location]. By coincidence, a young man that fit the description was living in your old room at the mess. He won't be as of Wednesday. So, check in after lunch on Wednesday and come and see me on Thursday at 0900. Okay, laddie, me boy?"

"Sir, thank you. I shall always be grateful to you. See you Thursday," said Higgs, then he hung up.

35

ANOTHER NEW BEGINNING

At best guess, there were over a hundred people gathered at the Lusaka Cathedral, at the top of King George Avenue, for Amanda's funeral. All of Higgs' mates and many more police officers, some of whom were complete strangers to Higgs, were present. All wore full dress uniform. Higgs had to choose whom he wanted to help him carry the coffin. Certainly, Van Rooyen and Baldwin, but also Swanny and Detective Chief Inspector Sythe. Then he chose Corporal Bryan Lygard, from the Northern Rhodesia Regiment. The team of six men looked like a million dollars. They were so upright, serious, and respectful. Their finest attire made them even more so; if only Amanda could see them all. Of course, the ladies looked gorgeous in their choices for outfits. Everyone was so young and handsome and beautiful. Anyone over the age of 40 stood out as being the "elders." And soon, the procession made its way up the Ridgeway, along past Government House, to the cemetery, where Higgs' darling Amanda was laid to rest.

Higgs stood at the graveside long after most had left. Swanny and Cindy stayed behind, as well as a handful of Higgs' closest police officer friends. Finally, and with great reluctance, Higgs left with Swanny and went back to his home.

That Saturday night was a very painful experience for Higgs. He was able to talk to his friends, Swanny and Cindy, and they were extremely helpful in their advice and suggestions. Without telling Higgs what to do, they helped him think clearly. They say one should never make important decisions closely after the death of a loved one. One's state of mind emotionally could mean a lifechanging decision today, which one would not have even entertained just a few months later. Higgs knew that but he did know that he had to get rid of all Amanda's belongings. He made a note to call Campbell Tribe, the local auctioneer, to sell it on his behalf. Higgs also did not want Amanda's house so he put that on the market. He would first offer it to the British company that had bought the business; they would surely want it for their manager.

By Monday afternoon it was all put in place. The British company "Floraworld" phoned him and asked if Higgs would mind selling him the house, as they had a new man flying out from England to take over. Also, they asked, could Higgs find some decent servants to help their man?

Higgs got £3,000 for the house and told Timothy that he would have a new bwana and all the servants could stay on. They would have to be very gentle and slowly train the new bwana, because he was new and from England and did not know the ways of the African. Timothy smiled and said, "Bwana Higgs. I can be sure that the new bwana will learn from the expert at training, me."

36

BACK TO SQUARE ONE

Superintendent Hamble greeted Higgs in his office on Thursday morning. "Higgs, I have had a bloody reporter call me yesterday, from the Central African Post. Wanted to know why four policemen were patrolling farming areas around Chisamba. I told him we were practicing a new routine for our horses, which would be combined with a team from Canada, the Royal Canadian Mounted Police, who are guests at the Royal Agricultural Show, in July. I said these Canadian police had a reputation for some charge on horseback and we want to show our skills. I think he bought the story."

"So, that's the line I should follow should I be confronted?" asked Higgs.

"Precisely," replied Hamble. "Now let us discuss armed response. We have to assume any attack will have the following characteristics: One, it will likely be at night two, there will be complete surprise and three, there will be more than two doing the attacking."

"Why more than two?" interrupted Higgs.

"Because studies of history, including recent Mau Mau attacks, show the Africans believe that more attackers show a force of strength – Islandwana, in Zululand, for one. There the Zulus used over 20,000 warriors to attack some 800 British troops. They, the Zulus, had calculated that they needed enough cannon fodder to overcome the heavily-armed British. Here, we can assume the attackers are not aware of how well-armed the farmer is, or if there is more than one person in the farmhouse that can use a gun. Think, Higgs, a farmer, his wife, and three teenage children, with a rifle each, in a brick building, is a formidable target to overcome. The attackers are outside, possibly with inferior weapons and no shelter."

Higgs responded, "Yes, but what if they have automatic weapons? What if they have inside information, from say, a disgruntled servant, or perhaps from a loyal servant but under threat? Maybe the attackers have a family member they are threatening to kill if the servant does not comply. That is exactly what they did in Kenya. The biggest enemy was the loyal and long-term trusted servant."

"Hmmm... good train of thought there, Higgs. Of course, the first few attacks may be a bit amateurish, with a high casualty rate; maybe the farmer killed some and brushed off the attack, but they'll be back, with more men, better weapons, and a new methodology. If they win, there is one less farmer and the attackers steal all their weapons. This is a dangerous and very real possibility. Alright then," said Hamble. Let's take this scenario: One, we have a call from A1. They say the dogs are restless and they have seen movement in the bush, about 200 yards away. Mr. Uys says he knows an attack is imminent. There are perhaps ten men about to break every window in his home and some are carrying guns. What should our response team do, Higgs?"

"This is maybe the biggest problem. Is he or is he not being attacked? Is this a ploy, a test if you will, by the terrorists to see what our response is?" said Higgs.

"Yes, good point. But what do we do?" said Hamble.

"Maybe we use four helicopters and send three to A1 and have one circle over all farms in a fivemile circle. Maybe we land one at Uys' farm and offload three armed police, who make their way into the house. I guess it would depend if an attack is happening or if Uys is still waiting. The helicopter pilot will know as he circles to land, as it is at night and he would have spotted flames, or sparks or gun-flashes, before touch-down. By the way, I assume that we have the law on our side so that when we arrive, and see bad guys shooting toward the house, we can fly in with all arms firing at the attackers, without any warning?" Higgs then suggested a couple of security ideas to pass on to all parties.

"Farmers should consider installing spotlights so they can illuminate the outdoor area from where the main attack is coming. These spotlights could either be rotated from indoors, and they operate from batteries, in case the attackers cut the power lines. A generator should be installed indoors as well."

Then Higgs suggested that each farmer install a screeching sound system, where hidden speakers were strategically placed, in trees or almost buried, and the volume button be inside the house. Higgs had seen a film where American troops used this strategy in WWII. The enemy could not stand the noise, which was so high-pitched it would deafen them. The government could surely locate such equipment and either provide it at no cost to the farmer, or it could be heavily subsidized. Hamble was mesmerized by Higgs' suggestions. "Poor terrorists," he responded. "They don't stand a chance against you, young Higgs."

A very important point was that, if these ideas were accepted by the government and installed, then the whole delivery and installation simply had to be a well-kept secret. The farmer must not allow any servant to be aware of their existence and the location of them. Higgs added, "In an old John Wayne film, Sir, they ran out of ammunition. We need farmers to tell us what ammo they use and we must make sure they have more than an adequate supply."

"Loved his films," said Hamble, "he walked a bit funny though!" They had a short tea break at 1100 and then carried on. Higgs asked if a perimeter alarm might work. "You know, about a mile away in a circle around the farm, a wire or a rubber hose. Someone steps on it and the farmer is alerted," he said.

"But, Higgs," responded Hamble, "this is Africa. There's all sorts of things doing a walkabout in the bush. Every bloody deer, elephant, and snake, will be setting off alarms. Nope, don't think so."

Higgs suddenly stood erect and stated, "Sir, I don't think we can do this. The bastards have the element of surprise as well as the complete choice as to which farm, how many farms at one time, how many attackers per farm, and what type of act. A stabbing from a servant in the house, or a full-on battle with an army of attackers outside, confronting a well-defended but small armed force from inside the house. We don't have the equipment and cannot spread out what we have to cover all farms in the Lusaka area alone, never mind those south to Livingstone or north to the copper belt. Frankly, we need to get the army in here now. They have the manpower and the arms. They need our knowledge and some helicopters. Well, do we even know how many helicopters they even have?"

"Higgs, I hope you are wrong, but your thinking is clear and important," said Hamble. "It's not that I haven't thought of these things as well, but when combined with your other comments, I must say you have raised some frightening situations. Any suggestions now as to where to head next?"

"I believe this must be a joint venture. Get the army in now and get Southern Rhodesia into limited discussions about what helicopters they have and if they will lease any to us; Treading carefully with each extra party we allow into our den," Higgs replied.

These discussions became a mammoth task each day. Finally, the British government was consulted. It was their idea in the first place, as Northern Rhodesia was a protectorate and thus their problem. The conclusions by all parties was what the Brits needed to know, if they did not want another Mau Mau on their hands, which they determined from the outset. If they wanted to fight off any attempt at changing the present government by any means other than a democratic vote, then they needed to pay attention. The Brits would need to train and pay for a team to fight off terrorists. The money would be substantial and needed for weapons, ammunition, transport, and attack helicopters.

Unlike the Belgians, who had slipped out of the Congo on June 30, 1960, without any preparedness for a new amateur government to take over, the Brits needed a strategy to save lives, save face, and maintain respect in the international community. All of this while outwardly appearing as if nothing was going on. Some Kenyan refugees drove to Lusaka and the press got hold of their stories. It did not take long, just ten days after independence, on July 9, 1960, five whites were killed in the Congo. No longer could the populace carry on believing that the horror stories were all way up north. They were up north all right but the Congo was on the border.

Of course, all the brightest students in Europe and the USA blamed the colonial powers for drawing borders that bisected tribal lines, which was causing wars between the natives, as if no wars existed in Africa before any white settlers arrived. There was some truth to this but not the real issue.

The police were heavily involved along the Congo border, helping refugees on their way to protection in the South.

37

A LONG SLOW CLIMB OUT
OF THE MOURNING

Higgs had been without Amanda for nearly three months. Every day had been miserable. He had his room back at the mess. He had declined Hamble's offer to take a horse team out to all the other farms, but he had helped in providing names of police officers he thought would do a good job. All now had to sign the "Official Secrets Act." Van Rooyen and Baldwin were selected and they had completed their tasks already. The community at large was simply waiting for the first incident to happen.

Senior Inspector Paddy Dickinson was given the task of recording all meetings by the new political troublemakers. As all meetings with more than six people attending had to ask for, and receive, government (police) permission to hold such a meeting, Dickinson found it easy to know where and when to attend, and where to place his microphones. The meetings were many and well attended, but, generally peaceful. There was a name that appeared more frequently than others in the press – Kenneth Kaunda.

He was cooperating with one political party, the African National Congress (ANC), and then he split to form the United National Independence Party (UNIP). He was arrested one early morning, charged with sedition, and spent nine months in jail. He seemed to be a peaceful man but his followers were not trustworthy. Certainly, he had charisma. One day when Kaunda was about to address 50,000 people, he actually stood on the stage, tapped the microphone and looked over at the Land Rover saying, "Are we on, Paddy?" Paddy gave him a thumbs up and away Kaunda went.

One day Kaunda was yelling, "We have been mistreated ever since Adam was a schoolboy!" Paddy could not resist. He yelled out, "And what bloody school did he go to?" Higgs was with him that day, and when 50,000 or so faces turned to glare at the police vehicle, Paddy suggested a quick departure. Leaving the microphone where it was, the vehicle backed up for half a mile then left the scene.

One night, in his room, Higgs realized all his mates were at a rugby dance to which he was not invited. He phoned Swanny but Swanny was on his way out to another function. It was 1800 and Higgs did not want to be alone that night. He remembered he had borrowed a very nice thermos flask and it needed to be returned. Marjorie was not far away, on Birdcage Walk, in the Longacres Apartments. It was a short drive and, if she was not in, he would bring it back and deliver it on a later date. He stuffed the thermos inside his leather jacket and soon arrived at Longacres. He got Marjorie's room number from the receptionist and drove his motorcycle around the building and parked right outside her door. It was nearly 1900 when he knocked and she opened the door.

She was in her nightie and said, "Oh, my God! It's you! I was about to go to bed as I am needed for the five o'clock weather meeting at the airport. Great job; weird hours. But come on in. I have some beer in my fridge, want one?" Higgs felt very uncomfortable being alone with Marjorie. He felt guilty. He said yes to the beer and grabbed the only chair in the room. "I...I just came to return your Mom's thermos. She said she wanted it back and to drop it off to you and you can take it back. How have you been?"

Marjorie got up from the edge of the bed and straddled Higgs' thighs. "And if I take it from you, will you then just leave?"

"Well, yes, if you asked me to leave. I have nothing special on so we could talk for a while. I must say I enjoyed your company on board the ship, but then we were on board a ship, weren't we?"

"So, you wouldn't want me then, you know, like on the ship. By the way you were amazing then. How about now?" She reached down and felt him getting aroused. She undid the ribbon on her nightie and pulled his mouth to her nipples. Higgs needed her and, within seconds, she was naked under him as she pulled off all his clothes. He climaxed and then burst into tears. He told Marjorie everything about his life since the ship. He especially told her about Amanda and how he had not touched or smelled a woman since April. He had gone from a very active sex life to nothing for over three months. Marjorie made him happier that night.

She had him dressed and out on to his motorbike by 2200. She gave Higgs her phone number and said next time they should go away together so they could be free to do whatever they wished. And, yes, she would take the thermos back to her mother the following week. He smiled and rode off into the cool evening on his purring Norton.

Being at the mess, fooling around with his mates and becoming involved with his new responsibilities, Higgs felt he was emerging from the dark hole he had been in for the past three months. His nature had changed a little. He was more aggressive and re-joined the rugby club; not because of their parties, but to tackle and get into rough-housing on the field. He noticed it in sex as well. With Marjorie, it had become frequent and, because she could take it, and often demanded it, he was rough with her.

Higgs decided to rent a small storage unit not far from the police station. It was a new building and this unit was on the ground floor. It was 12 feet x 20 feet, plus a full-sized car garage attached, with a door from the garage into the unit. He took Amanda's desk and office chair, as well as a pulldown Hollywood bed. He had some bedding, and a small wardrobe, as well as a stand-alone bookcase. It only cost £5 a month and this could be his little refuge; his "get away from it all." He had a supply of jotters and pens, and as well as he was having a phone installed.

He decided to sell Amanda's 1958 Morris Oxford station wagon. He wanted a car that was sexy and completely impractical. He would ask Swanny if he knew a good car dealer. That evening he spent at Swanny's. Cindy said the improvement to Higgs' mood was noticeable; he was almost back to being the Higgs she remembered. They were all great friends and were simply cozy with each other. Higgs tried to explain his new job, which he could not explain because it was so secretive, but he was at least able to explain why he was all over the place and hardly a regular cop.

38

NOTHING HAPPENING

During the month of October 1960, Higgs was involved in planning Hamble's plan of joint border patrols. The Northern Rhodesia Regiment and the police, would henceforth have joint patrols near Ndola, Solwezi and quite near Jadotville, near the Congo/Northern Rhodesia border. It was assumed many white refugees would be seeking safety in Northern Rhodesia, and the desire was to ensure these people were vetted carefully.

There were a dozen foreign spies in every bar in Elizabethville and Northern Rhodesia certainly did not want them sneaking across our borders. They could do tremendous harm from a vantage point in the copper belt. If they were agents of Russia or China, they could provide support to potential terrorists within Northern Rhodesia. To be blunt, if the spies were Chinese they were easier to identify. The Russians could look like any other European.

Higgs was flown up to the border one late day in October. Van Rooyen was with him, at his request. They landed in Ndola and were driven out to a camp, about 30 miles away, where they were assigned a tent to share. Also in the camp were 100 European NR territorial soldiers, doing their national service. As Higgs was strolling around to get himself acquainted with the camp layout, he ran cross a young man who yelled out, "Hey, copper! Remember me? I was in an argument with you at the Star Drive-in restaurant a year ago. Things have changed now, hey, can we shake hands? I've grown up a lot since then."

Higgs stuck his hand out and said, "I am getting too old to have grievances. Sure, I remember you. You were eating your food off the floor at the time, weren't you?"

"Yaah, man! That's the way they feed you in the army. I got called up and I figured I would show the army how strong I was. I think I was not quite as tough as I thought. I punched the un-armed instructor in the face. He grabbed my fist and actually spun me in the air and landed me on my back. Three days in hospital to recover. I now understand discipline and, look, I am a Lance-Corporal now. I live in tent 12 over there. Come and visit any time. Must go, my sergeant is glaring at me; they do that if your lips are moving but your feet aren't. Cheers! Just call me Basil."

Higgs and Van Rooyen took mental and written notes of their observations. They determined that the army had sufficient troops, well trained and motivated to handle threats at the border. The United Nations were now involved and while there were troops from many countries not one was deemed more of a problem than another. Higgs could not explain why one of the young conscripts was patrolling the border with a young chicken tied to his boot laces; companionship or potential future food source, perhaps?

The next afternoon, while standing at the pill-box that was deemed the border patrol office, a young soldier yelled out, "Speeding car approaching, Sir!" All eyes turned to his pointing arm. A VW Beetle, with a corkscrew of dust following it, was racing toward them, fast. "Squad, line up and stop him right in front of the gate." The "gate" was merely a telephone pole hinged over another set of poles, and a placard nailed to it, saying, "You are now entering Northern Rhodesia."

The VW was now still coming at them at at least 70 miles per hour. It did not look like it was prepared to stop. And, moments later, with a dozen soldiers leaping aside, the VW crashed through the gate and stopped. "Right, you bastard! When we tell you to stop, you bloody well stop!" yelled a Northern Rhodesia Regiment captain. He rushed up to the driver's side window, on the left, and a very old frail man was collapsed over the front passenger seat. In that seat sat his wife; she was dead, riddled with at least 50 bullet wounds.

"Those bastards the Simbas (Lions...a name the terrorists gave themselves.) just came to my farm this morning. I had packed my car the night before, ready to leave at a moment's notice. As they came through the front door, my dogs held them off for a few necessary seconds, and we made it.

The men simply riddled our car with automatic weapons and they killed my wife. They got me in the stomach and a few in the legs. I'm so sorry I didn't stop. Here are my papers.

My great-grandfather was born in the Congo. We grew food for the government, and this is how they thank us."

Higgs got the army medics over and they pulled this old man out of his car and laid him in the shade. His wounds were deep, and he had lost a lot of blood, but they were not life-threatening; the wounds were cleaned out and dressed. His wife was taken away to the temporary morgue by the air-strip. Antoine and Marie Francine were the first of many refugees to enter Northern Rhodesia.

Higgs and Van Rooyen had seen enough and they flew back to Lusaka in the afternoon DC3, along with Mr. and Mrs. Francine; both were aged 78. They got a lot of helpful information from poor Mr. Francine. "Beware of the UN troops," he said. "Those guys may be here to fight the Simbas but they were from Ethiopia and I think they are worse than the Simbas. They rape and loot as well as any I have seen; worse than Gerry in Belgium in WWII," he remarked. "Do not trust them one bit."

Higgs and Van Rooyen discussed these latest events and felt it was important to pass on a message to each farmer under their care, to also have their car packed and ready to go, spare tire, full tank, etcetera, as well as the bit of gossip about UN troops. Van Rooyen would get to that by radio telephone to each one, first thing in the morning. Still, in spite of their preparedness, nothing was happening. No rumours, no sightings, no mobs anywhere. It was very off-putting to be ready for something and nothing was going on.

Back at the mess, Higgs noticed Swanny standing at the bar. Of course, it was July 21 and Higgs had a birthday. Baldwin had phoned Swanny and a dozen beers and maybe that many gin and tonics were consumed. Housekeeping had prepared four dozen Cornish pasties, which all disappeared.

Higgs was forced to sing a dirty song; his choice was, "*Two German officers crossed the Rhine, parlez vous. Two German officers crossed the Rhine, parlez vous, two German officers crossed the Rhine to up the women and drink the wine, inky, pinky, parlez vous.*" The rest of the gang immediately started the next one. "*Oh, Mr. Fisherman, fisherman of the sea, have you a lobster you can sell to me, singing oh tiddley oh, shit or bust, never let yer bollocks dangle in the dust.*"

Then a short pause, then the crackling sound from a gramophone and one teary-eyed Scotsman played "Land of Hope and Glory." No new songs just the same old well-known songs, and all joined in. Nobody bought a drink for themselves but everybody bought lots for everyone else. Van Rooyen picked Higgs up over his shoulders and yelled, "This is my bloody rooinek (redneck) matey and I love him to death!"

Then Swanny picked up Higgs, yelling: "No, he's mine, all mine, and I am taking him back to Seth Afreeca soon. He is the finest pommie I know." Then Baldwin tried to pick up Swanny and yelled, "You are a nice bloody yaapie but I can't pick you up. So there!"

Then he staggered backwards into the sofa and promptly passed out. The party ended at two in the morning. The building had been specially designed to handle all the stress from the mass snoring that ensued.

Like a queue of zombies, men appeared at the breakfast table the next day. Bleary eyed and tongues weighing a ton, they gently sat down and ordered their own peculiar choices for curing hangovers. Most plucked up courage and had a piece of dry toast. Some had a boiled egg in a cup with bread and butter. A few tried corn flakes with ice-cold milk. Most had coffee; some had tea.

Nobody slapped anyone on the shoulder and no loud noises emanated from anyone. Swanny had been sent home by taxi and it was assumed that he too was being tended to at home.

But, in spite of it all, those who were on duty at 0800 were on duty at 0800. Higgs and Van Rooyen went back to bed. They had a meeting with Superintendent Hamble at 1300. Both men had discussed their current jobs and the lack of any excitement, so they were both going to ask to be put back on general duties. They would be available at a moment's notice should an activity occur that warranted them being present somewhere else. And that was the exact discussion Hamble wanted to see them for, and was the end result of their meeting. Hamble warned them as they left about the "calm before the storm," which all acknowledged.

Higgs was now 23 years old, back in uniform, and in his original room in the mess. It may seem that he had gotten nowhere since he joined the force, but he was surely a well-rounded and knowledgeable policeman now, compared to those early days. He was told to report at 0800, "A" shift, the following day. Saturday, July 23, 1960 was a very quiet day. When there was not much going on and one had a police station filled with young energetic men, trouble could surely arise.

The first indication was when a group of three officers approached the on-duty inspector and asked what sounded like an innocent question. "It is true, Inspector, isn't it, that a person can lie down on his back and be able to sit upright? Yet, if one was blindfolded it is impossible to sit upright?"

Hamlyn overheard this and stepped in. "Bullshit!" he yelled. "Are you saying if I was to lie down right here on the floor, and was blindfolded, I would not be able to sit upright?"

"Precisely," said Van Rooyen. "In fact I would wager £5 that you could not."

"Right," said Hamlyn. "Here, Inspector, you hold the money. Here's my five quid and, Van Rooyen, you hand him your five pounds too."

Higgs took the money. Hamlyn lay on the floor. Somebody tied a kerchief around his eyes and then let him lie flat on his back. Within seconds, Van Rooyen stood over Hamlyn, facing his feet, with his pants and underpants down. Somebody yelled, "Okay, sit upright!" Hamlyn sat bolt upright and his nose ended up between the cheeks of Van Rooyen's rear end, with his hands pushing away from each cheek. He sat upright and grabbed the money from the inspector's hand and yelled, "See, I win!" Van Rooyen had his pants on again and seven or eight officers were hanging on to each other with laughter. They could not believe there was anyone left in the world that had not fallen for the old "military-sit-ups" trick. Just as another practical joke was being formulated, a call came in and it was the officer-in-charge, who needed a driver. Higgs had answered the phone and was told he would do.

"Go to the ladies' dress shop, Truworths, and ask for Mrs. Ellenby." She had been awoken one night by an African male masturbating in her bedroom. She had managed to get out of bed and locked the bedroom door. She phoned the police and they arrested the man, charged him with breaking and entering and lewd activity. Today was her day in court and coincidentally it was the opening day of her annual sale. All she had to do in court was identify the accused. She knew the officer-in-charge and found out she would actually only be in court for a few minutes, but might be waiting outside for hours. With friends in high places, she persuaded them to persuade the courts to break while she was called and reconvene as soon as she arrived, possibly a ten-minute interlude at most. As the court was about to break, Higgs got the call. He drove a few blocks to the store, which was filled to the brim with society ladies tackling each other over bras, skirts, coats, etcetera.

Worse savagery, Higgs remembered, than any riots he had attended. He parked outside and walked in the front door. He was convinced there was a step up into the store and he lifted his leg. There was no step. Higgs fell on the floor and slid a good five feet, beneath the skirts and legs of the fighting women. His badge, sunglasses, and notebook skidded across the floor. Getting up and straightening his tunic, and placing his belongings back into their respective pockets, he asked, "Mrs. Ellenby?" "That's me," said this attractive woman. "By chance, are you in the police?" The crowd began yelling, "Do you have another like him?" and "How much is he going for?"

Higgs extricated himself from the store and had the lady at the court and back to the store within 40 minutes. She smiled as she left the vehicle, "Don't worry, lad. None of us had a gun. You'll be in more dangerous places in your career."

Higgs was glad that duty was completed, as his blood returned to his face. Someone had squealed. Higgs thought it was Mrs. Ellenby who likely told the officer-in-charge and, well, pretty soon everyone knew the story. Higgs could hardly wait to get to insurrections and terrorist activity where it appeared more tranquil.

The days drifted by and, on a steamy hot night in September, two men and two constables brought in, under arrest, Mr. Harry Nkumbula. He was driving while intoxicated and had been responsible for killing a police constable because of his inability to control his vehicle. Nkumbula was a British-educated and very socially-accepted gentleman who happened to be the leader of the African National Congress, the political party most assumed would be a contender in forthcoming elections.

He was assumed to be the leader of an independent country if Northern Rhodesia voted to leave the United Kingdom. Higgs and a few others were in the jail cell, interviewing Nkumbula, when he made a statement that was hauntingly appropriate. He said, "If every European got on a train and fled south, out of Lusaka, leaving just us Africans in charge, 10,000 black people would be dead in Lusaka before the train passed the south roundabout on Cairo Road." Mr. Nkumbula was sentenced to 12 months imprisonment and his political ambitions were dashed forever.

With events in the rest of Africa – Ghana, Kenya, and the Belgian Congo – and this thinking by Nkumbula, one can see why the white population was beginning to panic.

39

NOTHING ROUTINE ABOUT THIS LIFE

Weeks flew by. It was a hot and very sticky October. There was nothing happening on the political and violence front, at least not here. In the Congo, there was savagery and murders daily. Patrice Lumumba, the leader, had been arrested and nobody could find him. That meant bad news in Africa. Then Moise Tshombe stuck his hat in the ring and declared the province of Katanga, the richest province, independent from the Congo and started hiring mercenaries to fight for him. He persuaded the President of France to send him 1,000 ex-Foreign Legion members, in a pretext to guard western interests in the minerals of the state of Katanga. He had copper and other minerals, so he could pay them and, he had the western powers fighting over whether he was a good guy or not.

Northern Rhodesia still had domestic squabbles, drunken cyclists, and lots of little crimes that had to be dealt with. So, while the world could explode just a border away,

Higgs had to attend to whatever was called for each day. One such day, his friend from the regiment contacted him to say the military had decided not to buy twenty light armoured vehicles as they would be less effective than an alternative vehicle, being designed in the UK. He mentioned this as nobody else was aware of the, soon to be, cancellation, and frankly it was thought these vehicles would suit an urban police force's needs.

If Higgs could tip off his bosses, they could probably get a very sweet deal if they went for the vehicles then and made an absurd offer, which will probably be accepted, because the manufacturer was stuck with them. Higgs phoned Superintendant Hamble to ask for a meeting. Hamble agreed and they met in the gentlemen's bar, in the Ridgeway Hotel, at 1500. Hamble chose a shady corner with two large shiny leather chairs.

It took Higgs a while to adjust his eyes from the bright sun to the dark corner. Hamble half stood and waved. "Over here, old boy. How are you doing? Managing to get by after terrible news like that? I hear good things about you from my spies. Now just what is this hush-hush thing you need to tell me?"

Higgs passed on what his army friend had revealed. Hamble was very excited.

"You know, we did look at those vehicles. They were actually designed by a former major in the Southern Rhodesian Regiment, while in Malaya, in the 50s. He is still alive, living in England now, and this vehicle of his has some innovative and simple designs. The trouble is they wanted £6,000 for each and, while they may well be worth it, can you imagine me trying to get funds today, when absolutely nothing is going on?" said Hamble.

"Look, Sir. A dozen farmers have been killed in the Congo, just in July. I bet the Kenyan police thought they were well prepared and we can see now that they were not, and still are not. We would be caught with our pants down if something happened this week. Right, Sir? If we are serious about this business, then 'someone' has to do something. In this case, spend money. We really need these vehicles. I believe I can get twenty of them for £2,500 each. That means for under £50,000, we can get what we want, compared to over £100,000. This is a one-time opportunity. If they cannot sell their inventory for break-even, they will have to scrap them. They cannot auction them off because they have certain, should we say, 'things' in them, which we do not want others to know about. Could I be given the chance to make the pitch to our brass here, and then perhaps go to the UK and make the pitch there, to the manufacturer?"

"Hmmm ... I was only partially aware of this news; you make some good points. Leave it with me. I will check with the deputy and get back to you later tonight. Now, where the bloody hell are you these days? Same phone number? Like another beer?" The two sat back and each ordered another Castle beer, and then Humble said he had to go.

They left together and Higgs went back to the mess, where he changed into casual pants and a light cotton shirt. Then made his way down to the bar, leaving a note on his bed for Petrol to come and get him if anyone was looking for him. He also called the switchboard and told them to put all his calls through to the bar.

Hamble called at 2100. "Seems the deputy also has contacts in the army. He did not know the information you had but he told me that we should make an offer to the manufacturer, in England. We were not to let on that we knew they were 'stuck' with them, but simply put in a bid of £2200 per vehicle for twenty. UK Government wanted payment immediately, and we pay the freight. We will not place the bid until three days hence, when the army will have broken the bad news to them."

Higgs was excited, "Does that mean I can go over there?"

"No, Higgs," said Hamble, cutting him off. "Thank you for the detective work. Ye shall be rewarded somehow in some fashion, but keep your feet firmly planted and do your job until I call you. And, Higgs, thank you very, very much for your support and enthusiasm. I am afraid, for the time being, you are going to have to be a simple policeman; not as romantic as this work, but stay available. Okay?"

As a signal to all, the British Government showed how they viewed the world and how important the "big picture" was. They scrapped all the vehicles. Thank you, Mother Britain! Thank you very bloody much for showing us how important we are in your future plans! Higgs found out about this decision and realized he was growing up. He had to wear his big boy knickers and be more of a realist and, regretfully, less of a dreamer.

That evening a group of fellow officers were going to the local sports club to witness a revenge wrestling match. Lusaka had a contestant named Fred Coates. Fred was a plumber and was extremely strong; he was revered by the native population. He was fighting the champion from

Southern Rhodesia, "Mad-Dog Bezuidenhout." Fred had long arms and the chest of a huge male gorilla. He was like the Pied Piper, as he was followed by dozens of fans everywhere he walked. He once joked that he could rob a bank and his followers would simply wait for him and then continue to follow him afterwards.

That night, Higgs and a few other cops were in the front row of a crowd of about 500. Also in that front row was Detective Superintendent "Big Jim Morrison," a wrestling fan extraordinaire. He was tall, 6 foot 4 inches, with red hair and, that night, dressed in a three-piece suit. He may well have been a wrestler himself, when younger; he was 42 now. On one side of the ring, in the front row, were twenty fold-up seats, all of which were occupied by policemen. Big Jim was in that front row which was, conveniently, close to the bar. Jim was in the mood that evening. His jacket was on the back of his seat; he was sweating from the hot still air surrounding the ring. A one litre bottle of Castle beer was between his feet, under his seat. The other beer was in his fist as he drank from it. The crowd of about 500 locals was getting restless. The main bout was about to begin; money was on Fred. Then a roar was heard as Mad-Dog entered.

Bezuidenhout was a bigger man than Coates. His main occupation was a train driver for Rhodesia Railways. He looked as if he could dispense with the big steam engine and pull the train with a rope, all by himself. He would be no pushover that night.

Then, a roar resounded as Fred jumped into the ring, athletically, over the top rope. He ran around the ring waving at his fans; they roared their approval and waved back. The referee collected all the parties into the middle of the ring and gave them instructions and the rules and regulations. Frankly, he appeared to be saying, "Hand over your knives and guns and fight fairly; ten 3-minute rounds."

By the seventh round, the match was pretty even. Blood and sweat were everywhere, and then Mad-Dog picked up Coates, over his head, swirled twice and threw him completely out of the ring. Unfortunately, Detective Superintendant Morrison had just returned from another trip to the bar and had two bottles of beer under his seat, between his feet, while slurping on yet another beer.

Then Fred Coates came sailing through the air and landed on Morrison's stash of beer, spilling the contents on the floor. His flailing arms also knocked the beer from Morrison's hand and splashed beer all over Big Jim's tie, shirt, and waist-coat. "Right, you bastards!" yelled Jim. "Enough of this bullshit!" And, with that, he leaped up of his seat, jumped up and into the ring, and punched the grinning Mad-Dog Bezuidenhout right in his face. Mad-Dog fell backwards and on to his back and was knocked out cold.

The referee stepped in to get Jim out of the ring and Jim punched him with a huge haymaker; the referee was out cold. Five or six fans jumped into the ring and Big Jim simply stood there punching anyone who got within range. It was explained at a later date that Big Jim had been some boxing champion in Belfast, when he was 18, so now it became obvious why he was able to throw such powerful punches.

Fred Coates, meanwhile, had scrounged a cigarette from a nearby fan and stood outside the ring, puffing on the cigarette and watching the melee. Then he jumped into the ring, grabbed Big Jim around the waist and got him out of the ring and outside the building. At the front entrance, outside, a car was waiting and "somebody" grabbed Big Jim and drove him home. Fred went back in, jumped into the ring, and helped throw everyone out of the ring except the replacement referee and Mad-Dog. The bout ended with a victory for Coates. Another fun-filled evening!

The entire episode was, coincidentally, being filmed for a newsreel called "African Mirror," shown in cinemas before the intermission. It was a way of showing cinema-goers across central and southern Africa what our quiet little City of Lusaka was like. No charges were laid against anybody. The two policemen on duty that night could not identify anyone and the dozen or so cops who were present, in the front row, were merely fans that night, and unable to assist in the meagre enquiries that followed.

Not a week later there was a huge riot outside the Lusaka Hotel. Hundreds of the local natives had decided to break into the hotel bar, where there was a strict "right of admission reserved" policy. They said, and they had a point, that this was "apartheid"; it was simply a way for the white owners to prevent black people drinking in their bars. While it was true, the bar owners did not want hoards of black labourers drinking beer (the cost of which was at least five times the cost of a beer in an "African" bar) while driving out white people drinking expensive cocktails and eventually making their way to the dining room for an expensive dinner. It happened to be racist but was really a business class decision. In any event, 20 or 30 police members could not get a wedge into the hotel to start moving the protesters out; the police were really outnumbered.

At that moment, a guest in the hotel, an American opponent to Fred Coates in the following week's wrestling match, decided he wanted to go walk-about. At 6 feet 9 inches, "Sky-Hi-Lee," in full cowboy regalia and with twin fake six-guns strapped to his belt, came walking down the stairs from his room. His voice boomed, "Get out of my way, please," and all the protesters stood aside and, like the Pied Piper of Hamlyn, followed Sky-Hi-Lee out of the hotel and down the street in awe of his presence. The protesters simply forgot what their complaint was all about and they dispersed, presumably to go home? Aah! Another tense situation resolved.

40

IT'S BEGINNING TO LOOK
A LOT LIKE CHRISTMAS

Every day a bulletin was posted on the various notice boards in each police station. The contents were generally reminders of wanted persons, traffic issues, stolen material to watch out for, and so on.

That day's bulletin also included a reminder to all patrols that the festive season would soon be on us and shoplifting incidents would increase dramatically; police were also to expect more drunken driving and traffic accidents. Foot patrol officers were asked to go inside stores and make their presence known to the owner. Apparently, the presence of a policeman inside a store would put a would-be shoplifter off their original objective. Imagine!

In any event, the heightened tensions were present all over the city. It was as if the shoplifters had a calendar handy and showed up for work on the first day of November. Shop-lifting incidents went from a handful of thefts a day to above two or three dozen. Higgs, who was on foot patrol, found a man with two large boxes of chocolates inside his shirt.

He was leaving a chocolate shop and bumped into Higgs. He was shocked when Higgs asked about the chocolates; the man said he had no idea where the boxes came from! "I never see these things before, Bwana," said the doomed thief. As it was near Christmas with "goodwill to all men," etcetera, Higgs dragged the thief into the store and returned the chocolates to the owner. "Do you wish to press charges?" asked Higgs.

"Lock the bastard up for life," was the owner's comment. Being the eighth shoplifting in his store in the past five days, Higgs fully understood the owner's attitude. Higgs called the station and a vehicle showed up 10 minutes later to take the thief away, to face a week in jail, probably. As the thief was handcuffed and placed in the back seat of a Land Rover, he smiled and said, "Thank you, Mister Policeman." Frankly, free board and lodging for a while, courtesy of the law, did not seem such a bad deal.

Swanny phoned Higgs in the evening, after dinner. "Hey, you pommie bastard! We're having a party tomorrow, seventh of November. Haven't seen you in forever man, so show up. And listen, bring those two cops you always hang around with Van Rooyen and Baldwin; we have extra women and you can keep them happy. There'll be about 45 people. By the way, all three of you can sleep over if your shifts don't interfere. You haven't seen it but I bought a big RV and it sleeps six people or up to 50 drunks. On Sunday, I want to play with my new toy, a skeet machine. I have shotguns so we can all have a go. Okay, see you Saturday, around five P.M. The three of you can stay for the braai on Sunday afternoon."

Higgs decided that day to cancel his plan to buy a car. He loved his motorbike and was beginning to think more maturely.

The Austin Healey he had ordered would cost about £1,300, about two years' annual salary. He realized that this job, in this country, was likely not going to last forever. The dealer was quite pleased to refund Higgs' deposit, as he had another anxious local businessman who really wanted an Austin Healey. The new buyer paid £1,500 for the car; the dealer smiled, as car dealers do.

Politics and independence were becoming more prevalent each week. Higgs had sent money to his mother to help her in her latter years. He had found a financial adviser, on the island of Jersey. He wisely invested in a sensible and balanced portfolio with 70% in blue-chip stocks and 30% in government bonds. He had remitted nearly all of the money he received from Amanda's estate. He was set, perhaps if not for life, then for quite a while, should he find himself out of work and, likely, out of Africa.

Dan Baldwin could not make the party but Chris Van Rooyen could. Chris borrowed someone's car, probably Baldwin's, and Higgs went on his Norton. They both arrived about 1700 and Swanny greeted them with huge bear hugs and a cold Castle beer each. Out in the backyard, were nearly 30 guests, many had long legs and short skirts. Van Rooyen was hard to restrain. Swanny pointed out to both men who the single women were and left them to greet some guests.

Meanwhile, Philimon, Swanny's houseboy, wearing his red fez and a starched white jacket, circulated with a silver tray of smoked salmon on slices of cucumber as well as Boerewors on a stick, all to help the appetite and encourage conversation.

Chris, as subtle as ever, was already chatting up a lovely lady, who was divorced and looking extremely delicious. Chris used a worn-out line, "If I told you you had a nice body, would you hold it against me?"

She, who had obviously never heard that line before, replied cooingly, "Just give me a few more drinks and you can make all the moves you want." Chris, subtle though he was not, generally, always got results. A few hours, later he got them.

Higgs, who was trying to be a little more classy than Van Rooyen, sidled over to a nice looking lady, in her late 20s, and volunteered to refill her drink. She willingly accepted and asked, "Can I come with you to the bar, so I don't stay here on my own?" As they walked over to the bar, she asked, "Are you the English guy who lost his girl in a crash in England?"

Higgs replied, "Yes, she was in a taxi going to the airport, to fly home to me. Bloody shame. She was a great lady! Still, let me ask about you." The two got on well together and both Higgs and Chris left the party very early, but returned around midnight, to take Swanny up on his offer to sleep over. By 0200, the two men were fast asleep in a very comfortable RV, parked in the back garden.

The next day they went out to the backyard to practice on the new toy and do some trap shooting. They were out there from noon to nearly sunset.

Philimon kept up a delivery of roast beef sandwiches and cold beer. Chris was brilliant with the shotgun, shooting 19 out of 20 clay pigeons each round. Higgs managed an average of 14 out of 20; Swanny never missed any; his accuracy came about, he said, because he pretended the clay-pigeon was a terrorist, riding a bike.

Swanny volunteered to take them all in the car to a small clear pool, about a mile away, where they could swim naked, freshen up, and relax before closing down the weekend. Twenty minutes later, they were cooled down and lying on the grass, drying off, and feeling very ready for whatever should come their way.

After an hour, and with darkness soon to envelop them, they were about to get in the car when a bunch of African youths, a group of seven thugs, walked down toward them.

They say "never take a knife to a gun-fight," but the gang leader, pulled out a big knife and said, "We just want your money. No trouble if you do what we tell you." The gang formed into a semi-circle around the three men and ordered them to "Pick up all your clothing."

The three men had their shotguns on the ground, with their clothing thrown over them.

As they picked up their clothes, they also picked up their guns and swung them around and pointed them at the youths. Swanny said, "You poor stupid bastards! Not only do we have guns, we have badges. We are policemen and you are all under arrest!"

The black faces became white with fright and they got on their knees and started pleading. "Can you please, in your heart, remember Jesus and forgive our silly mistake?" begged the leader of the group.

"Get up and start jogging," ordered Van Rooyen, "up that road and into the sunset." The group slowly made their way back to Swanny's house. Van Rooyen drove with Swanny and Higgs jogging behind the group. It took about 10 minutes, but soon they were home.

The police were called and charges were laid and all gang members were taken away.

The three men started laughing and Philimon brought out a dozen ice-cold beers, which they polished off. They ate Boerewors on freshly-baked buns. Regretfully, they had to call it a night at about 11 P.M., as early shifts were in store the next day.

Higgs often thought of the irony and bad luck for the little group of thugs embarking on a robbery spree. Such an easy target, they must have thought, out in the bush, three naked white men, nowhere near any telephones; sitting ducks? Who would imagine that they were cops with guns.

As they had weapons, during the attempted robbery, they were all sentenced to one year in prison.

41

THE HEAT SLOWS DOWN EVERYTHING

Christmas Day was particularly hot this year. There were many parties to attend, in the weeks before, from the more formal police "galas," to very informal outdoor braais. Higgs ended up attending two military functions, then CID's famous annual party at the Ridgeway Hotel. At least three parties at Swanny's and a special "friends only" evening dance at Longacres on Christmas Eve. The latter was at the residence of the single women who worked for the government, in various occupations, mostly medical workers such as hygienists and nurses. Marjorie was a government employee at the weather department and she arranged the invitation. Higgs reluctantly attended because he felt like he would be the "boy on show." Well, the first person he met as he walked through the door was Chris Van Rooyen. He had been invited by some woman he met a week or so before. There were perhaps fifty other men in attendance, all dressed up, all Brylcreemed up, and being leered at by the women. Everyone knew what was going on there.

The whole idea for this party was that you paid 10 shillings each and got to drink all you wanted. There were about forty women who lived at Longacres, and this usually brought them a small profit, which paid for subsequent events. It is doubtful they made a penny with Van Rooyen being there.

The night was hot and by 2000 the music and the women were just as hot. Christmas was never better. Higgs had to drag himself out of Marjorie's grasp in the early hours. He drove home to the mess at around 0500 with the Norton swerving across each road. How he managed to ride that bike at all was a feat of wonder. Not such a smart decision for a policeman, but he managed to drive the three ish miles without incident. He found his room and fell on the bed, asleep before he stopped bouncing on the mattress.

Petrol knocked on his door at about 1400 and opened the curtains. He placed a steaming hot cup of tea on the bedside table. Higgs tried to get his eyes in focus but the machinery that opened his eyes caused the gears in his head to react in pain. Petrol also handed him a bottle of Aspirin, "Take three of these pills and soon you will feel well. Happy Christmas, Bwana Higgs. Here is a gift from Santa." He then handed Higgs a beautiful man's bracelet, made from silver coins that had been flattened by a train, and then cut into filigree wire and formed into a rugged bracelet. "The women from the village near Mazabuka made this for you. I hope you like it."

Higgs loved it and, after he had his Aspirin and hot tea, he said, "Now I have a very special gift for you. This is a £20 note [Petrol was earning about £7 a month] and I want you to go and buy whatever you want and enjoy having the money for Christmas. Okay?"

Petrol reached forward, with both hands in the customary manner, and accepted the gift. "Oh, thank you, Bwana. I really need this because I have a new baby which is my sister's but she needs help. This will buy food and clothes for the child."

Then Higgs' phone rang and it was the charge office inspector. "Look here, Higgs. I know your shift starts at 1600 but we have a shortage of men now. We need you right away. A bus has been attacked near Emmasdale, about six miles up the Great North Road, and there are reports of children being tortured or even killed. Get down here in riot gear ASAP!"

"Well, Petrol, a Merry Christmas to you, and help me find all my riot gear," said Higgs. After a quick cold shower, he ran down and reported for duty. It was exactly 1500.

Three other men were waiting and with a quick explanation of what they were expected to do, they jumped into a Land Rover and rushed to the crime scene. On the way, the dispatch radio filled them in on latest events, and who else was attending. When they arrived they found a school bus, which had been rented by the Evolution Christian Church, to take forty children to a party. Some group of newly-formed political bastards, who hated organized religion, especially this church, were waiting for the bus at its drop-off point.

As the children, all under 12 years of age and all African, emerged from the bus, they were captured, tied up, and taken away. Then screams emerged from the nearby bushes as these thugs started hacking the poor children to death with pangas. (A panga has a blade about 30inches long and was used initially to cut down sugar cane, it is a perfect killing weapon.) A senior officer at the scene, who Higgs did not recognize, knew exactly what to do; he called in the canine unit. It had been determined that about 12 thugs had been involved. They had dragged off and hacked to death 12 of the 44 children on that bus, as well as the driver. The thugs had run off into the bush. A helicopter had been called in and it had discovered the murderous bastards trying to hide in an outcrop of rocks, about two miles away. A typical vehicle could not drive to them and capture them, but the average native was petrified of dogs. Furthermore, they had no guns so they might try to defend themselves with their pangas, but, by then, they would be surrounded by armed police officers.

Within twenty minutes, four dogs and their handlers had arrived. They picked up the scent immediately. Two German Shepherds, a Doberman, and a Rottweiler were soon yelping through the sparse bush and running at a fast pace. Four Land Rovers, filled with a total of 16 policemen, armed mostly with Sterling machine guns, followed the dogs. It was not too long before the screams of the thugs could be heard. Flailing pangas had proven worthless as these trained dogs, ducked and charged and avoided being injured. Then, typically, they lunged and got their jaws locked onto the thugs' genitals. The natives actually call the police dogs "impotence makers," because they do grab the perpetrators by the crotch. The police encircled the group and walked toward them, firing a few machine-gun rounds in the air.

One thug threw his panga at the dog handler controlling the Doberman. The panga hit the dog and bounced off the handler. A nearby officer fired about eight shots from his Sterling, and not one bullet missed the thug, who fell dead on the spot. Two others tried running off but the Rottweiler chased them and brought both down. The dog, as if it knew how cruel these thugs had been, was particularly nasty when tackling these two.

One nearly died from loss of blood and the other will never win any good-looks contest with his ripped open face. The Doberman needed only two stitches on its flank, while the controller ended up with a small bruise on his thigh. In any event, all but one were captured alive and a large prison van was summoned to take them all away. It should not happen, and training forbade it to happen, but the thugs were thrown into the prison van with fierce and forceful accuracy.

Their fate would be determined by a civilized court system. The job now was to retrieve the bodies of the deceased children and to find the parents and break the sad news to them. Over twenty African constables who thought they had two days leave at Christmas, were called back to duty, to help clean up the site and help locate next of kin.

Higgs went back to the mess at 1900 and was given the rest of the night off. He collapsed onto his bed and only woke up at 1000 the next day. He discovered he had another two days off until his shift change. He wanted to be away from anything "police" so he called his mate at the military. The two men and their motorbikes spent the day riding down to the Kafue River, and using another friend's boat, went fishing until sunset. They spent the evening at the military mess in Kafue, eating the fish they had caught (over 30 bream averaging three pounds each) and sharing stories, and the fish, with other police and military members in the mess that night. They both stayed overnight in a spare room at the mess and drove back to Lusaka at noon the next day.

42

IT IS 1961 ALREADY.

Amazingly, Higgs was now considered to be one of the more senior officers due to his length of service. He now had two and a half years under his belt. No longer the young inexperienced youth from England; he was now tanned, experienced, and looking older than his years.

That night was New Year's Eve and he was not on duty. A huge party was arranged at police headquarters and Higgs, et al, would be in attendance. Unlike other parties, no guests were invited. This meant more drinking and likely more fun attempting to run off somewhere with somebody else's spouse or girlfriend.

The cover charge was only twenty-five shillings and that covered all the buffet food you could wolf down, and bar drinks were included. The music was supplied by a local band, "The Aces," and, at any given time during the evening, about forty couples could be found gyrating on the dance floor. Forty, or so, others were either standing at the bar or seated on the sidelines.

At midnight, the customary "Auld Lang Syne" was sung and a lot of smooching was carried out, as were some young maidens, to cars in the parking lot.

At about 0130 a car screeched to a halt outside the main door of the Ridgeway Hotel. Four men leaped out of the vehicle carrying a large brown canvas postoffice mail bag. Inside the bag was some young, new recently-graduated recruit who had consumed enough Scotch to diminish Johnny Walker's supply for a year.

The bag was padlocked through reinforced metal rings and the bag was dragged to the front desk, while nobody was looking, and left there. Nobody knows how many people stepped over the bag during the next six hours, but the matter was called in to Lusaka Central Police Station at 0730. The man inside was still fast asleep when he was finally cut free at 0800, when a dreary-eyed policeman arrived. This was called a "joke."

Later on that day, another young recent addition to the force was found sitting on the curb. It was 0800 and on the corner of Church Road and Cairo Road. His hands were behind him and handcuffed around the lamppost. Being January 1st there was little traffic and, it seems, nobody paid the poor sod any notice. The "grapevine" hinted that he was placed there at 0200, by the Ridgeway Hotel Mob, as they were subsequently named.

The next Saturday there was a wedding between a police officer and a female police officer. Weddings were a big deal for members of the police. They were all dressed up in full-dress uniforms and with the ladies looking their finest. Lusaka was a growing community and events like this welded people together. The service was terrific and the reception lavishly catered with food and drinks, and then, it was over.

The small Ford Anglia, with tin cans, boots, and suggestive signs tied to the rear, drove off with the newly-weds waving frantically. They assumed they had escaped, unscathed, from the usual pranks customary at police weddings; how little they knew. Everyone cheered as they drove off to the Nyanga Mountains, for their honeymoon.

Thirty miles South of Lusaka was the small Kafue Police Station. There was one white officer in charge there, but he was at the wedding. He did, however, phone his African sub-inspector, who had been placed in charge during his absence, to report the wedding party's car stolen. "Inspector Chirabula, the car is a Ford Anglia, driven by a white male; his passenger is a white female. The driver will tell you he is a policeman, and may even have fake I.D. His female partner may also have fake I.D. Ignore their stories and detain them until I get there, in about an hour."

The dutiful sub-inspector set up a roadblock and, sure enough, when the car rolled up the not-so-amused couple were detained 20 minutes later, despite their objections and waving warrant-cards around.

The officer-in-charge arrived, an hour later. While he was calming down the couple, telling them that he would get to the bottom of this and it was not his doing, other police officers had arrived and had the wedding car's engine compartment open; they proceeded to wire a large kipper to the manifold. Within minutes, and with smiles and apologies, the couple set off again, begrudgingly accepting the practical joke.

The smell from that kipper became very apparent just a few miles down the road. The couple had to flag down other vehicles to borrow tools, like pliers and wire-cutters, to get every last remnant of that kipper off the engine. Aah, yes! A perfect start to a happy wedded life! Police pranks are usually a bit more comprehensive than just a typical pie in the face.

43

WARNING SIGNALS

Higgs was now a very busy man. Thursdays was rugby practice and Sunday afternoons there was a match. Monday and Tuesday evenings he had been practicing with the motorcycle display team. Up to a dozen men in full uniform would race around a field, on Triumph 650 speed-twin bikes, while their fellow officers would climb up and form a pyramid of men. This team generally visited various festivals across the country, but mainly at the show grounds in Lusaka, and thrilled the crowds. Higgs managed to attend all but one practice, then, on the day before the first show, he injured himself. He slipped while standing up-right on the saddle and almost snapped his elbow. A substitute was brought in and Higgs, who was the best candidate for the team, had to pull out. One small but nasty elbow wound and Higgs was no longer a rugby player or a bike rider on the display team.

He had to pay for more drinks as his dart game suffered. The poor man could not even play cribbage, and at the cinema he had to sit on the right-hand side of his date, as he was still able to get his left arm around her shoulder. Higgs started going to each movie that was showing each week, at each cinema; four films a week. He saw *Psycho*, *The Apartment*, *Spartacus*, *La Dolce Vita*, *The Magnificent Seven*, *BenHur*, *North by Northwest*, *Some Like it Hot*, and *Pillow Talk*. He also discovered his dates loved the movies and he was always thanked profusely. He contemplated banging up his elbow again, but did not wish to be associated with the guilt.

He had been assigned light duties, which was mainly on patrol, with someone else driving, or desk duties. The beginning of 1961 was the usual routine – a few robberies and a slight increase in cycling thefts and moving offenses. There were a few more incidents of multi-racial drunken driving too. As the native population became wealthier with increased wages and longevity at the same job, they were becoming car owners. With that came an increase in car thefts and African driving accidents.

In April, Petrol knocked on Higgs' door and announced that five teenage African men were downstairs asking for him. Curious, Higgs put on his shirt and shoes and ventured out into the bright sunlight. At first he did not recognize who these men were, but the spokesman for the group soon reminded him who they were.

"Do you remember us, Bwana?" he asked. "We were at that fire in Matero village and you instructed us to let you know if we found out who caused the fire."

"Aah, yes! I remember you well. And have you discovered who did it?" asked Higgs.

It was not as if Higgs had forgotten about the fire, because every few weeks some detective would phone him and ask him if he had received any clues. Also Chris Van Rooyen, who was with him on the night of the fire, was also getting calls from CID, and that would prompt him to call Higgs. So, while it may not be foremost in Higgs' mind, he always had it at the back of his mind, and now and then the switch would turn on and he got to wondering about the case. He hoped these teens had some credible evidence.

"Yes, Bwana. We have exactly the evidence you need. At first we were frightened to even ask about the fire. But for a long time now, these new politicians are bullying our people. They do not bully us because we are many and we are strong. But now my sister was threatened. She was told that her mother, which is my mother, would be burned if they did not vote for them, when the elections happen."

"My God!" replied Higgs. "Is this kind of stuff happening in every village?"

"Yes, Bwana, except not at the village where Thomas lives," was the response.

"And, who is Thomas?" asked Higgs.

"He is this man here," he said, pointing to one of the five. "He lives in another village, and also that is where the bad men also live. So, we acted like policemen and found out, after questioning nearly all the villagers, if they knew who the bad men were who threatened them. Everyone knew. They had all been threatened in some way, and many were told that they should remember the five whose house was burned down a year ago."

Thomas spoke up. "These men have started a new political party and they want to rule the country, when it becomes independent. They even want me to join their group and go around other villages threatening everyone. They even have a membership card which costs ten shillings to join. If they find you walking at night time, they will ask for you to show your card. If you don't have their card they will slap your face and tell you to get one. If you have a card from another political party, they will rip it up and beat you, maybe even kill you."

Another man spoke up. "I am Moses. If the police arrive with all your men and guns, these men will hide inside the houses of frightened neighbours and you will not find them. But I think I know how to catch them. In our village, next to Matero, they are coming to have a meeting with the leaders of our village. The men who burned down that house will all be there. I even know the hut number and it will begin at seven P.M. I think we should have plain-clothes men from CID start filtering into the village in the afternoon. No uniformed police. Then about three or four come to one house nearby, to visit. Then another three visit another house an hour later.

By seven o'clock, you would have about 20 men surrounding the meeting place, then you enter the house where they are meeting and handcuff the bad men. Then you can radio your uniformed police to take everyone away."

Higgs was stunned. "How do you know how to plan like this?" he asked. "I must say that is a perfect plan but we need to coordinate back at the station. Now when was the meeting to be held?"

"I heard it was April 22nd, on a Saturday night."

"Okay, so we are now at Thursday, April 6th, which gives us two weeks to plan," muttered Higgs. "Now you realize that all five of you will have to come down to the police station and give us statements. I assume all of you are, or have been, students? And have you thought about these men and the threats they will make, because of you reporting them?"

"They are all Cirombos," said Thomas. "We are educated and they are not. We obey the law and they do not. We all would value life and they do not. They should all be hanged – and good riddance! If we have to live under their rule then we don't want independence. We prefer to stay with you policemen. We are all ready to give evidence."

Higgs arranged to meet all of them the next day, at the drive-in restaurant. He would introduce them to a senior CID officer, as well as a few African detectives. The police would pay for their transport back and forth, and their lunch. Of course, nobody must know about this meeting.

When Higgs phone Detective Chief Inspector Sythe that night and revealed the details, Sythe was delighted. "You know, old boy, we have a lot of evidence from that fire. Many fingerprints on petrol cans, as well as blood and shoe markings. It's just that we have had no luck matching them to anyone. If these lads are right we should have no problem putting the arsonist murdering bastards away. Good job, Higgs! Now, tell Van Rooyen. I want you both in my office tomorrow morning at 0900. See you then."

After a number of meetings, and arranging for a dozen undercover African detectives, along with armed police waiting just outside the village, the meeting on the 22nd began, in hut 44. Two of the teens, Thomas and Cephas, were with four detectives in hut 47. They could see everyone arriving or leaving hut 44. They pointed out the bad guys to the detectives, as they arrived. Once all five had arrived, using hand signal and very quiet radio messages, the police made their move. Seven detectives barged in to the hut, while another seven stood outside to apprehend any who tried escaping.

In the end, all five were arrested and, after being processed at the police station, the CID confirmed finger-print matches from their evidence. One of the five also turned against his friends and struck a deal to avoid the death penalty. After a brief trial, a month later, three were sentenced to life in prison, in a prison 200 miles away. Two were sentenced to be hanged. The five teen witnesses were each given £100 and also a personal recommendation, should any of them ever wish to apply to become police officers.

They were also given a special day of honour, in the main stadium at their village, with free food and soft drinks for all attendees.

As the winter slowly left and spring began, in August there seemed to be something in the air that nobody could put their finger on, but something was up. Take, for example: Thursday, August 31st 1961. Higgs, elbow all better now, was on duty at Lusaka International Airport. A Brittania from BOAC landed and a few businessmen emerged and strolled across the tarmac to retrieve their luggage, and to see customs and immigration, in the terminal building.

One man was Mennen "Soapy" Williams, a state official from the USA, whose responsibility was "Africa." He was a tall man with a bow tie. Suddenly, a big man, a local farmer, who did not like Williams or his comments about "Africa for Africans" came running past Higgs, onto the tarmac, and punched Williams flat on the nose. Williams dropped quickly and had to be helped up. The local farmer, who happened to be drunk, was taken into custody by Higgs. He was charged with being drunk and disorderly and with common assault. Many whites in Africa agreed with this farmer and he received many thousands of pounds, from around the world, to help his court costs.

Frankly, how does some American, who makes underarm deodorant, state that only Africans belong in Africa. This farmer who had hit Williams had parents whose grandparents were born in 1845 in South Africa, and they were all most certainly "Africans." Williams tried to wriggle out of his statement by saying he meant white Africans as well. It did not go over well. A few weeks later, at the courthouse, the sentence was a £50 fine and a year's probation. The magistrate was also a white African, so a lot of empathy was present at the trial. Williams threatened to appeal, but he was back in the USA and never returned. The local Barclays Bank, on behalf of an anonymous donor, made a huge donation to the school for African orphans, within days after the trial's conclusion.

The USA was very critical of the way the colonialists had educated the native population, or, should we say, NOT educated them. Once again, with their hearts in the right place, but their ears and brains in the off position, the Americans had the solution. "You see," they said, "most of the black children live in the bush, hundreds of miles from any schools. So we are bringing portable buildings and will build schools right next to their villages." Why didn't the British simply tell them to get lost? Not right you know. Some weeks later, a convoy of trucks, holding material to build one-room schools, set off into the bush.

A week later there were at least 30 schoolhouses erected hundreds of miles away, in remote areas like Mongu, Fort Jameson, and Mazabuka. Then they produced young school teachers, all volunteers. The police decided then that especially the female teachers (mostly blonde and with teeth) needed protection. Many police officers volunteered to help.

The problem was, as the white Africans had been explaining, once the novelty wore off, there would be no kids attending class. Oh yes, they meant well.

But, on that first day, 30 children ran into the class, took their seats, and waited. They were each handed a comic-book style schoolbook. Few words but lots of pictures were in that book. Page 1: A picture of twenty black youths, in a vacant lot, adjacent to a 20 storey building, in downtown New York City. They were playing basketball. "*Look at Johnny slam that ball into the hoop.*" "*See how the opposing team snatches the ball away and dribbles it down to their end,*" were a couple of caption examples.

Well, the children enjoyed the pictures but had no idea what was going on. Higgs thought, "If that was me designing those books, I would have a drawing of African children, under a tree and yelling "*Watch out for that snake!*" or at least some incident they could relate to.

In any event, by about nine o'clock in the morning, the fathers all came along and dragged their children out of school, telling them, "C'mon, it's time to milk the goats" or "strip the corn." By 1000 some police were playing poker with some of the teachers. Within a few weeks, all packed up and left the buildings behind. A week or so later, there were no longer any buildings; they had been stripped for windows and firewood. Africa was back to "normal."

The United Nations were more involved than ever with African issues. The Congo war, with its increasing number of mercenaries and the United Nations troops being sent there, was not working out. Eventually, the UN Secretary-General, Dag Hammarskjold, decided he wanted to see, first-hand, what was going on. He was convinced that he could resolve the issues. The "issues" were, of course, foreign owners, supporting selfimposed President, Moise Tshombe, who was protecting their investments in the Congo's mines. The entire debacle was a loselose matter.

This was Africa, not a Wall Street bank. Imagine what all those huge international investors must have thought when they discovered Dag Hammarskjold was flying in? Whatever the outcome, their money would be worth less in the future than it was at that time.

18th September 1961: Dag was in a four-propeller-driven DC6. It flew low over Ndola, Northern Rhodesia, on a banking turn toward the airport in the Congo, just a few miles away, across the border. Then, it disappeared. The wreck was discovered later, far off into the African bush. All souls onboard had perished. The NRP attended the crash site and tried to determine the causes, but really, it was difficult right from the start, Rumours are that "somebody" shot down the plane. No locals had sophisticated equipment to do that, so who was it? No credible reason has EVER been presented as to the cause of the crash.

Sadly, the end of 1961 was the beginning of more frequent clashes between various factions. These factions had really not existed until that time. Not only was each trying to figure out what they stood for themselves, simultaneously they could not stand the other groups, even though they were not really sure what they stood for either. The Governor, Sir Arthur Benson, had likened these groups to "Murder Incorporated."

The only similarities were the posturing for position if and when independence came about. Some were political parties while others were religious groups.

A most troubling group was run by Alice Lenshina. Religious and demanding of her plentiful followers, she caused much trouble. Essentially, she said, she had formed a religious group and wanted to be left alone. She had a trip to heaven and got a message that all her followers had a "Passport to Heaven." Each follower had a small piece of paper in their pockets. This would guarantee that they would be protected from police bullets. Starting with small fisticuff fights on a Sunday afternoon, the skirmishes went to thousands attacking groups, leaving dead and wounded in the streets.

This became a police action. Somebody else, as usual, started all this and the police had to clean it up. Also, some say "experimental" native ministers, had joined the government. Alice Lenshina really did not like this situation. One young white policeman was speared to death. Later, another white policeman was hacked to death as he was testing the strength of a small bridge over a flooded river. This lovely country was never going to be the same. Atrocities in the name of democracy were simply becoming too frequent and unnecessary. One could get very angry at the thought of these new politicians ruining such a beautiful place. It is not that this was "their" country and we whites should not be allowed to rule it, it was that "they" had also been invaders and that was okay, because they were black. So "they" were able to say they were the owners of the country because they appeared to belong? Frankly, nobody really cared who ran the country, providing we all could get on with our lives.

44

BACK TO BEING A COP

While the friendly populace of Lusaka kept on giving us work, we policemen continued to keep the city safe. Burglary, stealing livestock, and coveting thy neighbour's wife (wives?) were still daily deeds, not forgetting the stolen bicycle section. There was no let-up as officers still had to attend to these daily crimes and misdemeanours.

Human Resources had contacted Higgs to remind him that his three years' duty was up, and he had to take his six months' leave as soon as he could arrange it. Higgs contacted them and spoke to Muriel Hardman, Chief Human Resources Officer. He asked if he could visit her soon to ask some important questions. She said he could if he could make it that day. He said he could and an hour later he was in her office at Police Headquarters. She was a lovely lady, about 45-ish, with milk-white skin and red hair. She stood up and stuck out her hand. "Aah! You must be Higgs," she said.

Higgs stood at least a foot taller than Ms. Hardman, and took her hand gently, and said, "Yes, I am he."

She asked him to sit and offered him a cigarette, which he took from her, then gently took her lighter from her slightly trembling hands, and lit both their cigarettes.

"What do you wish to know?" she asked.

"A couple of things really," he replied. "One, can I get pay in lieu of my local leave?" (local leave was two weeks a year – long leave was, in addition, six months every three years).

"Sorry. No, you cannot. However, we can shuffle your dates around so you don't lose any days." She smiled. "Your leave should have started back in July. Did you forget?" she asked.

"Well, I suppose I did. My fiancée died some time ago and our plans were dashed. I haven't thought of going anywhere since," said Higgs.

"And, you had a second question?" she asked.

"Well, yes. It was sort of the same thing, but it was about long leave. Could I shuffle that around?" he asked.

"As a matter of fact, yes, you can. If you take your two weeks' leave before November this year, you should be able to extend your date of departure up to July 1962. If you speak nicely to me, I could arrange July 1962 right now and include your pay increase due to you. I was about to write to you anyway, in two weeks' time, on October 5th, your pay was going up by £13.14.6 a month." She put out her cigarette and brushed some ash off her bosom, and asked, "So, what do you think of all that?"

"Bloody hell!" exclaimed Higgs. "That's terrific! Can I buy you a drink later?"

"You can buy me one now. It is late and I missed lunch so I am off home early," she said. "Wanna join me?"

Higgs figured what was going on. He had no need to be caught with this charming lady, so he lied. "Aah! What a shame!" he squirmed. "I have to check out the horses right now, as we are off to inspect farmers' security arrangements and we're away for a week."

Whether she bought the story, or not, he had at least escaped. Higgs picked up the papers she had given him and fled.

He was soon sitting at the mess bar downing an ice cold Castle beer and enjoying the company of the few colleagues in there. Higgs brought the conversation around to questions about fishing on Lake Kariba; from all came a positive response. In fact, Higgs discovered that he and Chris Van Rooyen were the only two that had never been.

And, just like that, Higgs contacted his pals in Kariba. They knew people in the tourist business and arranged that three of them, plus Chris and Higgs, go on a houseboat and spend ten days just lounging around, drinking, sleeping, and fishing. Chris had a car that he had borrowed from a girl-friend who was in Europe for a month, a twostroke 1956 DKW, front wheel drive and very fast. The date was set for the end of November and, with all their gear in the back seat, they drove out of Lusaka at 0430. They would be in Kariba by 0900. After a very bumpy and dusty ride on some of the country's famous corrugated roads, they reached Kariba.

They parked their car in a reserved spot at the Kariba North Police Station and off-loaded all the essential requirements on to the boat. Firstly, of course, a large Coca-Cola

KEN SWAN

freezer, bought from an old petrol station auction, which would hold almost 200 bottles or cans of beer, then a large freezer to hold all the fish they caught. Another freezer was filled with beef, chicken, sausages, and lamb chops, all frozen and mostly in sealed vacuum bags in a marinade of some kind.

The boat was a 66-foot fishing boat that had started its life in Florida. There were four cabins and another two semi-open areas for sleeping. A total of ten could sleep aboard. This was a friend's boat and he had lent it to the Kariba boys for six days. It was named "Cointreau" and she was beautiful. Hippos lay in the shallow water near the boats and a few crocodiles swam past lazily as the Cointreau slipped out of the dock, heading for a small inlet about four miles upriver.

Mike Dunn and Lance Frazer were both on ten days' leave from their jobs with Impresit, the builders of the Kariba Dam, and Chris and Higgs had two weeks' leave. Also onboard were Jonathan and Ciphas, the captain, and his helper. The two black men knew the boat and the lake as well as anyone. They looked after the four guests and treated them like royalty. They shared a cabin together, up front of the Cointreau, with twin beds and about 170 square feet. Each guest had their own cabin which had a private shower and twin beds, with a small porthole and sized about 200 square feet; very comfortable indeed. At the rear was an open deck, covered with a canvas roof, and where ten people could sit around, in the shade, enjoying the slight breeze and enjoy food and drinks. And that is exactly what they did most of the day.

356

They trawled for tiger fish, and most caught at least two each day, weighing about 8 to 12 pounds each. Ciphas scaled them and ripped the flesh off the bones, slipped chunks of fish into a lightly seasoned flour, then deep-fried the fish. It was served with fresh vegetable salads, baked potatoes, and home-made bread, dripping with garlic butter.

When they stopped each night and tied up to some rocks or trees, they would hand over all the leftover food to the African children, on shore, who gathered around out of curiosity (and the expectation of free food!). The beer was ice-cold and the atmosphere was glorious. The stories began and, as the consumption of beer increased, the stories became more bizarre and funnier. Mike said, "What did the copper say when he came home and found his wife in bed with three men?"

"Okay, what did he say?" asked Chris Van Rooyen.

Mike, who could hardly talk as he was laughing so much, said, "Allo, allo, allo."

Captain Jonathan, cleaning up at the sink, said, "Bwana, I have never heard such a bad story. Maybe another Bwana has a funnier one?"

Chris said, "I know one. What did the giraffe say when he walked into the bar? The high-balls are on me!" That did get a laugh, except Ciphas wanted it explained. Chris' explanation was funnier than the story.

Higgs told the story of 2 old Brigadier-Generals, ex Indian army, a bit sloshed at the club. "I say," said one, glancing around the room , making sure nobody was listening, "have you hear old Farqhar is having an affair with an Elephant."

"You don't mean Major-General Farqhar of the 44th Dragoons, do you?"

"Well, yes, precisely,"

"Oh, my God!......bad show, what? Tell me, 'um, Male or Female Elephant?"

"Good God, what sort of question is that? Female of course. Nothing queer about Farqhar."

On the fourth evening, after a typical day of cruising, fishing, and eating, they tied up in a very remote spot, about 12 miles from the Kariba Hotel and Marina. The day had been very hot. Lake Kariba was 200 feet below sea level and November was a hot month; it reached 108 Fahrenheit that day. All decided to have a shower and a nap; it was close to 1700 and all were very tired and sunburned.

At about 1830 another boat filled with half a dozen rough-looking African teenagers, bumped into Cointreau and started to climb aboard. They were either pirates or terrorists or simply troublemakers. In any event, they were not there to bring good news. All were carrying knives or pangas and one had a rifle.

"We want money now or we kill you all!" yelled the supposed leader. He grabbed poor little Ciphas around the neck and threatened to kill him first. Chris was, unbeknown to the bad guys, just getting dressed after his nap. He heard the ruckus upstairs and he grabbed his Webley .38 police issue revolver and cocked it as he edged up the five stairs, peeping to see what was going on and who was where. He saw that one of the bastards had a .303 rifle in his hands, so he pointed his revolver straight at the man's head and waited. If it came to action, that man would be the first to go.

At that moment another fast speedboat came zooming up and it was filled with six white teens. "Hey, you guys, is everything okay?" one yelled. Then pointing at Higgs said, "Aren't you a cop? Didn't we meet at the drive-in restaurant a long while ago?

Are these muntu's bothering you? We're coming onboard right now!" The water became very turbulent as the white teens started climbing aboard from varying directions. These kids must have completed their national service as they were very fit and moved very fast. The few hippos lounging nearby in the lake became hostile and they evacuated the area immediately, causing the three boats to toss violently; it was difficult to just stand up.

The lead thug yelled, "Anyone try coming onboard and your friend here gets shot and anyone else that moves also we shoot him dead. Here!" he pushed Ciphas in front of the man with the gun, who raised it and aimed to fire, which he did. He hit Ciphas in the stomach. Chris fired his revolver and hit the gunman between the eyes. The youths from the speedboat jumped aboard. They tackled the thugs and, frankly, beat the living daylights out of them. There were certainly broken bones and missing teeth. Higgs threw one into the water and he was not seen again; crocodiles must surely have grabbed him. It was not long before every bad guy was bloodied, tied up, and pleading for forgiveness.

The six youths introduced themselves as those awful young buggers from the Star Drive-In restaurant, who had spilled Higg's food off his tray and threatened revenge. "Listen, man. We were just kids back then. We have grown up now and let us help you escort these guys to the local cops. And I hear you met my mate on the Congo border. You know, the one with a chicken tied to his ankle?"

Higgs chuckled, "Yes, I do remember him. I forgave him and his past behaviour as I will now forgive you. Help yourself to a beer."

Jonathan said, "I have radioed police and they are coming by boat very soon. We can all stay here and enjoy our drinks and food until they come. The bad men we can lock in the storage room with their hands tied behind their backs." Meanwhile, Higgs and Van Rooyen, having been trained in St. Johns ways to help injured people, managed to get Ciphas out of pain (three Aspirin and a cup of cane spirits helped) and bandaged him up. He would live and was taken to hospital when the patrol boat stopped by twenty minutes later. The two most senior officers in Kariba were on board. They took charge of the crime scene. The patrol boat left, rushing Ciphas off to the hospital and came back an hour later to pick up the two senior officers.

Of course, it took an hour or so to provide statements, take photographs, examine Van Rooyen's revolver, and so on. In the end, the criminals were transferred into the cell on the police boat, when it returned, and they were handcuffed to the bars. These "ne'er-do-wells" were well known to local police and they carted them all off with a roaring thank you. Everyone was instructed to appear at the police station at 1100 the next day, to be interviewed by an inspector from CID flying in from Lusaka. It was not quite a routine matter, but as two police officers were onboard, and had been victims and participants in the "piracy," they could be trusted to show up.

Back onboard the Cointreau, the party began. All were fortunate that this incident had not happened on the southern side of the lake, where the British South African Police Force (BSAP), of Southern Rhodesia, would have been in charge of the case.

Not that there was anything wrong with the BSAP, but the matter might simply have been more complicated. There were now ten young men plus Jonathan, and the dirty jokes and songs continued way past midnight. Lake Kariba, however, was a tourist attraction and if thugs were robbing people and the police were overwhelmed, this was not good and needed to be stopped. Perhaps the word would get out about what happened that night, and the enthusiasm for lake piracy might diminish? Might?

The following day the group of men attended the police station, right where their car was parked anyway, and were interviewed for about three hours. All were put on notice that they would be needed as witnesses, when the trial began, likely in about three months' time. With that, the fishing trip was cut short and Van Rooyen and Higgs said goodbye to all their fellow partygoers, and everyone headed off home.

Back in Lusaka, Higgs was greeted in the living quarters by his loyal batman, Petrol.

"Aah! Bwana Higgs. I am so pleased to see you! My friend, Detective Bwalya, told me you were shot in Lake Kariba, but obviously, you are here and you are not shot. The Lord was listening to me last night when I was praying for you."

"Well, thank you, Petrol, I must remember to consult you when I am on my next dangerous mission. Sit down and I will tell you the whole story," said Higgs.

Petrol beamed but asked if he could bring in his co-batman, Moses, who also wanted to hear everything. "And, it is better if he hears it straight from your horse's mouth."

Okay," said Higgs. "Bring him in. He's probably right outside my door now, correct?"

"Yes, Sir. You know everything about us African people. We are very busy-bodies." Petrol went to the door and cracked it open an inch or two and yelled for Moses to enter.

"Hello, Moses," said Higgs. "Sit down over there, and would you like a Coca-Cola from my fridge while you are listening to my story?"

And so, the three sat down, sipping soft drinks, and the two Africans listened and now and then would nod, or grunt, or say "aah haa, my way." Higgs made the story a little longer and a little more dramatic than had been the case. It took two bottles of soft drinks each, for the story to end.

Petrol exclaimed, "If these bad men ever come into my sight, I will surely kill each one!"

Moses said, "I am ashamed of what these men did. I am sure you don't know which tribe they belonged to?" In any event, it was around 1800 when the trio left the room. Higgs headed down to the dining room and the two batmen went to the downstairs parking lot, to retrieve their bicycles and ride home. They would be telling this story all evening. No doubt they would not have to pay for their beer that night.

45

NEW HORIZONS AND BIG DECISIONS

The lavender Jacaranda trees down Cairo Road were beautiful. The main dualcarriageway, a mile long, was filled with shoppers and cars and especially drivers who seemed frustrated at not finding a parking spot. Higgs wondered why the African population used drums when they were sending messages; white folks used car horns! The city was growing rapidly and the police were hard-pressed to fulfill all that was needed of them.

Higgs, Van Rooyen, Dan Baldwin, and Pete Sapphire were playing darts in the police mess one lovely evening. The ice-cold beer was flowing and the stories were shamelessly dirty and mostly true. Then the Officer-in-Charge, Paddy Alton, dropped by to say hello. "This bar is the closest and I need a cold Castle," he bemoaned, "and this bar has the best patrons." Paddy was a big Irishman, known for his sense of humour and, after three or four beers, he started with his usual habit of telling tall stories.

"This man was charged with drunken driving, somewhere in England," he started. "He had hired a pretty good toffee-nosed lawyer, who started cross-examining the policeman who had arrested the defendant. The lawyer, in his fancy wig and using his best upper-class voice, glared at the young policeman and said, "Now then, Officer, was my client driving erratically when you pulled him over?"

"No, Sir," replied the policeman.

"And when you asked him to pull over and stop, did he comply immediately?"

"Yes, Sir."

"And when you asked for proper identification and all his vehicle details, did he comply immediately?" the lawyer asked.

"Yes, Sir."

"Did you see him staggering when he emerged from his vehicle?"

"No, Sir," replied the policeman.

"And did you smell alcohol on his breath?" asked the lawyer.

"No, Sir."

"Did he slur his words?"

"No Sir,"

"Well, my man, pray tell me why you came to the conclusion that my client was drunk."

"When he urinated in my pocket, Sir," was the reply.

By this time there were about twelve off-duty policemen in the bar and were now falling about, and hanging on to each other, with laughter. Of course, there had to be a followup. Now it was a story that Paddy swore happened while he was on duty in Limerick, as a young constable.

"It was Friday night and the local rugby club were winding up their annual get-together, in the "Loyal Cockerals Arms." Perhaps thirty men had consumed almost that many gallons of beer. We decided that our duty was to keep drunk drivers off the roads that night. Four Panda cars were parked across the road, skulking in the trees, in the dark, just waiting for the drunks to emerge. It was close to 2330 and suddenly the front door flung open. A big man wearing a too-small tweed coat, with his tie crooked and undone, and his fly open, he staggered from the pub. He had a bunch of keys in his hand, swinging them over his head. He was singing some dirty rugby song about some machine made of steel. He crossed the road towards us and tried his keys in the police car doors. Peering in each window, he yelled, "Allo, sailor!" We sat there in the dark not responding."

Then, our drunk found a car that his keys fit. He got in, started it up, squealed his tires, and reversed back towards us. With a wave, he put the car into first gear and took off, toward the exit to the expressway. Well, we were not going to let him get away! So all four Panda cars, sirens screaming and lights flashing, chased him around the roundabout and a mile later had him pull over.

I went with my sergeant up to the driver's window. My sergeant tapped on the window and the driver rolled it down. He said, "Good evening, officer. And what is the problem?"

"Well, Sir, do you have your papers with you?" asked the sergeant.

"Certainly, officer. Here they are. And just exactly what is the issue here?" asked the driver, in a clear voice.

"Have you had anything to drink tonight?" asked the sergeant.

"Two beers. One at 1700, the second and last at 1945," was the reply.

"Sir, what is your occupation?" asked the sergeant.

"I am, Sir, a professional decoy. Why do you ask?"

"Naturally, the pub and its parking lot were closed and empty by the time we got back." Alton lamented.

Once again, the men roared with laughter. Then the African duty-sergeant arrived and approached Paddy Alton. He said, "Sir, your wife is outside in her car and she wants you to leave here and come home with her, and now." Paddy jumped up and said his goodbyes, and left. The rest of the men split into groups and ordered more drinks; some played cards, while some others played darts, and some left to go to bed.

Higgs phoned Swanny and they chatted for ten minutes. Swanny invited Higgs to come over the next evening and join them for dinner. It had been a few weeks since the two friends had seen each other. Higgs checked his next week's shift dates and saw he was on "B" shift, 1600 to 2359, on Tuesday, and each night thereafter until Sunday. That day was a Sunday.

A few of the bar patrons asked Higgs and Van Rooyen about the big shoot-em-up at Kariba, but nobody else had any stories at all. The city was quiet. One thing everyone had noticed was a change in attitude among the African police-men. Many were saying that troublemakers were starting rumours in the villages about the police. Constable Phineas said one day, "It is as if they want everyone to stop trusting us. They are trying to turn even our own families against us."

A sergeant, with 15 years of service, said, "I feel very nervous these days, when I cycle home to my village. I used to have fellow villagers wave at me as I came home at night. Now, they walk by me with their heads down. I think they feel guilty about shunning me, but they are also feeling that befriending me may turn against them."

In fact, these feelings were real and it was the beginning of the manner in which terrorism is trained in Moscow or Peking. Get the population to distrust the authorities; when they do not know who to turn to, they will turn to their new friends, the troublemakers. Higgs was quite disturbed at these new revelations; *his* country was falling apart.

Higgs needed to get away from the police that night. He phoned Marjorie. She said, "I am about to go to bed, but drop by as I have tomorrow off and could stay in bed all day, if I had to." Higgs left on his Norton at about 2330 and was soon at Marjorie's front door.

She was looking very pretty that night and she greeted him wearing a short kimono-type gown. She welcomed him in and took Higgs' arms and flung them around her. She knew why he wanted to see her and she had been thinking of him a lot, lately. Sex with Higgs was almost legitimate, but also terrific. She kissed him hard and they stumbled over their falling clothes as they made their way to her bed. Tonight, she was particularly eager and they made love until about three in the morning; stopping only for a drink and a shower and then again and again. Marjorie woke at about

1100 and made some coffee. She waited for Higgs who had just arisen and was now wet and fresh, from the shower.

"What are we going to do about us?" she asked.

"Us?" he replied.

"Yes, us," she said. "Are we just about sex or is there something more?"

"Well," said Higgs, "I am too young to think about 'us' right now. One day I will know. Right now, I think you are a beautiful woman and I love being with you. Can I take a rain-check on your question?"

"Sit here and have a coffee," she said, as she patted the cushion on the sofa. "If that towel around you makes any move, I will be on top of you in a second. I do love being with you and if it is just for sex, then it's okay with me."

He needed another shower before he left Marjorie's place; he left around two in the afternoon.

Higgs arrived at Swanny's place at about 1800. His Norton had a distinct engine sound and Swanny was waiting in the driveway. "I could hear you coming up Leopards Hill Road, a mile away," he said. Swanny hugged Higgs and they both went in to the veranda, where Connie was waiting with a drink tray. Higgs grabbed a cold Castle beer and gave Connie a kiss on the cheek. She returned one to him on the lips, saying, "I miss seeing you, man! It's been nearly a month since you were here."

Swanny said, "I have something serious to tell you, my friend. Connie and I are selling up and moving to South Africa. I have a business opportunity in Cape Town, at the docks, where I will be the only company in charge of maintenance of the roads. The money is great and the future is bright. This place will not be recognizable in five years' time. I also have information, on pretty good authority, that the new government here will begin nationalizing all companies, such as mine. There is no chance I would ever let that happen to me, after 12 years of breaking my back building up this business. I employ 5 white guys and 135 local Africans. If the government can run this business better than me, then good luck to them! So, I have been offered £200,000 by a guy from Kenya. I guess everything is relative, but he figures this country will be more stable than Kenya has become."

Higgs sat down. "Wow!" he uttered. "That is a shock! What will I do? You guys are solid friends; in fact, truly the only real friends outside of my buddies in the police."

"Well, we have talked about you a lot. In Cape Town, the company in Cape Town, that I am buying out, has about 110 vehicles, of all shapes and sizes. I need a very reliable man to head up my transport division. I will pay £3,000 a year, provide subsidized housing, and pay 5% of the company profits as a bonus. I want you to come with me and work in the company. What do you think?" Swanny asked.

"Can I have a brandy and Coke? A double, please. That is the second proposal I have had today. This is out of the blue and I need to think. Notice, I am not uninterested. In fact, maybe I am very interested, but I need time to think. Can I tell you in a day or so?"

"Hey, my friend, come and eat and take a week to let me know. I believe being a policeman must be a fantastically interesting line of work. You will miss all the antics you guys get up to; but, you will never make money like private business can bring you. As always, there are choices in life, and very few are black and white. So, you take a pad of paper and draw a line down the middle of a blank page, from top to bottom. In the first column you write each part of your present job that you like and in column two you write each part of my job offer that you like. Somewhere at the end of one page, or twenty pages, you will total each column up and determine which makes more sense, for you. Now, try a piece of this curried tiger fish, as an appetizer; it is an old Boer recipe, and they have it often, as an appetizer in South Africa."

Swanny placed a piece of cold fish, which had been marinating in a sauce filled with onions and apricots and green chillies, onto Higgs' plate. The fish was addictive. The meal was a roasted Guinea fowl, surrounded by roasted fennel, roasted carrots, and cauliflower cheese. On the table was also corn-on-the-cob, along with a green mealie bread. By 2230 the table was bare. Cold pineapple sorbet was the dessert. The three friends sat around slurping KWV Van der Hum liqueur, and enjoyed each other's company.

"What shift are you on?" asked Connie.

"Only four tomorrow afternoon," answered Higgs.

Swanny said, "Have another drink and stay here tonight. Okay?"

"Okay," replied Higgs.

All were fast asleep by midnight. The next day, at the table where a small breakfast had been laid out, Higgs asked, "When do you actually think you would move to Cape Town?"

Swanny thought a while, and said, "If the buyer also wants my house, and it is worth about £8000 more, then it would be quick. Maybe July 1, 1962. No sooner than that, but certainly before 1963. Why, does the time affect you at all?"

"All our police contracts are based on a 'tour' of three years. My three years were just completed, but I can get an extension, or just sign on for another three years. I just need a day without a hangover to sit down and plan this all out."

"Do not worry about money. I can employ you here and get you living quarters. There is lots of stuff you can do for me here. Or, if it is next year then, if you have a gap in income, I can advance you until you are onboard, full time. Anything else, then it is you that must decide; I can't help you," Swanny said.

Higgs gulped another mug of black coffee down. He picked up a scone, slathered it with apricot jam and shoved it all into his mouth. He left, with a quick thank-you kiss to Connie and a handshake to Swanny. "Gotta go, my friends. I will be in touch very soon."

With a wave, Higgs roared off on his Norton and enjoyed the sunny day, reaching his quarters at about noon. He parked his bike and made his way up to the stairs and his room. Higgs lay down on his bed and fell asleep. At 1530 Petrol staggered into his room and yelled at Higgs. He sat upright and found Petrol with a lot of blood dripping on the floor.

"Petrol, what has happened?" Higgs yelled, as he lay Petrol down on his bed.

"I have a knife in my back," moaned Petrol. There was a vicious looking pocketknife with most of its 4-inch blade sticking into Petrol's back, just below his left shoulder blade.

"I was in a fight with a man who wanted me to help him to bomb the police station. So I told him I would report him and he knifed me."

"What does he look like?" asked Higgs, as he reached for his phone to get the medics up to his room.

"I think you can find him. He has a broken face. I punched him very hard and I split open his nose and broke both eyes," said Petrol. Within two minutes, the police ambulance attendants were in Higgs' room. They removed the knife and dressed the wound, with a lot of Dettol disinfectant doing the job of killing every germ, while smelling up the entire building with its distinctive hospital-like smell.

Higgs also phoned CID and an African detective came up to the room to get more precise details from Petrol. He was able to identify the other man and the CID found him, that night, in an outpatient emergency room, with stitches all over his face. More importantly, it was obvious that this man belonged to some terrorist group and the police were able to pick up many of his associates. This was their first case where they gained insight into these newly forming terror-cells. It was a big break for the police and gave them a heads-up on these bastards who were now starting to use violence to get their way, politically. As usual, it was the very people they said they represented who suffered, and would continue to suffer, under the leadership of these thugs.

Higgs reported for his shift that night at 1700, an hour late. But he had sent down word that he was in a problem. Nobody berated his tardiness.

"Say there, Higgs," said the shift officer, Inspector Harlow, "why don't you take constable Phineas here, looking very glum, and go on patrol in the latest Land Rover. You would be the first to drive it officially."

Higgs stood up and grabbed his cap. "Alright, Phineas, you lazy sod! Let's go and breathe in some excitement."

Phineas replied, "Bwana Higgs, I will be the one bright and alert by the end of the shift, and then I will find you sleeping on my shoulder. I am just using my willpower to look like I am half asleep, but I am very alert. Wait and see."

"Come on, my boy, you can't bullshit a bull-shitter! Let's go!" said Higgs.

And, with that, the two got into the vehicle and drove off. Phineas noticed the tag over the radio was now in metal, not a piece of sticky tape like all the others. He exclaimed "We are growing rapidly, Sir. We are Lusaka 9" The city was starting to cool down as the sun crept down beneath the trees. But rush hour, which hardly existed when Higgs arrived just three years ago, had started. Flagrant violations of every traffic regulation were happening with just about every car.

Phineas said, "You know, Sir, if we tried to give a ticket to every violator, we would have to stop them all and make them line up along the road, as we processed each one. They have not been drinking yet, and they just want to get home and have a cool beer with their families. Maybe we should give them the Bwana Van Rooyen method of punishing them for bad driving."

"Oh, really? And what is this Van Rooyen method?" asked Higgs.

"If it is a male driver, you just drive next to them and yell, 'You are an idiot and if you do that again I shall give you a double ticket!' Mr. Van Rooyen says the drivers don't know what they did and they don't want a double ticket, so they change every driving habit and obey the law. Also, Mr. Van Rooyen says his blood pressure stays at good levels and he has more fun!"

"So, are you saying we should not bother with tickets tonight, or just give them to women drivers?" asked Higgs.

"Oh, no, Sir! I just did not finish. Female drivers, he would drive by slowly and make sure the woman driver was looking at him. Then he would just waggle his finger and slowly shake his head. They would get a red face and start driving more carefully."

Higgs said, "Alright. We shall follow Assistant Inspector Van Rooyen's rules of the road tonight. Meanwhile, what flavour of ice cream do you like? I am stopping here at the Star Drive-in and ordering two cones. I am having raspberry, and you want what?"

"I want chocolate, Sir," replied Phineas, smiling.

There really was a bond between all members of the force. This relationship with Phineas was simply a relaxing indication of the complete trust and faith in each other, especially if an incident, more challenging than buying ice cream, should come along.

Not one incident had occurred when the two men stopped back at the mess for an hour's break. Higgs found sausage rolls on the buffet table in the mess. The ice-cream had dampened his appetite, but he grabbed four rolls, wrapped them in a napkin, and took them out to the patrol car. "Phineas, if you get hungry, here are some sausage rolls for you. Did you get something to eat or drink during your break?" asked Higgs.

"Yes, I had two very large mugs of tea with sweet condensed milk. I am feeling very full now," replied the constable.

They parked near the roundabout at government house, and kept the engine idling so the radio would still operate. The two men talked about their lives, families, favourite sports, and every subject one can imagine.

Higgs wanted to know how Phineas felt about white men invading his country, in the name of colonization. Did it bother him or his family, and what about the entire indigenous population? Did he have any idea about this subject?

Phineas thought out loud, "I suppose every country has some kind of leader and even if that person was the same race there would be some who like the leader and some who do not. It is like you being my boss. If you were black and I liked you or I did not like you, then what difference does it make?"

Higgs answered, "Yes, but we are a completely different bunch of people and we are running your country. Doesn't that bother you?"

"Well, Sir, I don't have enough skills to run the country myself, so I will always have somebody bossing me around. As long as my bosses treat me fairly and I can live my life without fear, then I just enjoy myself and get on with my life. How many tribes are there in this country and where did they originate? Anyone from any tribe could be our leader and we accept it. Even this voting that people are discussing means people will just vote for who their chief tells them to vote for."

"Okay, not much either of us can do about this stuff, anyway. Let's get back," said Higgs.

They returned to the station at 2345 and clocked out

The next morning, Petrol, who had just had the stitches removed from his back the previous day, knocked on Higgs' door and brought him a note. It read: "Superintendent Hamble wants a phone call before 1000 today." Higgs had a quick shower, then a good breakfast, and then, at 0930, he phoned Hamble.

"Can you come and see me today, say around 1500?" asked Hamble.

"Yes, Sir. At your office?"

"Indeed, my boy. See you then," replied Hamble.

Hamble wanted to give a message to Higgs, right to his face, without any correspondence in writing. He greeted Higgs at his office, later that day, and said, "You have less than three years left before this country will, no doubt, become independent. We have actually stopped recruiting new officers as of now. There will be a push to persuade existing officers to sign on until the end.

I want you to know that if you re-sign, you will be making a big mistake. I'm sorry to say this, because you are one of the best policemen we have, but I think you should quit, when your contract is over. I gather it is over, officially, with six months' extension being worked on. Is that right?"

"Higgs said, "Well, you do tell it like it is, Sir. Yes, I am in that situation now. Can you give me details or is that just your opinion?"

"I don't like anyone knowing my business, Higgs, but I have been asked to step down and I know why. We are getting pressure from jolly old England to take it easy on persons who may well become future leaders of this country. In other words, they believe we are planning to be too tough on these rotten bastards who are bumping off anyone who opposes their views. So you would be left hanging out to dry without me, and before I go I can make sure you get treated with some fair terms. That's all," replied Hamble.

"I am pleased to get this information, Sir," said Higgs. "I was at a cross-road with my plans and my choice is now much clearer, and easier. It is a shame that we cannot put into effect all our plans, but everything is moving so fast, we have little choice."

The two men shook hands and Higgs saluted, saying, "It has been a pleasure knowing you, Sir. Thanks for the advice. I hope we meet again."

Then he walked out of Hamble's office, with a small tear running down his face.

46

A NEW LIFE

Higgs phoned Swanny. "Hey, my friend, can you wait for me for two months? I am saying yes to the job but need about two months to make final arrangements. I am going to England to check on my mother and put other things to rest. Then, I will contact you to give you details of my arrival date and so on. Okay?"

"Look, Higgs. I still don't know where I am going to be in two months, but your plan sounds good. Drop by this week and have a visit and then we can exchange addresses where we can always get hold of each other. I have my address here and two in Cape Town. Maybe your mother's address in England, or some other place where I can find you. Is Friday night okay?"

"See you at 1800 at your place, on Friday. Cheers!" said Higgs, as he then dialled for the Human Resources office. That day was Thursday, December 14, 1961 and Higgs wanted to depart on his "long leave," his official six-month vacation, as soon as possible. He spoke to Muriel Hardman. Between the two of them they decided on Monday, January 15, 1962 as the date to depart Lusaka. Higgs wanted to do it now, no waiting around.

He had made up his mind and would have left that day but, he had things to end and business to finish, so January it would be.

He contacted the BOAC ticket office and booked a flight on the Britannia, departing on January 15, 1962, the ticket paid by the Northern Rhodesia Government. Then Higgs contacted his financial advisor, who lived in Jersey, in the Channel Islands. He sent a telegram explaining his actions and asking what to do with his money, given different circumstances. Next, something he really was not happy about, he contacted Marjorie, and asked for a date; she happily agreed.

Then Higgs had to think about how he would say goodbye to all his colleagues. He could simply sneak away. He could arrange a going-away party, or he could see each friend and say goodbye, man-to-man, face-to-face. All of this was making Higgs extremely sad. Frankly, he would rather stay in this beautiful country, as a policeman, forever. He loved the country. He loved Lusaka. He loved his job and he loved his fellow police officers. Why the hell should he be forced to leave? What right did these communist-trained bastards have to run this country?

Friday night was lovely. Higgs rode up to Swanny's place and brought a bottle of Argentinean Malbec wine, which contrasted well with the usual South African wines, which were also wonderful. Dinner was a prime rib of beef with

Yorkshire pudding and roasted mixed vegetables. The three friends slowly ate the meal and talked about life and plans for the future.

Higgs explained how he had decided to go back to England. He needed to sort out his mother's living arrangements and finances. At the same time, he had arranged to see his financial advisor, to sort out his own finances. The first of which was to buy a house that his mother and a caretaker could live in. When Higgs' mother passed away, the management company would take it over and rent it, placing the profits into Higgs' savings and annuity account.

Swanny asked, "What are you going to do about your Norton?"

"Oh, Jees! I forgot about that! Hmmm...any ideas?" mumbled Higgs.

"Oh, hell! Don't worry about it," said Swanny. "We have so much to ship down to Cape Town, we will ship it along with my Merc and my bike. And you get employee shipping costs; in other words, free. Just bring it here, along with any other stuff you want to keep, and we shall get it done for you."

"Oh, man, you really are a good mate! Connie, if you ever leave him, I want to marry him! Okay? Higgs continued, I am guessing that around March next year I will have accomplished what I want to do in England, and I will contact you, wherever you may be, and we can set up a plan. There could be something, job-wise or personal, that you need me to look for and bring with me to Cape Town; if so, just let me know and it shall be done. Now pass me some of that grilled pineapple dessert."

Higgs stayed the night, in the guest room, and left just before noon on Saturday. He was on the committee to arrange a Christmas party, in the mess, and Christmas was only two weeks away. For whatever reason, Higgs decided to go about his work and not announce his departure in January. He did tell Chris Van Rooyen, which was an extraordinary conversation. The Christmas party meeting was to start at 1600 and Higgs called Van Rooyen's room at about 1300. Chris answered his phone and invited Higgs down to his room for a cold beer and a chat. The two friends shook hands and each took a long swig of beer before Chris said, "I don't know what you want to talk about, but I have something to tell you. I am leaving the force and returning to South Africa. My long leave has to begin within two months and so I am going in the middle of January. There is a lot of work available in Cape Town, so that's where I am headed. So, what is it you want to chat about?"

"Hmmmm...funny you should ask," replied Higgs. "Let me see now....okay, I am leaving the force and going to Cape Town. How's that for starters?"

Chris nearly fell off his seat, "Jees, man, tell me all about it."

The two talked for hours, until Higgs noticed the time and they had to spruce up a little and go down to the mess, for the meeting.

After the meeting was over, and it only took twenty minutes or so, Higgs excused himself and went to his room. He phoned Swanny.

"I must tell you about Chris Van Rooyen." He went through everything and said, "He is a good man, and if you ever needed, say, a strong guy with a police background, for a security head in your company, he might be a good fit. What do you think? Can I tell him that he is welcome to apply with you?"

"Better still," replied Swanny, "you can tell Chris right now that there will always be a job for him with my company. You can tell him just that, and he should phone me and come and talk to me within a week. Okay?"

When Higgs told Chris about the job opportunity in Cape Town, Chris began to cry. "My God!" he said. "Who knew that I could find such good friends? I will thank you for the rest of my life! I will call Swanny, right now."

Meanwhile, Higgs was getting paid a salary and had work to do, keeping the streets in Lusaka safe for all mankind. He was assigned to "A" shift, starting at 0800. He lay his head down at 2000 and set his alarm for 0700. Higgs awoke, showered, dressed, and had a quick breakfast, slipping into file at 0758.

"Higgs," said Inspector McCloud, "you are needed in Lusaka 3, along with Sub-Inspector Chimfwembe, to pick up two political boffos at the prison, and run them over to the courthouse. They are the leaders of the mob that burned to death the opposition back in Matero. If they jump out of the vehicle, then find a gun and shoot them."

Chimfwembe was a first-class man and the duty that morning was refreshing and enjoyable. They handcuffed the two prisoners to the frame inside the Land Rover, and dropped them off at the courthouse, handing them over to the custodians there. They then drove off to the deserted show grounds and parked under some shady mango trees, and just enjoyed each other's company, chatting about events and careers and political probabilities. Chimfwembe had strong and negative opinions about the way he viewed upcoming events.

"You know, Mr. Higgs, these people who have had training in China and Russia are black people who say they will help their fellow black brethren. They must mean me as I am black and their brethren. But all I know is that they have a lot of nice shiny black skin, covering nothing. They are a waste of skin! They will sink this country into the drains and then blame you white people."

Higgs was quite taken aback by the strong feelings he was hearing, but he had heard similar sentiments elsewhere. He was almost glad now that he was planning the move to Cape Town. At least there he was immune to the possibility that any black government would ever depose the stability of the white government, already in existence.

The shift was over and they checked out at 1555, going their separate ways. Higgs, still in uniform, walked into the bar, which was empty. He ordered a cold beer from Ngoni, the new barman, and picked up a copy of the Central African Post, to read about the events of the day. This was a good newspaper, printed locally, and had world news as well as local. He read about a policeman who was killed in the USA and discovered that the officer had never, in 23 years of service, ever drawn his gun. This time he drew his weapon and fired at his killer, but he had also not loaded his pistol; his inattention to discipline and training cost him his life. Higgs daydreamed for a while, wondering if this force, as well as the UK police, would ever carry weapons, like the Americans.

He also read that a farmer in Broken Hill, just 90 miles north of Lusaka, had been attacked and killed. Apparently a mob of about 30 local teenagers had attacked the farm at about 0200 and killed the poor farmer, who was still in his bed. Lusaka CID were on scene, investigating. This farmer had hired over 100 local natives when he first built his barns and homes for labourers, back in 1924. He had over 200 labourers working for him at the time of his death. Nobody knew why the death was necessary and finding the culprits would not be easy.

At that moment, five women arrived, two off-duty police-women and three officers' wives. They set about decorating the mess with Christmas decorations. Higgs ordered another beer and some drinks for the ladies. He helped when he was needed, like placing the star on top of the tree, but mainly he listened to gossip and bawdy jokes. The decorating was soon completed and the women left. Then a bunch of officers checked in and the evening began in earnest, with cards, snooker, darts, and drinks. The dirty jokes began and the details of curious activity during each officer's day. That was really the best part of being a cop, to escape the depressing events by making fun of them and hearing the adventures of the others. Higgs was going to miss all this, he thought.

A day later, Higgs phoned Marjorie. It had been some time since he had seen her and he now needed to break the news that he was leaving, and probably never coming back. She answered the phone, and said, "Oh, hello, Higgs. I was going to phone you tomorrow. You see, after our last conversation, I realized there really was no 'us.' We needed each other for sex, which I wanted as much as you, but there was nothing else. For the last week I have been sleeping with a man who works at my office. I love him and he wants to marry me and I agreed. I know you will understand and I will never forget you; you were damn good, my friend, but it's over. Goodbye, sweetheart."

Higgs sighed with relief. He had figured that he would have one last romp with Marjorie and then have to break the news to her. Now it was all done and, aside from no more romps, he felt great. He then decided that the quickest way to tell his friends that he was leaving would be at the Christmas dinner. That Monday was Christmas Day and the dinner was planned for single men who lived in the mess.

And so it was that after the dinner, Higgs stood up and made the announcement:

> "My friends, and I truly mean my friends. I have come to a crossroad in my life. I arrived here, as most of you did, from the UK, just over three years ago. I could not believe my luck at finding such a beautiful city, in such a pleasant country, and working in a first-class outfit, with friends like you. But, we each have our lives to live. We each have to make decisions and, for all of us, it is whether we get married, and to whom; whether to stay as a policeman, here, or somewhere else; and whether we choose another career that pays loads of money. And I have now made one very important decision. I am going

to England next month, on January 15th I fly out of here. Then, sometime later, maybe two months or so, I have accepted a terrific job in Cape Town.

This was not an easy decision, but I had imagined being a policeman here for the rest of my life. Circumstances now make that a pipe-dream that won't happen. A once-in-a-lifetime job offer was presented to me and I simply could not reject it. I can hardly speak now, my emotions are very high, and I could not stand being in a going-away party, which is why I chose this opportunity to say farewell. I still have three weeks' work left, so, no doubt we shall see each other during that time. But please, all of you, understand how I have welcomed and enjoyed knowing each and every one of you."

Higgs sat down and everyone stood up and applauded and wished him well. Higgs was not the only one with a few tears streaming down his face. Higgs thought to himself that having to break the news was over with Marjorie, and now it was over with his colleagues, but the worst was still to come. He had to tell Petrol.

The next morning, as Petrol arrived, to go through his usual morning chores, Higgs asked him to sit down. "Petrol," he said. "I have an important message for you. I am returning to England next month and I am not coming back.

I need to take care of my mother and I need to find a new job. You have a good job here and my leaving will not affect your work at all."

Petrol had tears running down his face. "Why can't I come with you and be your servant anywhere you are?" he pleaded.

"Well, it is not that easy. I am flying over a huge ocean and you do not have a ticket for the plane. Also, you know the British will demand immigration papers, and you don't have any."

"But I can save my money and buy a ticket and also fill in the forms. Then I can come and look after you." Petrol was sobbing.

Higgs was trying hard to not sob. He said, "With all the changes going to happen to this country, you will be promoted and you will be the batman for a senior African police officer. Don't you want that?"

"No, I do not want this. They are all rubbish people and only you can be my Bwana. I will be no good without you," Petrol replied.

There was nothing Higgs could do, of course. He said, "Let's think about this and talk another day. Okay?"

Petrol left and Higgs started planning his move. He would pack only the items he really wanted, such as a few items of clothing, plus a few souvenirs of his police work, like buckles, badges, etcetera. Everything he did not want, he would give to Petrol. Then he needed a secure box and he could ship the box to Cape Town, via Swanny. Soon, he had the packed box dropped off at Swanny's as he drove by his home one night, while on patrol in a Land Rover. A week later, he rode his Norton to Swanny's place and parked it in the huge garage, next to Swanny's SL 300. A land-rover picked him up.

On his way back to headquarters, that night, at around 2100, Higgs, still on duty, came across a traffic accident. An African woman, in one of the vehicles was about to give birth. Higgs radioed in for help and asked for two ambulances. One was for the pregnant woman, the other for the other victims of the crash. Alcohol was the obvious cause of the accident. One of the cars had strayed across the white line and hit the other car, head-on. He estimated both cars were speeding, from the debris and skid marks, perhaps over 50 miles an hour each. In any event, the lady could not wait. Higgs had her in the back of the Land Rover, sitting on an extra spare tire. Within five minutes, she gave birth to a screaming, but healthy, boy. The woman asked what his name was and Higgs replied, "Higgs."

"Then, Bwana Higgs, he shall be called Higgs," she said.

By this time, both ambulances had arrived as well as another patrol car. Two tow trucks arrived to take away the metal fragments that were once nice cars.

One man had since died from injuries while the other was in critical condition. It was not more than an hour later that the scene had been cleared and there was nothing left to show there had been an accident there. Now, all the paperwork had to be completed, back at the station. Higgs managed to get to sleep at about 0100.

Christmas came and went. The usual number of parties, only this time with many colleagues approaching Higgs and wishing him good luck, etcetera. Detective Chief Inspector

Sythe was particularly saddened to see Higgs was leaving, but all understood that they too would have to make plans for themselves, one day soon. And then it was all over. January 14, 1962, Higgs gave his planned box of clothing to Petrol.

"Goodbye, my dear friend. I wish you well in your new country, which will happen soon. Here is an address in England that you can write to if you wish to contact me. Wherever I am, I will get all messages sent to this address," Higgs said. They shook hands, and even hugged briefly, and Higgs went down the stairs with his suit bag and got into Swanny's car. Swanny had Higgs stay over at his home that night then he drove him to the airport the next day.

The Britannia arrived on time and, without any fuss, Higgs said goodbye to Swanny. They had exchanged phone numbers and addresses the night before, over a wonderful dinner and copious amounts of good wine. Swanny said, "I believe we shall see each other soon. Let me know if you need anything. Totsiens, my friend!"

Higgs boarded the plane and found his window seat, three rows from the front. Nobody was seated next to him, and he vowed to sleep the entire 17 hours of the flight.

47

CLOSE ONE DOOR AND ANOTHER ONE OPENS.

It was close to 1100 when the plane landed at London's airport. Higgs had actually slept nearly the entire flight. He awoke for breakfast and some bathroom breaks, but he was feeling fresh. He walked out of the aircraft, down the long corridor, to the baggage claim. He only had one suit bag to collect. He showed his UK passport to the immigration officer and headed for the exit that read: "Taxis."

Higgs noticed, near the bus exit, a small booth with a sign that read: "Union-Castle Line Passengers. Transport to your ship, in Southampton. Check in here." An attractive woman was waiting at the booth, in her Union-Castle uniform. Higgs caught her eye as he strolled by and she yelled, "Higgs, is that you? It's me, Yolanda! Come here!" Higgs realized who she was. She was still jaw-droppingly beautiful and her figure was still magnificent. He rushed over, dropped his bag, and the two met in an explosion of hugging, fondling, and terminally hot kissing.

"Are you alone?" she asked.

"Yes, of course I am," Higgs replied.

"What are you doing here and when did you arrive and where are you going and when?" Yolanda blurted out.

"And you – are you living nearby and did you get married and what have you been up to? Tell me all these things," said Higgs.

In between an occasional interruption as cruise passengers checked in their luggage and got on the bus, the two talked for an hour.

Yolanda suggested that they should talk some more.

"Look. I am off duty in half an hour. The bus leaves at 1300 and then I go home. I have my own flat about twenty minutes away, and my car is just down below in the underground parking lot. Come with me and have a nap and a chat and then we can go for a meal somewhere. And, no, I did not get married. I waited for you."

They were at Yolanda's flat by 1600. They talked for hours. They got to know each other again. They really were meant for each other.

Higgs asked if he could use Yolanda's phone. He used a card to charge the call. Swanny answered. It was 0800 in Lusaka. Higgs said, "Howzit, my friend? Do me a favour, please. When you said you would provide living quarters for me, in Cape Town, there will be a woman in my life and she will be living with me in that house. Okay? Her name is Yolanda. Yeah, you will really like her."

The End

KWACHA EPILOGUE

There was a while, after Higgs left Lusaka, that it was very peaceful. Northern Rhodesia was a lovely and satisfying place to live. The only unpleasantness came from the antics of Alice Lenshina's party. Her bandits caused the death of two police officers. One was hacked and speared to death by her followers as he attempted to serve a warrant. The other was attacked and hit by knives and axes, by teenage thugs, scouting for her party, looking for targets. The general populace lived their lives, mostly unaware of these incidents. The NRP continued on with everyday policing. Increased house break-ins and traffic incidents were typical.

Chris Van Rooyen spent weeks in court, as a witness to the incident in Kariba. He resigned from the NRP in May 1962 and arrived in Cape Town within a week. He became the head of security for Swanny's company and lived in an Adderley Street condominium.

By 1964 he had married a cute nurse from Australia and now lives with her and their two daughters. He retired as general manager of security, in 2000. Chris now lives in Stellenbosch, where he is dabbling in growing grapes for making wine. His family all found occupations and share a lovely farm house nearby. Both daughters are married.

Higgs and Yolanda were married in England, in April 1962. Higgs' mother died in the same month, two days after the wedding. Higgs put a manager in place to rent out his mother's house and transfer the rent into his Jersey financial account. Along with his other investments, Higgs was well off financially; not a rich man, but enough wealth to live a secure life.

For a second honeymoon (or was this a third?), Higgs and Yolanda took a Union-Castle ship, the Windsor Castle, to Cape Town; the cruise lasted 11 days. They reminded each other, as often as possible, how they first met. Swanny met them at the port in Cape Town and took them to his home in Sea Point. It was a magnificent 3,800 square foot former mansion of a former governor, in 1877. The two stayed as guests for a week. Each day they were shown various homes that Swanny had thought were suitable and, finally, they saw a lovely cottage, with three bedrooms and three bathrooms, which is now their home. A huge veranda surrounded three sides of the house, just overlooking Clifton Beach. It is a pretty house with almost 2,400 square feet and a big garden.

To this day, and past all the politics and changes in country names, Higgs and his family (two daughters born in 1966 and 1969) are all quite comfortable and healthy, in the very new Africa.

Higgs retired as vice president of Swanny's company, in 2007. He had been the transportation head, starting in 1962 with over 96 pieces of equipment. In 2007 there were over 300 vehicles. Higgs was in good health when he retired and once a day he rides his Norton, just a few miles around de Vaal drive. Yolanda turned out to be the best thing for Higgs. The two spend a lot of time gardening and now and then go on a cruise, just to see the world and remember old times.

Swanny is now a healthy retired man. He still drives his beloved Mercedes 300SL and his motorbike, at least twice each week, often with Higgs, around the beautiful roads around Table Mountain. He and Connie, Higgs and Yolanda, as well as Chris and Laura, meet "somewhere" at least weekly, to enjoy each other's company and have a decent meal. May they stay this way forever.

As for Zambia? Higgs still gets emotional over that land. The jewel it was and the potential that was there, simply disappearing every year. About 800 policemen are gone and now living in many parts of the world, with most making a living at work unrelated to their NRP experience.

By comparison to the rest of Africa, however, the government of Zambia is doing reasonably well and crime and corruption are the lowest in Africa. Europeans now represent less than 2% of the total population. Recent disturbances caused by the opposition, may cause Zambia to become similar to its neighbours? One can only hope they can resolve the issues at the ballot box, but. Like the rest of Africa, democracy may simply be a doubtful proposition?

Rover Patrol Car

Rail Trolley

Northern Rhodesia Map

This map of Northern Rhodesia will enable readers to imagine each loacation mentioned in the book, and distances involved. This was a large country and prior to 1900 (almost before the first white settlers "europeans as all whites were called" arrived) there was no transportation routes, roads, railway. This really was raw Africa that was untouched and had not changed since time had begun.

This map was drawn circa 1956.

What the Police do to amuse the public.

A daring stunt performed by Assistant Inspector M. Bestic (top) and Assistant Inspector D. G. H. Marnham during the motor cycle display at Northern Rhodesia Agricultural Show in Lusaka

Members of the Northern Rhodesia Police Motorcycle Display Team performing astounding tricks.

Police Band

African Training Course

Lusaka Central Police Station

First Day – Author

Very Raw Recruit – Author

KEN SWAN

Full Dress Uniform

CRIMINAL INVESTIGATION DEPARTMENT,
P.O. BOX RW.104,
RIDGEWAY,
LUSAKA.

POLICE CERTIFICATE

    Mr.
Certified that Mrs..............Kenneth Charles SWAN...............................
    Miss

resides/has resided in Northern Rhodesia and has not been convicted of any felony or misdemeanour in this Territory.

DATE STAMP   -8 SEP 1964 LUSAKA

....
Assistant Commissioner (C.I.D.)

Tax certificate – Author

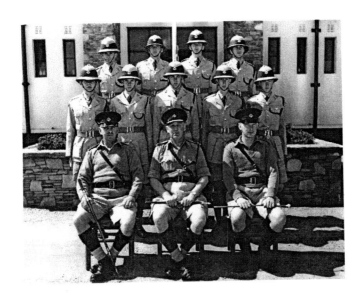

New Mans Training Course

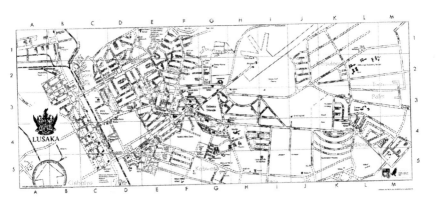

Lusaka City Map

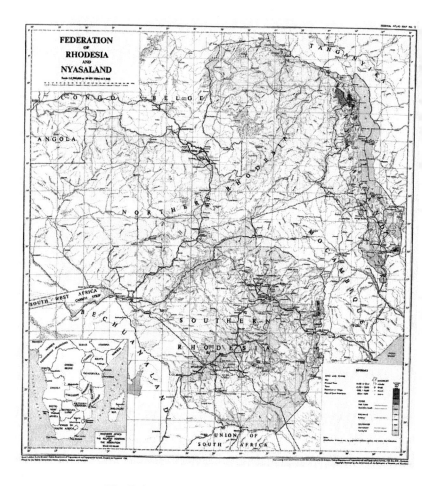

The Federation of Rhodesia and Nyasaland
A failed British attempt to increase their standing
in Central Africa. Disbanded in 1962.

AUTHOR'S NOTES

KWACHA

Before I joined the Northern Rhodesia Police (NRP), I worked for a year as a structural engineering draughtsman, for the Northern Rhodesia government. in Lusaka. I gave up that work when I watched the senior man (my bosses, bosses, boss) bring a soggy sandwich to work each day, in the same stained brown paper bag; a new bag was used each Monday. I dwelled on that for a long time. I wondered if that would be me forty years hence? I wanted better than that.

During that first job, just before I quit in 1958, a meeting was held in Lusaka, Northern Rhodesia's capital city. Tribal leaders from the largest tribes, the Chiefs (eight of them if I recall correctly) were summoned as well as medical staff, architects, engineers, and so on. In the centre of a large table was a Balsa-Wood model (about 24x30x10 inches). It was a model of a proposed multi-racial hospital, to be built near Lusaka. The Chiefs saw that the roof could be removed and asked why. "This shows you the ward lay-out," said my boss (everyone then was my boss!).

One chief asked, "What are those small things?" pointing to small model beds lining one wall. He was told they were beds. "But, my people cannot sleep on beds," said the chief, "they dream of falling off, so they like just a mattress on the floor."

Another chief asked why all the windows were closed, and could they be opened. He was told that they could be opened but the air-conditioning needed them closed. "Oh no," he said, "my people like fresh air when they sleep, so no air-conditioning for them."

Imagine the practical nightmare for Doctors and nursing staff to have such variety in the wards. As a result, the decision was made to have one ward with no air-conditioning, open windows and mattresses on the floor. Next door would be a ward with closed windows, full sized beds and air-conditioning. That ward would be for the non-native people. Then a chief asked where the fire was for the kitchen stove. "As you know, our people like sadza (a white corn meal thick porridge) and they cook it in a huge cast iron pot; they like the smell and taste of the wood smoke."

An engineer explained that there was no outside kitchen and the inside one was all electric, where sadza was just as easily cooked. The chiefs did not like that. The engineers explained that It was possible to include an outdoor facility that could accommodate a large wood fire. The chiefs liked that. These chiefs represented the best, most knowledgeable and influential Africans in the country and here they were, brutally honest and practical, endearing and friendly, yet, and not knowing or caring allowing the 20th century to glide by. Not their fault but just a reality. This is the way they are and, frankly, who are we to change that way of life?

A while later, an American magazine reporter said, in his article about the proposed hospital, "*I don't know who these colonists are kidding, but I saw the model of a proposed multi-racial hospital. The whites get real beds and air conditioning.*

The natives get a mattress on the floor and an open window. The whites get their food from a spotless electric kitchen, while the natives' food is cooked over a fire outside."

The hospital was never built. The reporter kept his job and the chiefs went back to their villages.

The point here is not to scoff at the Chiefs, after all, the Africans had developed their style of 'managing their people (Government) over hundreds of years. They were quite comfortable in their way of life. Us white folks were not trying to change their lifestyle, either, but we needed to understand it and live with it. Most white Africans living there barely understood it/them? The Brits figured they did.

These chiefs would be involved in running an entire country within six years from that incident; really unfair to them and certainly a mistake by Britain for assuming they could handle it. England handed over a whole country to people whose main qualification was that the country was "theirs". A question still remains about just who are the rightful owners of South Africa, Southern Rhodesia or Northern Rhodesia? It is sad to watch events in Africa today; the transfer of power should have been handled more sensibly.

Tales in this book are based on actual incidents. It is not a history of the NRP, simply my own recollection of events that occurred during my brief career as a member of it. I joined on April 1st, 1959 and was an Assistant-Inspector pending my departure in 1962. I have invented all names in this book, to minimize litigation and embarrassment for a few. I do not include my name although every incident involved me, in some manner. I am in here somewhere. Do not try to figure out which is me; I really wasn't that important. I also took liberty with some dates of events, to blend a story. In some cases, the character is a composite of a number of people.

Every person in that force, that I met and knew, were terrific. Some eccentric, some, perhaps, a little whacky, but all dedicated and well-meaning and individuals one would want to hang around with, on and off duty. Many still hang around with each other, decades after it is all over. And, ex members can be found across the world.

The daily life of an NRP officer was enjoyable and inspiring. We were seldom involved in terrorist activities, until later on as unrest began to brew, after other African countries gained independence.

The NRP was a good force; I was not aware of any bad officers. Today former members of the force, members of the NRP Association, visit Zambia periodically and are welcomed by the modern Zambia Police. This relationship cannot be found anywhere else in Africa. African members of our police force were brave, loyal and dedicated to their duties and their fellow officers. They were professional and pleasant to work with. Perhaps *they* should have been asked to run the newly independent country?

Since October 24, 1964, Northern Rhodesia is called Zambia. The country has been, compared to its neighbours, quite stable. The former Rhodesia, now Zimbabwe, is drowning in corruption and brutality. Meanwhile the once most advanced country in Africa, South Africa, has a corrupt and incompetent government. All three countries could be in peril before the first quarter of the 21st century is over.

I know Zambia was left in a far better condition than it was before any white settler stepped over its border. The NRP, helped the population of Northern Rhodesia to enjoy freedom and happiness. Frankly, and for me somewhat surprisingly, the peace in Zambia, lasted over 50 years from the takeover from Britain. I hope it lasts but recent events lead me to believe there is a crisis looming; the opposition parties have never tasted the thrill of governing, and they want to taste power. They are making moves *now* to achieve their goal; let us only hope it is by "one man, one vote" and not by violence.

I was born in Bristol, England. My family emigrated to South Africa in 1948. I grew up in a small village, Umlaas Road, in Natal. (1948-1952). We then emigrated to Lusaka, Northern Rhodesia (1952-1964). I was well educated in Lusaka, in modern schools, sponsored by Cambridge University. I think I know Africa quite well. I believe the western world, the UK in particular, in spite of any well-meaning intentions, ruined the African continent. The western-world politicians were either inept, or were using "know-it-all" policies, knowing little about Africa and convinced that once "democracy" took hold, all of Africa would become "Shangri-La." Well it did not.

411

The way the world handles African issues now shows a lack of understanding and is shamefully and obviously maladroit. To be fair, the new governments in Africa, have done little to help progress either. Perhaps democracy, as we know it, simply does not work, in Africa? Well, actually, who or what works in Africa?

The title **"KWACHA"** means, in Cinjanja, "freedom." (The main language spoken by the majority of the population of Zambia). Since independence Kwacha is also the name used for the Zambian currency.

Goodbye Africa. I hope you get on with your new Bwanas, the Chinese and the Russians and the multi-national conglomerates.

Ken Swan
White Rock,
British Columbia, Canada
September 2017